The Luck of the Draw

A novel

by

Kale Gray

MAIN POINT PRESS
CHICAGO • LOS ANGELES

Designed and published by Main Point Press
Chicago • Los Angeles

To contact the author or the publisher,
email MainPointPress@gmail.com, or call (312) 912-8639.

Cover photo ©2007 Loren Hettinger

CONTENTS

Little Willie Stokes was a buckin' horse boy
Had a grip that could crush pure granite
An' when hangin' on tight is the thing t' do
A good grip can't hurt now, can it
It stood 'im in good with Calamity Jane
A Ray Hix mare he once rode
He stayed on that horse for a day-and-a-half
An' the kid never did git throwed.

—Nevada Swift

CHAPTER ONE
TRAVEL

Zeke Eckhardt and Sonny Valverde were cooling their heels in Zeke's pickup, listening to country music on the radio, impatiently waiting for Scooter Henry, their third traveling companion. Zeke told Sonny to get his feet off the dash, and Sonny slowly and reluctantly obliged, pushing himself to an upright position and then placed his arm partway out the window. The truck was idling, and their gear was stacked in the bed. Zeke was proud of his '59 Chevy pickup and had installed dual exhaust pipes with chrome extensions and, on top of the cab, amber running lights as if a semi-truck. He had placed a dark blue and silver sticker on the rear window that read *Rodeo Cowboys Association*. It featured the silhouette of a cowboy on a saddle bronc in the center of it. There were two stickers on the rear bumper; the one on the left read, *Cowboy Up!*, the one on the right read, *Zero to Naked in 6.3 Beers.*

Sonny looked over at Zeke and studied him for a few seconds. "Yer wastin' gas." Zeke acted as if he had not heard and continued to fiddle with the radio dial, trying to fine-tune a station.

"Don't get yer G-string wadded," he finally replied.

"G-string! . . . hell . . . whatever that is among y'white-eyes," Sonny said as he glared at Zeke. Sonny was from the Jicarilla Apache Reservation in New Mexico and often used the white-eye response to anything he did not understand regarding Zeke and Scooter's comments. Zeke grinned at Sonny.

Scooter had hustled into the lecture hall to turn in a chemistry lab write-up. He came back out from the building and ran across campus, cutting through the last patch of lawn to the parking lot. He ripped open the passenger side door and, after Sonny hurriedly slid over toward Zeke, jumped into the outside passenger seat, exclaiming, "Spur 'em out boys!"

"Eehaw!" Zeke responded and shifted his pick-up into low gear. They headed out of the parking lot and down the steep hill from the Southwestern State campus toward the south end of town.

Their trips to other colleges to compete in rodeos always started out for Scooter with high expectations, and this one to Fort Collins was no exception. It would take them across most of Colorado, driving east from Durango on Highway 160 past the livestock sale barn where they sometimes helped sort stock for extra spending money, past Bayfield and on toward Pagosa Springs, across pinyon-juniper and ponderosa pine-covered hills. Then, they started the climb on the snaky road into spruce-fir forest to the top of Wolf Creek Pass.

All three of the young men were trim with sloping, muscular shoulders. Scooter figured that stacking hay bales on the ranch, among other work, had been a good exercise regimen for rodeo, though at the time it felt like sweaty, endless work.

Zeke pulled his pickup over to the side of the road at the top of the pass and meticulously slipped on a pair of thin, tan leather gloves and dabbed powdered rosin on them from a bag, throwing up a small amber-colored dust plume. Scooter incredulously took in this activity. "What're you doing fer cryin' out loud?" he asked. "This isn't a bull riding or a race. Maybe Sonny and I should get out if you're thinking it is."

"I like firm control of the wheel," Zeke said, shifting the pickup into gear again, as they headed downhill on the curvy road toward South Fork. He mentioned that a tanker truck had gone off the road last time he was through the area. "Might 'a killed the driver, I don't know. It was squeezed into a gorge 'bout fifty feet lower'n the highway!" he said, glancing over at his passengers. Sonny and Scooter did not say anything immediately but were attentive to the road ahead of them just in case Zeke's attention wandered too much. The tires on Zeke's pickup squealed occasionally as he bent it around the curves of the road.

Scooter knew that Zeke scurried around some—much more than he or Sonny—often in detriment to his finances and grades. "What were you doin', chasing some woman over here?" Scooter asked.

"Yeah . . . what else?" Zeke quipped.

"Your pecker's goin' to fall off one of these days."

"Sheeit, that'd be the day!" Zeke looked over at Scooter with a wolfish grin.

Sonny chuckled in his deep voice at their exchange that had gone across him. "Be kinda like a steer, I reckon," he finally observed.

"Well, it ain't going t' happen t' this cowboy, cause I'm all bull!" retorted Zeke. "Y'all just don't have any kind of experience with the women to be sayin' anything 'bout peckers or whatever."

"Yer all bull alright," Scooter said. Sonny snorted at this.

"Sheeit!" Zeke responded with his favorite swear word, glaring across at Scooter.

Scooter continued to observe Zeke as he glanced ahead studying the road, his dark hair, long eyelashes, and ready smile. *No wonder the girls like him. Then he has a lot of nerve with 'em too.* Zeke was over six feet tall and worked the bull-riding event. Contestants in this event were usually short and wiry or compact. He was from the Midwest and was the rookie of the three, although a natural athlete and an ex-state gymnastics champion. Scooter and

Sonny had been raised on ranches and around rodeo.

Sonny wiggled against Scooter to get more comfortable. He moved over toward the door of the truck to give Sonny more room. Scooter had Range Management and Animal Science classes with Sonny, and they had become good friends during the current spring rodeo season.

Scooter studied the profiles of his two companions. *We make a strange trio.* Sonny was approximately five-seven, and rode saddle broncs, an event that often attracted, and was more suited to taller cowboys. He wore his inky, dark hair long, nearly shoulder-length and usually pulled it back into a ponytail. He had a narrow nose and high cheekbones, perhaps from his Native American heritage, giving him an angular profile. Scooter knew from a few friendly tussles that Sonny was wiry. *Maybe like trying to hold onto a python.*

Scooter was between the two in height and figured the bareback event, his specialty, was the best, no matter the size of the person. His auburn hair extended onto his neck where it took an upward curl. Perhaps his most striking feature, however, was his light-flecked hazel eyes. He had high cheekbones and a slightly hawk-like nose. As a youngster, he had wondered if he might be part Indian, based on the caricature on his "Chieftain" school tablet. His mother had set him straight about this, explaining that he had inherited his nose from her father.

They continued to the bottom of the pass, through the small town of South Fork, across the sagebrush and rabbitbrush-dominated western perimeter of the San Luis Valley, into ranch and farm country.

The afternoon was warm; Scooter had his arm on the open window frame of the pickup as they turned north at Del Norte. He leaned back to relax and pulled his hat down over his eyes, thinking about a snooze. He wondered if they should stop in Saguache and have an early dinner, but then thought he smelled smoke, wondering through his closed eyes if some potato farmer was burning weeds.

Scooter continued to mull over potato farming in the valley, as he started to doze. *Wonder if we could raise them out on the ranch . . . if we irrigated of course.* He saw himself on the bed of a truck stacking hundred-pound sacks during harvest. *Guess not. Then there's the thing with Ron, who wants to be the boss with me as his hired man. If it were up to him, I would never have gone to college . . . if Mom hadn't pushed for it. Just what a guy needs . . . a big brother, who thinks he's boss of everything—can't wait until I get back this summer to order me to do stuff. Well, dad rodeoed too, so he is at least on my side a little bit. If I can qualify for the regional college finals and then the national championships . . . be so much of what I want to do. Ron is married to that ranch and loves farm work . . . course work, all the way through, even high school . . . well, let's just say he didn't take to it like a duck to water. I can still see him and Mom at the kitchen table struggling over some homework assignment . . . no way he was ever going to college. If I do qualify and go to the finals and other rodeos this summer, I mean being on the road aside from haying and then harvest in fall, well, that's where the shit hits the fan with him.*

"She's a smokin' some," Sonny grunted.

Scooter pushed his hat up, glanced toward Sonny, and then followed his gaze to the base of the gearshift lever on the floor of the pickup. Scooter could see a thin, white column of smoke rising along the gearshift lever.

"What the hell!" Zeke exclaimed. Sonny moved his feet away from the symptoms.

Scooter sat up and took it upon himself to move the gearshift lever slightly, hoping it was just a minor anomaly, instead of what he feared and thought it likely was. He liked the whole aspect of rodeo: preparing his gear, packing, traveling, and competing. He had felt like a warrior or being on a quest as they had left Durango, yet did not like interruptions and unforeseen circumstances. The specter of car trouble and being stranded caused him to offer an erstwhile, "Sonavabitch!" to the truck.

The smoke continued to spiral upwards from the floor, and Zeke slowed the truck. A whine gradually became evident, as if from a lonely wolf somewhere in the distance.

Zeke hit Scooter's hand off the gearshift. "Leave it alone! I'm hopin' we can make it into Saguache." The whine increased in volume and finally metamorphosed into a banshee-like wail. An acrid, hot metal, hot-oil stench came up with the smoke, causing Zeke and Scooter to stick their heads out the windows for better air. Sonny squashed in behind Scooter in a similar quest.

"Shut 'er down!" Scooter hollered. They coasted over to the side of the road.

All three naively peered under the open hood of the truck and then underneath the engine, as if they might magically identify and fix the problem.

"Let's take our gear and hitch. Johnny and those other guys from the team should be coming by sometime," Scooter said.

"I think they're ahead of us. I ain't leavin' my truck to be plucked clean by some cotton-pickin' varmints," Zeke said.

Scooter thought about this and said, "Hell!" to the whole problem.

Sonny, in his usual taciturn manner, had not said much, but after sticking his head into the engine compartment again, commented, "I think y' cooked 'er . . . smells like fryin' meat with no lard!"

This comment from Sonny softened Scooter's attitude slightly, and he grinned at the comparison. "I done that afore . . . the meat thing I mean."

Zeke looked at both and disgustedly said, "Sheeit!" He then put his thumb out. "Well, might as well get it towed in."

The few cars that went by showed no indication of stopping. Finally, a rancher with a truckload of hay stopped. They told him about the problem, and he also briefly looked under the truck, then offered them a ride into town.

"Sonny 'n I'll stay behind to guard the stuff," Scooter gruffly said.

"Okay. You girls don't go nowhere," Zeke said, as he climbed into the rancher's truck.

"Yeah, just hurry up," Scooter replied, "We ain't got all day to be sitting on our hands out here."

After Zeke and his ride left, Scooter noticed the silence and the peacefulness of the late afternoon. Only a few cars went by, barely slowing. He descended into the borrow ditch into a stand of tall grass to urinate. He talked back over his shoulder to Sonny, "This could take the rest of the day just to get this heap of Zeke's into that town." Sonny didn't respond and seemed to be at ease with their situation. He had sat down on a grassy area with his back against the bank of the borrow ditch. Scooter walked over and tried to follow suit, making himself comfortable beside Sonny, and reclined against the grassy bank, noting the warmth of the afternoon sun. Scooter pulled his hat down over his eyes to relax but took it off again to swat at some flies.

"Maybe we should jest head 'er back to Southwestern," Sonny mused. Scooter looked over at him. "Why? Hell, if we gotta hitch a ride or whatever, we might as well go north. I don't like to turn stock out anyway."

"Jeez man, take it easy. I was just sayin' . . . y'know, this might be one a those things . . . signs, y'know," Sonny said.

"Like an omen? You're not turning superstitious on me, are you?" Scooter asked.

"Well, what if'n we travel all the way up there 'n don't get there in time? Be disqualified anyways."

"We'll see about this. I mean we gotta find out if there's even a bus from Saguache or what. We might be stranded," Scooter replied. "I bet that Zeke never checked the transmission in his fuckin' truck since he's had it."

"Don't go blamin' him already. Chit man, he ain't had time with all the wimmin chasin' he's had t'do."

"Judas Priest, that's about right! But, don't be eggin' me on here. I'm already worked up!"

Sonny chuckled and started to add more fuel to the fire but leaned back and put his hat over his face. Scooter decided to do the same. *Might as well rest-up, because who knows how long we might be traveling or not. I should have taken my car.* He was nearly asleep, but noticed Sonny was softly snoring. He pushed his hat up from his eyes to observe Sonny who had his face completely covered, then relaxed again and finally dozed for a while.

Scooter woke to the buzz of several flies and tried to swat them with his hat. He checked his watch. 'Hell, it's getting late. Wonder if that Zeke is ever coming back?" Sonny removed his hat from his face and blinked, trying to focus on Scooter.

"What's it?"

"Well, it's getting' late. That Zeke better get back here!"

"He won't leave his ol' truck y'know, huh?"

"I guess not, but wonder what's going on?" He walked back up the bank of the borrow ditch to the truck, which still sat immobile with its hood open, a testament to their plight. Finally, Sonny joined him. Several cars and a truck went by, only slowing slightly. Finally, a car slowed and then stopped. A woman in the passenger's seat asked if they needed help.

"Well, one of us went into town to see about getting a tow truck. Guess he'll be back someday. So, thanks for stopping." The woman nodded her understanding, and the car resumed its journey.

"Chit man, we may never get t' that rodeo. Tough travelin' either way . . . either back or forward, innit?"

Scooter observed Sonny, figuring he was likely right. "Tough traveling is about it, pardner. That damned Zeke and his truck. It's only a couple of years old too" They both sauntered back to where they had been napping and sat down on the bank.

"Yeah, like we said though, he's had to do a lotta miles runnin' after all the women, uh?"

Scooter just shook his head, and then his attention was diverted as a tow truck with Zeke inside approached them. Scooter and then Sonny slowly stood up and both stretched, trying to get the kinks out. They slowly trudged out of the borrow ditch to Zeke's pickup.

The tow truck angled onto the shoulder and then backed up to the ailing pickup. The back of the pickup was soon angled skyward, and the operator, not wasting any words, said, "You guys get in." They squashed together in the cab of the truck with Sonny sitting on the edge of the seat and Scooter hanging his arm and shoulder out the window. They made a U-turn and headed back the way the tow-truck had originated. Zeke had to move his legs every time the driver shifted gears. This caused a ripple effect. Scooter felt the space contract and expand like an accordion, as Sonny pressed him against the armrest of the door. The compressed, jerky ride was not helping his mood any.

The tow truck driver stopped in front of a small wooden garage, which was surrounded by older cars and several broken-down trucks. "This here's yer best chance at getting a deal on any repairs," he said.

"Sounds good to me," Zeke nodded. Scooter opened the passenger door and the three clambered out. A shriveled, balding mechanic in black, greasy coveralls slowly limped out from the large open door of the repair shop.

"That's always a good sign," Scooter muttered as he watched the mechanic's approach.

The mechanic offered a "Howdy," and after being informed of the transmission problem, bent down to inspect the underbelly of the vehicle while the tow truck held it in traction. His cheery opinion, as he first spat a thick stream of tobacco juice out to the side, was, "Likely y'all fried the tranny like eggs in a red-hot skillet." Scooter noticed the mechanic was missing several front teeth.

"See, I told ya," Sonny said.

"How much do you think it would be to fix it?" Zeke asked.

"Depins on the extint eggzactly what y'all Pilgrims done to 'er—the tranny and maybe driveshaft," was the mechanic's proclamation.

Sonny, in his low, clipped speech exclaimed, "Pilgrims?"

The mechanic's dialect had aroused Scooter's interest and he had to listen closely to understand him. Scooter acknowledged Sonny's ire: "Travelers!" thinking this was a good time to avoid any confrontations.

"If'n it's just the tranny, I might know of a used un I kin git," the mechanic continued. "Course that there'n my labor will still come to several hunnert, I reckon."

Zeke shook his head. "Sheeit! Can you have it done by Monday?"

The mechanic thought maybe by Tuesday. He gave Zeke a business card edged with greasy fingerprints. "Phone me Monday mornin', en I'll give ye the news."

"Hell, I gotta know earlier. How bout I call you Saturday afternoon?" Zeke asked.

The mechanic scratched his ear and thought about it. "Fer you boys, I'll make an egzception. I should know sumthin then." He had Zeke sign a work order.

"What're we doing 'til then? I mean, are we gonna get to that town?" Scooter wondered. "Is there a bus depot in this burg?" Scooter asked the mechanic.

He pointed down the street with a thumb. "That there little gas station is it. You boys headed to a rodeo somewheres?"

"Yeah, we gotta be in Fort Collins tomorrow," Zeke said.

"Well, yer in luck cuz there's a bus here later . . . evenin' . . . heads north," the mechanic said. "Otherwise it's every other day. Tomorrow there's one headed south. Okay, guess I kin give 'er a look for ya in the mornin'. Good luck up there."

"Yeah, appreciate it," Zeke replied. He peeled off several twenty-dollar bills to pay the tow-truck driver.

The three gathered their gear from the vehicle. Sonny had his bronc saddle bundled up with the stirrups and cinches latched across the seat. He threw it on his shoulder, as Zeke and Scooter carried duffle bags with the rest of the gear. They hiked a block along the dusty street to the small service station.

After buying tickets from a matronly woman wearing an apron, Scooter sauntered over to use the small restroom, and then nearly bumped into Zeke on the way out. He was followed by Sonny, as they had no idea when another opportunity for a toilet stop would occur. Scooter then bought sodas and candy bars, which he distributed to the other two as they emerged from the toilet facility.

"We'd better go easy on the green," Zeke said, as he observed the purchase.

Scooter had been stewing over a question and finally asked Zeke, "Did you ever check or change the transmission fluid in that heap?"

Zeke took offense at this, and hotly replied, "Whaddya think, I'm dumb or somethin'?"

"Well, don't get yer shorts all in a knot. I was just wondering."

"Sheeit!" Zeke replied.

Scooter looked sideways at Zeke. He still had the idea that Zeke probably had never thought about it.

Their exchange seemed to amuse Sonny, and he smiled slightly, and said, "I been on a bus lots a times, en don't mind it. Takes me most a day to get from the rez to the college. Hafta go through Farmington usually."

"Yeah, guess we don't mind riding a bus either," Scooter grumbled. He asked for change from the woman at the counter and checked a slip of paper from his wallet. "We better tell those guys with the rooms that we're hampered here." Scooter walked back outside to a payphone on the wall of the building, dialed the number, and then fed a series of the coins into it. After ringing for a while, a man's voice answered, and Scooter tried to explain their situation. Finally, Scooter said, "Goddammit, look, some guys from Southwestern are coming into town later today to stay at your place. We've had car trouble and will come into town on the bus late tonight and will need a ride from the depot." The person asked again who was calling. "Tell the guys from Southwestern it's Scooter Henry." Scooter started talking louder as the conversation proceeded. Zeke and Sonny had come out of the service station and were taking in the one-sided conversation.

Scooter hung up. "That's comforting. Those guys don't know us from Adam."

"Well . . . is Johnny or someone pickin' us up?" Zeke asked.

"Judas Priest, that's what I'm telling ya! It'd be a miracle! I wonder how far it is from the bus depot to that house."

"None of us even know where it is, do we?" Zeke mentioned.

Scooter studied him for a few seconds. "Guess not. We know the address though, so can ask."

The three sat down on a bench in front of the service station, not saying much. Sonny opened a notebook and began to study. Zeke had pulled a bag of Beechnut chewing tobacco out of a pocket of his leather vest and placed a large pinch of it in his cheek until it bulged slightly. He occasionally spat on the ground between his feet. Scooter observed Zeke, thinking it was another thing about him that was suddenly irritating. *Wonder how all his girlfriends like that habit? Guess they must not mind . . . hmm, well, he's got that swagger and that smile . . . gift of gab too.* He glared at Zeke, then suddenly reached over and swatted the sack of tobacco out of Zeke's hand.

"Hey, goddammit! What're y'doin'?"

Zeke jumped up and put Scooter in a headlock. Scooter strained to pull his head out and when he could not, lifted Zeke off the ground. They became unbalanced and fell into the bench and onto Sonny, whose notebook flew onto the ground.

Zeke turned loose of Scooter to catch himself and Sonny exclaimed with a string of Apache words, then in English, "Youse guys act like a couple of kids . . . idjits!" He bent down to retrieve his notes. Scooter picked up his hat and brushed it off.

"Hey, it weren't my fault!" Zeke exclaimed. "You should watch it, afore y'get yer ass kicked," he said to Scooter.

"Hell, I'm just savin' your teeth from that poison," Scooter said. His ears felt hot and he rubbed one of them.

Zeke observed Scooter for a few seconds as if contemplating more follow up with him, but finally muttered, "Sheeit!" and picked the bag of tobacco off the ground.

He then walked back into the gas station to buy more snacks, and then impatiently paced the area in front of the station. Sonny seemed to be at home on the bench and continued reading his class notes. Scooter decided he better settle down, too, and he pulled his chemistry notes out of a duffle bag. Concentrating on the diagrams and configurations of the organic compounds gave him some respite from their car trouble. Organic chemistry was something he understood or could visualize, and it was a lot more certain than waiting.

Finally, a bus lumbered around a corner and stopped in front of the station. The three travelers thought they would immediately board and gathered their gear, but several passengers got off and the driver closed the door. He mentioned they would be leaving in ten minutes.

"Probably has to take a leak," Zeke grumbled.

After filing onto the bus and presenting their tickets to the driver, they spent most of the night among the other not so fortunate, down-in-the-heel travelers. Scooter likened the trip to a connect-the-dot puzzle, as the bus stopped in Villa Grove, Poncho Springs, and Buena Vista, Basin, Jefferson, Conifer, Bailey, and finally Denver, often picking up a lone passenger, or none. A different bus was to take them north to Fort Collins.

Scooter asked at the ticket counter about the connection north, but the answer was not comforting. They were told there had been a scheduling change because of a hold-up, and their connection to Fort Collins would be several hours late.

"When you say 'hold up,' do you mean like a robbery?" Zeke asked. The woman ticket agent told him to go sit down, which caused Sonny to laugh in a loud snort.

Scooter also smiled. "Well, so much for our ladies' man making an impression," he said.

Zeke wandered the waiting room like a caged animal. Scooter said to him once as he passed by, "You ought to sit down some and save your energy. You make me tired lookin' at you." Zeke showed him a middle finger.

Again, Sonny laughed, surprising Scooter. "What's so friggin' funny?" he asked.

"It's you two white-eyes; I think it's that love-hate thing. You like Zeke to get shot down by them wimmin. Whole thing makes me laugh!"

"Well, we get out of here and on that bus, I'll laugh with you."

CHAPTER TWO
A SMOOTH-TALKING DUDE

By the time they arrived in Fort Collins, it was nearly dawn. Sonny had developed a wing-like wedge of black hair from sleeping against the window but smashed it down with his hat and quickly slung his bronc saddle over his shoulder. Zeke and Scooter grabbed the rest of their gear and pushed through the remaining seated passengers with multiple warnings of, "Excuse me!" They stepped off the bus unshaven, clothes rumpled. Zeke's shirttail was hanging out of his pants.

Scooter had phoned again from a payphone in Denver to tell other members of the rodeo team they were delayed, but didn't know if Johnny had received the message, as the person had answered the phone with a sleep-thickened voice, asking who the hell was calling. Scooter called again and let the phone ring for several minutes. No one answered. The three travelers didn't see anyone who looked familiar, so drifted into the coffee shop. A few old-men patrons turned to check out the new arrivals, curiosity piqued by Sonny sauntering in with his saddle slung over his shoulder.

The three took possession of stools at the counter, cluttering the aisle with gear, and grabbed menus from a holder that was part of a jukebox song selector. A waitress in a peach-colored uniform came over to them, "Hello boys, you want coffee?" she asked.

Scooter noticed her thick auburn hair, which was weaved into a short single braid, and brown, almond-shaped eyes. Her uniform accentuated a trim waist that was offset by the flare of her hips and nicely rounded haunch. Her butt reminded him of a Quarter Horse. While he was making these observations and turning a coffee cup over for a fill, Zeke immediately began a dialogue and told her in short order that they had been forced to leave his truck in Saguache, had traveled all night on a bus, and were in town to compete in the college rodeo.

She poured them coffees while mentioning that she was taking some classes at the college, but hadn't heard about a rodeo.

"Yeah, one of the biggest ones on the college circuit!" Zeke offered. Scooter thought Zeke was trying to impress the waitress and wondered if it would work, thinking it unlikely. He looked over at Sonny, who grinned at Zeke's erstwhile description, but seemed oblivious to the male-female interaction while concentrating on his cup of coffee.

Zeke continued to flirt with the waitress, and she seemed to like the attention. "You should come to the rodeo!" he offered. "I could get you in, if you wanted."

She didn't know if she could but came back occasionally to pour them more coffee after serving other customers. She asked where they were from and what events they worked. Zeke inquired, and she gave him her phone number.

Scooter observed this, as he spread jam on a piece of toast, and changed his opinion about Zeke's technique. The ability to be free and easy with the opposite sex amazed Scooter, who had plenty of nerve while riding bareback broncs, but very little with women. Neither he nor Sonny had said anything to the waitress except an occasional, "Yes" or "Thank you."

Zeke knew about Sonny and Scooter's shyness, "You see how us urban cowboys operate while you ranch boys stand around suck'n your thumbs with your hands in your pockets?"

"Dude, you make a lot of sense," Scooter retorted sarcastically.

It was hard for Scooter or Zeke to read any of Sonny's emotions, but he smiled slightly at the verbal exchange, and said in his clipped speech and deep voice, "Ranch boys? I thought y' said I was a wild redneck."

The other two laughed at this remark. "Yeah, something like that. Come on, I'm going to call that place again . . . let's see about getting outta here and about catchin' some zees. We got stock this afternoon," Scooter said.

The three stood on the sidewalk near the bus depot and finally saw Johnny driving up the street. Zeke let loose a piercing whistle, and they piled their gear into the trunk of the car after Johnny had pulled over to the curb.

He complained about the time of day, asking, "What the hell you guys been doing all night?"

"We rode a Podunk bus stopping in every two-bit town," Zeke replied, and to emphasize his point, added, "all night!"

Scooter explained further, "There was a hold-up in big D-town, so sat in the bus station for a few hours with the other sleeping-upright dead beats. I phoned someone to give you a message."

Johnny stopped at a large house that served as an apartment for other rodeo-inclined college students. Johnny didn't know about sleeping arrangements, so Scooter crashed on a couch, while Zeke laid back in a recliner. Sonny had already taken to the floor and had covered up with a small rug. Scooter threw him a pillow from the couch. Sonny seemed to be asleep before Scooter had gotten his boots pulled off.

"Will y'look at this guy? He can sleep anywhere, anytime. Y'know he has a huge Big Ben alarm clock and puts it in a metal cake pan with silverware to wake up for early classes," Scooter said.

"That's what I'm going to need later today," Zeke yawned.

Scooter felt grimy as he washed from the waist up in a basin—what they called a cowboy bath—and then changed to a fresh shirt. He noticed Sonny didn't even do that, but he did flick his hair forward, plaited it out straight through his fingers, and then pulled it back into a ponytail, which he held in place with a thick rubber band.

Scooter watched Sonny fix his hair. "Come on, Hollywood, you look sweet! Let's ride some broncs."

Sonny twisted back and forth from the waist up and then leaned over to touch his toes. "I'm a little stiff."

Zeke sauntered in from the bathroom, his hair still wet. "Well boys, couple hours sleep an' I feel finer 'n frog hair!"

"Glad you do, 'cause I feel like road kill," Scooter replied.

"You look like it, too, but that's all the time," Zeke retorted.

"That's like two flat, road-killed frogs talking," Scooter said, showing Zeke a middle finger, and then stretching out for a series of push-ups.

"That flat frog 'bout sums it up," Sonny said. He was still trying to touch his toes.

Johnny bumped down the stairs with his duffle bag in tow and said, "You night owls ready to go?"

They grabbed their gear and followed him outside to his car. Johnny opened the trunk of his car for them, but Scooter had to push on the top of his duffle bag for it to fit. Johnny drove through part of town to the college campus and stopped at the student union. The rodeo office had been set-up in the lobby, and Scooter, Zeke, and Sonny tromped behind Johnny to check-in, to pick up their contestant numbers, and to find out which animals they had drawn for the first go-round.

The rodeo secretary exclaimed to Zeke, "Oh! You're the one who drew Double Ought! We were wondering. He's a National Finals bull from last year, you know!"

"Sonuvabitch! This could get interestin'," Zeke said nervously.

"Look at it this-a-way, you ride him, you win it," Scooter quipped.

"Well, that's it, I guess," Zeke said in agreement.

They continued to study the list of riders and their assigned stock, noting that they were on the list along with a host of other contestants from a variety of colleges.

"Be a tough competition," Scooter observed.

"Yeah, this draws everyone," Johnny noted. "Let's get some lunch. I think the other guys are in there." They followed him into the student union cafeteria where they said hello to a table of other contestants and joined Hank and Will, also part of their team. Scooter was not fond of Hank, who was in several of his classes, but currently ineligible to compete. He had come on the trip anyway. Scooter thought Hank should have stayed at Southwestern to study.

After lunch, they all piled into Johnny's car, for the short trip to the rodeo arena to get ready for the competition. Scooter was crowded into the back with Zeke and Sonny. He thought it might be like a clown's car from which a large group of people would emerge.

The arena was in an open area on the western edge of the campus with a close view of the mountains to the west. A tractor pulled a disc to soften the arena surface.

Bareback bronc riding was the first event, and Scooter immediately began to prepare. Johnny also worked this event and set his equipment bag next to Scooter's. "I think I have a pretty good horse, according to the guys from A&M here," he said.

"That's what they said about mine too, 'Pretty Boy Floyd.' Not sure if it means a guy can win on it or a guy maybe gets shot on it," Scooter said. Johnny and Zeke laughed at Scooter's analysis.

He pulled his rigging from his duffle bag, along with his leather glove, and then tugged on his riding boots. Spurs were next, and he strapped these on starting, as his usual routine, with the right foot. A second leather strap extended from the spur's shank and looped under the arch of his boot. He then threaded the spur strap through the buckle and latched it, which tightened the leather loop under the arch and created stability. He went through a routine of stretching out and then through a series of warm-up exercises. He tried to get his heart rate and breathing to accelerate as he completed a series of inverted push-ups with his feet part way up on the thick planks of a chute. He then unfurled his chaps, latching the belt first and then the buckles on each thigh.

The horses were loaded into the chutes and, with the help of the stock contractor's chute boss, Scooter located his draw—a large sorrel gelding. Sonny and Zeke helped Scooter set his rigging. He tried to stay loose during the grand entry and the playing of the National Anthem. He stood during this on the back of the chute with his hat off. The tension was building though, and he could feel the "butterflies" in his stomach. *Not really butterflies though . . . more like a cable tightening up through my core until it's humming . . . maybe like the telephone wires out along the road at the ranch on a hot day.*

Zeke and Sonny stayed close by to help. "Bear down on this one!" Zeke said. Scooter just nodded. He tried to concentrate on what he needed to do, barely noticing some of the other rides before his.

Finally, the chute boss said, "Yer next, bud." The horse was jumpy, and it took Scooter several tries to carefully thread his leather glove into the handhold and then slide up to the rigging He then placed his feet in front of the horse's shoulders. He was careful not to touch the horse with his spurs but slid up as close as he could to the rigging and laboriously finished threading his glove into the rigging's handhold. He tugged his hat down and then nodded for the gate.

The horse jumped and kicked in a wide circle of the arena, and Scooter was able to get in time with it, spurring up and out each time the horse left the ground. Halfway through the ride, however, the horse lunged side-ways, and Scooter nearly tipped over in the opposite direction. He felt panic but righted himself by pulling hard on the rigging and spurring ahead of the horse as it lunged forward. The tipping mistake and what he felt was tentative spurring likely detracted from what could have been a decent ride. Scooter could feel the burn of the rigging's handhold through his leather glove, and when the buzzer sounded to end the eight seconds, he quickly looked for one of the pick-up men as they rode alongside, to be set onto the ground. Zeke gave him a high-five for a successful ride when Scooter arrived back at the chutes.

Weren't especially pretty but survived!" Scooter quipped.

"Eh, I'd take it," Sonny replied.

They waited for the score. Scooter was hoping for a few more points than the announced *72.*

"I hope that holds up for some money, but it could set you up for some of the average, too," Zeke said.

"Well, me too," Scooter replied, meaning he was hoping to do both, but the score currently placed him in fourth. "It seems like the judges are marking low, but hey, better than nothin'. I thought I was coming off for a few seconds there," he said. Scooter was secretly relieved that so far, he was in the money and would have something to tell his dad and brother, too.

"Damn right! You were due!" Zeke exclaimed. "I better see if Hank needs any help for Johnny getting set." Sonny worked his way behind the chutes to a narrow aisle and retrieved Scooter's rigging from the contractor's roustabouts.

Scooter was interested and watched as Johnny came out on a large palomino. It seemed like he made a respectable ride, but the score was not in the top five. Scooter knew Johnny would be disappointed in not scoring better. "Well, a qualified ride, anyway," he told Johnny afterward.

"Yeah, it was a little stout, so never really opened up on it," Johnny explained.

Scooter and Zeke sat on the fence taking in the steer wrestling and team roping, while Sonny prepped his saddle while sitting in it on the ground, his feet in the stirrups. He rubbed rosin onto the swells and the inside of his chaps and used the strength of his legs to create friction and work the material into both surfaces.

"They're going to have to pry you off after the ride," Zeke observed.

"That's fine with me, innit?" Sonny replied, not glancing up from his task.

Scooter thought that Sonny was developing into a classy saddle bronc rider and had mostly been in the money at all the spring rodeos. He had told Scooter that growing up, he had ridden a bunch of unbroken horses on the Indian reservation. After the saddle broncs were loaded into the bucking chutes, Zeke and Scooter helped Sonny place his saddle and attach the thick-braided rein to the horse's leather halter. The horse was a large black with a Roman nose and large feet. Scooter had a vision of it pulling a plow.

Sonny never seemed nervous before a ride, and Scooter envied this. They watched as Sonny cautiously climbed down onto the horse when it was his turn, and carefully placed his feet into the stirrups and extended them out as far as possible. He pulled his chaps back to make sure they were free of the stirrup leathers and extended his riding arm out in front of him, holding the thickly-braided rein.

Sonny grunted an "Out!" and at the same time flicked his head in a nod for the horse. He rode upright, spurring from near the rein when the horse kicked out and then back to the cantle of the saddle as the horse again left the ground. Zeke let loose a piercing whistle from his perch on the chute fence to celebrate the ride. After Sonny had latched onto a pickup man to be taken off the horse and walked back to the chutes, Scooter gave him a high-five. The announcer exclaimed that the score was 78.

"Wow!" Scooter exclaimed, "Nice ride!" Zeke shook Sonny's hand and several of the other contestants gave him high fives. They watched the rest of the rides with interest to see what the other scores were. Sonny ended up in second place for the first go-round, which caused Scooter to think their initial poor luck on the trip north was changing for the better.

CHAPTER THREE
DOUBLE OUGHT

The barrel racing event preceded the bull riding, and as it started, Zeke began to prepare. One of his warm-up exercises had always amazed Scooter because Zeke would gradually lead up to a maneuver in which he held his body horizontal on the side of a fence using his arms as levers. Scooter knew this was a holdover from Zeke's gymnastic days, but he had never been able to duplicate the maneuver, even with Zeke's instruction.

Zeke strapped on his spurs and chaps, and then attached his bull rope to the top-board of the fence. He put on his leather glove and with some rosin in the palm of it energetically rubbed the handhold and then the tail of the rope to increase its tackiness. Other bull riders were doing the same, causing a disjointed symphony of clanking bells tied to the end loops of the ropes. The bells served as a weight to pull the ropes off the bulls at the end of a ride, although Zeke had told girls at Southwestern that the bells were to keep the contestants awake during the ride. The bulls were loaded at the beginning of the barrel racing event. Their bulk caused a clatter as they pushed through the narrow alleyway and entered the chutes, raising a cloud of dust. This activity, and the clanking of bells on the bull ropes being prepped, was like a harbinger of an oncoming storm. Scooter noticed the nervous energy that seemed to exude from the chute area. It seemed to him that the bull riders were a motley group. Many of the guys chewed tobacco, and a characteristic smear of manure on jeans from the bulls seemed to be an occupational hazard.

Double Ought was pushed ahead through the narrow aisle into the second chute. Scooter used a wire hook to reach through the slates on the chute gate under the belly of the bull and brought the loop up to where he could bring the tail of the rope through it. Zeke then reached down from above the bull and brought the tail of the rope up. He set the handhold just to the side of the bull's midline.

The bull, a large black Brahma, twitched its ears at the activity, but stood calmly, a veteran of many rodeos. The tips of its horns had been nipped as a safety measure for the riders, and possibly to help ease it through the narrow alleyways and into the bucking chutes. Even so, they were intimidating with their thick base and sword-like upward curve.

The first rider didn't last long, coming off a spinning bull near the open chute gate. After the bull had been cleared from the arena, the chute boss came over and said, "Go ahead and pull it!"

Sonny stood halfway up on the chute gate and pulled upwards on the tail of the rope until Zeke said okay. He then took the tail from Sonny and placed it across the handhold and the palm of his leather glove, then took another turn around the back of his wrist and brought the tail of the rope back across his palm once more, and then ran it between several fingers. He closed his gloved hand and hit it with his other hand—a signal that the hand was to stay closed. Zeke had his shirtsleeve rolled up; the veins in his forearm stood out. He slid up close to his hand and pulled his chaps back to the side to be out of the way when the gate opened.

"Bear down now and turn your toes out." Scooter meant for Zeke to concentrate and use his spurs.

Zeke scooted up even closer to his handhold, leaned forward slightly and grunted, "Okay boys, let's see some daylight!"

He seemed to be riding well the first of several high jumps and during the start of a spin. Scooter stretched out from the back of the chute to see better, as Zeke was into the middle of a great ride. Suddenly, the bull lunged and kicked his rear into the air, which whipped Zeke's feet back behind him, and he hung horizontally for a split second above the bull, as if doing a gymnastic pommel-horse maneuver, but then his head slammed into the bull's horns. Zeke tumbled to the ground and the bull turned, trying to butt the fallen rider until the bullfighters diverted it away. Zeke lay motionless on his back with one hand under his head, his feet crossed as if cloud gazing after a picnic.

The bullfighters continued to lure the bull away from the fallen rider and it lumbered back through an open gate. The arena had become uncharacteristically silent, as people observed the prone, unmoving rider.

"Damn! He smacked the dashboard!" Scooter mused to nobody in particular.

Several EMTs hurried into the arena to Zeke and, along with the bullfighters, bent over him. Scooter and Sonny also hurried out to where their comrade lay and looked on while emergency staff worked on him. After several minutes, Scooter was becoming worried, but then Zeke started to move and then an EMT helped him gain his feet. Another held gauze to Zeke's forehead; his nose was bleeding. He groggily hung onto the emergency staff as they led him out of the arena to the applause of the crowd, as the announcer said, "Give that cowboy a hand, 'cause that and a headache is all he's getting today, folks!"

Scooter and Sonny gathered up Zeke's bull rope and hat from one of the bullfighters. "Shit! He didn't look too good!" Scooter said.

Sonny shook his head. "Chit man, that there's a good reason to work a different event . . . innit."

You ain't just whistling Dixie there, pardner."

They picked up Zeke's equipment bag from behind the chutes and walked through the aisle to the small gate and over to the medical tent where they tentatively peered inside to assess the damage. The staff had gotten the bleeding from Zeke's nose to stop, and a man that Scooter realized must be a doctor was in the process of placing two pencils into Zeke's nostrils to set it.

The man, very business-like, explained to an EMT, "It's just gristle, so once we get it straightened out we'll tape it in place. I think now though he needs stitches to close that gash over his eyebrow and needs to be checked for a concussion, so I want him over at the university's medical center."

Scooter tried to amuse Zeke, who was groaning slightly as they worked on him, "Wait till that waitress sees you now, partner, she'll be runnin' for her life!"

Zeke stared blankly at Scooter, not responding. He still seemed unsteady on his feet and a medical technician put a hand on Zeke's arm to guide him.

Johnny came over and had a look at the damage. "Hell's bells . . . I'll take his tack and put it in the car."

Scooter nodded and handed over Zeke's equipment bag. "Can you guys stash our gear as well? We're going with him . . . see where this ends up. Guess we'll see you back at the student union or maybe we could get a ride back to that house from the infirmary."

Scooter and Sonny followed along and, after Zeke settled into a re-clined seat, climbed into a white van for a ride to the infirmary.

Scooter and Sonny lounged in the waiting room while Zeke was being attended. Scooter leafed through several magazines and then paced the room wondering how long it was going to take. He noticed that Sonny had fallen asleep on one of the couches and had gradually slumped over. A girl who had been sitting at the other end moved to a chair. Scooter grinned to himself and sat down again next to Sonny.

Zeke finally was ushered by a nurse out through the door of the examination area into the waiting room. It seemed to Scooter that Zeke's face had puffed-up some since they had arrived; one eye was nearly swollen shut. The eyebrow above it had become a prow-like wedge, giving him a Neander-thal look. Already a myriad of purple hues among yellows had set in. He had a large Band-Aid above the eyebrow on his forehead. His face, the manure, and dirt on his jeans, and the fact that he still had on spurs caused a ripple effect of interest among the other students in the waiting room.

"What happened?" one of the guys asked.

"Um, bull riding," Scooter replied

"Are you his friends?" the nurse asked.

Sonny and Scooter had stood up and nodded an affirmative. She mentioned that Zeke had stitches and gave Scooter a small bottle of liquid. "He'll need to have the bandage changed in a couple of days, so I've given you some antibiotics and here's some extra gauze. The stitches need to come out in about a week. He also has a slight concussion, so can you guys watch for symptoms?"

Having to watch for symptoms alarmed Scooter. "What are they . . . the symptoms?"

"Check his pupils . . . if they don't respond to light, for example. Here's a sheet of instructions for concussion and for the abrasion. If he wants to sleep all the time, too, then you should telephone." She handed Scooter several sheets of paper.

"Okay. Should he be in a hospital? Scooter asked

"Well, he refused, and the doctor thought the concussion is minor, but we still want to be cautious."

"But about sleeping, we haven't slept most of last night for the traveling."

"I mean if he won't stay awake."

Scooter nodded that he understood.

After the nurse left, Sonny asked Zeke, "How y'feelin'?"

"Not worth a shit! What'd I hit anyway?"

"'Bout had a horn sandwich, man," Sonny answered.

Zeke's nose was obviously stopped-up from gauze packing and he spoke with a nasal twang.

"You sound like a southern gentleman," Scooter observed.

"Yeah, well, the breathin' ain't too good neither. Anyway, y'know, he felt good, what I remember of it."

"Y'looked good too, up 'til the wreck," Sonny added.

"That doc said I have a concussion and gave me these super aspirins for later. He said somethin' about watchin' that I don't get worse or somethin'."

"Yeah, the nurse explained already. We have t'keep you awake." Scooter looked at Sonny and he just shook his head.

Scooter studied the instruction sheets further for a few seconds and stuck them into the back pocket of his jeans. "Come on, I'll look at this later. Can you motor okay? Let's see about some money and get something to eat, find Johnny and the guys."

"I can motor, but no sprintin," Zeke replied.

They slowly wandered across a parking lot and back to the rodeo office in the student union to pick up checks for Sonny and Scooter's winnings.

The rodeo secretary noted in viewing Zeke's face, "Double Ought takes no prisoners. He threw Jim Higgins, one of our bullfighters, out of the arena several weeks ago down in Lamar. Getting meaner with age."

"Yeah, I seen that. I guess I liked him for the first two or so seconds," Zeke mumbled.

She laughed at his remark and wrote out two checks. Scooter and Sonny inspected their winnings and put the paper into their wallets. Scooter noted the ninety-five dollars of the check: *Not too bad for a day's work . . . wonder what Sonny made for second in bronc riding?*

The three then ambled down the hall to the cafeteria to get some dinner. Zeke gingerly munched on a piece of toast and washed it down with a milkshake.

Johnny and Hank came over and gazed in wonder at Zeke's face, "Jeez pard, you could star in a Frankenstein movie." To Scooter and Sonny, Johnny said, "You know there's a rodeo dance here at the college tonight. We're going, just so you know."

As he slowly chewed his toast, Zeke mumbled, "Whaddya think? I'm goin' to be waltzin' around squeezin' some honey tonight?"

Johnny and Hank cut Zeke no slack, telling him they needed him to break the ice with the girls, who they thought would be struck with sympathy in viewing his face.

"Or fear!" added Sonny. Johnny and Hank laughed at this, and Scooter smiled. He had not contemplated going to a dance, though, thinking they would all turn in early after the previous, nearly sleepless night. He looked over at Sonny. "Whaddya think? A dance might be interesting."

"Naw, I don't know. I might hit the sack soon . . . them white-eye dances don't interest me much."

They continued to work over their meals. Zeke left most of his, and Scooter thought that he looked pale. "I think we better get him back to that house."

"Come on, I'll give you guys a ride back for a shower. Y'all a little gamey," Johnny said.

"Gamey!" Scooter protested. "You ain't seen nothin' yet!" But, it seemed his shirt was sticky with several dried sweat, starch-like patches, and he was relishing a shower.

Zeke perked up a little after showering and putting on clean clothes.

"I better phone that guy on the truck before I space it." He dug the card out of his wallet. Scooter observed Zeke, noticing his nasal twang.

After a short conversation, Zeke said, "Guess he'll have it done Monday afternoon. Be about three hundred though."

"This is an expensive trip," Scooter noted.

"We're layin' over until Monday morning. I hate leaving so late on Sunday," Johnny said, "anyway, could give y'all a ride that far."

"Tha'd help for sure," Zeke noted.

The phone call seemed to have tired Zeke, and Scooter watched as Zeke took a handful of aspirin and lay down on the couch. Scooter walked into the kitchen and found a tray of ice cubes in the small freezer. He found a sandwich bag in the cupboard and broke out a hand-full of ice cubes, thinking this would help Zeke's face. He had become very quiet, and Scooter remembered, according to the instructions, they were supposed to keep him awake. "Wonder how long we're supposed to watch him?"

Sonny seemed unconcerned and replied, "Make sure he's a breathin' should be okay." He had unbound the cinches and stirrups of his saddle to work over the swells with some rosin to improve the grip for his legs. "I'm hopin' to get a good bronc tomorrow, so maybe I kin win this thing."

Scooter smiled at Sonny's attempt at a joke about Zeke and sat down in a chair to observe him working on his saddle. "Shoot . . . breathing's always good. You're in good shape. I could use a nice jumping and kicking horse myself to move up some and for the average. Well, we'll see how our luck holds in the draw. I have no idea on that second horse for tomorrow . . . Contractor said it's a little rank."

Several other residents of the house walked in from outside and looked at Zeke's face with some concern. "I saw the wreck and figured he'd been knocked cuckoo. Is he going to be okay?" one asked.

"Well, he's a bull rider, so he's tougher'n lips on a woodpecker!" observed Johnny. The others chuckled at his analogy. "You guys going back to the college with us?" Johnny asked Scooter.

"I don't know now, as we're supposed to be watching Zeke for that concussion," Scooter said.

"What y'need to do?" Hank asked.

"Well, he wasn't supposed to sleep, but he is now, and that was several hours ago that we left that little hospital," Scooter replied uncertainly.

"If y'wanna go, we're leaving 'bout an hour," Johnny said.

"We might as well go for a while, see what's up there, huh?" Scooter said to Sonny, whom he knew would be reluctant.

"Might be a waste a time. We should get some sleep is what I'm thinking," Sonny replied.

"I know . . . already thought about it. We don't have to get up early, though. What else you going to do? You've already prepped that saddle all evening."

Sonny bundled up his saddle and said, "Okay pard, if'n yer set on it. I better chaperone you anyways . . . keep y'outta trouble!"

"Chaperone me?" Scooter smiled at the thought that Sonny could be a chaperone, as he had never thought of his friend in that way. "Why would I need a chaperone anyway?"

"Cuz yer so green is why," Sonny replied.

Scooter chuckled. "Judas Priest! That's another pot calling a kettle black, huh!"

CHAPTER FOUR
DANCING

The dance was crowded with a mix of rodeo team members from the different colleges, as well as other students who were mostly milling and standing at the edge of the dance floor. Scooter and Sonny lounged behind the crowd, leaning against the wall, checking the scenery as a band played familiar country and western music. Scooter was not poetic on the dance floor, as his experience consisted of scattered instruction for high school dances from his sister, Rachel, in the box step and occasional attempts at simple country two-step.

As they continued to slouch against the wall, Sonny mentioned that he hoped to see a girl he knew from the reservation who was a student at the college.

You could've let her know you'd be here," Scooter said.

"Well, I don't know her too good actually," Sonny mumbled.

Scooter observed Sonny, thinking he keeps things close to the vest. "If you see her are you going to go talk to her, maybe dance some?"

Sonny winced, and then said, "Yeah, I'll dance all over the floor with 'er." Scooter laughed at Sonny's comment.

Finally, a few couples swirled around the dance floor, and as if having broken the ice, more and more couples joined them. Scooter and Sonny continued standing against the wall noticing the variety of dancing abilities being exhibited. Suddenly, two girls in western attire appeared and asked if they wanted to dance. The taller one with dark hair said to Scooter, "I'm Charlene O'Brien, by the way," and put her hand out. He thought the girl was very attractive and was struck dumb by her smile and sudden presence. Scooter had no option but to take her hand. Charlene introduced her shorter blonde companion, as "Squirrel."

"Huh?" Scooter said. He and Sonny continued leaning against the wall.

"Oh, she's from a walnut ranch in California. She gets packages from home, so, her nickname."

Squirrel smiled at the explanation but seemed reserved. Scooter thought: *It'd be a cold day in hell for her to get Sonny out onto the dance floor, even if she were Miss Squirrel America.*

Finally, Scooter pushed himself from leaning against the wall and, as if on a leash, following Charlene onto the dance floor, as she lightly pulled him by his hand. "I saw you over at the rodeo in bareback. You rode well."

He noticed her turquoise, blue-green eyes, and involuntarily said, "Oh!" stuttered another half-thought, and finally said, "Thanks. Ah, did you compete?"

"Yes, I'm in barrel racing, but had a poor run today. My horse . . . well, we knocked over a barrel."

"Ah . . . hmm, too bad. It takes a while to train a horse." Scooter was still disconcerted by this girl and thought: *What a lame remark!*

"No, I've had this horse a while. Maybe we haven't been practicing enough."

They talked about the vagrancies of rodeo events, and what was luck versus skill. Scooter was having a hard time keeping in time with the music and talking, so explained, "We never learned dancing much out on the ranch." Scooter hadn't danced much in high school and now not much in college either. In fact, he had not worried about whether he could or couldn't. Suddenly, he was regretting it.

"Don't worry about it," Charlene replied after he stepped on her foot.

He mentioned that one of their teammates had gotten a concussion in bull riding and was at the house where they were staying. "We need to get back soon to check on him," he said.

"Oh! I saw him, I think, being taken out of the arena!" she exclaimed.

"Yeah, we left him lying on the couch with an ice bag on his head."

Scooter had started out dancing with several feet of distance between them, as if dancing with his sister. Charlene essentially indicated that this was not how she danced and moved into him. Her hair tickled his nose occasionally and he felt her hand on his neck. It felt hot there. After the music stopped, Scooter thanked Charlene for the dance and said, "Nice to have met you."

He found that she still had his hand and before turning him loose said, "Likewise, nice to have met you. But I'll see you later."

He bobbed his head as he looked into her sparkling eyes. He had an urge to follow her somewhere and said to himself, "Hell!" He saw Sonny still standing along the wall, so went over, and asked, "What happened to the girl?"

"I tol' 'er I don't know how t'dance."

"You mean to this kind of music. Why didn't you do one of your Apache dances to impress her?"

"Sure, that'd work," Sonny said and gave Scooter a hard stare.

"Well, dancing aside, we should probably find Johnny and make sure Zeke's still living . . . and get some sleep."

"I'm ready fer that sleep thing," Sonny said.

As they moved through the crowd, Scooter noticed Charlene and

Squirrel and he started to angle toward them, thinking he would at least tell Charlene, "So long," but hesitated when he saw they were with some other people, including several guys.

She looked over though as Scooter and Sonny started to walk by, and called out, "Hey, just a minute!" Scooter and Sonny stopped, and Charlene came over with Squirrel in tow.

"We thought we better go check on our teammate," Scooter said.

"This dance is kind of lame, maybe we'll all go," Charlene said.

Scooter didn't know what that meant and wasn't keen on a large group going to look at Zeke. "Well, we're afoot and were going to find a ride from this other guy on the team."

"Come on, we'll drive you guys," Charlene said.

Scooter and Sonny followed the girls outside. The air felt cool, refreshing. Scooter had not realized how hot it had been inside. He and Sonny followed Charlene and Squirrel to a large pickup truck with rear dual wheels.

Scooter was impressed and told Charlene, "Wow, quite a rig!" Thinking she must have some money coming from somewhere.

"Well, this is my tuition for next year, already spent. It's for pulling a horse trailer you know. It's used . . . I mean my dad let me, well, had me take over the payments." Scooter stood by the rear door with Sonny, but Charlene asked Scooter, "Are you afraid I might bite?"

"Naw!" Scooter replied. He changed direction toward the passenger side door and nearly collided with Squirrel and they did an awkward dance to miss each other. She and Sonny got into the rear seat.

As they pulled away, Scooter glanced toward the back to see how Sonny was faring, but he had his hat pulled low, as if getting ready to ride a bronc. He was sitting pressed hard against the door. Scooter smiled, knowing that Sonny was uncomfortable with the situation.

Scooter gave directions and they pulled up in front of the house, "You guys want to come in, meet the dude?" Scooter asked. They all traipsed into the house, first looking in the living room where Zeke had been when Scooter and Sonny had left. Scooter then went upstairs to check the small bedrooms.

He came back down the stairs and wondered aloud to Sonny, "Where the hell could he have gone?" and was thinking hospital, or Zeke wandering aimlessly around the neighborhood in just his jeans, or worse, his underwear.

"Y'know Zeke. He's likely carousing' around somewhere even with knots on his head," Sonny said.

"Well, he ought to've left a note . . . I don't think he was at the dance anyway."

"Should we go out looking for him?" Charlene offered.

Scooter thought about it but didn't know where. He decided Sonny was likely right, and said, "Naw, he'll likely be back soon."

Charlene pulled a piece of paper from her purse and wrote out her phone number. "In case you need us," she told Scooter.

Scooter took the offered paper. "Thanks, and thanks for the ride, and it was nice meet'n you both."

"I'll see you tomorrow, and good luck," Charlene said and unexpectedly stepped into him for a hug that in reflex he returned. Her gesture of affection had taken him by surprise.

"Uh-huh, guess I'll see you tomorrow," he mumbled and walked the girls to the front door.

After they had gone, Sonny bent over in a fit of laughter. Scooter shook his head and said, "Okay, you can quit anytime now. It wasn't that funny."

Sonny snorted a few times between breaths. "Chit man . . . you shoulda seen yer face. It was redder'n a drunk's nose. She's after yer ass pard . . . like a dog on a rat!"

Scooter did not know what to say, as he thought Charlene was the most attractive and the most forward girl he had ever met, but weakly replied, "Dog on a rat? Jeez! She seems nice though. What about that other girl . . . Squirrel?"

"She's just along, y'know. I'm hittin' the sack."

Scooter followed Sonny upstairs to their assigned room and said, "I wish Zeke would get back, so we could rest easy about him."

"I bet ya he's found some honey fer medical attention, if y'know what I mean." Sonny pulled off his boots and then piled his jeans beside them and draped his shirt over the footboard. He lay down and threw a blanket over himself. Scooter gazed at Sonny's bedtime actions and decided he might as well follow suit. He envied Sonny's ability to go to sleep so easily: *He just turns off a switch.*

Scooter had just dozed off when he heard someone come up the stairs and thought it must be Zeke, but a girl's melodious laughter confused him. He got up and yelled down the hall, "Hey Zeke, that you?"

After a pause, he heard, "Yeah!" and decided, as he went back to bed, he would have no more sympathy for his friend.

Scooter was lying in bed, thinking about Charlene—her lithe figure, thick, dark hair, and bluish or greenish eyes. *What color are they anyway . . .*

guess they're kind of in-between? His romantic experiences with the opposite sex were limited. One incident after the high school prom came to mind. The memory of the evening had stayed vivid.

He had been set-up with a date by his cousin, who thought, as a senior, he should have a date and go to the prom. Of course, he knew the girl, who was a junior and apparently interested in him. Although not smitten by this girl, he was okay with the arrangement and had tried to be a good companion. He had bought her a corsage and at the prom had danced—well, shuffled around—with her as much as possible during the evening. The prom had been held in the school cafeteria that had been decorated to mask the heating pipes along the ceiling with paper stars and moons. Afterward, at her suggestion, they had gone to a nearby park for some light, then heavy kissing, and she told him, "Come on, let's go for a walk!" In the midst of some evergreen trees, she clamped one of his legs between hers and pulled him close. Scooter had heard rumors from some of the guys of what supposedly happened after the prom but had dismissed them as myth or wishful thinking. The girl apparently had thought the rumors were reality. He had also realized she had shed her ruffled petticoat from under her prom dress and had wondered when she had gotten rid of the encumbrance. He remembered liking the feel of her pushing against him as they kissed; her leg against his. But after their kissing had become quite passionate, a scene had suddenly flashed somewhere behind his eyes as if on a cinema reel, of them in a sparsely furnished basement apartment, her with an alarmingly protruding stomach as if she had swallowed a watermelon, while he looked longingly toward open range through a small window. This vision had been like being hit in the face with ice water, or maybe having it poured down the front of his pants. He had used early chores as an excuse to reluctantly disengage.

He had lost track of the girl after he left for college, but his sister said that she had married one of the boys from her class at the end of high school. He wondered if they had a kid or more by now.

Sonny moved the mound of covers on his bed and grunted something, breaking Scooter's reverie. He pushed off the bed and pulled on his jeans. He then walked across the hall and cautiously looked in on Zeke, who seemed to be in a deep sleep; his mouth hung open. Scooter thought his face looked terrible—what he could see of it in the half-light from the hall. He then crept quietly downstairs in his bare feet and rummaged through the kitchen cupboards exploring for breakfast. He finally found an open box of corn flakes and filled a bowl. His initial optimism for food waned, though, when he checked the milk container in the refrigerator. Scooter first noticed lumps but confirmed the age by sticking his nose in the pour spout, said something unkind, and then proceeded to dump the buttermilk-like colloid down the sink and ran some water. He disgustedly poured the cereal back into the box with some spilling under the table. He gathered up the bulk of the spillage off the floor with his hands and funneled it back into the box.

Scooter continued to scrounge through the cupboards and found a can of coffee and finally, a small coffee pot. While waiting for the brew, he pulled out his chemistry class notes from a large zippered notebook to study for a final exam that was coming up in several weeks. He was hoping to do well enough on the test to bring a B- grade up to an A. Some of the other guys on the team, including Zeke and Johnny, thought him odd to be doing well in chemistry, when they had failed the introductory course and had to take it a second time. But, organic chemistry and the diagrams of compounds, the reactions and products were something innate and came easily to him, which he realized as soon as the class started. After going over the notes for an hour while sipping coffee, he clambered back up the stairs to shower and shave. He gave Sonny a punch through the blanket, saying, "Hey pard, let's get some chow." Sonny moved slightly and responded from under a blanket with a muffled reply. Scooter thought it was probably Apache for "Not yet!" or "Go jump in a lake!" or possibly something worse.

After showering, Scooter made a second effort to rouse Sonny, and knowing his hibernation-like sleeping habits, grabbed a foot from under the blanket and gave it a pull.

"Get up dude! Let's get ready to ride some broncs!"

Sonny slowly sat on the edge of the bed, mumbling something else in Apache, and followed it with, "White eyes." He slowly shuffled down the hall to the bathroom and turned on the water in the shower. The rest of the house was quiet. After getting dressed, they opened the door to Zeke's room down the hall and saw he was still asleep, so quietly closed the door again, and walked several blocks to a café. Scooter mentioned that he thought Zeke had come back to the house with a woman.

Sonny pushed his hat back off his forehead and nodded. "Well, like I told y', if he could ride bulls as good as women, he'd be winnin' this thing."

"Two different things ain't it?" Scooter replied.

"Innit, but just in case y'didn't know."

"Judas Priest!" Scooter said, as he observed Sonny, who smiled and then turned his attention to the menu.

Scooter shook his head and did the same. He ordered scrambled eggs, toast, and bacon, washing it all down with orange juice. Sonny restricted his breakfast to a large plate of hash browns and settled for toast, after initially asking for a tortilla. He liberally flooded the potatoes with hot sauce.

After breakfast, they walked back to the house and saw that some of the others were congregating in the living room. It might as well have been a tack room, as everyone was making sure they had all their equipment packed for the rodeo.

Zeke was reclining on the living room couch and asked in a nasal twang, "Why didn't youse wait fer me?"

Scooter smiled and shook his head at Zeke's voice and checked out his face, which exhibited the yellow and purple parts of the color spectrum, partially framed by the white tape on his forehead in a kind of modernistic art piece. "That's some nasty face y'got there, pard. We checked . . . you got in late . . . ah, who was the chick?"

Zeke looked at Scooter, not saying anything for a few seconds. "Well, that girl from the bus depot. Whad y'do with those pills?"

Sonny added his two cents to the conversation by telling Scooter, "See, I told youse it would take more 'n a horn in the head to slow him down with wimmin!"

"No shit!" Scooter nodded in agreement.

"You guys don't know anythin," Zeke replied.

"Come on guys, enough socializing, we gotta get," Johnny admonished.

The team gathered in the front room for a ride to the arena. Johnny told Hank, "I don't know about how far we should take this team thing. Those guys are still a little gamey."

"Sheeit! Gamey . . . hell. You ain't smelt nothin' yet!" Zeke said and hit Johnny on the arm.

They followed Johnny outside to his car. "That's right guys, we can get powerful gamey if we've a mind to. You think this is bad, wait till Monday!" Scooter quipped. The three scrunched into the rear seat with their gear.

"I like being gamey, jus' ask Scooter here," Sonny smiled.

Johnny looked back from the front seat. "Don't overdo it, cuz we could sneak out of town without you guys." Hank laughed at this remark.

"Well, you guys are no Georgia peaches either, so we'll just be a car of gamey, fartin' dudes, I reckon," said Zeke.

"That's another thing I don't allow in my car," replied Johnny.

"Well, good luck enforcing that one," said Scooter.

Zeke and Hank laughed at Scooter's comment, and he heard Sonny snort.

"Well, I better not hear it anyway," said Johnny.

"Yeah, but we'll make sure y' smell it," said Zeke.

All of them laughed again at Zeke's reply, but Scooter nearly doubled-over, not only at the comment, but his Daffy-Duck nasal tone. It took Scooter several tries to catch his breath.

"Damned bull riders!" Johnny grinned back from the front seat.

"I ain't in that group," said Sonny.

CHAPTER FIVE
PIEFACE

Scooter and Sonny hoisted their gear bags, and Sonny slung his saddle over a shoulder. They then angled across the parking area, threaded their way through other contestants' vehicles and horse trailers, and then twisted through a small wooden gate to an aisle behind the chutes. After depositing their gear, they climbed over the thick planks of the adjoining fence and walked over to a pen of horses. Scooter had asked the stock contractor and now knew which horse he had drawn—Pieface, a sleek, muscular pinto mare with a ghost-like head. Scooter thought it looked like a blooded pony and told Sonny that he thought it might be a spoiled saddle horse.

Sonny snorted a short laugh at the thought, "Yeah, sure . . . fer you, be like gettin' on a rockin' horse."

Scooter grinned and climbed up on the fence of the holding pen to have a closer look. The horse rolled its eyes and flinched, belying any saddle horse tendencies.

"Hey Pieface, it's just me, your friendly cowboy." All the horses in the pen twitched their ears and shifted nervously at the sound of Scooter's voice. He had already heard from several contestants that Pieface was a tough draw—gnarly in the chute and one that switched gears as it bucked—a ducking, diving horse.

Scooter studied Pieface for several minutes and then backtracked to the narrow alleyway that separated the bucking chutes and stock-holding pens. He greeted several other contestants as he pushed through them. He moved his equipment bag to the shade of the fence and opened the heavy zipper. His bareback rigging was near the opening and he pulled it out. His leather-riding glove had been tucked into the hard, prow-like leather handhold. He draped the rigging over the top board of the fence and started to stretch, working the kinks out of his legs.

Finding a place near the fence that was out of the way of the other contestants, he flattened out on the ground and did a series of push-ups. He worried about a tendency not to spend enough time warming up, so he tried to focus on working his arms and legs for the explosive nature of the bareback event.

"Hey, guys . . . check out Henry," he heard one of the other contestants exclaim. "The woman went home 'n he don't even know it!"

Several of the other contestants chuckled, and Scooter smiled at the comment, "Yer a regular comedian," he grunted. Satisfied with his reply, he continued until he felt the muscles of his arms and shoulders burn and then hopped back onto his feet, taking in a deep breath.

He dug through his equipment bag and pulled out a pair of angled, long-shanked spurs. He strapped these onto his boots, placing a foot up on the fence, stretching out his hamstrings. He forced the leather thong attached to each spur under the arch of his boot in front of the heel and tightened the strap across the top of his arch. As usual, he put the right spur on first. He splayed his feet out wide and reached between them toward the ground to stretch his groin muscles.

He again rifled through his equipment bag and pulled out a rolled-up pair of tan-colored chaps. He unfurled them, showing the black trim and fringe. Scooter liked their leather smell. This and the earthy, yet aromatic smell of the horses in the near-by pens reminded him of his family and the ranch—maybe the smell in the old barn. Thinking of his family calmed his nerves somewhat. The term "butterflies" was too mild for what Scooter felt before a rodeo. It was more like an electric current pulsing through his core. It was not as bad as what Zeke sometimes felt though before a bull ride. *Causes him to toss his cookies . . .* Scooter had gotten too close to Zeke at the first spring rodeo before he knew of this tendency and had to scramble out the way. *What a gross habit . . . like a farm dog, all hunched up like that . . . I'm glad I don't enter the bull riding anymore.* He remembered that Zeke was to inform the rodeo secretary about not being able to take his bull. *They should know just by looking at his ugly mug.*

Scooter clenched his jaw to focus on the task ahead. A good score in this second go-round, along with his fourth place in the first, would put him in a good position to win the average and the championship. Any score though would help his chances of qualifying for the regional finals. His riding had been up and down all spring.

He hoped his luck would hold out though. *But luck . . . fickle, like how this trip started . . . Zeke's truck breaking down, and us riding a bus all night . . . then Zeke being slammed into the horns of that bull the first go-round. What a mean-lookin' face!* Sonny and Scooter had called Zeke Mr. Halloween, but Zeke hadn't found this very amusing. *Course, the flip side of the whole thing was meeting those two girls at the dance. Well, meetings not the right word . . . was like they fell out of the sky and plopped right in front of our faces . . . liked to gave Sonny a heart attack . . . me too, I guess.* He smiled at the vision of them . . . *But that willowy barrel racer, Charlene . . . those strawberry-like lips, cat eyes . . . dark hair . . . wonder if she's here yet?* Scooter thought about what Sonny had said—about her being after him like a dog on a rat. Scooter thought there was likely a better analogy, but guessed it was better than the one they normally used of flies on shit. He wouldn't mind, though, if she was after him.

Scooter shook the thoughts out of his mind. He had to concentrate on this horse; on how he was going to rear back and spur it. He continued to loosen up—extended his arms out and twisted back and forth from the waist like a weather vane in a swirling canyon wind.

Several angular amber-colored pieces of rosin were nestled in a side pocket of Scooter's equipment bag, and he fished one out. He used his glove to crumble it onto the handhold of his rigging and then fumbled with a package of matches and ran a flame across the powdered material. He worked the melt-ed goo into the handhold with his glove. This was the last part of his prepara-tion. The tacky feel of the handhold and the piney scent focused his mind and his being as if into one central point of energy for the eight-second ride.

He looked up as the roustabouts started loading horses into the chutes. Zeke, who had been joking with several other contestants, sauntered over and asked, "Y'ready?"

Scooter grunted an affirmative and pulled his rigging off the fence. "Let's saddle a horse." He climbed up onto the side of the chute and carefully set the rigging onto Pieface's withers. The horse flinched and canted her ears back toward the activity. Zeke took a long wire hook and reached underneath the horse's stomach to snag the D-ring. Pieface flinched and kicked forward and then for good measure, let fly with a loud bang into the back of the chute.

"Hell's bells, man, damned horse nearly got my hand!" Zeke ex-claimed.

Scooter shook the horse's mane and talked softly to it, saying over and over, "Hey Pie, hey Pie." The horse continued to fight them, and he asked it with more force, "Are you some kind of a rookie or what?"

Sonny climbed up onto the side of the chute to see if he could help. He had told the other two that with his Apache heritage he innately knew how to handle horses. Scooter had matched his friend's boastful attitude, say-ing that he was from a long line of bronc riders. But now, he wasn't so con-fident. Finally, Scooter was satisfied with the set-up and stood on the back of the chutes, absently watching the other riders that came out before him. Scooter noticed one make a decent ride. The current humming through his core was strong. He felt like a coiled spring and did a series of deep-knee bends to relieve some tension.

As the bareback horse in front of Scooter's was cleared out of the arena, the chute boss from in front of the chute gate said, "Yer up next, bud." Scooter stood above the horse, straddling it, and meticulously threaded his gloved hand into the handhold. He slowly crouched down onto the horse, but it reared, nearly throwing him out of the chute. Zeke pulled him away from the danger.

Scooter swore forcefully and started over, but Pieface continued to fight. The chute boss was growing impatient at the hold-up. "Yer as timid as a naked man goin' through a barbed-wire fence, son."

The comment fanned Scooter's temper. "Goddammit! I'll take 'er when I'm damned good 'n ready!" he hotly retorted.

Sonny slid up to Pieface's head, folded one of its ears over and squeezed. "Take 'er now, pard."

Scooter felt his anger subside slightly and threaded his hand back into the handhold, then slowly crouched onto the horse's back. He carefully slid his spurs ahead of the horse's shoulders, pulled his chaps away from his feet, and then again tugged his hat down, squashing his ears out.

"Get the mark-out," Zeke reminded.

Scooter nodded, "Let's go, boys!" The horse exploded out in a high jump upon the chute gate being opened. Scooter was not sure if he had followed Pieface back to the ground to have his spurs in front of its shoulders for the first jump to complete the mark-out rule. Pieface soared high into the air a second time and then whirled, causing Scooter to spur over the horse's neck, suddenly sitting sidesaddle. He reared over toward the horse's rear to get it back between his legs but was nearly spun sideways the other way. Realizing he was flopped onto the side of the horse away from his riding hand, he tried to spur back into the middle. He felt the horse whirl again though and he remained over on the side of it, not having any luck getting back to the middle. He sarcastically thought: *This ought to score real high* and continued to flop on the side of the horse, to be jerked violently along each time the horse left the ground.

Scooter double grabbed to save himself at the sound of the buzzer that signaled the end of the ride and looked for a rescue from the pick-up man. Pieface continued to buck, letting out throaty grunts with each effort, whipping Scooter back and forth. He desperately lunged with his left arm and grabbed the pick-up man as he galloped alongside. Pieface leapt away from the pick-up horse, stringing Scooter across the intervening gap. The force dislocated his shoulder, causing him to lose his grip on the pickup man's saddle, and he plowed a furrow between the two horses into the gravelly surface of the arena.

Scooter spit out bits of arena dirt as he slowly regained his feet. He could feel the bones of the joint grind together. The injured arm hung limply, and he held his wrist as he gingerly walked back to the chute area to scattered applause from the crowd. On the way, he retrieved his hat, which had sailed away early in the contest, a lonely reminder in front of the chute of what had been scripted by Pieface. Zeke and Sonny met him at the chutes with an EMT. "It's been out before. Have t' pull it straight out 'n over," Scooter told them.

The EMT gazed at the sloping shoulder. "Just a minute, we need the doc to look at this."

Scooter followed the EMT to the emergency tent where a man in a white lab jacket was treating a large abrasion on another contestant's elbow. Scooter noticed it was a different person heading the treatment center than the day before. Scooter and the other contestant nodded at each other. "Been a tough day on the ranch, I reckon," said the contestant as he left.

"Yeah, I reckon," said Scooter. He was feeling a little nauseous.

The doctor checked Scooter's sloping shoulder. "We'll see if we can get it in." To Zeke and Sonny, he said, "Help him with his shirt."

Scooter gripped the top board of the fence with his good arm while the doctor tried to reduce the dislocation by placing a foot under the injured arm and then pulling it out over the joint.

Finally, as sweat began to form several muddy rivulets down the side of his face, Scooter grunted, "Ain't no use doc, sonsabitch's stuck . . . give me a second, I need to relax it." He shook his arm out and let it relax against his leg. "Okay, try it again."

He felt light-headed, but forced himself not to tighten the shoulder muscles as the doctor again pulled out on the arm. Scooter had to let it go, not worrying about the pain. He clenched his teeth and uttered another, "Sonuvabitch!" as the bones of the joint crossed each other. Suddenly, his arm felt better. He moved the shoulder back and forth to make sure that it worked. "Hey, thanks, doc." He followed the doctor back into the emergency tent.

"It needs to be immobilized for a few days, and then you need to start strengthening it," the doctor told him.

"Like?" Scooter asked.

"Lots of push-ups, for example."

"I do some already," Scooter replied.

"I'm thinking you need to get up to a lot . . . eighty or more, eventually pull-ups, but start out light after a week or so. Otherwise . . . I mean if you don't extensively strengthen the shoulder, you're going to need surgery." He wrapped an Ace bandage around Scooter's shoulder and strung it around his chest and back, and then pinned the end.

Scooter shook his head to the surgery, but said, "Okay," meaning that he understood about exercising.

"Every time you dislocate it . . . well, that stretches the ligaments," the doctor continued to explain.

"My beat-up face don't feel so bad now," Zeke said, having watched Scooter's shoulder treatment.

The doctor looked up from writing Scooter a prescription, "This is for inflammation. Here's some aspirin for pain." He handed Scooter an envelope. "Don't take more than two every four hours . . . they're strong. Both of you should take it easy for a few days."

"I know, and thanks again," Scooter said, but figured they probably wouldn't take it too easy. He slowly pulled his shirt back on, first tugging it over the injured shoulder; the bulk of the bandage. He had to leave the sleeve unfastened and rolled it up onto his forearm.

"Y'goin' to live?" Sonny had retrieved Scooter's rigging and brought it over.

Scooter didn't answer and instead replied, "That Pieface . . . more moves than a snake in a fryin' pan." They drifted back to the alleyway behind the chutes.

"Sunfishin' bitch is what!" Zeke said, "Judges said y'slapped 'er." Zeke meant Scooter had touched the horse with his free hand and had been disqualified.

Scooter smiled at Zeke's quip, but said, "Yeah, thought I might've. That horse had me flapping around like a damned ragdoll!"

Sonny grinned and shook his head. "That flappin's good!" Scooter and Zeke laughed.

"Y'need any more help gettin' unsuited?" Sonny asked. He rolled Scooter's chaps and stored them in his equipment bag.

"Naw, it's alright. I'm just goin' to rest up for a while. You guys go ahead and get ready."

Sonny unlatched the wrapped-up stirrups and cinches on his saddle, while Zeke watched.

Scooter made sure all his equipment was stored in his bag and moved it to a shady spot along the alleyway, then sat down on it with his back against the fence, contemplating the frustrations of his outing. He realized a cowboy could not ride all the broncs and injury was part of rodeo. This trip had been tough luck so far. *But, maybe Sonny will win big in the saddle broncs—the average. He's been riding well all spring.* They still had to pay for the repairs to Zeke's truck on the way back. He brushed the dirt off his hat and tried to re-crease the crown.

"You okay?" a girl's voice asked. Scooter looked over and saw that it was Charlene. She had climbed partway onto the fence near the edge of the chutes and was peering over the top.

Scooter contemplated the view of her for a few seconds. She looked . . . *What was the word? Expectant . . . pert, maybe.* His mouth was dry, and he said, "I guess . . . you got any water?" His voice sounded hollow, frog-like. He cleared his throat.

"Come on, I have some in the truck." Her smile jolted him, and Scooter suddenly thought of a cool breeze on an otherwise hot summer day.

He laboriously stood up and walked to the end of the alleyway, and then slowly climbed the fence. He still had his spurs on and was careful not to snag them as he climbed down to join her. Charlene had on tight jeans, and Scooter was suddenly struck with her tall, good looks and thought: *Wow . . . nice buns!* He liked her thick, dark hair and how she had wound it into a single braid, which hung down between her shoulder blades.

"I was sorry to see you get hurt. You had a tough horse . . . at least I thought so." She smiled at him as she said this. "Come on, my truck's this way."

He nodded as he studied her; her arching eyebrows, sparkling smile, curved mouth, and her full pink lips. *Maybe she put on lipstick.* Her eyes especially mesmerized him, and he was not sure whether they were blue-green or maybe they would be called turquoise. He nodded again and mumbled, "Uh-huh, thanks. Yeah . . . tough."

Scooter had nearly forgotten Pieface and barely felt the throbbing in his shoulder.

CHAPTER SIX
CUCUMBERS AND FRESHLY CUT ALFALFA

They sat on the running board of Charlene's truck, both sipping water. "That horse was pretty wild, you know," Charlene said.

"Yeah, it was nasty to get any kind of timing. Zeke said it was like a belly dancer on wheels." Charlene laughed. "I've dislocated this shoulder before," he continued.

"Well, it can be a tough life," she said.

"I know, but it gets in a person's blood. I'm going have to bear-down on strengthening this thing though, so it's not an issue. That's what the doc here said."

"Like exercising?"

"Yeah, we do some stuff already in the weight room, but I gotta do like about five thousand push-ups." He smiled at her with his exaggeration.

She laughed. "You're funny."

Scooter noticed that Charlene had a nice smell about her, perhaps like diced cucumbers, or maybe fresh-cut alfalfa. He suddenly had a soft feeling inside, as if Charlene had melted something in his chest. He thought he probably smelled like horse manure, or at best, horse sweat. He was wondering if, or why, Charlene was interested in him. Desperate came to mind, but then he thought: *No, that ain't it, she's too attractive.*

He started to speak, then cleared his throat, and surprisingly heard himself ask, "Are you interested in me?"

She looked at him, smiling at the question, "Whatever gave you that idea?" and laughed, which made him smile. "I saw you ride at the rodeo down in Alamosa, and thought, 'Well, there's a nice guy.' I have to admit, I was attracted . . . wanted to meet you. I said 'Hi' later, but you were talking to some guys. I think you told a joke because the other guys were laughing. Anyway, I veered away and regretted it then. I asked a girl I know about you. She goes to Southwestern, too. We were in high school together."

Her statement about the girl perked Scooter's interest and he asked, "Oh yeah? Who is she?" Charlene told him the girl's name, but he did not know her. "So, what'd she say?"

"Oh, that you seemed to be a nice guy . . . kind of quiet," Charlene smiled at him and continued. "So, do you have a girlfriend?"

Scooter didn't want to tell her that so far in his life, girlfriends were rare. "Not right now," he said. "I think you're nice, though," amazing himself with his nerve. "Do you have a boyfriend somewhere that I should know about?"

"Well, no, not right now either. I was going with Billy Hall for a while. He's on the team here. Do you know him?"

It seemed to Scooter that a shadow passed across Charlene's face, as she asked the question

"I know of him. He's a good steer wrestler."

"Yes, but I finally realized that he thinks the world revolves around him. We just didn't mesh. He thought he owned me, like one of his horses."

"Well, I'm glad about you getting loose from being one of his horses, to be a wild, free mustang, I reckon."

Charlene laughed at his comment and studied him. "Yeah, a wild mustang. That's okay!"

Like a cloud had passed and the sun is out again, Scooter thought and smiled at the sunny weather.

"Well, I'd like to visit more, but guess I better get back. I'm supposed to help Sonny with his saddle bronc . . . if I can."

Charlene seemed to be thinking about something and her smile had tightened. Scooter thought she was very beautiful and gazed at her full, curved lips, finally realizing that his gaze had fixed on them and he shook his attention away.

"How 'bout I treat you to dinner after the rodeo?" Charlene asked. Scooter had started to get up but sat back down. "Well, that'd be nice, but the other guys . . . would Squirrel want to come along? 'Cause Sonny's with me." He was thinking about Zeke but decided he would probably be hanging around with the waitress.

"I'll see. They're so shy with each other. He never said anything to her last night."

"Yeah, Sonny hasn't been out in the world . . . well, among white women I reckon."

She laughed at his remark and asked, "How's your bullrider friend?"

"Oh yeah . . . Zeke's better'n a person would think. He and a waitress from the bus depot hooked up it seems, and he was with her last night. Neither Sonny nor I . . . well, me at least, could believe it."

"You guys were worried about him. That's kind of funny. I mean about him being out on a date with a concussion."

They both laughed. "I guess it is when you think about it. Would'a given her a start if he'd a keeled over!" He pushed his hat up off his forehead. "But about dinner . . . let's see later . . . I mean, I'd like to go! It's not every day a guy gets asked out by a good-lookin' woman."

Charlene smiled at his comment. "You think so, huh?"

Scooter nodded. "Yeah, it's quite rare I think!"

Charlene linked her arm through his. "I think you're joshing me. But here's what you can do. I need to feed and water my horse after the barrel racing. You want to help?"

Scooter was thinking about the luck of the draw, and maybe he was luckier than he had thought after his bareback ride. "Yeah . . . okay. I'd like that." Charlene stood up with him. "So, good luck today on your run," he said.

Thanks! I'm always pretty nervous before. I need to start getting ready, so I'm not rushed and have a good warm-up."

"Yeah, tell me about it. I get like a coiled spring, could about bounce all around the arena before bareback."

Charlene let out a peal of laughter at his explanation. "That's pretty tightly coiled! I just get those butterflies, as they say. Well, can we meet back here at my truck and you can help me with my horse?"

Her laughter at his comment made Scooter laugh too and he felt happy. "Okay, you have a deal. I better get over there."

Scooter thought about Charlene as he walked back through the pickups and horse trailers, and through the small gate to the area behind the chutes. *She's better than I thought at the dance . . . after. She likes to laugh. I like to make her. I love that wide, bright smile . . . the smiling eyes. That could be her name if she was Apache. Wonder what happened with her and that Billy . . . probably a possessive jerk.*

Sonny was sitting on the ground in his saddle, checking the length of the stirrups by extending his legs forward, and then kicking back to the cantle board in the back. Scooter knew this was part of Sonny's normal routine—a way to limber up and to get his mindset on being in the saddle on a bronc.

Their attention centered on the horses as they were loaded into the chutes. Sonny's was placed in the last one, and he climbed onto the chute to attach his thickly braided hack rein to the halter and draped it over the chute gate. Zeke came over to help and used a wire hook to snag the cinch ring under the horse's stomach, then reached through the gaps in the chute gate to thread the latigo through and pulled it up to where Sonny could reach it. He and Zeke set the saddle and cinched it down to where it was snug by rocking it back and forth. They then did the same with the back cinch but left some sag. The big black stood patiently. Sonny then measured the rein back to the swell of the saddle trying to figure how much of it the horse would need as it bucked. Taking the rein too short would pull him over the front end into a header. Too much and he would have no point of contact for balance and leverage. He plucked several strands of hair out of the horse's mane and threaded these through the soft weave of the cotton rein as a marker for the correct length. He then calmly sat on the top of the chute with his feet on the seat of the saddle watching the other rides and buck-offs.

Scooter observed Sonny to see if he was nervous. Sonny looked back and smiled. Scooter thought: *It must be nice to be so calm—he might as well be sittin' in church.*

"Both you and this horse are way too calm."

Sonny smiled. "The calm afore the storm, innit."

"Yeah, it's a storm alright!" Scooter replied. *Maybe he goes into some kind of concentration trance before he rides . . . I need to find out and do it, too.* His throbbing shoulder though was detracting from any good feelings about the "storm" and he took a deep breath.

Finally, the chute boss came over and said, "Valverde? We're goin' to you next, buddy." Sonny stood up on the back of the chute and did several deep knee bends, then climbed over onto the saddle. Zeke came over and held onto the halter from the back of the chute as a safety measure in case the horse reared. Scooter had not done much to help. It seemed like the other guys were excluding him some from their usual routine.

Sonny placed his foot into the right stirrup first, pulled his chaps out of the way, and did the same with the left; his usual routine. He took the rein, looking for the hair marker, and at this mark ran the rein between his third and little finger. He threw the tail of the rein over his shoulder.

"Get a good mark-out on him, pardner," Scooter reminded.

Sonny pulled his hat down and extended his feet in the stirrups to be in front of the horse's shoulders. He then pushed the hand holding the rein out in front of him. "Let's go!" he said.

The horse wheeled out of the chute with a high jump, but Sonny angled his feet up with it to have his spurs in front of the horse's shoulders to complete the mark-out. He then got in rhythm with the horse, spurring in an arc from the front when the horse's front feet hit the ground and then to the cantle board of the saddle in the back during the apex of the jump. As Sonny had stated earlier, the horse jumped and kicked straight ahead for the eight seconds, and Scooter thought Sonny had made a great ride. So apparently did Zeke, who placed two fingers into his mouth and from his perch near the top of the empty chute let out a loud, piercing whistle.

After being plucked off by one of the pick-up men, Sonny walked back to the chutes. Scooter heard the announcer indicate a score of seventy-five and thought it was low. He told Sonny, "I think it's five points too low, pard," and wondered if Sonny would be in the top five to receive money.

"I think yer right, the score'ns been low, but our boy got gypped some," said Zeke.

Sonny didn't know. "It felt like a good ride, en it's better'n a kick in the teeth, innit? I should be in the average anyways en I need these points to make sure 'bout regionals."

They retrieved Sonny's saddle and rein from the unsaddling pens behind the chutes, and he started packing his gear.

"Those girls we met last night might want to go to dinner with us, what you think?" Scooter asked.

"Are any of the team headin' back tonight?"

Scooter realized that Sonny was ready to head back to Durango and would rather do that than go out to dinner. "No. Sounds like Johnny's still planning on leaving early tomorrow morning, and we can jam in with those guys to Saguache."

"I doan know about that girl from last night . . . Squirrel. She never hardly said anythin."

"That's what she said about you," Scooter replied. "She's a tame squirrel, y'know . . . she ain't goin' to bite you!"

Sonny grinned at Scooter's comment. "Well, maybe! Me an' her ain't likely to be on no date."

"She and I ain't," Scooter said.

"Yeah, whatever. Doan give me any that white-eye bullshit."

Scooter grinned at Sonny's comment, "White-eye? Crying out loud!"

CHAPTER SEVEN
PURE COUNTRY

Scooter watched the barrel-racing event and saw Charlene make a respectable run. It didn't seem like she was in the money, though. After the event was over, he walked through the parking area toward her truck, but didn't see her. He didn't want to be too obvious, so he went over to use a port-a-john and then went by the concession stand and bought a soda. His shoulder was aching, and he threw down two of the pills the doc had given him. He walked back toward Charlene's truck and then saw her leading her horse.

He angled over to her. "Hey, a pretty good run, huh?"

"Oh, it was okay I guess. We went wide on the last barrel, so it was a little slow." She looked at him and continued, "We just need everything to come together for one run sometime . . . no mistakes. You know what I mean?"

"Absolutely . . . we're all looking for perfection . . . me, too." She studied him, searching. He smiled again, her eyes mesmerizing, unsettling him.

"Yes, perfection . . . I like the thought. Help me load her and we can go over to the stable." He set his soda inside the truck on the dash and helped load her horse. That completed, she said, "Hop in!" and he got in on the passenger side.

After he closed the door, she grabbed his soda and took a drink. He smiled at her, as this seemed to him an intimate act. "I can get you one."

She smiled and handed it back. "Nah, I just needed a sip."

Scooter observed her profile; her curved, slightly upturned nose and dark lashes. Her ear was partially covered by her hair, which had been pulled back into a long single braid, but he noticed a round turquoise earring. She turned her head and smiled. He inadvertently nodded but was not sure what he was trying to communicate.

As they slowly drove to stables west of the arena, Scooter asked, "What's your major?"

"I'm in education," she replied, "but I took an animal science course with Squirrel and liked it. I better make up my mind though, because this is my third year. Squirrel is in animal science. Says she's going to raise pygmy goats in California and make a fortune. I don't know why I'm telling you this . . . she's a goat-roper on the rodeo team and I guess she likes them."

Scooter thought the idea of raising goats was interesting. "So, would she raise them for hair or to eat?" he asked.

Charlene laughed. "That's funny . . . the way you said it. Well, maybe both, I don't know. Maybe milk . . . you know, cheese."

"Are you going to throw in with her?"

"No, probably not, but animal science seems more exciting than teaching right now."

"Oh, I don't know about that, twenty-five or thirty screaming first graders. I can see you there, actually," Scooter replied.

She laughed and then asked, "How about you?"

"I'm in agriculture, but it's just a two-year program down there and I have to transfer somewhere like here next year if I stay in it."

"What do you want to do, stay in it or do something else?"

"Well, I'm like you. I see there are other things out there, and I do well in other stuff—English composition, chemistry . . . I don't know. I guess I take after my mom more than my dad. He figured I would take animal science or husbandry and come back to the ranch. My older brother is entrenched there. But . . . well, Dad would be disappointed if I went off to do something else. He wants to put in some additional wells and raise more crops . . . you know, alfalfa . . . hay."

"So where is this ranch?"

"Out east, south of Bunting, if you know where that is."

Charlene nodded, but asked, "Do you have any other brothers?"

"No, I have a younger sister who's in high school . . . a sophomore. What about you?"

"I have a younger sister. She is nothing like me. Not a girl jock. She had a horse for a while, but is now mostly interested in shopping, and lately, boys," Charlene smiled at him as she said this.

"Well, guess that's normal." She grabbed the can of soda from him and took another sip. He watched her; liked her doing it.

She handed it back with a sly look. "Thanks, I'm parched!"

"I like sharing actually . . . with you."

"You do, huh?" Charlene smiled at him as she said this; the center of Scooter's chest felt warm again.

They approached the stable, backed the trailer up toward a gate, got out of the truck, and unloaded Charlene's horse, a sleek sorrel Quarter Horse mare that had a splash of white on its forehead. They took it through a small gate into a corral. Charlene stripped off the halter.

Scooter stroked the horse's neck. "I like your horse. What's its name?"

"She has a long name . . . registered, but I call her Star. Yes, this is my baby. I've had her for about three years."

Scooter helped run water into a small tank, while Charlene broke open a bale of hay and tossed some into a feeder in the center of the corral. He studied Charlene without trying to be obvious. She looked lithe. He liked her long legs and trim waist. She smiled at his obvious interest. Her sparkling eyes sent something into him—like a shock wave. He noticed her pinkish lips and mouth that tilted upwards at the corners, wondering what it would be like to kiss her. *If she knew what I was thinking . . .*

Charlene brought out a comb and brush, currying the horse's mane and then across it's back, concentrating on the sweat marks from the saddle. Scooter stroked its nose and its forehead while he observed her.

"What about teaching school and raising, maybe training Quarter Horses . . . you know, barrel racing horses?" Charlene stood on tiptoe, peered over Star's back, and gave Scooter a serious look.

"Well, the thought crossed my mind before. A person would need a ranch though, some acreage." She continued currying Star.

"Yeah, I know," said Scooter. The horse became tired of the attention and pushed over to the feeder. Scooter followed Charlene into the tack room.

He jumped up slightly to sit on the end of a hay bale, and asked, "So where's your place in Colorado Springs?" he asked.

Charlene hung the bridle on a wall-peg and then placed the curry-comb on a shelf. "My folks have a small place east of town. I grew up there. It's kind of like a small ranch, but town is moving out toward it now, surrounding us. I bet you've driven right by it when you go out east to your place."

"Next time I do, I'll stop in." he grinned at her as he said this.

"Yes, you'd better!" she smiled and moved over to him.

"Why don't you bring your horse out to the ranch sometime and I'll give you a tour . . . or you can ride one of ours. It's not so far out there from Colorado Springs . . . maybe a couple hours, a little more."

"That'd be nice. But what would your folks say?"

"They'd be mighty surprised . . . I mean that I have a girl . . . ah . . . I was going to say, girlfriend. Anyway, I think they would really like you, and you would like my mom. She's very cool . . . might have you help her make apple pies or something. Dad . . . as long as I did my work he wouldn't care, I guess."

Charlene looked at him intently and then moved to stand between his legs and put her hands on his shoulders. Scooter could feel his heart thumping. He looked up at her. She was studying him through her lashes.

"We don't need to get over to the rodeo yet, do we?" she asked.

"Not right away . . . till the bull ridin's over.

He continued to be surprised at his nerve, but he had already made up his mind that he had to take some chances. He had been thinking for a while what it would be like to kiss her. He put his arms around her shoulders as she stood over him, and then moved the hand of his uninjured arm into her hair and pulled her to him for a kiss. She leaned into him, and they kissed again for a longer period.

Her lips were soft and pliable. She tasted sweet. Scooter was conscious again of her fresh smell. "You know, you smell good . . . like cucumbers or fresh-cut alfalfa."

She laughed and said, "You're funny . . . and you really are country."

He laughed with her. "I know I must smell like . . . ah, well, horse manure."

Charlene laughed again at his remark and said, "Well, you smell like horses, and I don't mind that. You still have sand in your hair." She gently brushed the back of his neck.

"We're heading back to Saguache to pick up Zeke's truck tomorrow morning, then to Durango. I wish we had more time."

"I already know about the time. Are you guys going to Laramie in two weeks?" Charlene asked.

"Well, I think so, but I'll have to see how this shoulder is and get ready for finals. I know I'm going to the last one down at La Junta, 'cause our semester's over then and I'll just head home after."

"So, bring your homework to Laramie and we can study together."

"That sounds like a good plan. I may need to place again in the last two rodeos to have a chance of making the regionals. Are you going?"

"No, I haven't been consistent enough."

He continued to muse, "That'd be nice if you and I both did."

"Well, let's try to do Laramie anyway."

Scooter nodded. "Laramie's good. I suppose we better get back to the arena."

They kissed again. Charlene pushed into him until he could feel her breasts on his chest and her fingers on the back of his neck. He laced his fingers through her hair again. It felt soft.

He again surprised himself with his nerve, saying, "You're doing things to me!"

"Yeah, I mean to," she replied, and they both laughed.

He studied her to see if she was teasing him and to determine if he was being led down some strange, dead-end path.

She pulled her hand from the back of his neck in a caress and lightly rubbed his sore shoulder. "Guess we better go though. I still have to find

Squirrel and make sure she'll go to dinner with us and your friend"

"Yeah, Sonny. And vice-versa," said Scooter.

They closed and locked the door to the shed and climbed into her truck.

The bull riding was nearly over when they arrived back at the arena. "Let's meet back here after the rodeo, and I'll give you guys a ride over to your house," Charlene said.

"Well, we want to get some of this arena dust off, but you don't have to drive us. We'll probably ride over to the house with Johnny . . . the team guys. I'm thinking Sonny will get a check, so we'll need to go by the office. We just need to find out if Sonny and Squirrel are going. I'll meet you here, after, and we can see about it. We might have to go without them, hint, hint!"

His comment made Charlene laugh. "Yes, hint, hint at what?" she asked.

"We have a date, no matter what. There's no backing out."

"Okay cowboy. That's fine by me."

Scooter just nodded. She squeezed his hand. He thought: *Judas Priest, this girl! What have I got myself into here?*

He walked across the parking area to the chutes and found Zeke and Sonny. "Hey! Where y'been? Sonny ended up third in the go and third in the ave, so we gotta stop by the office for a pretty good payout," Zeke said.

Scooter doubled up his fist and hit Sonny's in what had become their traditional congratulations greeting. "Awesome! That's better than we were thinking after that score."

Sonny wryly grinned, "Take it when you kin get it, I say."

"No kidding!" Scooter said. He told Zeke, "Sonny and I have to see if we're going to dinner with some women. We gotta meet up to make arrangements in a few minutes, so tell Johnny to wait up for us to go to the office. He must be getting some pay for that bareback ride."

"Yeah, he got fifth in the go-round, but where'd you guys find any women? The earth must've switched poles or something," Zeke said.

"Yeah, something like that. Actually, they found us at the dance last night. Even offered to help us find you when we went back to the house to check on whether you were alive or dead, not realizing that you were screwing your damaged brains out with that waitress!"

"Now, don't go assuming anything about me 'n her!" Zeke's voice went up an octave.

"We know you," Scooter replied. To Sonny, he said, "Come on let's see about this date."

"I ain't sure about this," Sonny said. He hung back, not making a move to go along with Scooter.

Scooter stopped and faced him. "Here's what you do . . . tell her something of your culture. You don't have to do anything else but tell her a little about yourself . . . teach her some Apache words, and then ask her about herself . . . you know, what she's majoring in and stuff like that. She's a goat-roper y'know."

"Sheeit, you guys are like babes in the woods. This date ought to be real interesting!"

Scooter absorbed Zeke's comment, thinking he might be right.

"Come on, let's at least talk to them." Sonny didn't reply, as they slowly walked toward Charlene's truck and approached Charlene and Squirrel.

Scooter spoke first, and said, "Hi, Squirrel!" He still thought it was a strange name for a girl but made a mental note to remind Sonny that she already had an Indian-like name.

"Hello, you look the worse for wear," Squirrel said.

"Yeah, it's been a rough day in the arena, unless you're mister bronc rider here." But wondered if maybe his hat was on backwards or maybe he had forgotten to zip the fly on his pants. He looked at Charlene, but she just smiled at him.

Finally, Sonny said something in Apache.

"Not yet! Scooter said, and then explained to the puzzled girls, "I told him he ought to tell you something about his culture . . . just to make things interesting."

The two girls started to laugh, and Squirrel said, "You guys are funny." And to Sonny said, "Yes, I saw how good a bronc rider you are, is it part of your culture?"

"Sure," then added, when nobody else spoke, "well, in my family, anyways. They live in the mountains . . . northern New Mexico . . . near Jicarilla. Y'ever been there?"

"I never even heard of it."

Sonny and Squirrel continued to talk, and Scooter looked at Charlene. She was smiling.

"What are you thinking?"

"That I like this moment." She put her hand in his.

The gesture softened him toward her even more, yet he was still skeptical and wondered if something this good would last very long; perhaps it was fleeting, like a fresh spring shower.

Instead of voicing his thoughts, he said, "We better get back to our ride. We still have to stop at the rodeo office to get Mr. Bronc rider's money, and then clean up so's we'll be all slicked up for dinner."

Charlene smiled at his use of words and said, "Okay cowboy, you better get slicked up. We'll stop by that house around seven-thirty. Is that good?"

"That should give us enough time. We'll see you then."

As they walked back over though the parking lot of horse trailers and trucks, Scooter said to Sonny, "See, she hasn't bitten you yet."

"Naw, she's okay I guess. I'm gonna see if she can send me some of them nuts."

"What? You just met her, and you want to take advantage of her already. You're corrupt!"

Both laughed at their little joke. Scooter was glad Sonny was in a good mood about the dinner date. They rode over to the rodeo office with Johnny and Zeke.

"Where are the other guys?" Scooter asked.

"They went to a bar for beers with some guys from here," Johnny replied.

Sonny received nearly three hundred dollars for the go-round and average placing in saddle broncs, and Johnny received eighty dollars for placing fifth in the second go-round of the bareback event.

The rodeo secretary and stock contractor wished Zeke and Scooter better luck at the next rodeo.

"Let me know when I draw that Double Ought again . . . before I leave home!" Zeke said. Everyone laughed at his comment.

CHAPTER EIGHT
CITY LIGHTS

Scooter and Sonny hustled to get their gear upstairs to the small bedroom. "Hit the shower while I stow this stuff. I got to get this mummy casing off my arm," Scooter told Sonny.

Sonny stripped off his jeans and shirt and then ambled down the hall to the bathroom in just his skivvies. Scooter wondered if Sonny was going to put on clean ones. He unsnapped his shirt and unwound the bandage from around his chest and shoulder. He then painstakingly rolled the bandage up again for future use and then laid out clean clothes, including his best shirt and a pair of new Wranglers that he had carefully creased.

Sonny came back into the room with wet hair. "Bout good as the sweat lodge on the rez."

"Ain't you going to change underwear?" Scooter asked.

"Why? She ain't gonna see 'em."

"Yeah, but dude, you been in 'em two, three days. Talk about gamey."

"Quit stewin' man, maybe I ain't goin' t' wear any. Y'act like yer my mother."

"That could be your first and last date, if you advertised it, I mean."

Sonny laughed at Scooter's comment and said, "Worry 'bout yer own underwear." He then proceeded to pull a tin-can lid out of his duffle bag and bent over close to the mirror on the dresser. He had folded the lid into a sharp angle so that two edges of it touched and used it as a tweezer to pluck out any stray hair of his sparse beard.

Scooter watched the process fairly amazed and finally said, "I wished shaving was so easy, but why don't you use real tweezers instead of that soup can lid?"

Sonny stepped back from looking in the mirror. "Why? This works. Instead a worryin' 'bout me, y'better get yerself fluff'd up fer that woman."

Scooter took his clean clothes and sauntered down the hall toward the bathroom only to see Zeke scurry in and to then hear the shower running. He was cognizant of the ache in his shoulder and shook his arm for relief as he backtracked to the bedroom. "I don't believe it . . . two minutes and that Zeke ran in there. He better hurry."

"You were worry'n 'bout my underwear en all, so that's what y'get." Sonny was still studying his image in the mirror to make sure there were no stray hairs left.

Scooter watched Sonny pull his hair back as he looked in a mirror.

After waiting for what seemed like an hour, he finally heard the shower stop. He hustled down the hall again and waited at the door, finally giving it a kick and hollered at Zeke to hurry.

Zeke opened the door and smiled through his mangled face. "You better not have used all the hot water," Scooter said.

"Of course, not, pard. I'd never do that to you."

Scooter turned on the shower and found it was tepid, so hurried to soap up, and rinsed as the water turned cold. It wasn't long before he was jumping in and out of the cold spray and plotting revenge on Zeke for being so inconsiderate. He got out, quickly toweled, and then shaved, also with cold water. He had to stop the bleeding from a small razor nick on his chin and finally stuck on a small piece of toilet paper.

Johnny approached the bathroom, but Scooter said, "You're going to have to wait a while, 'cause I just took a cold shower."

"Shit, I might've figured you guys would use all the hot water."

"Don't blame that one on me. Mine was cold the whole way," Scooter lied.

He fluffed his hair with a towel and walked back to the bedroom, then pulled on a pair of creased jeans. Sonny sat on the bed, watching, and commented, "Man, she's got you. Ain't that yer best shirt?"

Scooter turned toward Sonny, as he pushed an arm into the sleeve of his shirt. "Y'know what? She smells like fresh-mowed alfalfa." Scooter grinned as he said it.

Sonny shook his head and said, "Fresh-mowed alfalfa . . . chit man, I knew she's trouble."

Scooter suddenly regretted that he had shown his softer side. "Don't tell Zeke I said that, okay?"

"He already thinks yer cuckoo." They finished dressing and trundled downstairs. Zeke followed them down the hallway and down the stairs. Scooter turned at the bottom of the staircase. "Thanks a lot, you moron, for using all the hot water."

"I don't know what you're talking about. There was plenty when I showered. You apparently didn't realize it, but y'missed your butt and hit your face with TP!"

"Just wait, pard, revenge will be sweet, and it will be applied when you least expect it."

Sonny said to Zeke, "He would've beat ya in the shower, but he was worried 'bout my underwear."

"I always knew he was weird but didn't know he was fruity, too," Zeke said.

Scooter finally smiled, and said, "Just remember what I said about revenge."

He went into the downstairs bathroom and used water to remove the toilet paper from his chin and dabbed the cut to make sure it would not bleed again. He ran a comb through his hair, as he looked at his image in the mirror. Finally, he was satisfied and joined Sonny and Zeke in the living room. Zeke had reclined on the couch with his head back and had once again placed the icepack on his forehead. Scooter rechecked his shaving cut just to make sure it didn't ooze.

A horn honked outside, and Scooter said, "That must be them. Keep your powder dry tonight, and don't wait up," he said to Zeke.

"Sheeit, you guys'll be back by eight-thirty," Zeke answered with his "Daffy Duck" voice, not taking the icepack off his head.

"Why don't you come out for a minute? We'll introduce you to 'em."

Zeke slowly got up from the couch and followed Scooter and Sonny outside to Charlene's truck. Scooter looked into the driver's side window. "Hey girls. Wow! You both look great." He noticed that Charlene and Squirrel had applied make-up, including eye shadow. Charlene's lips were glistening with red lipstick, and he felt like leaning his head into the window and sampling them.

"Hey cowboy, you guys slick up pretty well yourselves," Charlene replied.

Scooter smiled and looked back to Zeke and said, "Zeke, this is Charlene and Squirrel. Girls, this is the maniac bull rider we call partner when he behaves."

Everyone exchanged greetings. Zeke shook hands with Charlene and reached across into the truck to shake hands with Squirrel.

"We heard all about your nasty ride on that Finals bull," Charlene said.

"I think I can ride him . . . someday . . . in my next life," Zeke said.

They all laughed at his comment.

"I don't know about this," Zeke continued, "I need to warn you girls. These guys act all shy and green like newborn calves, but don't let that fool you. That's how they get women to fall for 'em. Anyway, nice meetin' y'all."

"Nice meeting you, but take it easy on those bulls," Charlene replied.

"Shoot, comes with the territory, huh." As Zeke started to head back toward the sidewalk, he said quietly to Scooter, "Sometimes a guy gets lucky . . . wonders never cease, man."

Scooter nodded, "I know."

Squirrel seemed rooted in the front passenger seat, so Scooter slid into the back seat with Sonny.

Charlene put the truck in gear. "His face looks awful!"

Squirrel agreed. "That's an advertisement for all you guys to wear football helmets."

Sonny had been quiet, but her comment brought him to life. "That'd look real good out in the arena, runnin' around in helmets." Scooter laughed.

"Well, it's not funny when you see damage like that!" Charlene had turned her head toward the back seat.

Scooter stopped chuckling, thinking his laugh was suddenly inappropriate. "Well, helmets would be hot, huh. It's part of the sport, isn't it?"

"Yes, not the good part of it, though. You guys have to admit it."

"Well, I guess," said Scooter, admitting what he already knew.

Charlene looked back at him and smiled, "What's your pleasure . . . I mean what kind of food?"

Scooter had assumed he would ride up front with Charlene and now thought: *One hour and she must have cooled off already.* "I don't care, whatever you girls want. You know the places."

"What about that Mexican place on the north side?" Charlene asked Squirrel.

"It's pretty good . . . good margaritas!"

"Are you guys twenty-one, 'cause we're not," Scooter said.

"We're just," Charlene said. She looked over at Squirrel and winked.

"Yeah, like my little sister en a fake ID, innit?" Sonny said.

Squirrel looked back from the front seat and stuck her tongue out at Sonny. Scooter thought: *She's saucy!* "Guess it's okay by us," he said, "we're famished anyway."

They stopped at a restaurant with a southwestern adobe décor and were able to get a booth. Charlene sat on one side and Squirrel slide in beside her. Scooter was wondering about the exclusion arrangement that was taking place but slid in on the green vinyl seat to be across from Charlene. Sonny sat on the outside across from Squirrel. The waiter came over and asked about drinks.

"We need large glasses of water to start with," Scooter said.

"Don't we need some margaritas?" Squirrel held out her ID to the waiter.

Scooter looked from the ID in Squirrel's hand to the waiter to see if there would be any doubt. "It's okay with me, Sonny doesn't drink much. He's in hard-core training."

"Nah, it's not that so much," replied Sonny. "Alcohol does a job on me . . . well, on us Native American types."

Squirrel stuffed her ID back into her wallet and asked, "Why's that?"

"I think they, I mean scientists, have found that we have a strong reaction to alcohol or are missing somethin' t'break it down. Scooter, you mentioned it to me."

"Well, Boyd—that's one of the chemistry profs—had this in a lecture. It may be an allergic reaction to grains or derivatives, so supposedly, it's cultural—grains come from Europe, see—something like that . . . not a natural part of North America. Guess I'll have to do the team duty and stand in for him."

"Corn's from North America though, huh?" Squirrel mentioned.

"Yeah . . . shoot, never thought about it. Guess we need some white lightning!" Scooter studied Squirrel, as he suddenly had the idea she was sharper than he had been thinking.

Charlene pushed one of her legs between his and said, "Anyway, I'm sure you will go above and beyond the call of duty on that!"

He looked over at her, and she smiled mischievously at him. He pushed back, placing one of his legs between her knees and she squeezed it. He smiled at her. "I like this place already."

"I can tell you do."

Squirrel asked Sonny about the Jicarilla area and about Native American culture; about some of the Jicarilla Apache traditions. He was telling her about the old days when the tribe raided the Spanish settlements throughout northern New Mexico. "The warriors took a lot of prisoners. We used 'em as slaves mostly," he said. His statement grabbed Scooter's attention.

Squirrel seemed mesmerized. "You mean women and children?"

"Well, mostly, but maybe guys, too. Cheap labor. But probably more women. Keep the tribe diverse y'know?"

Squirrel nodded slightly and said, "Diverse?"

"Yeah, more kids then, innit?"

Charlene looked at Squirrel and said, "Wow! The good ol' days."

"Sure, you guys would 'ave been highly preferred I reckon."

Squirrel blushed and said, "No way! I'm not getting captured!" Sonny shrugged.

Scooter could not keep a straight face any longer and laughed. "You should see your faces. You don't know whether to believe him or not. I say, 'not', 'cause yer lookin' at a number one straight-faced bullshitter."

"Naw, it's all true," Sonny grinned. "I'm pure Apache, though . . . my great granddaddy traded all them women fer livestock."

Charlene and Squirrel let out peals of laughter, and Scooter grinned at his friend. He felt it was turning out to be a fun evening. He could feel Charlene's knee against the inside of his. He pushed against her again, and she pushed back.

The waiter finally brought water and a pitcher of margaritas. "I didn't realize how thirsty I was," Scooter said, and then poured the water. He was aware that the waiter had not asked for additional IDs. Squirrel helped by pouring four glasses of drinks.

"Here's to rodeo and new friendships," Charlene said. They touched glasses.

Sonny barely sipped on his drink and put it down. "You weren't kidding," Squirrel observed.

"Naw, I wasn't," Sonny replied, "I get completely shit-faced on one drink."

"He ain't kiddin' is right," said Scooter, "I've seen it, and it's ugly."

The girls laughed, and Charlene said, "You guys are too funny!" She squeezed Scooter's leg between hers again and looked intently at him. He found the situation interesting, but also disconcerting. Yet, he had an urge to reach under the table and run his hand up her thigh.

The waiter came back to their table and they ordered smothered burritos and sopapillas. After dinner, Scooter and Sonny wanted to pay, but Charlene said it was her treat. They compromised and the three others anted-up for the tip. Over half of Sonny's margarita remained.

"I thought you were going to stand in for him . . . take one for the team," Charlene said to Scooter.

"I get completely shit-faced on two drinks," Scooter replied.

Yeah, same as me . . . I seen it and it ain't pretty. We're a couple a lightweights," Sonny said.

The girls laughed, and Charlene said, "Well, you're fun anyway! You want to drive?"

"Sure, I have a license y'know . . . real too!" Scooter said. Charlene hit him on the arm and climbed in beside him. Sonny and Squirrel clambered into the back seat.

"Tell me where," Scooter said.

"Hey Squirrel, let's go up to Horsetooth . . . okay?" Charlene said.

"It's okay with me."

"Sonny, we haven't heard anything from you for a while. What about it?"

"I guess so . . . I don't know anythin' 'bout a horse's tooth, though," he replied.

Charlene and Squirrel laughed. "Yeah . . . funny! The guys on our rodeo team are all too serious," Squirrel said.

"Well, I'm glad we can entertain y'all. We aim to please," Scooter quipped.

They skirted west around the town and, then headed south and drove up a steep twisting road to the top of a dam. "Pull in here, and we can see the lights," Charlene said.

Scooter drove past another parked car and then parked the truck farther up the road. The lights of the city spread out below them to the east. "Hey! Pretty damn nice," Scooter said.

"I thought you'd like it," Charlene replied.

Sonny and Squirrel got out and went to the edge of the parking lot to view the expanse of lights on the eastern horizon. They came back to the truck. "We're going fer a hike, so doan leave us," Sonny said.

"Well, don't be all night," Scooter replied.

After they had left, Scooter and Charlene looked at each other. "What are you thinking?" she asked.

"Well . . . I was wondering, did you tell Squirrel to get lost for a while?"

"That's something just between us girls, I mean arrangements and plotting."

Scooter smiled. "Yeah, I hope you were plotting. About what I was really thinking . . . you know, I'm trying to figure this out. I don't know whether this is just a temporary thing and it's suddenly going to disappear like a puff of smoke. Or maybe I just got lucky all of a sudden, and a nice girl decided to come along. What do you think about it?"

Charlene didn't respond for a few seconds. "I think we have to take destiny in our hands sometimes . . . to do what we think we need to. To take a step . . . to take a chance and meet someone nice, who perks our interest. How else can we know things to expand our horizons about what might be?"

"Wow! Aren't you the deep one," Scooter said. "I like what you just said though about taking chances with someone that you want to know. I feel, ah . . . I don't know . . . I'm comfortable with you."

"I know! Do you think it's dangerous?" she asked.

"Yeah, very dangerous, I reckon," Scooter teased.

Charlene slid across the seat to be closer to him, and he put his uninjured arm around her. She turned toward him, and he kissed her neck and her ear, nuzzling her earring. "So, we going to take some chances, cowgirl?"

"Hmmm, we'll see." She placed her hand on the back of his neck and then kissed him. The intensity increased; their tongues touched, which gave Scooter a strange, but erotic sensation. He decided he liked it. He was aware of her fresh cucumber smell again. They both started breathing heavily, finally breaking apart for some air.

"Goddamn!" Scooter exclaimed.

"Let me see your shoulder." Charlene unsnapped his shirt, and then moved her hand across his chest and massaged his shoulder. "You're ropey!" she mused.

"Is that good or bad? Might be like twine."

She laughed at his joke. "It means you're wiry, silly."

He found he had plenty of nerve now and placed his hand inside her shirt. "I like western shirts for the snaps . . . I never thought about them this way before."

"Are you saying you haven't been out with one of the ranch girls or college girls and explored some? Zeke was right, I better watch out for you."

"Nah, I'm inexperienced . . . really. You're going to have to show me."

He felt the front of her and ran his hand inside her shirt over her smooth stomach. He felt it quiver. "You're kind of ropey too," he said.

"Tell me more about the girlfriend you don't have right now."

He paused in his intentions, wondering how to answer. "Well, not really a girlfriend, I guess. We have a class together and I usually borrow her notes when I miss it. She had a boyfriend earlier in the year and he was in my way."

Charlene laughed at his explanation. "In your way, huh? Well, I think that's good."

He smiled at her response and then felt her lips on his neck. She tickled his ear with her tongue. He resumed his exploration, feeling the lacy edge of her bra and then the satiny fullness. She held his hand against her, stilling it as they kissed.

"Sure, inexperienced . . . tell me about it," she huskily said. He was going to reply, but she covered his mouth with another kiss and then said close to his ear, "I know you have to leave tomorrow . . . and I don't know if you'll be back. I wanted to know you, so that's what I'm talking about . . . taking chances."

"You said something about destiny and I agree," Scooter replied

He pulled her to him and they kissed again, as he continued to explore. He felt her hand lightly stroking him through his jeans over the fly of the zipper and felt an involuntary jolt go through his abdomen. He stopped what he was doing, as her attention diverted him. "Be careful, that thing is loaded!" he exclaimed.

Charlene laughed and then said, "Bang, bang!" She continued to tease him, and he gritted his teeth at the sensation.

"I mean it . . . it's going to be a big mess!"

"Okay . . . I guess we can save it for later," she teased.

He smiled but wondered when. He noticed his hand was on her upper thigh and he moved it upwards and said, "Okay then, how 'bout one good turn deserves another?"

"You better be careful too . . . or there could be another 'bang'!" she teased back.

They both laughed at her remark. "You have strong hands, but gentle, too. I think you better quit though before my resolve gives way, and before the hikers come back. Come on, I need some air."

Scooter opened the drivers-side door and slid out, saying, "Yeah, I need some cooling off alright." He caught Charlene by her waist while she put her hands on his shoulders in stepping out of the truck. Scooter's injured arm throbbed some. He adjusted his pants and tucked his shirt back in. He was still aroused, "This is hard on a guy, y'know."

"It's not only a guy thing," Charlene replied.

Scooter was amazed that their making out had gone so far, so quickly. He liked the excitement but thought Charlene was the fastest girl he had ever met. The quick progression unsettled him, yet he wanted to see where it led. She grabbed his hand, and he turned, trying to see her. Even in the dark, he felt she was beautiful and wondered if he was suddenly going to wake from a dream. He pulled her closer to him to ensure a sliver of reality.

They walked up the road to a small rock outcrop. Scooter climbed on top of it and gazed at the lights spread out below them. He extended a hand to pull Charlene onto it, and they sat down; she scooted back toward him to sit between his legs.

She placed her head back into his shoulder, and he kissed her hair, breathing her essence through it. She turned her head toward him and he kissed her; a natural connection now as if they could not get enough of each other. He dislodged several of the snaps on her western-styled blouse and held her in a close embrace. She placed her tongue in his mouth as they again kissed. He was aroused again, wondering if this was going further or what. They were both heavily breathing. Suddenly she broke apart from him. "Listen, honey, I'm sorry, but we better quit again."

Scooter became still, wondering about the moving ahead and then retreating. Charlene seemed to sense his uncertainty. She turned toward him. "I'm not just teasing you. I like what we're doing, but honey I think we better put a damper on it some. I mean, plan some . . . well, I'm not explaining this very well. You're doing things to me . . . ah . . . does it bother you . . . me telling you these things?"

He liked her calling him "honey." "Well, I like this making out, that's for sure! What would we do if we kept going? Make love on this rock?"

Charlene laughed. "How you said it."

The thought excited him, yet it was a relief they hadn't made love, as he wasn't sure he knew what to do and it seemed to him making love—going all the way—was like jumping off into the deep end of a pond into unknown water. Instead of voicing these thoughts, he said, "Guess you're right though, but going to the edge like this is tough, 'cause I'm frazzlin' myself."

She laughed again at his use of the word. "Frazzling yourself. Making love on a rock! You are so funny. Anyway, I don't want you to be frazzled, whatever that is, forever. We just have to slow down a little. Snap me up . . . it's part of my instruction."

Scooter had trouble refastening Charlene's bra. "It needs to hook—fishhook-like." She instructed.

"Well, that's an apt description." She laughed at his comment and adjusted her blouse. He pulled her to him for a kiss. They then turned and ambled along the road holding hands. Scooter wondered where Squirrel and Sonny had gone. "They've been gone a while, huh?"

"Well, seems like it. Is Sonny trustworthy?" Charlene asked.

"She's in good company with him. He won't do anything. He's ten times more bashful with women than I am."

"You don't seem bashful to me." She again intertwined her fingers with his.

"Like I said before, I guess I'm not so shy with you, but tell me about this. I mean . . . ah, I know we said we were going to take chances, but talking about love-making . . . well, this has accelerated faster than I anticipated."

"Am I scaring you . . . scaring you off? I'm sorry. I'm not like this with other guys. Do you believe me?"

"Why wouldn't I? So, what are you telling me?"

"Okay, here it is. I really like you and I'm willing to take chances with you."

"Are you talking about love?"

"Well, of course. But, is it big or is it small? I don't know that, and I don't think we better get into such a deep subject yet. We need to see each other more to find out, see? I just know I really like you and I'm willing to take some chances with you. That's all."

Scooter stopped them. He tried to see her in the dark, as her take on love amazed him—about it being big or small—a completely new concept. He took a few seconds to try to form a response. "Well, I was just saying it accelerated. I didn't mean that I was getting scared. I don't know how big it is either. What an interesting way to look at it . . . to define it . . . Anyway, what the heck, this is our fourth date, isn't it? I think we've just compressed time is all," he finally said.

"Fourth? I wasn't counting, but, how do you?"

"Okay, let's see . . . there's the dance and after, talking by your truck, at the stables, and now tonight."

Charlene laughed at his analysis. "Well, that's one way to look at it."

"Don't worry, I guess I like taking chances too, especially with the right one—a nice, beautiful girl."

She kissed him softly on his cheek and then put her arm through his to be close. They continued to walk along the road. After a few minutes, they finally saw Sonny and Squirrel partially silhouetted against the lights of town.

"We thought maybe you guys were headed on down to the reservation," Charlene said. "You know, part of the diversification program!"

"Jeez, Charlene!" Squirrel exclaimed.

"We got lost," Sonny said.

"That'd be the day. You're supposed to be a scout . . . a guide for this young lass," Scooter said.

"Actually, we hiked down to the reservoir and he showed me how to skip rocks . . . I mean to get bunches of skips, and I now know how to say "*Ndee Biya'ti Bigoch'Iaah*. Which means, in case neither of you know, 'I'm learning Apache," Squirrel said.

"We been discussing goats, too . . . she likes to raise 'em, I like to eat 'em. So, I'm goin' to rename her from 'Squirrel' to a nice Apache name, like 'Goat Woman,'" Sonny added.

Squirrel hit him on the arm, and they all laughed.

"I'm always amazed at what skills my partner here has, and wit, too," Scooter said.

"So, what have you guys been doing?" Squirrel asked.

"Just looking at the lights," Charlene replied.

"I'll bet!"

Charlene gave Scooter's hand a squeeze. He thought: *Squirrel's suspicious.*

Except for the statement about goats and names, Sonny didn't say anything else. Scooter couldn't discern any expression under the shadow of Sonny's hat, but it seemed he had a slight smile. *He's a sly fox.*

Charlene said, "We better go, I have an early class tomorrow. We're exchanging addresses and phone numbers, okay?" Charlene pulled out a pad of paper from her purse and handed pieces to everyone.

Scooter waited for a pen from Squirrel and wrote his address and telephone number on the paper and gave it to Charlene. She gave him one in return and he looked at what she had written and then folded it over and slid it into his wallet. Sonny had done nothing with the paper. Scooter noticed this, and said, "Sonny has no phone, so just contact me."

Squirrel said to Sonny, "You are in the backwoods apparently."

He responded with a wolfish grin and nodded slightly. "Yeah, it's aways out there. We still start a fire with two sticks!" The girls laughed.

Scooter thought: *That's my partner . . . the fox.*

"Well, that's okay. We'll see you guys in Laramie in a couple of weeks . . . right?" Charlene asked.

Sonny said, "Yeah, that's another big un fer us."

Scooter took in all the interchange and watched Charlene to see if her face reflected any feelings. She looked at him and smiled, so he leaned over and tipped her head up, then kissed her. "Don't forget me!"

"That's my line cowboy. Get that shoulder strong for me." She lightly grabbed his arm and returned a kiss.

"Yeah, it'll be ropey just for you."

Charlene laughed. "Okay, but I'll test it." Charlene placed a hand on his neck and pulled him to her. They kissed again for a longer period, and it felt to Scooter as if a progression had occurred, where kissing was becoming a natural part of their relationship.

He got out of the truck as Squirrel was also getting out of the back to move into the front seat.

"I don't know what you did, but you better do right by her!" Squirrel told him. Her voice had an edge to it.

She surprised Scooter with her admonition and he only mumbled, "Yeah, take care."

He was still wondering what Squirrel had meant, exactly, because he didn't think he had done too much yet—not as much as they nearly had. He caught up with Sonny, and they went into the house, not looking back.

"So, what did you really do down by the reservoir?" Scooter asked.

"Skipped rocks—talked some Apache. I took her hand once to help her over some rocks. She's a nice girl, but I doubt if'n we'd ever . . . um, be a couple. I don't have time fer it. We're friends, though . . . seems. She's goin' t'have her parents mail me some them nuts though. Now you and that Charlene . . . that's different."

Scooter didn't know if Sonny was kidding about the walnuts, but he said, "Nuts! Judas Priest! But yeah, I think I got into something deep."

Yeah, like quicksand for you, pard."

Scooter looked at Sonny to see if he was kidding, but it seemed he wasn't, that now possibly Scooter was getting sucked into something quite complicated. Yet, he liked the excitement and the strong feelings that occurred when he was with her.

"Quicksand, huh?"

They trudged upstairs and threw off their boots. Scooter folded his jeans for the next day, hung his shirt on a hanger, and finally peeled the covers back. He was going to comment on when they should get up, but Sonny seemed to be breathing heavily already. One of his feet stuck out from under the blanket. Sonny had not taken off his sock.

Scooter lay awake for a while thinking about the events of the last few days, how things had changed suddenly in his life. It used to be so simple: working out, going to class, studying, getting on a few practice head of horses out at the fairgrounds . . . now things were getting complicated, and exciting. Even more exciting than riding bareback horses, if that was possible. He liked thinking about Charlene, and now was wishing she had given him a picture of herself. His shoulder was throbbing. He flexed it several times and then got up and took two of the pills the sports doctor had given him, and then went into the bathroom for water and to relieve himself. He hadn't noticed the shoulder much while he and Charlene had been making out. *Must have been mind over matter.* He wondered if she was teasing him about making love. *Those nice, long legs . . .* it didn't seem like it, and he didn't think she was a tease, but everything just happened so fast. *Yes, fast and exciting.* Back in the bedroom, he noticed Sonny was snoring. Scooter climbed back into bed.

CHAPTER NINE
EARLY MORNING LIGHT

Scooter rolled out of bed around four. There was no position where his shoulder didn't hurt, and there wasn't any use trying to sleep. He took several of the super aspirins, walked down the hall to use the bathroom, and downed some water. He quietly crept downstairs in just his jeans and tried to relax on the couch, massaging his shoulder muscles and the aching triceps of his arm. He knew from past experiences it might take a week for the shoulder to quiet down. *Guess I better have the college trainer look at it and tell him what the doc here said about strengthening.* Eighty push-ups were a lot, but he could already do about fifty.

He continued to muse while lying back, looking toward the ceiling and thinking he might as well get out some class lecture notes in a while and do some studying. He heard before he saw someone coming downstairs and realized in surprise it was Zeke's waitress.

He watched her without saying anything. She came into the twilight of the room and then jerked when she saw him. "Oh, you scared me!"

"Sorry . . . I couldn't sleep so came down here. I saw you at the bus depot the other morning. I'm Zeke's friend."

"Yes, I know. Zeke told me about you. You guys live a tough life is what I think, both getting beat-up. I have to get to work."

"Okay, see you around."

"Take care of yourself," she said, and quietly went out the front door.

Scooter could not believe that Zeke was so brazen to have this girl in his room all night, just down the hall. He continued to think about it: *He's a nervy guy, that's for sure. I wonder if Charlene and I would do that. I bet not. I mean she wouldn't spend the night—but she did mention, "sometime." I wonder what she meant exactly. We did go a long ways in being . . . ah, intimate. Wonder what she told Squirrel anyway? She doesn't like me for some reason. What about Laramie? Charlene said we could study together, so that would be good . . . making out maybe, too . . . I hope I get some good bareback horses there and can get to the regionals . . . that fourth in the first go-round here will help.*

After sleeping several hours, Scooter got up, stretched, and rubbed out the fabric pattern that had transferred from the sofa to his back. He wandered into the kitchen, first brewing a small pot of coffee and then paging through his chemistry notes. Rewriting lecture notes helped him memorize key points. After going through several chemistry lectures, he switched notebooks and started working on an English composition outline that he had prepared earlier. Suddenly he stopped. *I should write a paper about this trip. Well, not about Charlene and me, but about college rodeo and what it's like.* Thinking about Charlene, he wondered whether he should phone her some time, then realized he would before Laramie, but whether he should in the next several days. Maybe it was a good idea not to seem too smitten . . . or was it? No, better be cool, but he would phone her at the end of the week. Maybe he would write her a note saying thanks for everything. He could mention her shiny raven-black hair and blue-green eyes, perhaps figure out some metaphors. *You are so sappy . . . you better straighten out . . . toughen up.*

He redid the outline and started the composition with Zeke, Sonny, and him sending in their entry fees, packing their gear, their unexpected car trouble in Saguache. After working for another hour and downing several cups of coffee, he clumped upstairs to shower and shave.

Sonny was still sleeping with his head under a blanket, as usual. After showering, Scooter quietly opened Zeke's door and observed a lump under the blanket. He was getting bored. *We might as well get this show on the road.* He went back into his and Sonny's room and pulled the blankets off the bed. Sonny reached for them, mumbling something.

"Come on let's get some chow and get ready to roll. Johnny said we're leavin' at eight." Scooter said. After several attempts, he finally got Sonny to sit up, and said, "Get moving. How you going to help Squirrel raise goats if'n you can't get up in the mornings?"

Sonny peered at Scooter with his dark eyes. "What'n hell you talkin' 'bout?"

Scooter didn't bother to reply but instead reminded Sonny that they were supposed to strip the beds and put the used sheets in the laundry room on the first floor. He grabbed his shaving kit, walked down the hall to Zeke's room, stuck his head into the doorway and said in a falsetto voice, "Hey handsome, let's get some chow!" There was no response. Scooter retraced his steps to the bathroom. Sonny had stripped his bed and was packing his gear when Scooter came back to the bedroom. He did the same while Sonny showered.

They piled their dirty linen in the laundry room, left Zeke a note on the living room coffee table just in case he wanted to join them, and then walked several blocks down the street to the same café they had patronized the previous morning.

"This shoulder was really bothering me last night and now too, but that happened last time as well. Anyway, I was downstairs in the wee hours of the morning and Zeke's waitress came down from his room to go t'work. I wish the bus depot wasn't so far, we'd go over and have her give us some preferential treatment." Scooter said.

Sonny took in this information. "Y'mean she came downstairs an' you were there to greet 'er?"

"Yeah, she's pretty good lookin', but her hair was still kind of . . . well, stickin' up in back. I figured she had been in there with Zeke, but I sure never heard 'em. I gave her a scare when she saw me lying on the couch. She appears to be older than him . . . us."

"You'n Zeke, you both goin' down . . . your days of riding the rough stock's 'bout done."

"Wait a minute," Scooter protested, "I'm not hooked up with anyone . . . yet."

"Yeah, but that Charlene has you in her sites. You're like a fly on the edge of a sticky web . . . like a love-sick calf, innit . . . waller'n around, look'n fer mommy."

"Waller'n around . . . Judas Priest! I have to admit, she's really nice. Why can't a guy rodeo and have a girlfriend too?"

"It ain't never the same, pard. Your mind gets mushy . . . one-half of it's on yer bronc, the other half's on yer honey. I seen it with good bronc riders on the rez."

"Yeah, but many of the pros are married . . . have families," Scooter mentioned.

"Sure, but that's after they got good."

Scooter rarely had such long discussions with Sonny on anything, unless it was bucking stock, and he took a good look at his buddy as they entered the café. He realized that Sonny had strong feelings about being sin-gle-minded toward rodeo and not letting anything get in his way. It bothered Scooter that Sonny seemed to be more serious than he was about making it a career, or that now there was a slight diversion in their pathway.

The two friends placed their orders and turned their discussion to a safer topic, of the stock that would be at the rodeo in Laramie, and what would be good to draw in their respective events.

Zeke wandered in as they were about halfway through their break-fasts and sat down with them at the next stool along the counter. He ordered scrambled eggs and toast without looking at the menu. "We gotta hurry 'cause Johnny's getting his underwear all wound in a knot 'bout getting going."

"We're about to snarf this all down, so you better hurry," Scooter said. "By the way, I gave your honey a start this morning as she was leaving." Zeke looked at Scooter without saying anything, waiting for him to contin-ue. Finally, Scooter said, "I was having major shoulder throbbings and was downstairs lyin' on the couch."

"Well, yeah . . . we kind of hit it off. She's trying to get over a nasty divorce. Might as well tell y'all, has a kid too," Zeke said.

"Jeez, a ready-made family. What a lazy bastard you are, not even wanting to make your own kids," Scooter said.

Sonny snorted a laugh at this and spewed pieces of egg back onto his plate.

"Oh, I can make kids alright, you doan have to worry none about that!" Zeke said gruffly.

"See, I toll youse . . . y'both goin' down," Sonny said. "That ground's goin' t' seem hard as a rock when you get throwed . . . it ain't never the same . . . you're minds on fuckin', innit, and not on what you're ridin'."

"What's he mumbling about?" Zeke asked.

"He's on this kick about you'n me getting hooked up with women and not being worth a shit again on the rodeo circuit."

"Hell, it ain't never bothered me before." Zeke's stuck his jaw out as he said this.

"It ain't ever," Scooter replied,

"You'll both see," Sonny said.

Scooter glanced at Sonny but continued to press Zeke. "So, did y'have her kid with you or what?"

"Don't be such a dumb ass," Zeke responded.

Sonny snorted a second laugh at this exchange. "You guys both gettin' soft in the head on these wimmen is what. Rodeo guys gotta be tough!"

"Sheeit!' Zeke exclaimed and got up, stuffing a last piece of toast into his mouth.

They paid their breakfast bill at the counter and walked back to the house. Scooter made up his mind that he was going to prove Sonny wrong and was going to do maybe one hundred fifty pushups or whatever else the college trainer thought he should do.

Zeke broke his reverie, saying, "Johnny said to tell you not to forget, we gotta settle up with him 'cause he paid the guys fer the rooms."

"Probably some for gas too. We'll help you out on the repair bill since we earned a little cash this week," Scooter said.

"Thanks, that'll help . . . at least until I can get some money from home," Zeke said.

Johnny's car was bulging at the seams with passengers and gear. Scooter, Sonny, and Zeke occupied the rear seat. Johnny, Hank, and Will, a teammate who had competed in steer wrestling, were in the front. Will still owed money to a local competitor for using his horse in the rodeo. Scooter was wondering how this was going to work out because Will had not placed in either go-round. Scooter was resting his feet on top of his duffle bag and had to look between his knees to see the road. Sonny held a duffle bag on his lap.

"I'm sure glad it's only three hours down to that place," Zeke said, "otherwise this could get uncomfortable."

Scooter was thinking it was already uncomfortable and they had yet to clear Fort Collins. Will and Hank were talking about some of the girls they had met from the college and Hank said, "Those dudes from up here are mad at Scooter."

The comment got Scooter's attention. "What'd I do?"

"You were hanging around one of their primo girls. I think one of the guys likes her . . . might be her boyfriend."

"Judas Priest . . . is she like some kind of property?" Scooter asked. "She came over and asked me to dance and dinner. Sonny was there."

"Hey, don't get mad at me, I'm just saying what I heard."

"So, who's this dude, anyway, so's I know what I'm dealing with?"

"Don't know. You'll have to ask around. Next rodeo up at Laramie, I guess."

Scooter was wondering if the guys were jerking him around, and said, "Well, it's a free world here in the USA yet as far as I know. Guess she can go out with who she wants!"

"Doan worry 'bout it. She loves ya," Sonny said.

Zeke chuckled at Scooter's agitation. "Your first love, and it's already complicated for you. That's life, kid. One day they love ya, the next they leave ya."

Since when did Zeke become doctor love? Scooter thought but didn't say anything. He wiggled against Sonny to get more comfortable, pulled his English composition lecture notes and his outline out of a zippered notebook, and opened them using his knees as support. Finally, he said, "Y'all be careful what you say from here on in, I'm writing this trip up for an English assignment."

Hank responded from the front seat saying, "Just don't put us in it. We don't want to be in any of your funny papers." Will and Johnny laughed at Hank's comment.

Zeke echoed the statement. "Yeah, be careful, you better change the names to protect the innocent."

"If there were any innocent, I would," Scooter replied.

Scooter was still stewing silently over the news, real or not, about a guy on Charlene's team being sweet on her. *He could take her out whenever, while I'm four hundred miles away. There's probably stuff to go to—dances, movies. A person can't expect a woman to wait around for too long. Maybe I should write her a poem. Well, that may not work, as I've only written one for class and it got a C. Let's see maybe that 'thank you' note I was thinking about. How syrupy would I seem though? Well, she said, sometimes you have to take chances. Let's see . . .*

He wrote in the margins of his notebook, erased and started over a few times, finally writing:

I know someone,
Who has shining, raven-black hair, like midnight,
Magical eyes that ignite my soul,
Dusky-rose lips, my heart's desire.

Zeke was saying something to him. "What?" Scooter asked. He covered the cursive scribbling of the poem with his hand.

"That guy better have my truck done like he said."

"I got a class at eleven tomorrow that I better not miss," Scooter replied.

Sonny, who was also studying, looked up and said, "I got a class at eight, en I missed two today. I should continue on with these guys."

"That's okay, if'n you got to," Zeke said. "Scooter can keep me company."

"Guess I will," Scooter finally said, "but we better make sure that truck is reliable. I can't miss my Tuesday classes either. We gotta make sure we stay eligible."

Grades usually weren't a factor for Scooter, but Zeke had problems with some of his classes, and in applying himself. They all had to keep at least a C-plus average to be eligible to compete in the rodeos. Sonny plugged along, just doing enough to get *Cs*, but occasionally rose to the occasion and did enough work to get a *B* and remain eligible.

Johnny and the other guys in the front seat had been telling jokes and stories, but heard the dreaded "eligible" word, and joined the conversation. Hank was ineligible currently, and Scooter didn't know why he had come along on the trip. He was the one that had mentioned someone being sweet on Charlene. Scooter had several classes with him. "We got that composition paper due next week, so I gotta get it done this week. It counts as much as a mid-term," Scooter said.

"Yeah, hurry up so I can copy it. I need to get my grade up somehow. You can just change the title for me," Hank said.

Hank's attitude was starting to steam Scooter and he replied, "Fat chance on that, dude!" He had an urge to smack Hank in the back of the head. Johnny and Will laughed at this exchange, and Scooter continued, "You ought to try studying for a change, instead of being such a dumb shit."

Hank turned and tried to grab Scooter's arm, but he caught Hank's and twisted it instead. Will in the front seat and Zeke in the back hollered at them to quit, as the tussle spilled over onto them.

"Goddamned kids!" Zeke said.

"Watch yer mouth," Hank said to Scooter.

"Uh-huh, uh-huh," Scooter responded.

As everyone settled back down, he went back to work on his essay.

Johnny pulled into a service station at Basin to fill the car with gas and for a pee break. They all got out and stretched, went inside to the restroom, and bought some snacks. Scooter gave Johnny five dollars for gas.

Afterward, as they continued to head south, Scooter, Sonny, and Zeke either studied or occasionally dozed. Zeke had a spring-loaded gripper that he occasionally squeezed. The three in the front seat were telling stories about bad "wrecks" in rodeos, either ones they had been in or seen. Scooter tried to tune them out, as he had heard most of the stories before. He continued to work on the essay, writing about the past two days. He looked at his drafted prose to Charlene. *I need another line. Let's see . . . she said something about destiny and taking a chance.* He wrote: Taking chances opens destiny's door.

He looked at the five lines. *Not too bad for an amateur. Now I'll have to see if I have the nerve to send it.* He figured he would have to in order to quiet his mind about having competition. *But not right away. I don't want to seem to her like a lovesick calf, as Sonny said. I'll wait a few days.*

"I gotta bear down t' make up any classes," Sonny said, "'cause I'm sposed to go to a family thing Saturday. You guys should come with me. We'll ride some stock at a jackpot 'n hit the sweat lodge. You both need it."

Both Scooter and Zeke stopped studying and looked up contemplating Sonny's offer. Zeke continued squeezing a spring-loaded gripper. "I think I'm supposed to work that bull sale out at the sale barn Saturday. I need some green to help pay for this trip, the truck, and to go to Laramie. That's even farther."

Scooter was interested. "Would your family care? Do they have room?"

"Yeah, there'd be room. I can send word down t'the trading post. My folks doan have a phone out there yet. I mean at the ranch," Sonny said.

Scooter thought this was a big step for Sonny and appreciated being invited. "I don't know if I will ride anything, but the sweat lodge sounds good. Maybe it will be good for this shoulder."

"There's a person who can help that, innit," Sonny replied.

"What you mean?" Scooter asked, wondering if he was getting into something more than just a sweat.

"Doan worry," Sonny said, "It's just herbal stuff."

Zeke broke into their conversation, "He's going to cure you of having any thoughts about women, that's what!"

The guys in the front seat and Zeke laughed. "Good luck on that one," Johnny said.

"Yeah, doubt if'n it'll work," Sonny said.

The laughs continued. "You guys are idiots!" Scooter said and continued to work on his essay.

CHAPTER TEN
BLUE PLATE SPECIAL

They arrived in Saguache at noon. "Head over to that garage," Zeke told Johnny, "let's make sure that guy has the truck ready."

Johnny parked the car in front of the garage and Zeke got out. The large garage door was shut, so Zeke tried the small door to the side of it. It was locked. He checked a sign on the door's window that had a clock face. The hands indicated one o'clock, and at the top, it read *Back Soon*.

"Sonovabitch! He must'a gone to lunch!" Zeke said, walking back to the car.

"Well, we might as well gas up and get some lunch ourselves," Johnny said.

They filled the car with gas and asked the attendant about restaurants. He told them the one on Main Street was okay. Sonny paid for the gas. Scooter noticed this and thought Sonny was reserving his ride with Johnny. Sonny had mentioned to Scooter that he thought Johnny and the other two guys were weird about him or maybe of his bronc riding ability. Scooter thought Sonny was right—jealous, and him being Indian.

They parked the car in front of the restaurant. Scooter wondered if the itinerant mechanic would be there also, as they tromped inside. The patrons, mostly elderly people, looked up from their meals at the group's invasion. Zeke, never at a loss for words, said, "Howdy, we're part of Southwestern College Rodeo Team." to answer the patrons' silent question.

"How'd you do?" An older man, sitting at a table, asked.

"Well, we won some and lost some," Zeke answered.

"I coulda figured the 'lost some' part!" the old-timer said.

That broke the ice, as everyone laughed.

Zeke asked about the garage and the mechanic. If he always closed for lunch.

"Yeah, he goes home for it. Sometimes I think he might take a nap too," another of the old-timers said.

"Sheeit!" Zeke said, "we got a truck to get out of him."

"He lives in a trailer on the edge of town if you need to get 'im," the older of the fellows said.

"Well, we'll see after we eat, I guess," Zeke said.

A waitress brought over menus and glasses of water. "We have Swiss steak as a special today," she said.

Scooter had noticed some of the other patrons were eating what he thought was the special. It looked gristly and greasy. He continued to study the menu and then ordered a cheeseburger and home fries. Sonny ordered a taco and a salad. Scooter then decided to change his order to substitute a salad for the fries. He was going to make sure Sonny didn't get ahead of him in training and in being dedicated to the rodeo profession. The others ordered the special. Quickly chewing halfway through the burger, Scooter thought he should have ordered two of them.

After lunch, they told the other patrons to take care, paid the bill, and squeezed back into the car. The large door to the garage was open, and Zeke and Scooter went inside. They said hello to a pair of overall-encased legs sticking out from under a car. The legs became a body as the mechanic slid out on a floor dolly.

"I figured y'd be here today." He noticed Zeke's face and asked, "Jeez, whad y'run into up'n there?"

Scooter replied before Zeke could, saying, "He'll tell you it's from bull riding, but he got his ass kicked by some little skinny guy in a bar."

"Yeah, right. It was a bull . . . really," Zeke said.

The mechanic shook his head and said, "She's a rough sport. Let's go take a look at 'er."

They went over to Zeke's truck and got down on the floor to look underneath. It looked like an old transmission to Scooter, as it was scuffed and had yellow paint marks on it.

"It's used but should be okay. I drove 'er around town before lunch," the mechanic said.

Zeke got in and started it up. He ran it forward and then backed up slowly. He hopped out and said, "Let's settle up, 'cause we got a ways to go yet."

He and Scooter followed the mechanic into the office, and he took an invoice from a metal file slot tacked to the wall. "I tried to keep it low fer you boys. I used to rodeo some, long time ago . . . she's a rough life. Anyway, it comes to three hundred fifty."

"I thought you said on the phone three hundred!" Zeke exclaimed.

"Sure, but thas just en estimate. Took me longer, en I worked most'a Saturday."

Scooter studied the mechanic. He was missing several of his front teeth, and the remaining few were stained. "Let's pay the man," he said, and gave Zeke a one-hundred-dollar bill.

Zeke got down on his knees to peer underneath the truck. I don't see any leaks, anyway. We'll settle up, and then I wanna take it for a spin around town just to be sure." He paid the mechanic with cash and received a receipt.

"Hell, I reckon there won't be any leaks," the mechanic noted.

Scooter nodded and then walked out to the others at the car. "I think we got a functional truck, but Zeke's going to check it out first."

Zeke drove the truck out of the garage and headed it up the street until he was out of sight. Johnny said, "Shit, where's he going? We ain't got all day to be sittin' around here."

Scooter leaned against the car, while the others sat inside waiting. He looked over at the mechanic, who was also waiting for Zeke to return. He said to him, "Thanks for helping us out . . . we appreciate it." The mechanic nodded an acknowledgment.

Finally, Hank said to Scooter, "I think yer good buddy done left ya here with us."

"He'll be back. He ain't that trusting of his ol' truck."

Zeke came roaring up the street from the other direction and pulled into the parking area, raising a cloud of dust. Johnny hollered a "Hey!" at Zeke for being inconsiderate.

Scooter and Zeke took their gear out of Johnny's car and put it in the bed of the pickup. They shook hands with the other guys. "Thanks for the ride," Zeke said. "Watch out for the 'smokies.'"

"See y'all in the morning," Scooter told Sonny.

The car pulled away with a few waves. Someone from the passenger side gave them a middle-finger salute. Scooter said, "That's that fuckin' Hank, I'm going to break that off for him!"

"Yeah, he's got a chip on," Zeke said, "just because he couldn't compete. He thinks he's tough."

They said so long to the mechanic, who was still watching from the door of his garage, piled into Zeke's truck, and went back to the service station to fill it with gas. "I'll pay this time," Zeke said.

As they headed south out of town, the truck seemed to purr; no smoke, no stink.

"I hope it stays running this way," Scooter said. "We got Wolf Creek Pass to get over yet."

"Yeah, you 'n me both, pard."

They rode in silence for a while. Scooter asked, "You like that waitress?"

Zeke didn't answer right away, but finally said, "Yeah . . . her name's Molly."

After several more minutes, Scooter asked, "How do you know she likes you?"

"Well, it's pretty obvious. I mean . . . y'know, all the sleeping together . . . lotsa times, what it was?"

Scooter scrutinized Zeke. "You mean making love? Maybe she was just lonely for a grand adventurer cowboy like you."

Zeke smiled at Scooter's comment. "I'm going to see her on the trip to Laramie. Her mom takes care of the kid some, so maybe she'll go up there with me. I don't know. Why all the questions?"

"Well, I was just wondering. If you go with her, Sonny and I will have to drive up separately."

"Yeah, have to take two cars."

Scooter was thinking about the added expense and if Zeke's truck was going to hold up for another long trip, but then about the real question on his mind.

"Here's the thing," said Scooter, "Charlene suggested we get together at Laramie, y'know, like study together. I'm just wondering."

"Well, take her up on the offer," Zeke said. "It ain't no rocket science, y'know."

"Yeah, I guess," Scooter said, "maybe I got lucky!"

"You ain't just singing soprano there, pardner. Just don't fall in love with the first honey that comes along. You're too inexperienced. She's a look-er, too. Trouble."

Scooter took a long look at Zeke but didn't say anything for a while. "I've been on dates this year."

"I'm talking about taking the big plunge . . . bitin' the dust," Zeke replied, glancing for a few seconds at Scooter. "The thing is . . . well, here's one thing that nearly got me once. I thought this little honey was really into me. She was hot! Then I found out she was just trying to get a boyfriend jealous. Typical movie script . . . at home, last Christmas vacation. My sister knew her . . . knew the score . . . were both on the cheerleading squad. I mean, we sort-of knew each other, cuz she's friends with my sister. I felt like a sap at first. Kind of like getting on a bull with your chaps on backwards or somethin'! But being clued in, I decided to turn the tables on her."

Scooter took a hard look at Zeke, who continued to study the road ahead. "What you mean, turn the tables on her?" he finally asked.

Zeke looked over at Scooter and smiled, "Ah, well, you know, went on the date intending to seduce her."

Scooter looked at Zeke again to see if he was kidding, and then said, "Ha, right! I'm sure she fell for that one." Zeke looked over with a wide grin but didn't reply. "So, you're telling me it happened?" Scooter asked.

"That's what I'm telling ya."

"Okay, Mr. Lover . . . how? How could it happen if she was only interested in you for ulterior reasons, 'cause I don't believe you."

"Man, I should charge you a fee. I mean, I'm telling you things that some guys never learn their whole lives. Who said she was only interested in me for alternate reasons, or whatever? That's your first mistake. You have to realize, she wanted an adventure, at least subconsciously. Second, you need t'know that girls want to have fun in any event. A guy just doesn't take them to a dark lane and hope."

"So, what was the fun thing?" asked Scooter.

"We went to a dance. I figured this was the deal . . . where her boyfriend was supposed to see us. I put that out of my mind and we danced up a storm . . . we were both sweating. I actually don't know if he was even there. Got us some hooch punch too . . . y'know to cool things off again."

Scooter knew that Zeke was a good dancer. "So's that it? Just dancing around?" he asked.

"Okay pard, here's what you need to know too. You need to get into their heads . . . feelings."

Scooter had no idea what this meant. "Keep talking," he said.

"Well, like . . . I asked her stuff like if she could be anywhere she wanted to be and be anything she wanted, what would it be? If she had control of her life; if she had found her kindred spirit in a guy, what would he be like?"

"You're deeper than I gave you credit," Scooter said, and sarcastically asked, "So then what? You ran outside and screwed on the front lawn?"

Zeke laughed. "No, dude! You need to keep turning up some heat . . . take some chances. We talked about other things. I had to get her talking about her feelings, see. We talked about her issues at home with her folks— her dad's a dick supposedly. She wants to move out, but they fight about it. I told her she should go to college . . . a natural way to cut the cord. I told her to come to Southwestern. I'd show her the ropes. Those were the slow tunes, y'know. Then we did some special moves to some rock tunes . . . had fun just twirling around. She's a good dancer. Finally, I think I asked her if she had ever made love to a buckaroo . . . a wild bull rider. She said something like she had a midnight curfew. I told her buckaroos don't do curfews, we take chances!"

Scooter laughed at this. "So, then you went out on the lawn and screwed."

"Not yet! You need to let things simmer, to allow for the imagination to overcome fear or reluctance. I mean we were having fun and laughing, so that was a plus . . . sweet girl. Anyway, we finally left the dance after some more cutting a few wild dance steps and hooch punch. We did it twice in my mom's car . . . the first time for me . . . the second for her. She tore the headliner of my mom's car with her foot somehow, and I got her home around three, so we were both in trouble, but man it was worth it! I couldn't figure out what kind of story would explain the tear in the roof . . . like hittin' a huge bump in the road, which no one believed. Fortunately, I saw that she had abandoned her panties . . . were on the floor. Good thing I noticed!"

"Abandoned . . . jeez, didn't she need 'em?" Zeke didn't answer but smiled and shrugged his shoulders. "Both'd be hard to explain, but twice? You're such a bullshitter. I like the story, though. What happened after, did you ever see her again?"

"Naw. Well, just before I left to come back here . . . to Southwestern . . . met at the drive-in for a while . . . I worried for a few weeks . . . I mean, y'know, if she had got knocked-up. 'Cause I hadn't used anything . . . poor planning actually. We thought we would get together over Easter break. I talked to her about considering Southwestern for college again but never went home Easter break . . . too short. My sister said she's going steady now with some local yokel."

Scooter didn't say anything, pondering Zeke's story. Finally, he said, "I don't think Charlene would do that. I mean set me up to make a guy jealous. It's kind of disconcerting though."

"Well, she's a honey, must have guys wantin' to hang all over her with those long legs and all, y'know?"

Scooter shifted uncomfortably on the seat. "Believe me, I know. She said she recently broke up with Hall . . . that steer wrestler there."

"Yeah, the lookers can be a challenge. I say ride 'em when y'can!"

"Jeez! You talking about rodeo stock or women?" asked Scooter.

"Both!" Zeke said and chuckled at Scooter's reaction.

After another few minutes, Zeke changed the subject. "Thinking of which . . . that bull kinda gave me a dose of reality. I thought I was riding better'n that. I got to the whistle at Alamosa, an' that bull was no slouch!"

"Those bulls that are selected to be in the NFR," Scooter said, "you can bet they know how to get a guy on the ground better'n others . . . just goes to figure. You going to keep at it aren't you?"

"Yeah, I'm just getting started."

With that settled, they lapsed into silence again with occasional talk about rodeo, if they would try to go pro, if they should save up money to go to more rodeo schools. Scooter had already been to one put on by an ex-bareback NFR champion. "Yeah, we should. That one I went to last fall by

Tureman and those guys was the best thing because I learned so much about technique. Otherwise, I was just continuing bad habits."

"I know, just takes money," Zeke said, "my folks aren't so keen on this double life I'm trying to lead, so I have to twist their arms to send some green once in a while. I'll have to tell 'em it's tuition."

"Well, wouldn't be a complete lie."

They stopped in South Fork on the east side of Wolf Creek Pass and put gas in the truck. Afterward, Zeke asked, "Y'wanna drive? I'm feelin' a little punky."

Scooter was glad to drive, as he was getting bored just riding. They started up Wolf Creek Pass when Zeke suddenly said, "Pull over!"

Scooter glanced at Zeke and decided he looked a little pale. Scooter stopped the pickup on the shoulder of the road, so his friend could get out. Zeke ran down the road embankment into a small ravine. Scooter let the truck's engine idle but then realized that Zeke was hollering something. Scooter shut the engine off. He got out and asked, "What?"

"Hey pard, y'got any toilet paper?" Zeke hollered up from behind some willows.

"Jeez, man, like what?" Scooter replied.

"Well, I need something. See if there's a napkin or somethin' in the truck!"

Scooter scrounged through the truck, not even finding a used tissue. Finally, he tore some unused pages from his notebook and wadded them into a ball. He wasn't going to get any closer to Zeke than necessary. He walked partway down the bank and saw Zeke with his pants down. His strikingly white, bare ass was visible through the shrubbery and reminded Scooter of a rising, full moon. Zeke was hanging onto the trunk of a willow with one hand.

"Here!" Scooter said and threw the paper at him.

"Thanks," Zeke said, as he retrieved the wads of paper. "Get some more!"

Scooter went back to the truck, tore out more notebook paper, and repeated the procedure. He went back up the road berm to the truck. Zeke finally came through the vegetation of the ravine. "Y'feelin' better?" Scooter asked.

"What a fuckin' trip this has been. It's probably the lunch we ate," Zeke said.

"It didn't look good to me," Scooter replied, "but you been takin' lots of aspirin or whatever, too. We'll have to see if Johnny and the other guys got sick."

After a few minutes Scooter said, "One thing, though, you met that waitress and got some lovin'."

"Yeah, that's one thing," Zeke gruffly admitted.

They got back into the truck and Zeke put his head back on the top of the seat. Scooter started the truck and continued up the pass. "I hope you're not getting the flu, 'cause I don't want it," he said. "Neither of us has time for it."

Zeke didn't reply and seemed to be dozing. Scooter was thinking about stopping somewhere for a sandwich but kept driving. They arrived in town after dark. Scooter stopped at his small apartment and retrieved his gear from the back of Zeke's pickup. "Take it easy and get some of that Pepto-whatever in you . . . or something. You nearly killed me with the 'gas-o-rama!'"

"Yeah, see ya tomorrow," Zeke said as he yawned and crawled into the driver's side of the pickup.

CHAPTER ELEVEN
COLLEGE LIFE

Scooter dug through his gear bag and a side pocket for his key and unlocked the door to his apartment. He unloaded his overnight bag in the small closet of the bedroom and sorted the dirty clothes out from the few that were still fresh. He shook out a single shirt that he hadn't worn and slipped a hanger in it, hoping some of the wrinkles would disappear. He pushed the duffle bag of gear with his riding tack into the closet corner. The gear could be sorted out later. He was tired and very hungry, so opened the door to the small refrigerator, taking out a jar of strawberry jam and then some bread and peanut butter from the cupboard. The bread had an edge of green mold, but he tore this part off and made two peanut butter sandwiches with the remaining pieces. He drank a large glass of juice to chase the sandwiches down and then went into the bathroom where he splashed hot water on his face. He took two of the aspirin the doc in Fort Collins had furnished and climbed into bed.

He had been alone in the apartment since Christmas when his roommate had left college—flunked out, actually. However, it had been small for the two of them. He and Sonny had talked about moving in together, but never had. Sonny was still living in the dorms on campus.

The next morning, Scooter downed several aspirins again to ease the ache in his shoulder, and drove up the winding road to the campus parking lot. He walked across to the cafeteria for breakfast. He looked for Sonny, but didn't see him, so he sat down at one of the tables and started plowing into a large pile of scrambled eggs and toast. He had asked for extra. Several other students he knew sat down at his table and told him, "Good job in Fort Collins!"

He wondered how they knew about the rodeo. "Who told you?'

"Oh, Johnny and Hank were in earlier and said y'all kicked butt."

"Well, sort of. Wait till you get a look at Zeke though. It was the other way around. He looks like a raccoon!"

"Yeah we heard about him getting hooked," one of the other students said.

"Well," said Scooter, "it was more like getting a horn in the kisser. It gave him a concussion." The other students nodded. With that settled, he again attacked the eggs.

The student he knew the best, Marty, was in his range management class and said, "That bull riding . . . pretty risky!"

Scooter washed down a bite of toast with a swallow of juice and nodded, "You got that right."

Marty continued, "I entered bull riding over in Mancos last summer. Y'know, that little amateur rodeo they have there. I never been so nervous in my life . . . just gettin' down into the chute. It was on a dare, so I couldn't back out!"

Scooter took a harder look at Marty, and then when it looked like he wasn't going to continue, he asked, "So what happened?"

"Oh, never made it very far, I have to admit. Maybe one or two seconds. Climbing up on a fence after getting thrown never felt so good!"

Scooter laughed along with several others that had been listening.

"Well, see you in class," Marty said. Scooter nodded.

He scanned the cafeteria to see if he could spot Katherine to borrow Monday's English class notes. Katherine was one of the best students in the class. He had worked on a paper with her earlier in the semester and had finally asked her out a few times. That was what he meant when he had told Zeke that he had been out with girls before and whom he had been talking about when Charlene had queried him. Katherine was nice, and Scooter had noticed how trim she was and how she moved so . . . maybe cat-like. He liked how the outside of her calves showed the long muscles and thought it was probably a result of running. Actually, he had wanted to ask her out early in the semester and it had taken two weeks for him to get up the nerve. He knew she had been on the cross-country team in the fall and had seen her on campus with another runner. He figured the guy was her boyfriend, so he had veered away from the whole thing, but now it didn't seem like she was seeing anyone.

He had been shy, though—afraid of something. He had berated himself about it after their last date. Well, it was a study session, really, but he had walked her back to her dorm. Was it not knowing how to proceed, or was it being afraid she'd react negatively if he did anything? He had been thinking about holding her hand or about kissing all the way back to her dorm, but hadn't done anything. He had felt like a junior-high kid walking around with an erection and not knowing what caused it, or what to do about it.

He had finished his plate of eggs when he saw Katherine come into the cafeteria and sit down at another table. He told the others, "So long," and carried his glass of juice over to sit across from her.

She looked up from eating. "Okay, I know, you want notes from yesterday's English class."

"What are you, a mind reader? Maybe I want to talk to you."

"So, talk!"

Her frosty attitude was disconcerting. He wondered what Zeke would do in this situation. "I do want your notes but wanted to say 'hi' also. What've you been up to?" he asked.

"You mean besides studying and working in the cafeteria, while you and your buddies go rodeoing and leech off others to get your work done?" Her eyes were dark. Scooter had thought of them before as obsidian. They were radiating some heat at him now, though.

Her strident comments put him on the defensive. "Sheesh! What's going on? Is this beat-up-Scooter day?"

Katherine looked at him for a few seconds and finally said, "Okay, I'm not really mad at you. I'm in a situation . . . my mom has to go into the hospital in Cortez and I may have to go home. I'm trying to put it all off for a couple of weeks until after finals. My aunt may be able to help out for a few weeks. But it's all a mess!"

Katherine had told him that her dad was Hispanic and her mother was Anglo, *or was it the other way around? No, her last name is Sandoval.* She had mentioned siblings and that her dad worked for the Forest Service, but otherwise, he didn't know much about her family.

"Gee, I'm sorry! Do you need me to drive you? I could, you know," he said.

"Thanks, but I don't know if I'm going or not. I'll bring the notes at lunch because I'm working . . . Are you going to the dance Friday?"

"I hadn't thought about it." He had forgotten there even was one. "Are you going?"

"I don't know."

Katherine looked away as she said this, and Scooter noticed her high, angled cheeks and long eyelashes. He liked her dark hair with its reddish undertones. It changed color depending on lighting, or how she turned her head. It intrigued him. She kept her hair short, but it swept upwards in the back. Scooter thought like a ducktail. He asked before he thought about it, "Well, you wanna go?"

She looked back at him. "Meaning with you? Are you asking me out?"

"Hmm, well, sure, let's go. We'll cut a mean rug," he said.

Katherine smiled, and said, "You think so, huh?"

"Well, actually, maybe you could teach me some steps. Okay?"

"I guess I could. By the way, I heard you did well in Fort Collins, so I guess congratulations are in order."

"Yeah, thanks. I had kind of a wreck the second go-round and dislocated my shoulder, so that was the other side of the coin."

"You guys . . . why do you want to do that, anyway? Seems like a good way to get hurt. I heard about that bull-rider friend of yours."

"Jeez, word gets around quick here. But yeah, comes with the territory," Scooter said, "the good with the bad. You see, if there wasn't any danger, everyone would do it 'cause it's so fun!" He laughed as he said this, and Katherine smiled. "But yeah, let's go dancing. I mean, if you want to!"

"Well, I said yes, didn't I?"

"Yes, I know . . . just making sure, I guess." He smiled at her. "I better hit it," he continued. "See you at lunch?"

Katherine returned his gaze and smile. "Okay, you cowboy, see you."

Scooter thought as he left: *I shouldn't have asked her out, but all of a sudden, she seems so attractive, even when she's a little angry . . . yeah, good-looking and she's nice. Well, I'm not going steady—yet, thinking of his conversation with Charlene, and Katherine's not really a girlfriend . . . is she?*

Still thinking of his emerging conflict and the two girls, Scooter wondered about his intention of sending Charlene a message. He paused, wondering about it, but decided he better and walked over to the bookstore. He bought a card with a picture of a horse and colt on the front. It seemed completely appropriate, as the horse resembled Charlene's. He then walked across campus to the Library to study for his class at eleven. Some other students also told him, "Great job up north!"

He modestly said, "Thanks," but was thinking: *They never said anything when I came in sixth down at Lamar.*

On his way to the chemistry class, he spotted Sonny and yelled at him. They met up and asked each other, "How're things?" even though they had just seen each other the day before.

"I been like a hero today," Sonny said. "Word got around about placing in the ave."

"Yeah, I've been hearing a little of that too. It's nice for a change. Take it while we can get it pard, 'cause fame is fickle."

Scooter then asked Sonny if he had seen Zeke yet, but Sonny hadn't. "Y'know, Zeke got sick on Wolf Creek Pass. Had to stop fer 'im!"

"Pukin'?" Sonny asked.

"Naw, not that. He was blasting the shrubs in a ravine with the squirts! That habitat's ruined. Said it was the 'blue-plate special' stuff from the café, but who knows. If I see Johnny or Hank, I'll ask 'em if they had it too." Sonny just shook his head. "Anyway, after our range class, we better phone Zeke and see if he survived the night."

Sonny grunted a reply that Scooter figured was a "Yes."

Scooter headed across campus to the science wing and his chemistry class. The lecture was complex, and near the end of the period, the instructor dealt a pop quiz, accompanied by groans from the class. Scooter was relieved that he had studied the notes during the weekend. There were 12 points available from six questions, including several asking for diagrams of compounds. Scooter smiled, as he viewed these and then worked on several reaction diagrams. He thought he did okay, maybe a few points off, as he wasn't sure on a catalyst.

Afterward, Scooter met Sonny in the hall of the cafeteria and they phoned Zeke's apartment from a payphone. The phone rang for a while. Finally, Zeke answered with a sleep-drugged voice. "You gonna live?" Scooter asked.

"I tell ya, that food or somethin' was poisoned. I been sleepin' since we got back, hardly knew where I was when you phoned."

"Probably all that screwing you did with that waitress. Don't you have a class this afternoon? You better bear down these last few weeks."

"Sheeit! Okay, boss, whatever you say. Look, I know, I'll try to get moving. I'm feeling kinda empty though," Zeke answered.

"Well, get some soup or something . . . maybe see ya later."

After he hung up, he told Sonny, "Well, he's still livin', but just got up."

He and Sonny stepped into the cafeteria line to grab some lunch. As they approached the serving area, Katherine brought out a notebook and gave it to Scooter. "Here cowboy," she said, "I need it back tomorrow . . . in class." She had her hand on his upper arm.

"Okay, I'll guard it with my life. Sonny, this is Katherine."

Katherine laughed. "Yes, I see you two guys together all the time. Another good bucking horse rider I'm told."

Sonny seemed tongue-tied and just bobbed his head. After they had gone through the line and worked their way to an empty table, Sonny asked, "What's goin' on with you? Another squaw wants yer bod."

Scooter paused as he was about to sit down. "What're you talking about? She and I are friends . . . have a class together."

"Keep on thinking that en she's goin' t' be disappointed. Chit man, she's in love."

"What kind of bullshit are you trying to feed me? You and Zeke . . . hell, I don't know how you guys think you know everything about women. You go tell her that and she'd laugh in your face."

"No," said Sonny, "she'd turn red as a berry, 'cause it's true."

"You don't know what you're talking about. I did ask her to the dance on Friday night though, so maybe . . . well, I don't know." he confessed.

Sonny started laughing through the last of Scooter's statement, nearly falling off his chair. Scooter had never seen him laugh so hard and lamely explained, "For borrowing her notes." Sonny laughed even harder until tears were running down his face. Scooter uncomfortably looked around the room to see if anyone was wondering what was going on.

"It must have been a great joke," a student said walking by their table.

Finally, when Sonny could talk, he said, "Frens', huh? Y'act so dumb. But, what I doan know is why all of a sudden you're tryin' to get yourself between a rock 'n a hard place, and these wimmen are falling all over ya. That's something to ponder en your scientific mind. It's the wild bronc rider coming out in ya. They're either lovin' the danger of ya, or mor'n likely wanting to tame yer wild mustang ass and harness you to a wagon! You'll be all spavined, out in some garden pullin' a plow."

"A plow! Are you done with the biggest speech of your life?" Scooter asked. "It's about time I had a few dates, isn't it? That's all! I have to get over to the gym." They continued to eat in silence for a while. Scooter could not believe that Sonny had such strong opinions about the girls who had recently come into his life. *Well, wait a minute . . . Katherine and I have been out some earlier in the year, well not really dates . . . I never kissed her or anything. This dance though is a little different. I guess—a real date!*

After finishing, they took their trays to the discard area. "I'll see you later," Scooter said to Sonny. He grunted something, and Scooter ambled across campus toward the gym. He knew Sonny and Zeke would give him a hard time about women. They gave each other a hard time about everything for some reason. He knew it was just bantering though and didn't usually mind, but girls were something new.

He had a P.E. class on Tuesdays and Thursdays after lunch, which he knew was poor timing. He had already tried to work out after eating too much, and it was not fun. He wanted to arrive early though to talk with the instructor about his injury.

The P.E. instructor, Mr. Anderson, told Scooter to see Mr. Taylor, the trainer about the shoulder injury. Scooter thought the instructor mostly just took roll, so he wanted to make sure he had an excused absence. He had to wait for the trainer to come back to his office, so he sat on the floor against the gym wall reading Katherine's class notes.

After several minutes, Mr. Taylor came in through the gym, and Scooter asked him if he had a few minutes. He invited Scooter into his office.

It smelled like wintergreen. Scooter told him about his injury and what the doctor in Fort Collins at the rodeo had said about strengthening his shoulder. He thought Mr. Taylor still worked out. He had close-cropped blonde hair and was trim. He often wore T-shirts and the lean muscles of his arms were evident. Early in the school year, he had set-up a fitness program for everyone on the rodeo team, but Scooter didn't think many of them followed it very well. Part of the regimen included running, and he never did that anymore and knew that Zeke and Sonny had done even less. They saw the benefit of the weight-lifting program though.

Mr. Taylor had Scooter remove his shirt and flex his shoulder, asking what hurt. "Yes, that doc was right about it. You need to strengthen the muscles across the front, but also across the back into the triceps to help those stretched ligaments." He then went to a file and pulled out a sheet with some illustrated exercises on it.

"Push-ups are good, but you need to do the exercises shown on this as well." He circled four different illustrations on the sheet. "But, don't start until next week, and I want to see you before you do, to walk you through them . . . to start kind of light."

Scooter mentioned that there was another rodeo in two weeks. Mr. Taylor looked at him and said, "I doubt it. I mean it's going to take like a month to get over the initial trauma and then to even begin to strengthen it. Don't get your hopes up."

"It's not my riding arm," Scooter explained.

Mr. Taylor ended the session by saying, "It's the torn or stretched ligaments I'm worried about and getting it stable. I'll talk to Anderson about using this for the class, but you need to talk with him as well."

Scooter nodded. "Thanks."

Scooter left somewhat discouraged but thought he had ridden a week after when the shoulder had been dislocated the previous summer. He checked his watch and then hustled back across campus to his range management lab. This class was one of his favorites, partly because he saw the application of it to his family's ranch, but he liked to identify the mounted specimens of grasses and other forage plants that were part of the lab requirement. He needed to know these as well as other weedy plants detrimental to range, and in some cases, poisonous to livestock. A lab test on these was scheduled for the next week.

He entered the classroom and sat down near Sonny, then saw Hank, so stood back up and walked over to him. "Hey knucklehead, did you or Johnny get sick yesterday from the lunch?"

Hank just looked at Scooter. "It'd take more'n that lunch to have an effect on my iron stomach."

"Yeah, right . . . you're always so tough." He twisted Hank's ear between the fingers of his fist. "That's for giving us the finger yesterday!"

Hank hollered and wriggled free. Scooter thought Hank was going to tussle with him, but the instructor came in and gave them a questioning look. They hurriedly took their seats. Hank's ear was red, and he said in a quiet voice, "I'll get you for that!" Scooter just smiled and nodded at him.

"Jeez man, take 'er easy," Sonny said.

Scooter had planned to head back to his apartment, maybe having a TV dinner, but Sonny said, "Let's have a good meal tonight over'n the cafeteria."

Scooter thought about the cost, as he had been eating out all day, but then thought about a boring evening. They sat with Johnny and Will, mostly discussing the upcoming rodeos and if the Blue-Plate Special had made anyone else sick. It seemed not.

Scooter went back to his apartment after dinner, recopied notes for the next day's Animal Science class and worked on the English composition paper. He opened his English class notebook and saw the prose that he had written, thinking about Charlene. Scooter thought about sending the note, so she would have it by Friday when he was planning to call her. He took out the card he had bought, and then his English notes. The prose now seemed mushy. He instead wrote:

> *Charlene, Just wanted to say thanks for a stellar weekend I miss feeding your horse with you! Scooter*
> *PS: I'll call Friday evening to make sure you're studying and not goofing off!*

He sealed the envelope and found a stamp among the clutter on his desk and then walked outside and down the street where he dropped the envelope into a mailbox on the corner of the block. He walked back to his room thinking what Charlene was like. *Tall or willowy, huh? . . . And those eyes . . . oh, those lips, too. I bet that guy that Hank mentioned has called her . . . probably has a class with her . . .*

Scooter closed and locked his door and then put his class materials together for the next day. He took Katherine's notes and copied them into his notebook. He noticed she wrote with rounded cursive. She had even written in italics for titles that the instructor had said needed to be underlined or italicized. *Amazing she could do that . . . must have studied penmanship . . . bet this stuff is on the final for one thing. She's nice too. I think she liked that I asked her to the dance.* He shook his head thinking about Sonny's impression and wondered too if he was getting into a deeper part of the quicksand. After he finished transferring the notes, he realized it was getting late.

He went into the bathroom, threw cold water on his face and then dumped several aspirin tablets out of the envelope—there were only a few left—and washed them down by drinking from the faucet. He stripped off everything but his underwear and flopped unto the bed. He decided it had been a long day. His shoulder ached. *That Pieface . . . wonder if I could ride it now, knowing what it's like . . .*

Wednesday was a long day of classes. Scooter looked at his English class notes as he ate cold cereal. *Sentence structure, gerunds, infinitives . . . A lot of stuff to know.* Scooter placed his empty bowl in the sink and ran some water into it and then hurried to his car and drove up the winding road to the college parking lot.

He had planned to give Katherine her notebook and then sit by her. Linda, one of her friends who Katherine seemed to pal around with was in his preferred chair. He walked over, offering her the notebook.

"Thanks, Katherine. I wished I took such good notes. Could I borrow it again after class?"

She smiled at his joke. "Don't get too comfy in this. I'm not your servant girl." Linda laughed at their exchange.

"Hmm, now that's a thought!" He moved to a chair farther back in the room. After class let out, he told Katherine he would see her later.

On Thursday after chemistry, Scooter hiked across campus to the gym and first looked in the weight room. Zeke was already lifting and then Sonny came in to join him. Sonny was going to work out in his jeans and boots but stripped off his shirt and hung it on a rack of weights.

"Anderson sees you, you're going to get hollered at about that," Scooter said. They were supposed to change into gym clothes.

"I ain't got time," Sonny said, "besides, they stink anyways."

Scooter started to walk down the hall to find Mr. Taylor but met him coming toward the weight room and followed him back toward it. "Does it still ache?" he asked.

"Not too much now," Scooter said.

"Well, certainly not today. Come in tomorrow afternoon . . . let's see, around four, and we'll start out. All you rodeo guys need to do more on your legs anyway. You're spending too much time trying to look like Charles Atlas. More on your trunks too." Zeke was doing bench presses and Sonny was spotting him. "Do you guys still have the handout I gave you in the fall?" Mr. Taylor asked. "That's the program you should be following." The three silently looked at each other. Finally, Scooter said, he wasn't sure. Mr. Taylor shook his head, indicating his displeasure and said, "Remind me and I'll give you another copy."

Having a course of action toward competing improved Scooter's outlook. He and Sonny walked together to the range management laboratory, and there quizzed each other on the range and forage plants. Sonny said, "These 'r tough, I'm a struggling t'remember that Latin, innit?"

"Yeah, we gotta come back to some of these, especially those from earlier in the year. We need to make a list, common names first then scientific, huh?" They started to do this in their notebooks as they sorted through the pressed, mounted plants. "Let's say the scientific on these, huh?" Just to help put them in our brains."

"Chit man, my brain's too full fer that Latin."

Scooter laughed, then said, "It's not going to run over on you, is it? I gotta get." Sonny placed the last plant specimen back on the stack and shook his head.

"It's about to!"

"Well, let's capture that runoff, huh?" They both chuckled at their analysis.

In the evening, Scooter finished a rough draft of his English paper. Zeke's face-plant on the bull's horns was a key paragraph and he worked on increasing the graphic detail; he added how the dust had settled together with the crowd noise as if both had fallen onto the arena floor and were draped over Zeke. Scooter then added a description of the procedure when Zeke's nose was set with two pencils. Some of the students had thought Scooter made up that part of the incident when he had retold it. In reviewing the paper, he realized it needed more heft, and especially something on the background of rodeo and bull riding, so made notes in the margins to enlarge the lead-in.

He finally took a break and decided he better call home. He was supposed to after the weekend and here it was already Thursday. His mother answered the phone and said they had been wondering about him. He said he was fine and had placed, winning fourth in the first go-round. His mother relayed this to his dad, who then got on the phone. Scooter repeated what he had told his mom, and his dad asked for details about the horse and his ride. Scooter said he might be going down to Jicarilla for the weekend with Sonny, and his dad thought it was for another rodeo. His mother got back on and asked if he was keeping up on his studies. She said all this traveling around surely was not good for schoolwork, let alone money. He told her not to worry, as he was doing fine, and asked if Rachel, his sister was there. His mother said no, she was at school doing some project. Scooter asked to have her call when she got home if it wasn't too late. He was fond of his sister but had not talked to her for a while.

Scooter stuffed his dirty laundry into a pillowcase and walked down the street to a laundromat. He tried to decrease the amount of ironing by folding the shirts and pants as they came out of the drier. Back at his apartment, he placed his shirts on hangers and laid out clothes for the next day, and then his books for the morning classes.

He had just gotten into bed when the phone rang and figured it was his sister. He answered and at first didn't recognize the musical voice that asked, "How's my cowboy?"

After a few seconds, he asked, "Charlene?"

"Yes, are you surprised?"

"Well, yeah, I was going to phone you tomorrow."

"Yeah, I know. I got your nice note today. I'm going to the Springs on Friday afternoon. My folks want me to come home for some family thing. My grandparents and some other relatives are going to be there Saturday, so I wanted you to know before you called."

"So, that's good. Are you cooking?"

"Well, helping. Why? You want to come over?"

"Wouldn't I like to! I can smell the home cooking from here," he replied.

"Well, next time you're driving through we can arrange it. How's your shoulder?"

"I'm going to start working out with the trainer tomorrow, so that's good. I'm figuring on Laramie. Are you?"

"I said I was going. You better be there! I wanted to remind you, I think entries have to be in by next Wednesday."

"I think we're sending ours in this week. I'm going down to the rez with Sonny on Saturday. He said we're doing a sweat lodge thing, said it will help my shoulder."

There was a pause after he said this. "You better not go native on me," Charlene finally said.

"Go native?" he asked.

"I mean linking up with some sweet girl down there and never coming back!"

He laughed at the thought. "Naw, we're not doing that . . . well, I'm not anyway, and I would eat dirt if Sonny had some girl down there. How's Squirrel?"

"She's fine. I don't know if she is going to Laramie though. She's an alternate on the team, so depends if everyone else is going or not."

"I don't think she likes me," Scooter said.

Charlene paused. "No, it's not that. She's just worried about things."

Scooter had no idea what Charlene was getting at and asked, "What things?"

Charlene hesitated. "Well, that you and I were moving too fast. Or I was moving too fast maybe."

Scooter didn't say anything for a few seconds, "Ah . . . hmm, well, does that mean that someone could get hurt?"

"Yes, something like that."

"Are you worried?" he asked.

"I wasn't going to worry about it, you know, like we were talking the other night, but a person always does I think, at least a little . . . are you?" Charlene asked.

"I've been thinking about you . . . a lot!"

"I'm glad. I liked our talks," Charlene said.

Scooter thought the conversation was going in an interesting direction and decided to push how he felt slightly.

"I liked being close to you! Zeke told me to be careful. He thinks I don't know what I'm doing. Maybe that's true."

"Didn't we say we were going to take chances?" she asked.

"Tell me exactly so I know," Scooter said. "Does it mean that we like each other a lot and we want to be with each other to see where this pathway takes us? Is that what it is? Is that what you want?"

"Well, we already said what it is. But, you're close. I knew you were a smart guy."

Her comment made him laugh. "Okay, I just wanted to know some of the territory . . . while we're out there taking chances!"

She laughed at his explanation. "I liked getting your note. You don't waste words though."

"Well, did it make you smile?"

"Yes, it made me laugh a little."

"Well, that's good." He was going to let it go at that, but then remembered about someone on her rodeo team being interested in her, and said, "I had written a love note; a poem actually, but wavered . . . nerves I guess. Maybe I'm no good at taking chances."

"What did it say?" Charlene asked.

"Maybe I'll tell you in Laramie."

"You have to now. I mean that's only fair."

He continued. "You know, Zeke said he might drive up alone . . . to take his waitress with him . . . at least he's stopping in Fort Collins. I think he's smitten! Anyway, Sonny and I will likely go up together. Why don't you see if Squirrel wants to go anyway, just to hang out?"

"You and he are pretty thick."

"Well, we've been good buds all this year. I'm looking forward to meeting his family. Maybe he can come out to the ranch sometime to meet mine. Are you thinking about coming by after La Junta? I mean if you go an all that. It's on the way."

"We'll see," she said.

It seemed to him that Charlene was reluctant about visiting his family. Maybe this was part of moving too fast.

"I don't know about Squirrel going up. You're not match-making, are you?" Charlene asked.

"Well, they can be friends can't they, and hang out?"

"I guess that's okay. I mean it's up to them. Well honey, I better let you go. You guys be careful out there in the wilds of New Mexico."

"We are going wild y'know . . . only leather underwear all weekend!" Charlene laughed, and said, "Call me next week, will you?"

"Okay. How 'bout Monday?"

They both said, "Goodnight."

It was near eleven, and now Scooter wasn't tired. He asked himself: *Did we make a commitment to each other?* He wasn't one hundred percent sure, but it seemed like it. *Every time she calls me honey. I melt a little, but it gives me pause, too. Yet, the attraction is strong, and I look forward to Laramie and not just to the rodeo and riding bareback horses.* He thought of the making out they had done up at Horsetooth and it excited him. He had liked the exploration, the teasing, and wondered if it might lead to everything. This thought both excited him and gave him pause. *Maybe Zeke's right! Maybe Sonny's right! Now I have the date with Katherine! I think I'm in a pickle. Wonder if I should break the date with her?* He thought about her hot eyes. *Breaking this date would not go well . . . she'd be hurt no doubt. She sure is different than Charlene . . . pretty, but maybe more settled or not so impulsive. She's more like a good-looking Quarter Horse. Charlene, with her long legs, is like a Thoroughbred. Okay, we'll just go as friends . . . she'll have to teach me how to dance though. I hope she knows that.*

He climbed into bed still contemplating the two girls.

Scooter tried to concentrate on his classes, but there was a lot on his mind—his upcoming date, for one thing. He wondered if he should go after the conversation the night before with Charlene. He looked at Katherine though in English class and she smiled. He decided he couldn't do it—couldn't break the date. Instead, after class, he said he'd be by around eight.

"Put on your silver slippers 'cause we're going to be lighter than air!"

She laughed. "What? Have you been drinking?" Her eyes were sparkling.

"You'll see," he said.

He noticed Hank across the room. Hank mouthed something. Scooter mouthed back, "What?" several times, figuring that Hank was trying to say something obscene. Hank showed Scooter a middle finger.

"Aren't you guys friends?" Katherine asked.

"Hmm, well, not right now I guess," Scooter replied. "We're having a disagreement about study habits."

"Oh!" Scooter looked at Katherine and shrugged.

Scooter walked across campus to the physed building late in the afternoon and changed into his gym shorts and shirt. Both smelled of old sweat. He went by Mr. Taylor's door, but the office was empty, so he went to the weight room where he heard the clank of barbells. *No doubt some of the jocks.* He went into the room and saw Mr. Taylor working with one of the guys from the wrestling team. He had been in Scooter's P.E. course the first fall he was at the college.

"Start on the leg press machine, I'll be over in a minute," Mr. Taylor said.

The trainer showed Scooter the exercises he wanted him to do for his shoulder, but he also had him perform more leg presses, and then some leg curls, extensions, and calf raises. Scooter could feel the burn settle into the muscles.

"You see why I want you to do more of a complete program?" Mr. Taylor asked. He had Scooter finish with ab curls and back extensions until he couldn't do any more. His shirt was wet, and the stink had accentuated.

After showering, Scooter spent several hours in the library, mostly working on chemistry, but he had an assignment to recopy for range management as well. He headed out to his car near evening and drove down to his apartment.

Once inside, he put a TV dinner into the oven. He ate while reading a new edition of *Rodeo Sports News*. He studied the photos of bareback bronc riding and checked the standings, based on earnings in the event. He thought the top contestants earned a lot of money. After putting the empty dinner tray into the trash, he pulled a clean shirt out of the closet and worked on it with an iron. His mother had shown him how to press shirts and pants before he had left for college, but he noticed there were a few unwanted creases on the sleeves. He tried redoing these, but a scorch mark appeared. He said a swear word and hung the shirt on the door jam. He grabbed a pair of western-cut slacks, and after turning the heat selector to a cooler setting, pressed them as well. It seemed hot, and Scooter was about to take a second shower when someone pounded on the door.

"Just a minute!" he hollered, and grabbed his jeans, quickly pulling them on. He opened the door to see Zeke standing there with a six-pack of beer.

Zeke barged in past Scooter. "Yo pard, looks like you're ready to party. Girls like a guy to go shirtless, bare-foot too. Brings out the motherly instinct in 'em. Let's go out on the town some, shake off the class-work dust!"

"I have a date . . . girl from one of my classes . . . Katherine," Scooter said. He was still standing at the open door.

Zeke set the beer on the counter. "Yeah, I heard . . . Sonny. Y'got time for a beer, though," and proceeded to open two of the cans and thrust one at Scooter. He sat down on a stool and took a sip while Scooter leaned against the other side of the counter. He lifted the can and said, "Here's to you and all yer women!"

Scooter reluctantly touched Zeke's can with his and said, "What y'mean all my women? You and Sonny are getting weird about me having one date!"

"No, I don't care how many dates you have," Zeke responded, "but you don't know what you're doing, do you?"

"Don't read anything into this date. I'm not going to seduce her . . . or try, like you would. We're more friends than anything, so there."

"She's going to be disappointed if you don't try to seduce her a little. She's a college girl, you know, not some high schooler. Anyway, be careful, that's all. I mean, do you have anything?"

Scooter was getting agitated. "You mean condoms?" He straightened up. "Hell! I'm not doing that for Christ's sake! Don't start mothering me."

Zeke backed off saying, "Okay, okay, don't get your temper up, I'm not looking for a fight. I'm just trying to give you some advice. Anyway, the main reason I came over . . . we need to get our entries in for Laramie as soon as we can. Johnny called and there are a lot of colleges coming in for it."

"Yeah, I heard it, too. I have my entry filled out and a check ready, so let's send them all in together."

"Give me yours and I'll get Sonny's too," Zeke said, "'cause I think Johnny's going to send them in for the whole team tomorrow—certified mail or something."

"I was going to send it in on Monday," Scooter said, "Sonny and I are still going down to the rez tomorrow." He lifted some papers on his desk and found his form and check and clipped them together before handing them over to Zeke.

"Well, Monday might be too late. Tomorrow I gotta work the sale barn. I'm not so flush as you guys."

"Do you need some green, 'cause I could loan you some," Scooter said.

"Well, maybe for the trip north," Zeke said. "I'll see next week, so thanks. Okay, I'll let you get ready for your second honey." He laughed at his comment and took the rest of the beer as he headed out.

"Yeah, yeah, you guys are both so funny," Scooter said.

He closed the door and went back into the bathroom to shave and shower. He thought his teeth needed brushing again and he swished some mouthwash to get rid of the beer smell. He then put on his shirt and placed a string tie around the collar. He hadn't worn one for a while and had to retie it several times. He got out his best boots and decided they needed buffed some, so used a wet towel to take off the dust. It was still too early, so he read more of the *Rodeo Sports News*. He was a little nervous and went back into the bathroom to put on a second application of deodorant.

Finally, he decided it was time and drove up the hill on the winding road to the college parking lot near the girl's dorms. He walked over to the lobby and told the woman on duty he was there for Katherine. She told him to make himself comfortable while she phoned. Several other guys were there waiting for dates as well. He grabbed a magazine and was leafing through it but looked up as Katherine came into the room. He got up to meet her, and said, "Wow, you look completely . . . ." He was lost for words and she smiled at his predicament. Finally, he said, "Sensational!"

"Thank you, my prince," Katherine replied, "notice . . . not silver, but gold." She stuck one foot out from her dress to show him a sparkling gold shoe with a small heel.

"I like them!" he said.

He was quite amazed, as Katherine had slightly transformed herself with eye shadow and lipstick. Her lips looked moist. He found himself staring at them. She had a gold hairband that matched her shoes. Her dress was black and had a slit up one side to above her knee.

"You do look very nice. Maybe I should go get a tuxedo," Scooter said.

"No, you're just right . . . a cowboy, but a dressed-up one at that." She smiled up at him as they walked toward the student union ballroom. They brushed hands. He pulled his hand away from hers, but then, as if his hand had a mind of its own, it took hers and they walked hand-in-hand the rest of the way. He asked her about her mother, and what she was going to do.

"My older sister is taking some time off until I can go home after finals. She has a husband and a baby, so she can't stay for too long. My aunt is going to pick me up tomorrow and we'll go to Cortez . . . to the hospital. She's bringing me back Sunday."

"It must be serious, so I'm sorry," Scooter said.

"It might be serious. That's what they're going to find out I guess. Let's put this behind us for tonight. Okay?"

As they approached the ballroom, he could hear the music and said, "That's fine with me. I hate hospital stuff, growing-old stuff. We came to kick-up our heels."

Katherine squeezed his hand. Scooter looked around the dance floor to see if he knew anyone. None of the guys from the rodeo team were evident, although he saw and said hello to several guys that he knew from his classes. They stood on the sidelines for a while. The music was varied, but mostly rock-n-roll.

"Can you jitterbug?" Katherine asked.

"Well, I doubt it, since I don't know what it is," Scooter answered. "I guess before we can glide on air, you'll have to do some teaching."

She grabbed his hands and showed him how to step to the music, how to spin her around under his arm and then behind his back. He was quite amazed by all the moves and tried to concentrate on the twirling and how they would then come back together. After a few songs, he thought he was getting the hang of it.

They then did a slow dance and Scooter noticed the fresh soapy scent of Katherine's hair. She nestled into him and they danced as if one person. He viewed the other dancers over her head. She felt good to him. Her hand was on the back of his neck, in his hair. *Just friends, remember. Quicksand, isn't that what Sonny said?*

The music stopped, and Katherine led him over to say hello and introduce him to several of her friends and their dates. One of the girls, Linda, he already knew from their English class. They walked over to the refreshment table and he filled two glasses of red punch for them. "Sorry, no hard stuff for a princess."

She smiled at him and asked, "You think so, huh? Where have you been all semester? I mean . . . we had a study date and then you disappeared. I thought maybe you didn't like me."

"No, it wasn't that. I don't know. I've been dedicated to becoming a monk." She smiled at his joke and he continued. "Okay, not really, but I did dedicate this year to courses . . . the Dean's List, and to working out for the rodeo thing. You know, Sonny and I want to join the pro ranks someday, maybe even this summer if we can get a card. But no, I saw you. Why don't you have a steady boyfriend? I can't figure it out, now that I think about it."

"Maybe the right guy had to come along." Her tone of voice caused him to wish he hadn't asked. She continued, "I've been out with a number of guys. One asked me to this, but I told him I didn't know if I wanted to go. The next day you changed my mind. Did you know that?"

"No, I didn't know anything. As my buddies tell me, apparently, I know horses some, but I am naive about women.

"Maybe so or maybe you just think you are." Katherine smiled. "I knew you were shy, it was kind of cute—at first." She took his arm and said, "Let's hit it again. Okay?"

They danced the next set and came back to the refreshment bar. "See, you dance fine."

"You're a good teacher," he replied, "I do think we lifted off a couple of times."

Katherine laughed. "Let's get some air. We need to walk." They went out onto the veranda and continued into the night air. It was refreshing after the closeness of the dance floor. They stopped near a railing and looked out toward the horizon. A bright swatch of stars spread across the northern sky. They held hands while gazing.

"Sweet view," he said and put his hand over her shoulder to point out the North Star and the Big and Little Dippers. The moon to the east was nearly full.

"I was a Girl Scout, so I already know them," she said, "but I still like to look." Some of the other couples were embracing in the shadows of the building.

"Come on, let's keep going," she said. They walked down the stairs to the sidewalk. He asked her what she was going to do during the summer, and she told him about a job she had in a large Native American jewelry shop in Cortez. He mentioned there was a rodeo in Cortez that he and Sonny had discussed entering.

"You better let me know if you do." They had stopped by some evergreen trees.

"You know, that monk thing I mentioned . . . well, it was true in a fashion, but I'm trying to break out of it. It's not that I didn't like you. In fact, I noticed you every day in English class. I like sitting by you. Did you notice that? I knew you had a boyfriend in the fall . . . a guy from the cross-country team. But then later, I wasn't sure."

Katherine turned toward him and said, "You talk too much." He viewed her up-turned face and they kissed. He could feel her against him; her breasts and the curve of her thighs pushed into him. They broke and looked at each other. He kissed her again. She pushed his lips apart with her tongue and he took it in. He moved his hand down onto her waist and then on to feel the swell and firmness of her hips. He increased the pressure between them. She didn't seem to mind.

"Let's go to the picnic grounds," she said.

You mean walk all the way over there?" he asked.

"No silly, don't you have your car? I have to be back to the dorm by midnight."

They walked to his car near her dorm and drove around the perimeter road to the other side of campus, and then turned onto a gravel road that led to several picnic spots. She sat close to him and he was conscious of her leg against his. The rodeo club had used the area for a barbeque in the fall. They drove in and saw a few other cars parked in some of the spots. "Great minds think alike!" he joked.

"Don't get your ambitions up too high, you cowboy," Katherine said teasingly. They parked between several large conifer trees.

"Hmm, I might be shy, but I am ambitious," he quipped.

She laughed and said, "I have no doubt about your ambition."

Scooter changed the direction of the conversation, wanting to know more about her. "What are your ambitions? I mean about a career and your life?"

"Do you have a couple of days? I mean that requires a long-winded answer. I do student teaching next fall. I'll be glad to get out and start a job. Do you have your essay done yet for next week?"

Scooter thought: *She's too smart for me.* He told her about writing about his trip to Fort Collins, Zeke's pickup breaking down and getting a concussion in the bull riding. Except he didn't tell her anything about Charlene and wasn't about to broach that subject, figuring that would ruin the evening for both.

"I have to fill in the middle with background research on rodeo and bull riding though, you know, the history. How's yours coming along?"

"Oh, it's done I think. It's good to let it set though, like over the weekend, and then I'll do a final."

"What are you going to do after you start teaching? I mean are you gonna get married?" he asked.

"Are you asking me? . . . Scooter, you sweet boy!" she teased. He felt himself stiffen, and she laughed at him.

He recovered. "Well, you had me there for a second, but there could be worse things I guess. I have a lot I want to do though before that."

"So, I gathered. You shouldn't become a rodeo bum though, okay?" she had her hand on his thigh. It felt warm.

"You know, my dad, well he figures my brother and I should take over the ranch someday. So, there's that. My brother is already entrenched there—like the boss . . . wants to be the boss. He can't wait to get me under his thumb. I see him giving me a list of chores every morning! But, I'm not ready to be in one place. I like the road . . . to see where it goes . . . but I realize a guy can't rodeo forever." He wanted to sway the conversation back to her. "I see you out running sometimes."

Well, I wouldn't call it running, now . . . maybe jogging. I wasn't going to go out for the cross-country team next year, with student teaching and all the class stuff. But now, depending on what happens with my mother, I may need the scholarship, so I need to do the team training yet. Or what if I have to drop out?"

He tried to reassure her. "I think it will all work out for you somehow. I mean that's what I want. You know . . . what we're talking about is freedom to form our own lives. Do you know that?"

Katherine did not immediately reply, instead placed her head on his shoulder, and he wondered what she was thinking. He noticed her leg peeking out from the slit in her dress. It looked shapely—what he could see of it in the near dark. "Yes, forming our own lives at this point is everything!"

He put his hand on her thigh and ran his thumb up and down. It felt silky. Katherine placed her hand on his to still it and turned her head to him for a kiss. The intensity of it increased, but they finally disengaged, panting slightly. Katherine had placed a leg over his and he was conscious of this and what he thought was the top of a stocking and wondered where it ended. The whole area seemed to be composed of silky-smooth topography; an area that he had only previously imagined. He heard her say, "Oh"! She kissed his neck and then his ear. They toppled over, and she pulled him toward her. He wondered where this was going to end . . . if they were going to make love. He had to bend a leg up against the door to make room for himself or crush Katherine and pushed back toward the steering wheel in order not to slide off the seat and onto the floor. He realized one of his legs was partially out the window of the car. The window was not all the way down and the top of it was putting a crease into his leg above his boot top. He moved the pressure point to a new place. His butt was wedged under the steering wheel. It was becoming uncomfortable. He tried to move away from the pressure, more onto Katherine. She moved under him and placed one of her legs around him, and he found himself merged with her. She had her hands in his hair and they kissed again. They had remained clothed, though, and he thought of this as a major hindrance, and then the concept of his foot being out the window took precedence. He thought it would be funny if Zeke could see him now and wondered how Zeke had made love to the girl in his mom's car. Scooter's two-door Chevy coupe now it seemed extraordinarily small. His desire waned as he thought of Zeke and their talk, and about Charlene. The pressure points of the steering wheel on his thigh and window now on his ankle weren't helping either.

Finally, he could not stand the cramped position further and lifted himself off Katherine. Like a contortionist, he jackknifed his legs under the steering wheel and, as they both sat up, he said, "I'm sorry, I wasn't quite prepared for this." thinking of Zeke's question about having a condom. "You have me super-hot though!"

"It's okay, and it's my turn." She unzipped his fly and felt for him. She then put her tongue in his mouth, while continuing her ministrations. The quickness of it all took him by surprise.

Suddenly he jerked free of her kiss and said, "Whoa . . . oh, damn!" He gritted his teeth at the sensation of her. He was panting as if he had just ridden a bareback bronc.

"Judas Priest, sorry!"

Katherine searched for her purse and took out some tissues. "It's okay, you don't need to be embarrassed," she said.

"Well, it is kind of embarrassing, but you did it to me!" He was amazed that he had lost control and felt as if his face was on fire.

"You were doing it to me though," she answered. Her dress was still up near the tops of her stockings.

He could not believe that this had happened. "How do you know how to do that?"

Katherine didn't say anything for a few seconds, but then replied, "Girls know more about boys than boys think. Boys always think they know everything about us, but they usually know very little, although I see you've learned a thing or two. I could ask you the same thing!"

"Jeez, though!"

"Don't worry about it . . . it's biology, isn't it?" She pulled his head toward her and kissed him. They broke apart and he was conscious of her softness, her femininity.

"Jeez, it seemed more than just biology." She laughed at his comment. "You have very nice legs. Do you know that?"

"You think so? You are some cowboy. You better get me back to the dorm before I get a demerit though." She tugged her dress down and said, "Turn on the light for me." She turned the rearview mirror to push her hair back in place and then applied lipstick. He watched her.

"I'm just going to kiss it off again."

"Well, I'll put some on your face again, so watch out," she teased. He smiled at her and started the car.

On the way back, he said, "I hope your mom's going to be okay."

"Thanks, I hope so too. My dad is really worried . . . me too."

He put his hand in hers and she snuggled against him.

Scooter walked Katherine to the lobby door among other escorts bringing dates back. They kissed again, and Scooter said, "I liked this date. Thanks for the dancing lessons . . . ah, you know which lessons I liked best even if it was kind of embarrassing."

She kissed him on the neck. "Yes, I know what you liked. I think you are an ornery boy! I'll see you on Monday. Be careful down there on the reservation." She smiled at him as she turned to walk inside.

Scooter drove down the winding road from campus to his apartment complex. He could still smell the scent of Katherine; some of her perfume or fresh soapy scent, but more than that. *Zeke was right, Sonny was right. I don't know what I'm doing. I think I trapped myself. I wonder if a guy can be in love with two women? No, not in love, or is it? But feelings for both—strong feelings. I never thought this date would be like it turned out. Now if Charlene asked if I had a girlfriend at Southwestern, what would I say? Man, what a mess. I think I want to turn the clock back to when I wasn't involved with anyone. Wonder what Zeke would do. Well, he would likely try to seduce both as much as he could and not worry about it. Sonny's right too. Why are there two women interested suddenly when for all this time there weren't any? That first year here, I was wet behind the ears . . .*

He unlocked the door to his apartment and walked into the bathroom. He very much had to pee and then flushed his face with cold water. It was nearly one. His shoulder had started to throb, probably from all the gymnastics he had attempted in his car. He took the last two of the prescription aspirins and slid under the blanket. He stared at the darkness toward the ceiling, still thinking about the two women in his life, not sure if this new development would get in the way of his rodeo goals, as Sonny claimed, as well as scholastic goals.

CHAPTER TWELVE
SONNY'S ROOTS

On Saturday morning, Scooter wolfed down a piece of toast and chased it with orange juice. The juice was a little fizzy. He made a mental note to pick up some next time he was at a store. He threw some clothes into a duffle bag and pulled his sleeping bag off the closet shelf. Sonny had told Scooter to bring extra shorts or swimming trunks and a sleeping bag. Scooter checked his car just to make sure there were no telltale signs left from the night before—thinking of Zeke's mention of the girl's panties in his mother's car, not that Katherine had discarded anything—and drove up to the college.

He parked in front of the men's dorms and walked toward Sonny's unit, only to be met by him coming out the main door.

"I seen y'drivin' up," Sonny said. He threw his bronc saddle and riding tack into the trunk of Scooter's car and told him, "S'posed to be a jackpot out there tomorrow."

Scooter was tempted to stop at his place on the way out of town to retrieve his bareback rigging but thought about Mr. Taylor's admonition about resting his shoulder. He told Sonny about working with the trainer; about the light upper-body work of "flys" and shoulder presses. The shoulder felt okay, but his legs were stiff and sore from the exercise routine.

"I guess I'm not in as good as shape as I thought," he told Sonny.

"Y'goin' to keep following his program?" Sonny asked.

"It probably would help us ride better. I think the pros do a lot of weight stuff now."

"How's yer hot date last night?" Sonny asked.

"Hmm, hot, huh? Did a lot of dancing, so it was alright."

"Yer becomin' a reglar dancin' fool, I reckon!"

Scooter looked over at Sonny and saw a wolfish grin. "Yeah, a dancin' fool is about it!"

They both laughed.

They drove through Pagosa Springs and turned south toward the New Mexico line and on to Jicarilla. They stopped in town at a small grocery store. "I better get some supplies," Sonny said.

Scooter went in with him to help pay. Sonny threw in a gallon can of salsa among other grocery items. He said in response to Scooter's questioning look, "My dad's partial to it." He also bought several toys. "I gotta always bring somethin' for the kids."

Scooter wondered if Sonny had a secret life on the reservation and asked, "What? Y'mean you have a wife and kids out here?"

Sonny laughed. "Yeah, got kids scattered all over down here." Scooter looked at him and realized Sonny was kidding. He explained, "Fer my younger brother and sister."

"Jeez, y'had me wondering about you for a few seconds," Scooter said.

From Jicarilla, Sonny gave directions to his parent's place. "It's out Sawmill Gulch, southwest of town."

They drove by a rodeo arena, and Scooter noticed the bucking chutes. Sonny explained that some of the tribe, including several of his uncles, would bring stock in the next day. The road became rough and Scooter was wondering about the wear and tear on his car, as they lurched through several areas of deep ruts.

"I'm glad it ain't muddy, or we'd have to walk," Scooter said.

Sonny looked over at him and said, "I've had to a few times. She gets gnarly . . . greasy."

Scooter noticed the deep ruts that angled out away from the road and back to it in several locations. "I can only imagine."

They continued to bounce slowly along, and Sonny finally said, "Take a left." They traveled down a double-track road to a small, white, frame house. There was a long, low barn and attached corrals several hundred yards farther out. A small camper trailer was parked at the side of a shed. A second small shed and an outhouse sat leaning slightly to the side of the house. A late-model pickup sat in the driveway and they parked beside it. Two rangy dogs came out toward the car. Scooter noticed one's hackles were up.

"Welcome home," Sonny said either to Scooter or to no one in particular. He got out and said something in Apache to the dogs, whose demeanor changed when they realized who it was.

"Come on, they're tame," Sonny said. Scooter wasn't so sure. A woman and several young children came out onto the small porch. Sonny said something to them in Apache. The woman replied, and a boy and a girl came running out to him. They appeared to Scooter to be about ten and eight years old. Sonny talked to them in Apache, and they clambered over him. "This's my rodeo buddy, Scooter," he said in English.

Scooter said, "Hi!" as they walked toward the house, the two children hanging onto Sonny's leg. He swung the girl up to his back for a ride.

At the door, Sonny said in English, "Mom, this is the guy I told youse about, Scooter."

She extended her hand and Scooter shook it. She was a slight, short woman and had her thick hair wrapped into a round bun. A long silver nee-dle-like clasp kept it in place. She wore a heavy silver necklace that Scooter thought looked Navajo.

"Welcome to our home," she said.

Scooter thanked her, and they went inside.

Sonny asked her something in Apache and explained to Scooter, "Asking where Dad and my brother are."

His mother responded, "We should speak English for your friend. Your dad and Frank went to look at the cattle up the canyon this morning. They took the horses but should be back soon. They'll be getting hungry. I have some stew on. You boys want some?"

"Yeah," Sonny replied and to Scooter said, "I'm always hungry for Mom's cooking."

"I can go for some," Scooter said.

The kitchen was the main room of the house and had two stoves. Scooter realized that one was a large wood or coal stove and the other one was propane.

Sonny remembered they had some groceries and he and Scooter went out to the car to retrieve them, with Sonny's siblings in tow. One of the dogs came over to get a better sniff of Scooter, who tried to pet it, but it was leery of him and came around behind him. Scooter checked to make sure it wasn't coming in for a sneak attack.

Sonny noticed Scooter's wariness. "I think he likes ya"

"Yeah, wants to take out a piece of my butt," Scooter said.

They went into the house and Sonny's mother put away the grocer-ies. She told Sonny, "You're always spoiling these two," when she pulled out the toys. The boy and girl just smiled at Sonny. It was obvious to Scooter their big brother was their hero.

Sonny's mother set two bowls of stew on the table and some fry bread. She said to Sonny, "Your Uncle John is having the sweat tonight and is expecting both of you to be there."

"We're expectin' to go. I talked Scooter into it."

"This is delicious by the way . . . I've never done a sweat before," Scooter said.

Sonny's mother said, "I think you'll like it. It's good for body and soul."

After they had eaten, Sonny said, "Let's go down to the barn and see if any of the horses are in."

They walked from the house with the youngsters still tagging along.

Sonny mentioned to Scooter that they would likely sleep in the camper along with his younger brother Frank. "He likes his solitude, so stays out here . . . well, except meals, y'know. There's no room in the house anyways."

They looked in the barn and there was a cow in one of the stalls and a horse in a corral behind the barn. "Bet this cow's got something, or why else Dad would have it here. Can y'figure out what from our Animal Science stuff?"

"Well, it ain't like we're learning to be vets." Scooter replied. "She ain't about to spring a calf, so maybe she has the bloat or ate some bad forage. She's kind of bloated or swelled up some." He was just guessing from the most common maladies on his family's ranch.

"Maybe some a that poison weed . . . y'know that locoweed, innit?"

"Well, not sure, but that stuff would likely put her down."

Sonny nodded. They went out to the corral and looked at the horse. It whinnied a greeting and then came over to the fence. "This is one of the horses I used to ride. It's always hoping for some grain," Sonny said. They petted it on the nose and neck.

While out at the corrals Scooter noticed two riders coming toward them from a valley to the east. "Bet that's Dad and Frank," Sonny said.

"Betcha it is too," his younger brother shyly said.

They waited for the riders to approach and Sonny hollered something to them in Apache. They returned the greeting.

After coming into the corral, both men dismounted. Sonny, Scooter, and the two children climbed over the fence and approached them. Both men shook Sonny's hand, and then, in turn, gave him a hug.

"This here's my rodeo buddy, Scooter, from Southwestern," he said. They greeted Scooter in Apache and then said, "Glad to meet you," as they shook hands.

They helped the two men unsaddle and water the horses. They then put them in two stalls in the barn to be brushed and fed. Scooter checked the horses out and decided not registered Quarter horses, but big, tough mountain ponies. After taking care of the horses, Sonny asked what was wrong with the cow.

"We don't know yet," his dad said. "She was stove up'n all hunched, so we didn't want to leave her out there to be coyote bait. I gave her a dose of antibiotics."

They walked through the yard to the house and sat down for some more stew. Sonny's mother had made a tossed salad with the groceries they brought out from town. Sonny's dad and his brother, Frank, talked about the cows out on range and the number of calves that had been born earlier in the spring. His dad mentioned that they were thinking about getting some sheep to better utilize some of the sagebrush areas.

"We been studying range plants and which're good fer forage—fer sheep, too—not just cattle. Sagebrush is not too bad, and winterfat, uh Scooter?" Sonny said.

"That's what the books say anyway. We got a test on the stuff next week, so maybe we can see if we know some of them here," Scooter said.

Sonny told his family, "He studies too much, trying to be an Einstein or somethin'." They laughed at Sonny's comments. He went on to say, "Sheep need someone to tend 'em though. Keep the coyotes off 'em."

His dad nodded. "Well, Frank's interested, and the two young uns need something to do in the summers."

Sonny had not told his family anything about their rodeo experience and Scooter was wondering about it. Finally, Sonny's dad asked, "How y' boys been doin' on the circuit?"

"Oh, pretty good once in a while," Sonny said.

Scooter knew how modest Sonny was and said, "He's been riding saddle broncs really good, actually. We were in Fort Collins last weekend and . . . well, I wish I could ride like that."

Sonny's mom and dad looked at Sonny with pride, his dad nodded. Frank's face was stoic, and Scooter got the impression he did not want to hear about Sonny's success.

"Well, I was lucky," Sonny meekly said. He deflected the attention away from himself, saying, "Scooter here rode pretty good, but he's nursing a bad shoulder . . . dislocated. Y'know that bull rider we travel with . . . Zeke? He got face-slammed pretty good into a set a horns. We had t'nurse him some."

Sonny's father shook his head. "That's the riskiest event. We seen plenty of injuries here in that, too!"

"He kind of amazed us though. He was able to get a date there even looking like a caveman with a purple eye!" Scooter said.

Sonny's mom and dad chuckled at this. Frank smiled, but Scooter thought that he remained reserved.

After they had eaten, Sonny's mom and younger siblings cleared the table. "You guys are supposed to be at John's around seven for the sweat," she said.

Frank said something to her in Apache and she said something back at him in a strong voice. Scooter thought it was a disagreement.

Sonny, his dad, and Scooter, grabbed extra underwear, a pair of shorts and towels, and climbed into Sonny's dad's pickup, heading out to the main gravel road. They continued south for several miles and then turned off onto an even rougher double-track.

"We don't pay enough taxes out here to rate gradin'," Sonny explained, tongue-in-cheek.

His dad added, "The grader couldn't get out this far even if'n it wanted." Sonny and Scooter laughed with him.

After about a mile, they came to a house with a set of pole and brush corrals to the side. There were several pickups and cars parked out front, and people were standing near them. The three newcomers parked and went out to join the others. Sonny took Scooter over to one of the men who wore a large black felt hat with a hawk feather in the band.

"Uncle John, here's my friend Scooter from Southwestern," Sonny said.

His uncle said something in Apache and said, "We welcome you to our country and to take part in this with us."

"I'm glad to meet you and appreciate the invitation," Scooter said.

Sonny's uncle continued, "We're going to start in a few minutes. Let me introduce you to these other yahoos!"

Scooter only remembered a few of the names but took a second look at a man named Slow Mink, because he never knew a mink could be slow.

The men went over to a low wickiup structure made of willow branches, which had been lashed together. A fire was burning, and smoke occasionally blew over to where they were standing.

Finally, Sonny's uncle told Sonny and Scooter to get ready. They went back to the pickup and stripped down to their shorts. Scooter was feeling self-conscious about his paleness as they went back toward the fire to join the other men. He wanted to make sure he didn't do anything wrong and followed Sonny's lead.

An elderly man with long, grayish hair came over with smoldering material and dabbed the smoke among them using a bundle of plants. Scooter noticed it had a pungent, cinnamon-like odor and thought it might be juniper. After the elderly man had circled the men several times, as he was chanting, another man transferred heated rocks using a shovel into the wickiup framework, and they were told to enter. A tent-like covering for the frame had been brought over to it.

Sonny, Scooter and two others, including the man named Slow Mink, crawled into the structure. The elderly man placed material on the rocks, added water and then pulled the covering down with the four men inside. The air in the lodge started to become thick and the temperature increased. Scooter was wondering how long he could take the heat and if he would "chicken out" before they could leave. After about five minutes he felt sweat running down his back and neck. Finally, someone lifted the covering slightly to let in some fresh air and then one of the men placed additional rocks into the center pit with a shovel, and the elderly man again placed plant material on top. Scooter thought the material looked like bark and sage, but the light was dim.

The covering again was placed over the framework, and one of the men poured water onto the heated rocks. The air again became heavy as the temperature increased. Scooter started feeling light-headed. He thought about getting out, but instead tried to relax. It seemed thoughts just kept running through his head as if on a cinema reel, random scenes spilling out into the steamy air. The reels jumped around from college course material, including chemical formulas to making fantastic rides on bareback horses, to Charlene and her turquoise-like eyes, which appeared to be overly large, and then Katherine with her hair fixed into an exaggerated ducktail. He wondered if he was hallucinating and if the smoke was inducing this. He tried to concentrate on one thing and to relax. He knew he was completely wet with sweat. Finally, one side of the covering was rolled up and the others began to crawl out. Scooter followed, feeling somewhat weak.

Sonny's dad and several others doused them with cold water, and after the initial shock, it felt great. They grabbed their towels, which they had hung on a juniper tree. Sonny asked him, "How y'feel?"

"I feel like all the starch's gone outta me," Scooter said.

The others laughed, and someone said, "That's how it is."

They were given bottles of water and sat in a circle sipping it and talking, mostly in Apache but sometimes in English. "This purifies the body as well as the mind, white-eyes, redskins, whatever!" one of the men told Scooter.

"Well, I felt lots of stuff leaving," Scooter said, which got a big laugh.

Sonny and Scooter finally toweled and cooled off enough to pull on their clothes. They thanked the men, and along with Sonny's dad, headed for home.

Sonny mentioned that he thought Emmett Fox was coming over to the jackpot rodeo the next day. Scooter didn't know who this was. Sonny explained that he was in the NFR finals a couple of times in bareback—quite a few years ago. "I thought it would be good for you to meet him."

"Is he gonna ride?" Scooter asked.

"Naw, he's too old," Sonny said. "He got injured—snapped an arm—just coaches some of us now, high school kids."

Sonny's dad mentioned Emmett was one of the best bronc riders out of the reservation for a time.

"Those two went down the road together for a while," Sonny said, meaning his dad and Emmett. "Kinda like you 'n me, innit." Scooter nodded his understanding and smiled.

They went into the house and Sonny's mother asked, "How was it?"

"Felt good," Sonny replied.

She looked at Scooter. "I kind of liked it," he said, "made me weak, though."

"It takes many of the bad spirits out of a person." Sonny's mother said. "I made some sweet tea and fry bread." The fry bread was sprinkled with sugar. It and the tea tasted great to Scooter.

Finally, Sonny said, "Let's get some sleep." They took a flashlight, their sleeping bags and headed to the camper. Frank was already rolled up in a blanket in one bunk. Sonny grunted something to him. Frank grunted in reply.

Sonny told Scooter to take the top bunk and he took a cot. Scooter rolled his sleeping bag out and hopped up on the bunk. He thought he smelled very smoky, but spicy, too.

CHAPTER THIRTEEN
PONDEROSA PINE

An overwhelming urge to urinate woke Scooter. It appeared that Sonny and Frank were still sleeping. Scooter found his boots in the dim light of the trailer and with some difficulty, jammed his bare feet into them. He hobbled out through the door into the chill of the morning and shuffled over to some rabbitbrush behind their sleeping quarters. *Cold, but still invigorating.* He noticed the aromatic sagebrush smell in the air and could see dark silhouettes of the mountain ridges against the morning sky. There was a brilliant swatch of stars out and he could make out Venus. He felt great.

He went back into the trailer and crawled up to the top bunk and into his sleeping bag to get warm. Frank moved in the lower bunk and sat up. "I didn't mean to wake you," Scooter said.

Frank said something unintelligible, followed with, "I usually get up early, anyways," and he started to dress. He went outside, shutting the door. Scooter crawled back into his sleeping bag. He woke up several hours later to someone moving around in the trailer and looked out to see Sonny putting on his boots.

"Y' must have been tired from that sweat. I never get up afore ya," Sonny said.

Scooter stretched and asked, "What time is it?"

"I don't know. Out here y'can usually forget about the clock. Let's go give the horses some hay, cause we're gonna ride. I wanna show you some country!"

Scooter got down onto the floor in just his shorts and grabbed his Wranglers and shirt. He found his socks and then his boots. "I gotta take a leak. That sweat has me goin'," he said.

"Sometimes I have that reaction. Y'need t'drink lots of water today," Sonny said.

Scooter went out behind the trailer again to pee, then came back around to the front and said, "I gotta get a jacket. It's cold out here!" He noticed Sonny seemed comfortable in just a shirt.

They walked over to the barn and went through the smaller side door, which Sonny left open for some light. "Shoot, Frank must'a taken one of 'em. Well, we'll take the other'n in the corral," he said.

He told Scooter to bring a bale of hay over and Sonny dipped a small pail into a barrel of oats. He asked if Scooter could give the one remaining horse in the barn some of the hay and bring some out for the one in the corral.

Sonny put the oats in a feedbag and put the straps over the horse's ears. He then placed hay in a feeder.

Scooter was still wondering about Frank and Sonny's relationship. "Frank got up early . . . when I went out to take a leak. Like five, maybe."

"Well, Frank wants to be a traditional Apache. I think that's his way of establishin' his identity. Y'know, t'go back to the old ways some. I think he's jealous of me goin' on to college. He never took t' school much."

"Isn't it good for some of the people to study the old traditions?" asked Scooter.

"Oh sure," said Sonny. "My Uncle John wants him t' study the spiritual way . . . maybe he will. I think he just needs to find himself in this." Sonny took the feedbag off the horse, and said, "Let's go get some grub." They walked toward the house.

Scooter noticed he still felt great, like he was efficient, lean, as if there was no unnecessary noise in his body. The dog that had cased Scooter the day before trotted up and sniffed him and followed along as they walked up to the house. Scooter thought: *This is a good sign.*

They went into the house and said good morning to the family. Sonny's mother told them to wash-up and to join them at the table. She brought over a large stack of French toast and some scrambled eggs. Sonny's dad asked how they felt after the sweat. Sonny just said, "Great!'

"I really slept good, and I'm trying to define it . . . like there's a difference or am I imagining it . . . but I feel lean or efficient . . . focused maybe," Scooter said.

"See what I mean? He's always thinkin' too much," Sonny said to his family.

Sonny's parents both laughed. His dad said, "No, I think that is one of the benefits of a sweat, to focus your life a little. It gets rid of the toxins."

As they ate, Sonny mentioned that he thought Frank had ridden somewhere.

"I suspect up the canyon. He sometimes brings some trout back," his dad said.

"We're going to ride up the canyon in a while. I wanna show Scooter some of the nice country. We'll 'av to head back to Durango after the jackpot.

"We're all going to town to the rodeo. We wanna see you ride." Sonny's mom said.

Sonny asked his two siblings, "Y'all doin' the mutton bustin' or calf riding?" They smiled shyly at him and shook their heads.

"We might at this summer's rodeo, if'n you show us," the boy said softly.

"It's a deal!" Sonny replied, and they smiled at him.

After breakfast, Sonny and Scooter saddled the two horses in the corral and rode up the valley. They followed a double-track trail for several miles through sagebrush and groups of scattered cows closely followed by their calves. The valley narrowed, and they angled the horses up onto a bench and rode through scattered pinyon and juniper trees. Sonny then led up a slope, following a game trail onto a second bench. This area was covered by large ponderosa pine trees and had a park-like aspect with grass cover in the open areas.

They let the horses blow for a few minutes. Scooter looked across the area. "This here area's never been logged and not burned for a while neither," Sonny said.

Scooter noticed the good grass cover between thicker stands of trees. "Pretty good grazing here," he said. They followed a small gurgling, tumbling creek and stopped at a large pool so the horses could drink.

"Look at that!" Sonny exclaimed. Several turkeys ran through the grass away from the intrusion.

Scooter had never seen wild turkeys, and said, "Wow! Were those wild turkeys? Holy cow, I didn't realize how big they are! You're lucky to have this wild country to live in."

"Yeah, we have all this, so it takes the place of bein' modern. But sometimes I got tired of not havin'."

Scooter looked at Sonny. "Not having?"

"Yeah, hot running water, telephone, y'know?"

Scooter nodded his understanding. "But maybe you can't have both," he said.

"Yeah, guess so," Sonny said.

Then as they continued, a large buck mule deer bounded for cover. They reined up again to watch it. Scooter continued to be impressed and said, "Wow, what a specimen."

"Yeah, there's lots in here. Y'know that stew you had yesterday?" Sonny asked.

"Yeah?"

"One a them."

They rode through a swale where the forest was dense and included large Douglas-fir trees as well as ponderosa pine. It was as if they had left the modern world behind and gone back in time. Scooter noticed that the air was cooler in the swale, and it was very peaceful. They dismounted to check out one of the larger trees.

"This here's the papa tree," Sonny said. "Don't it look like it?" Scooter agreed and sat down leaning against the trunk while looking at the other side of the cove.

A black squirrel with tassels on its ears moved along the ground between several of the trees. "I've never seen a squirrel like that. What is it?" Scooter asked.

"I don't know the English name fer it. I call it 'timid one.' We say the pine forests are healthy if y'see those squirrels."

Scooter watched the squirrel as it meandered along the ground through the long needles that the trees had shed, seemingly unconcerned about human presence.

Scooter thought he could stay for a while, maybe a long time, it was so peaceful, so different from the country of his family's ranch. They had a creek on the property with some tall cottonwoods, but nothing like this.

Finally, Sonny said, "We better header back. We'll get something t' eat en head t' town fer that jackpot."

They mounted up and retraced their route back through the sage-brush valley. The horses were quicker going back, as it was mostly downhill, and they knew the way to the barn.

After unsaddling, Sonny and Scooter brushed the sweat from their mounts and led them to the stock tank for water. They put the horses into the corral by the barn and placed hay in the feeder and then went to the house to see about lunch.

Sonny's mother had made Mexican tortillas, and they ate this with meat sauce and salsa. The ride had made Scooter hungry and after washing up, the two of them sat at the table to eat. Sonny's father and two younger siblings were already loading supplies into the pickup.

"Is Frank going with youse?" Sonny asked his mother.

"Who knows about Frank?" his mother said. "He may show up to watch you ride, though. He's quietly proud of you, I think."

"I don't know about that," Sonny said.

"You have to realize Frank and you are different."

"Oh, I know he is, but he doesn't have t' be . . . what's the word . . . resentful to me."

"Well, just let him know that you value him and that will make a difference. He sees you getting all the benefits of college and he's jealous of your rodeo abilities"

"I do value him."

Sonny's mother turned to Scooter and said, "Brothers!"

"I know. I have an older brother who thinks I'm wasting my time in college. He told me, 'You think you can learn to milk a cow by reading a book, you got another think coming.'" Sonny and his mother laughed at this remark.

Sonny and Scooter went out to the trailer and gathered their gear. On the way back, Scooter went into the house to thank Sonny's mom for her hospitality.

"I hope you can come out to our place someday for a visit," he said.

"Thanks, but we don't go very far from home, it seems," she said.

He went out to his car to meet up with Sonny, who told his dad, "See youse at the arena." Scooter backed his car around and they retraced their journey back toward Jicarilla.

They parked near several pickups and horse trailers. "There'll be a bunch of team ropers here," Sonny said. "Hope they 'ave bronc riding first, or we could be waitin' around, uh."

They got out of the car and walked over to the bucking chutes and holding pens. There was a group of horses and some steers in separate pens.

"Looks like they're going t' have steer riding t'day, probably the younger kids," Sonny explained to Scooter.

"Well, that's a good way to start," Scooter said.

Sonny introduced Scooter to some of the men, and then said, "I gotta take you over to meet Emmett. He coaches the kids fer bareback . . . actually, saddle bronc too."

They walked over to the chutes where some of the cowboys had gathered with their bareback tack. Sonny said to one of the men who had a trim build, "Hi Emmett," and they shook hands. "I'd like you to meet a friend a mine, Scooter, from the college rodeo team . . . rides bareback. Scooter, Emmett Fox."

Scooter shook Emmett's hand and said, "Glad to meet you."

"You ridin' today?" Emmett asked Scooter,

"Nah, I'm sposed to be resting a shoulder . . . dislocation." Scooter said. "So, trying to get ready for a rodeo in Laramie next weekend. I think Sonny's riding though."

"Well, you can help me with some of these high school kids."

"Okay," Scooter said uncertainly.

Additional people gradually arrived at the arena. Sonny saw his younger siblings at the concession stand and said, "I better see if they need something."

Scooter remained, sitting on top of the chute fence, taking in the events. Two men with heavy chaps rode into the arena, warming up their horses. Scooter knew they were the pick-up men. A man climbed up into the booth behind the chutes and another man handed up a cord for the sound system. Some of the cowboys that had entered the bareback event brought their tack over behind the chutes. Scooter had the urge to ride as well, wishing he had brought his tack, but remained sitting on the fence.

Finally, the announcer said, "Ladies and gentlemen, we're about to get this show on the road," and followed that with Apache. "We don't have music," he said, "but could we have a moment of silence as we honor our flag." People, who were in the stands and by the arena fence or the chutes, stood up and those wearing hats, removed them. They all faced the flag, which had been raised on a short pole above the announcer's booth. After a few minutes, the people went back to their original activities.

The bareback horses were loaded into the chutes, and Scooter went over to see what they were like and to find out what he could do to help. Several men were putting flank straps on the three that had been loaded. The cowboys who had entered the event came over to check them out, trying to figure which ones they had drawn. Scooter noticed a few of the riders had on chaps, but most did not. Several had on large leather, work gloves. He was thinking: *It's great to get back to the basics—just put on your spurs and ride!*

"Can you help some of these guys with their riggin's? I gotta make sure my high school kids are ready," Emmett said.

Scooter went to the first horse and helped several guys set the rigging and then pulled cinches. The first few riders only lasted a few jumps out of the chute, but the third made a qualified ride.

Sonny came over to where the action was and asked Scooter if he needed help with anything. Scooter said, "I really haven't done much."

Several of the high school cowboys were up in the next batch of horses. Emmett had a group around him on the chute. He got down onto the bareback horse and showed the group how a person should place their feet on the sides of the chute, to slide their butts up close to the rigging, and then to reach forward with their feet for the mark out when the gate opened. Scooter watched intently.

"I want you guys to rear back . . . lay your head on the horse's butt practically, and spur into the front, not into the cinch!" Emmett said and leaned back on the horse. The young cowboys nodded. Scooter thought: *That's good advice for me actually.* One of the high school kids made a fair ride and was leading the event until the third group. An older rider with some obvious experience won the event.

After the bareback event was over, Scooter followed Sonny to the stands where his parents and siblings were sitting, while the first group of team ropers competed. A girl, who Scooter had not noticed previously, was with Sonny's parents, and he figured it must be another family member. Sonny's mother introduced her to him as Lisal—at least that's what Scooter heard. Lisal was tall; kind of long and lanky. She wore dark glasses and had long hair that she had pulled back and held in place by a tooled leather barrette and thong.

"Let's get some grub," Sonny said and led the way to a concession area that contained a smoky BBQ grill. They ordered some chipped beef on bread. "These young 'uns are always hungry," Sonny said.

Scooter thought: *not only them*. Lisal had gone with them and it dawned on Scooter that maybe she was not a family member, but perhaps Sonny's girlfriend. Scooter studied the situation, but Sonny was hard to read—nonchalant as usual. The girl though was attentive to him and had linked her arm in his. *It would be so great if I found out he had a girlfriend out here. I could then turn the tables on him. Look at him there, not a care in the world while this girl is hanging all over him. What a sly fox is right . . . him telling Zeke and me how hard the ground was going to feel.* A smile crossed Scooter's face and he turned to take in a different view. He turned back to observe her again. She was a few inches taller than Sonny. He seemed oblivious to everything, including her arm through his and her closeness. The girl was lithe and had on body-hugging jeans that extended over the top of beaded moccasins. She was smiling—a perpetual smile it seemed. Scooter turned his attention away again, trying not to be too obvious.

The team roping was slow with many of the men going to a second loop if they missed with the first one. Finally, someone hollered to Sonny, "They're about to do saddle broncs." Sonny walked back to Scooter's car to get his saddle and tack. He stowed his gear behind the chutes and unfurled the stirrups of his saddle. He went through his usual routine of placing the saddle flat on the ground and then sitting in it with his feet in the stirrups and swinging them from the front to the back. Scooter wondered about this as the stirrups should have been the same length as the last time and Sonny's legs certainly would not have grown.

Sonny put on his spurs and chaps. He again got into his saddle and took some pieces of rosin, which he worked into the swells of the saddle with the insides of the chaps to increase the friction. He then got up, took his rein out of the bag and gave it to Scooter. They then waited around some more. Someone said something to Sonny in Apache, and they looked around to see

Frank. Sonny went over to him and they talked for a few minutes. Sonny gave Frank a pat on the shoulder and Frank returned it. Scooter was glad to see the brotherly gesture, thinking about their mother's admonition.

Finally, the men working the rodeo sorted some of the horses in the holding pen and drove three into the chutes. Scooter asked Sonny which one was his, and he said, "It's a big buckskin. It ain't in this group."

The first three riders tumbled off their mounts in spectacular fashion. The third drug a stirrup across the saddle as he was thrown, which hung his foot, and he dangled alongside the horse for several seconds as it continued to buck until his boot pulled off. The crowd voiced a collective sigh of relief, as the rider picked himself up, apparently non-the-worse for the ordeal, and he went over to retrieve his boot and then walked back to the chutes without putting it on.

Emmett Fox had come over and said, "That's a good way to get one leg longer'n the other." His comment resulted in a few nervous laughs from the other riders.

The next three horses were loaded into the chutes, including a large buckskin. "This un's it," Sonny said.

Scooter climbed up onto the chute gate, attached the rein to the halter and then draped it over the gate. The horse nervously twitched its ears but stood still. Sonny brought his saddle and handed it to Scooter who set it onto the horse. The horse flinched at the weight of it. Frank came over then and helped snag the cinch, so Sonny could thread the latigo through it. Scooter helped take the slack out of the latigo until Sonny said, "Good," and he then tied it off around the Dee-ring of the saddle.

"I've 'ad this ole pony a few times out here . . . called Golden Sunset." Sonny said. "Sposed t' be able to see over the mountains from atop 'im!"

Scooter glanced at Sonny and saw his grin. "He rank then?" Scooter asked.

"You rid him afore," Frank said to Sonny.

"Yeah, I practiced on him a few times, but . . . y'never know, innit?"

Scooter understood Sonny's comments to mean the horse could be rank today. Another rider was up before Sonny and made a qualified ride without much spurring.

The gate handlers came over to Sonny's horse and he got down into the saddle, taking his time. Frank had hold of the horse's halter as a safety measure. The announcer mentioned Sonny's name and noted he was a member of the Southwestern State College Rodeo Team.

"Bear down on him," Scooter said.

Sonny didn't acknowledge Scooter's admonition. Instead, he squashed his hat down, pushed his hand with the rein out in front of him and squeezed himself down into the saddle.

He said, "Le's go!" to the men handling the chute gate. The gate was thrown open and the horse took several quick strides and ran into the arena as if it was in a race. Sonny kept his feet and stirrups in the front end with his spurs over the horse's shoulders. Finally, the horse exploded into a jump straight up into the air and began to buck in a wide circle around the arena. Sonny sat nearly upright, slightly bent over in a mild arc, in what Scooter thought was becoming Sonny's style, and spurred from the front end near the rein back toward the cantle of the saddle until the whistle blew. The pickup men galloped alongside the still-bucking horse, and Sonny gave the rein to the pickup man to control the horse and then grabbed onto him, vaulting over the back of the man's horse to reach the ground. The crowd gave Sonny an appreciative round of applause. Someone added to this by honking a car horn.

"The kid's gotten good!" Emmett said to Scooter.

"Yeah, he's riding great right now. He won third in the average up in Fort Collins last weekend. He's taking it serious," Scooter said.

"Well, his ol' man was good on the broncs back in the day, so maybe the apple and the tree thing."

Scooter nodded and smiled at Emmett's comment. Sonny came back to the chutes to some high fives. No one was close to his score. Scooter and Sonny retrieved his saddle and rein and then packed his gear. He told Frank thanks for the help and good luck on his studies. Scooter understood this to mean in the old ways. Frank nodded an acknowledgment.

They told the other guys and high school boys at the chutes, "So long!" Sonny went by the rodeo secretary to collect his winnings and then he and Scooter walked over to Sonny's family. Sonny's dad clapped him on the back for the ride. Scooter noticed that Sonny gave his mom forty dollars. She and his dad told Sonny to be careful and study hard.

"That sounds like my parents," Scooter noted. "Thanks for everything. I'm glad to have met you. I'll try to keep Sonny out of trouble."

They told him to drive carefully. Sonny's younger siblings hung onto him as they walked back along the parking area to Scooter's car for the trip back. Sonny teased them that he was going to take them along and enroll them in college. Frank and Lisal walked over together. Scooter thought that perhaps he had been wrong—that she was Frank's girlfriend, then thought: *That can't be it after how she was hanging all over Sonny.* Frank took hold of his siblings though, and Lisal put her hand on Sonny's shoulder and whispered something to him. Sonny nodded and smiled at her, and then they kissed. He whispered something back to her and she laughed, and then placed her hand around Sonny's neck to draw him close and for another kiss. Scooter turned his head away from the intimate scene and thought: *Wow, my suspicions were right.* Sonny threw his tack in the car's trunk and got in.

As a goodbye, Frank told them, "Doan take any them there wooden nickels." Sonny nodded an agreement.

They stopped in Pagosa Springs for gas and picked up some snacks. Scooter remembered he needed orange juice, which he liked for breakfast, so added that to the purchases.

"Okay," Scooter said. "Who's the girl . . . Lisal?"

"Oh, just a family friend. We been out a few times, that's all"

Scooter, trying to turn the tables on Sonny, said, "Family friend, my ass. She had her hands all over you! She's in love, y'know."

"Yeah, all the girls on the rez are," Sonny matter-of-factly replied and showed Scooter a wolfish grin.

Scooter shook his head and said, "As Zeke would say, 'Sheeit'!" Sonny laughed at this.

As they left Pagosa Springs, they talked on the safer subject of rodeo and Sonny's ride for a while. Scooter mentioned that Emmett had been impressed. Sonny was modest about it, as usual.

"That horse doesn't usually throw anything weird at ya . . . never took a run like that afore!"

"Yeah, I thought he was headed for the fence and greener pastures for a minute there," Scooter said. "Before I forget, we gotta remember to get some room reservations for Laramie. I'm calling Charlene tomorrow about some places since I've never been up there before. Then we should call the rodeo committee on Thursday to make sure we're entered . . . afore we head out y'know."

Sonny nodded, "I'm glad yer takin' care all these details, cuz I'm not."

"What would you do if I wasn't? You need that Lisal to come along and take care of you."

"Now that there's a pretty damn good idea, innit!" Sonny said, as he leaned back in the seat and pulled his hat over his eyes.

CHAPTER FOURTEEN
CLASSROOM CHATTER

Scooter poured cold cereal into a bowl and mixed in a splash of milk for breakfast, and while spooning it in with one hand, looked over his English class paper. He scribbled several notes on his essay and some corrections and then wrote another paragraph, looking up several words in his Thesaurus. English was his first class; he left the apartment at seven-thirty.

He sauntered into the classroom and sat down in his usual chair beside Katherine—well, when he could beat Linda to it. He said hello and asked how things were with her family. She said her mom was still in the hospital, and they were doing more tests during the week.

"Jeez, sorry. That sucks y'know?"

"Yeah, it does. How was your trip to Jicarilla?" she asked.

"I liked it. Did a sweat ceremony. Have you ever?"

"No, you must be kidding."

"I'm not kidding," he whispered. "You can do one with me sometime. We'd both have to get naked though!" Katherine smiled at him but hit him on the arm.

Hank came in shortly before class was to start and he sat down across from Scooter. They grunted a greeting at each other. Scooter looked at him, and suddenly thought: *Why was I ornery with him the other day?* He walked across the aisle. "Hey, I'm sorry about the other day. I was just mad about something," Scooter said.

"I still owe y'one," Hank said.

"Yeah, I know. Why don't you come over to my pad tonight and I'll help you with the essay?" Hank looked at him to see if there was a catch. Scooter continued, "We need to get you eligible to compete, don't we?"

Hank thought about this offer for several seconds. "Okay, man, you're on."

"What're you writing about?" Scooter asked.

Linda walked into the room but saw Scooter's notebook on the chair by Katherine, so she sat on the other side of her. She was followed into the room by their teacher, Mrs. Starmire.

"I was going to write something about rodeo but couldn't get started. I don't know, maybe my family . . . my dad. He's all screwed up you know," said Hank. Scooter was about to find out more, but Katherine hushed him as Mrs. Starmire turned from writing on the blackboard to address the class.

Scooter thought that Mrs. Starmire was attractive, even if she was fairly old, and still had a nice shape. He figured she might be about forty-five but was likely a "fox" in her younger days. She had dark brown hair, which showed a few gray streaks. She liked large strings of beads. Sometimes they plopped into her blouse and cleavage. This mesmerized him, and he wondered if she noticed when the beads disappeared down her blouse. She wore pointy-framed, cat-like glasses. He knew from a chance glance in the grade book that her first name was Grace but bet that none of the students knew much about her personal life, and she never brought that into the classroom. Sometimes she wore a large diamond wedding ring, or at least had it on her left hand. Sometimes she didn't. He wondered about this too. She was known to be a good teacher and used imagination to inspire them about literature and language. Scooter quit daydreaming and began taking notes.

After class, Katherine asked Scooter if he would stop by later. "If you come over to the cafeteria for lunch, I want to talk to you," she said.

"You mean about studying for the final? Maybe you could help me finish my paper," he said hopefully.

"Well, we'll see, but I think you have to do that on your own. You're such a moocher." She smiled at him, and he liked her comment.

Later, Scooter joined Sonny and Zeke at a table in the library for a study session. The library was Scooter's study refuge, but it was rare for Zeke to be there. *Maybe he is getting serious about grades,* Scooter thought.

As he joined them, Zeke said, "So, lover boy, when the dam breaks it's a big flood."

"You guys should get a clue and zip it," Scooter retorted.

"Oh, we got a clue alright. Yer penis is workin' overtime, probably wondering what the hell's going on, not being used to anything but yer hand!" Zeke said.

Sonny silently laughed at Zeke's comment, his shoulders shaking like the last leaf on a tree. Scooter moved to a different table and opened his English essay to finish it. He glared back at them. Sonny was still silently laughing. Scooter looked around to make sure no one was watching and showed them an exposed middle finger. Zeke laughed at this, also silently shaking. Scooter shook his head and walked over to the card catalog desk to look up references on rodeo history.

After studying for several hours, Scooter drove down the hill to his apartment. He pulled a TV dinner out of the refrigerator and turned on the small oven. He drank a large glass of milk and, while eating, nearly completed the first draft of his essay. He wondered if Hank had chickened out. Finally, there was a knock on his door, and Scooter opened it.

Hank looked around and said, "Cozy." He carried a notebook and a six-pack of beer.

"Put that in the fridge until after. "Scooter said.

"You're no fun," Hank said, but complied.

They sat at the kitchen counter. "You mentioned writing about your family. You still want to?"

"Yeah, it's something I ought t'do. I mean it would be something I feel. I don't know . . . angry about, whatever. My dad was a drunk, y' know. But a great guy when he was sober. We used to do so many things . . . hunting, fishing. Then he'd go off the deep end. I could almost tell when I heard the car door slam . . . just the loudness of it. As I got bigger, I tried to protect my mom and the younger kids. I was in high school. I played football, wrestled, so was in great shape."

Hank had shifted on the barstool and then got up and paced some. Scooter watched him, wondering if he was going to continue. Hank seemed to be mulling something over.

"Well, I knew I was going to try and go to college and wouldn't be there if that happened, so I worried what might happen to the younger kids, my mom. One night he came in like so many times before . . . started hollering, slamming things, asking why his supper wasn't ready. It was like nine at night. I came out of the bedroom and stood there. I knew, never again. He said, something like, 'What're you lookin' at big boy?' I hit him right on the chin. I felt the jolt of it clear up to my shoulder. He went down like he'd been shot and hit his head on the stove on the way down. Kind-of went into convulsions. My mom and the kids were . . . like stunned, then mom started crying, saying, 'Oh no, oh no!' I made sure he was still breathing and then rolled him over to a rug . . . got some ice for his head. I was still mad about the whole sick thing, and told my mom, 'It's about time his face looks like how he makes yours sometimes!' Needless to say, he lived. He said he was going to make me pay but was leery of me after that. He even went into a treatment thing with his work, so it's kind of been better. I still worried about being gone, though. I told him if he ever did anything to Mom or the kids again, I was going to hunt him down. He didn't like that of course and said I should just get out. I told him to think about it."

Scooter was stunned by this story. Hank looked at him and became embarrassed.

"Sorry to give you the whole story of my life."

"No, write it down, just like you told it!" Scooter said.

I don't know if I remember how I told it."

"I'll help you."

They started, and Hank wrote with Scooter looking over his shoulder.

"Quotation marks go outside periods and exclamation marks," he said.

"Oh, yeah."

"To make it long enough, I think you'll have to give some more details as an introduction about what you and he would do when you were growing up . . . you know, like fishing, hunting, camping, whatever, and how his drinking changed things for you and your family," Scooter said. "Then it needs something for a conclusion."

"Like what should we put?"

"Well, that there might be hope for him, for your family, I guess. But, like I did on mine, give some background to it . . . you know like research."

Hank nodded his understanding, but said, "Research? What would that be anyway?"

"You know, a lot of people have issues with alcohol. Isn't it like a disease? That's what you need to do to cap it off . . . to make it mean something beyond your experience."

"Oh, getting it now . . . like cinching it all up!"

They worked for an additional hour. "So, here's what I think . . . look up some facts on the issue and then recopy this for Wednesday's class. I'll read it over for you if you want, then you can do a final draft for Friday. What's the title going to be?" Scooter asked.

Hank paused and thought for a while. Finally, he said, "I dunno, maybe 'My Dad?'"

"Write it down."

He got out the beer, took two cans from the six-pack, opening two of them. He gave one to Hank, and said, "Here's to eligible." They touched cans. "You better take the others along, I have to stay in training."

"You sure? I can leave 'em," Hank said.

"I'm positive," Scooter said. He was getting antsy. It was getting late, and he wanted to call Charlene.

"Thanks, man, now I really do owe you one."

"Hey, get ready to ride some bulls."

"That's the plan," Hank said. "Well, I gotta get. See you in class."

"Yeah, see you tomorrow." Scooter closed the door.

Scooter paused in dialing the phone, and then searched his wallet for the paper with Charlene's number on it. He waited while the phone rang, thinking that no one was home. Finally, somewhat breathlessly, Charlene said, "Hello!"

"Hey, Charlene, what's up?"

There was a pause. "Scooter, I was wondering about you!"

"I know, sorry. I got to studying with Hank on an English paper. How are you?"

"Well . . . fine. Are you okay?"

"I tell you, I never been better. For some reason, I feel honed, concentrated."

"Jeez, what did you guys get into down on the reservation . . . smoke something?

"Well, it was the other way around. We had the sweat lodge thing. I think it purified me, or something. I've felt great ever since. Anyway, how are you and how was your stay with your family?"

"It was nice. My grandmother and I had a nice talk. She understands me. And the rest of the family is fine. Mom and I cooked, so that was nice. What do you think about this weekend?'

"Well, we're primed to go. Johnny said there may be only one go-round in bareback and bulls, cause northern teams are entering too!"

"Yes, someone said rooms are going fast. I got one at the 'Palomino' for Squirrel and me on Saturday night, but I still don't know if she's going. Let me give you some motels and numbers on the strip there, including that one."

"Okay, I'll phone tonight. I don't know if Zeke's waitress woman is going or not. He didn't phone her like he was sposed to. If not, he will likely go with us."

"You guys! You never learn."

"What you mean? . . . Oh, about phoning. Well, I phoned . . . ah . . . finally. I thought about you a lot."

"Yeah, I'll bet!"

"No, really!"

"Well, I was worried. It's ten-thirty."

"I know. I really was helping this guy, Hank, from the team. I owed him one," Scooter said.

"It's okay, I know how it is. I thought of you too. I had a lot of time to do it I guess. I wondered what it would be like for you to stop in and meet my family and, well, just be there," Charlene said.

"I know what it would be like," said Scooter. "It would be like a soft, velvet evening . . . balmy. I'd sneak kisses to you somehow!"

"You're changed! Are you still my shy, unassuming cowboy?"

"More than ever."

She laughed. "I better go. I'm eating up my phone allowance. Do you have a pen and paper? I'll give you some numbers."

"Go ahead." Scooter wrote down several numbers on an old newspaper that was on the table.

"Thanks for that. I'm looking forward to seeing you again. We'll be to Laramie late Friday night, but I'll call about where we're at and all that soon as I know," he said.

"Okay, phone me!"

He hung up the phone and thought about their conversation. *She seemed reserved. Maybe it's me. Well, she was expecting me to call earlier—so probably was worried. Jeez . . . I don't want to seem so eager, like she has me wrapped around her little finger.*

Scooter telephoned the motels that Charlene had mentioned, starting with the Palomino. It had no vacancies. He found a room at the third one he tried, at the The Peak. He had asked for a double in case Zeke roomed with Sonny and him. He remembered that the rodeo teams were supposed to get room discounts, so he asked about it.

The desk clerk didn't know about it, but said, "I'll mark it on your reservation card and check with the manager."

Scooter concentrated on his classes the rest of the week. He met Zeke in their Phys Ed class on Tuesday, but had been excused to work with Mr. Taylor, the college trainer, who told Scooter to follow him into the training room. He threw Scooter a towel and told him to strip.

Mr. Taylor turned on a Whirlpool machine and said, "Let's work that shoulder some with this. I don't know about sweat lodge stuff, but I know this works."

Scooter immersed himself in the warm water of the tank, and the trainer adjusted the nozzle onto Scooter's left shoulder; first in front then later on the outer edge.

"It feels pretty good, but I'll see if it's as good as that sweat lodge," Scooter said.

Mr. Taylor laughed, "Yeah, maybe both work."

After range management lab, Scooter, Sonny, and Zeke met for dinner at the college cafeteria and discussed the motel arrangements. Zeke said he really was going to call Molly to see what's what and to see if she still wanted to go rodeoing with him.

"What if she wants to take her kid along?" Scooter teased. "Let's see, two years old, how're you at changing diapers?"

"Sheeit, I tell you somethin', if she wants to, she can. I'm going to meet him anyway. At least that was the plan last time we were thinking about this weekend. I'll start training him to ride buckin' stock."

It seemed to Scooter that this love interest of Zeke's was different. "Wow, meeting her kid! You're biting the dust," he said.

Zeke nodded. "She's different somehow."

"Yep, just what I tol' ya. Yer both lettin' wimmin get in yer way a ridin'," Sonny said

"Naw, you'll see . . . I know how to do both," Zeke replied.

Scooter smiled. "I think by now we got a kettle and the pot thing going on. I have t' get. See you guys tomorrow."

Zeke looked at Scooter and frowned. "What's that got t' do with anything?"

Scooter put his books on the small kitchen table and called Charlene. The phone rang several times, and he didn't recognize the person that answered. "Is Charlene there?" he asked.

"Hey Scooter," the person said, "this is Squirrel. Charlene's washing her hair, so you'll have to wait a few minutes."

"Hey Squirrel, how's it going?" he asked.

"Oh, okay. Just going to school and we had rodeo practice on Friday and again Monday. What have you and your bronc rider buddy been up to?" Scooter spoke tentatively, as he was leery about Squirrel's opinion of him. She seemed to have an edge toward him but talking about Sonny seemed to be safe territory.

"Well, we went down to Jicarilla on the reservation on Saturday for a sweat lodge ceremony. It was very cool. Ah, I mean, actually it was very hot, but I liked it. We rode up onto some amazing pine forests. Here's something you would be interested in, saw a black squirrel with long tassels on its ears."

"Now you're kidding me. What were you drinking?"

"No, really. We should look it up. Are you going to Laramie this weekend?"

"Well, not to compete, 'cause we have' a full team there. I may go up on Saturday night or Sunday. Anyway, here's your woman . . . nice chatting with you. Tell Sonny hello."

"Hello cowboy, so what's the word?" Charlene asked.

Scooter felt her musical voice in his chest. "Hey! We got some rooms at a motel there on the strip . . . called The Peak. The Palomino was full. Good thing you told me about calling, otherwise we might've had to sleep under the stars or move in with you."

Charlene laughed. "Three gnarly guys in the room with me? I don't think so. Anyway, yeah, it's going to be a big rodeo. I ran Star today. She went well. I think I'll run her on Thursday a little and then just keep her loose. What do you think?"

"Hmm . . . you know your horse, but I'd say don't overdo it before Saturday's competition. So that seems okay to me! So . . . I heard Squirrel's comment. What's this 'your woman' thing?"

"Oh, don't pay any attention to her. She's been giving me a hard time . . . you know, about you and me. She's just jealous."

"I was telling her about the nice mountains and forests on the Indian reservation. Oh, and about those weird, black squirrels, which she thought I made up. Anyway, another place we need to ride someday . . . if Sonny invites us."

"Well, you make it sound really nice."

"It's pristine country, nearly. Well, a few cattle get up there, but deer and turkeys, crystal clear streams too. Anyway, I'd like to take you."

"In that case," said Charlene, "I'd like to go."

"Yeah, it'd be a big adventure for us . . . riding among those large pines—ponderosa, actually."

"You make it sound very appealing."

"Yeah, we could have a picnic. Well, I better let you go, otherwise, I'll talk to you all night."

Okay, honey let's talk again Thursday night, okay?" she asked.

"That'd be good. So long 'my woman."

She laughed at this and said, "Okay. Be good."

CHAPTER FIFTEEN
THE MYSTERY OF WOMEN

Wednesday was a long day of classes for Scooter, with English, animal science, as well as chemistry and range management classes. He said hello to Katherine before English class started but went to the library with Hank after class. Scooter redlined Hank's paper with corrections.

"I don't know how you know this grammatical stuff. What y'doin', paying attention in class or somethin'?" Hank asked.

"I like composition. And, I like your essay. It's from inside you and that makes a difference."

After Animal Science class, Sonny and Scooter grabbed sandwiches from the snack bar and then walked back to the main building to the range science lab to study pressed mounts of range and forage plants. Both of them were having trouble with the scientific names.

"We got to think of some trick to help remember these names," Scooter said, "for example, rubber rabbitbrush. You have this on your ranch. I know, cause I peed lookin' at it. It's not very good forage. *Chrysothamnus nauseosus* . . . to me, it means a golden sickness."

Sonny looked at Scooter for several seconds and frowned. "Chit man, how y'get all that? Sounds like a bad beer hangover. I see the nauseous part I guess. It's harder even for me as this Latin's a new language."

"Hell, what do you think . . . that I talk this stuff at home?" Scooter asked.

They continued to go through the plants among several other students. Scooter decided he better make some notes on the features he might recognize of the new specimens.

"I think we better come back to this tomorrow before the class. I'm strugglin' some."

"That ain't the half of it!" Sonny said disgustedly, as he viewed one of the pressed mounts.

They stuffed their notes away and headed down the hall to their Range Management lecture. Scooter did not mind having so many classes in the middle of the week, figuring it was worth it to be free of classes early Friday afternoon.

After class, Scooter walked down the hall and through the main doors to the library. He scouted the room for Katherine, but did not see her, so sat down at a table, got out his chemistry notes, and opened his textbook. He wondered if there could be a "pop" quiz the next lecture and he needed to know the material anyway for next week's final. He sensed and then realized someone was standing beside his chair and looked up to see Katherine. He smiled, and she put a hand on his shoulder. It felt nice.

"I was here before and didn't see you. I wondered if you were going to stand me up," she said,

"No, I wouldn't do that. I have a lot of lectures on Wednesday and Sonny and I were studying for a lab . . . plant specimens. Anyway, I'm studying already, I'm ahead of you."

Katherine sat down next to him and said, "I'll catch-up." Scooter craned his neck toward her and noticed she had brought a history book.

He continued to work on diagrams of carbon chains and chemical reactions. He murmured aloud, "I bet the catalysts will be key." thinking of the test.

"Don't ask me about any of that stuff, it looks like Greek. You're a strange boy for a cowboy," she said.

Scooter was not sure if her comment was a compliment or a criticism. "You mean different?"

"You're different alright," she teased.

He moved his chair closer. "I can help you study," he said

"How is this going to help with you breathing in my ear?"

"I could explain about these chemicals. Organic chemistry is the basis of everything. Did you know that? If I kissed you, it would be a chemical reaction."

His statement caused Katherine to blush. "Quit it for now and get to studying," she said. She turned back to her notes but gave him a sly look.

They studied for more than an hour. He was getting hungry, checked his watch, and then said, "Let's go get something!"

"You don't have to take me to dinner. It's expensive," Katherine said.

"But I want to. It'd be nice not eating cafeteria food as I said, or like I do in my apartment, eating a tinny TV dinner or peanut butter sandwich. You need to get away from the cafeteria anyway." He stood up and waited for her. He thought something must be wrong.

"Okay, but we can go Dutch."

"We'll see. I wanted to treat you, that's all."

They walked across campus to the main parking lot and his car. He was hoping they didn't run into Zeke or Sonny. He'd had enough of those guys. He opened the door of his car for Katherine and they then drove down the hill on the campus road to the main part of town and stopped by the Branding Iron Steakhouse. Scooter had eaten at the restaurant before. It was not especially elegant, but one he could afford. The décor included booths of red vinyl seats and red tabletops. Scooter noticed that someone had squirted Ketchup on the wall behind Katherine's side of the booth and he hoped she wouldn't notice it. An older waitress brought them menus.

They talked about course work and getting out of college for the summer. There was a semester during the summer, as well as two during the fall and winter.

"I'm expected to work on the ranch during summers and guess will rodeo as much as I can," Scooter said. He mentioned that he would have to transfer somewhere to complete an agricultural major but hadn't decided yet if he would.

"Are you going to or what? Changing your major might require additional courses," Katherine said.

"Yeah, I know. I think my family expects me to finish and come back home . . . y'know to help run the place. Well, they're paying for part of my education. My dad doesn't mind me rodeoing as long as it doesn't get in the way too much. He was on the circuit when he was young. But, sometimes the ranch and my brother being the boss seems like a trap, sort of . . . do you know what I mean?"

"I think so. I may have a similar problem if something happened to my mom. I might have to go home and help my dad. We'll know this week what they found out. They did surgery on Sunday. They're checking to see if it's cancer."

"I figured . . . jeez, such a downer. I hate that stuff. I'm sorry for you about this. You know that?" Scooter said,

Katherine looked up and Scooter noticed tears in her eyes. He wanted to reach over and brush them away, but instead covered her hand with his.

"Sorry I'm being such a girl." She took her napkin and dabbed her eyes. "Anyway, I hope for the best, but like they say, prepare for the worst."

Scooter nodded. "Hey, I understand." He covered her hand with his again, and she gave him a smile

They concentrated on their food for a while. His steak seemed a little tough, so he chewed on it for a few minutes. "Is your steak okay? I think mine must be from some old has-been rodeo steer."

Katherine laughed and said, "It's okay. Mine's from a young rodeo steer." Her comment caused Scooter to laugh in return. He noticed that her foot had come over against his and he left his there—a kind of connection to her.

She continued, "I need to say something . . . about Friday night. I wanted you to know that what happened surprised me. I mean that I let it go so far. Do you think I'm easy?"

Her question took him unaware and he stammered, "No!" he tried to recover as Katherine looked intently at him. He continued, "I could ask you the same thing about me. Do you think I'm easy? The answer should be 'No,' cause I've never been quite that far before."

"I just wondered about what you thought is all."

"I thought it was a special evening and wanted to make love to you, if you want to really know."

"I wanted you to at that moment. You could have. Did you know that?"

Scooter looked at her and they locked eyes. "You mean even without . . . isn't that dangerous?" he asked.

"Yes . . . well, I'm telling you too much. You will know too much. Anyway, after, I was glad we hadn't."

"I wasn't sure if I was glad or not, especially at the time. Talking about this gets me to thinking about you again," Scooter said.

"Well, I don't want to do that to you, at least not right now." She smiled at him and continued. "It isn't the time anyway, so let's talk about other things. You said something about hiking a trail. Have you been there and hiked it?"

Her comment about the time not being right puzzled him, but he replied, "No, but I know where it is. You want to go now? What do you mean it isn't the time? That we haven't been together enough?"

"Well, sort of. It may not be a good thing for us yet, I don't know, but there are aspects of time too, you know, biology."

He tried to absorb her statement but couldn't figure out what biology had to do with anything. "Well, I've had biology," he said uncertainly and then finally realized she might be talking about female biology.

"Am I embarrassing you with too much information?" she asked.

"No, it's okay. I can take it."

"See, we haven't been going out long enough for there to be a natural progression. I'm scaring you off. I can see it in your eyes. You're thinking about mounting up on a fast horse, like a cowboy in a movie," she said.

"Jeez, I wasn't really thinking about retreating. You have me puzzled though. I'm trying to take this all in and I'm still thinking about the other night!" *She's a quick study. I bet she's been on the Dean's List each semester.*

"Well, it's complicated and some about commitment, which I think scares you!" Katherine said and laughed at him. Scooter wasn't laughing. "It's okay, we'll see where this goes," she continued.

"Are you going to date other guys?" he asked.

"I don't know. I might while you're off on your rodeo quests. Are you going to date other girls? I know some of them hang around rodeo."

"I might. Do you think we should?" He couldn't figure out where this was going but didn't like the direction. He continued, "I thought we finally had a date where I was more myself; not so timid, walking on egg-shells. I used to beat myself up after we kind of went out before, for being so sucky."

"I think we should do what we feel is right. If you're off doing rodeo, I might go out. I know you are going to be somewhere this weekend. Guess I will be home again."

"If I was here I'd take you," he said.

"Yes, but you're not."

"Are we having our first fight?" he asked.

"No, we're just setting some ground rules," Katherine said.

"If I asked you out next week towards the end of finals, would you go?"

"I guess I'll have to see what else is going on."

Scooter was getting perturbed and said, "What? I don't get it. I thought you liked me . . . at least I got that impression Friday night. I thought we had a good time, at least I did. Now you say you may not want to go out again. You're right, guys, or at least me, know very little about women! Are we breaking up already?"

Katherine's eyes again glistened with tears. "Look, I'm just being cautious. I don't like to be hurt!"

They looked at each other in silence for a few seconds. Scooter said, "Okay, I know. I understand that. Do you still see that guy from the cross-country team?"

"No, that's one of the things I'm talking about."

"I have a warm feeling for you. That's what I was talking about from Friday night," he said.

She smiled at him. "I know, I think we both got carried away . . . we better go. I still have studying to do.'

Scooter thought about what had happened. "Maybe we did, I don't know."

He asked for the check and they walked to the front of the restaurant to pay the cashier.

"I said we'd go Dutch," Katherine said.

"No, you can treat me next week at the end of finals . . . could be a big bill too." She smiled at his comment.

They drove back up the road to the campus to her dorm and talked about things other than their relationship. He parked and started to open the car door. Katherine grabbed his arm and said, "Look, don't be mad at me about this, okay?"

Scooter shut the car door and said, "No, it's okay, I understand what it is." He observed her; a completely soft feeling about her flared through him. He tilted her head toward his and they looked at each other. He kissed her and finally she kissed back. They broke for a few seconds, and he kissed her again.

"That's what I really think," he said.

"The shy boy is no longer. Walk me to the dorm," Katherine said.

On the way back to his apartment, Scooter thought about how complex his relationship with Katherine had suddenly become. *I think we did kind of break-up. Well, maybe just as well . . . she's saving me from myself!*

Scooter had been right. Chemistry was getting tough. The instructor was trying to show them three-dimensional aspects of polynomials. Then at the end of the class, there was a pop-quiz. Scooter took silent pride that he had predicted the quiz, but thought he may only have gotten seven of the ten questions. He hoped to have gotten lucky, or at least some points, on the rest.

After lunch, Scooter and Sonny hustled to their range management class. The last half-hour of class was for the identification test. Scooter was suddenly worried that he had not prepared very well. The instructor had placed the plastic-covered mounts of pressed plants on the lab tables and had clipped a numbered paper over the identification labels. He handed out test sheets with corresponding numbers and a column for the common names and another for the scientific name. The students started going to each plant. The instructor told them to stay spread out, not to congregate at any one place.

After turning in their test sheets, Scooter told Sonny, "What a friggin' effort that was. I got muddled up on one and it affected others . . . shit! I blanked out on one that I should have known and it about threw me for the others for a while. But, I left it and went on. You know what it was?"

"No," Sonny said.

"It was winterfat, but I couldn't even get the genus all of a sudden, then the next plant was Great Basin wildrye, and I started to blank on that one too, then remembered my crutch!"

"What was it?"

"You mean the crutch."

"Yeah."

"Well, the way I remembered it was that it had something to do with a cinema . . . y'know, like Elias at the cinema, and then the name came to me . . . *Elymus cinereus*. I know, weird, but it worked. And then . . . ah, I remembered winterfat had something to do with sheep—like lanolin—and the name for it came to me, *Eurotia lanata*. Lanata means wooly. So, I got lucky on a few, but shit, overall there were some I just couldn't remember."

"Chit is right man, there were a lot . . . that Latin stuff killed me, innit? I mayn't 'ave passed it," Sonny said.

"You always say that. I may not have done too well either, but I think I passed."

"Yeah, you always say you didn't do good either. I should have the instructor learn 'em in Apache! Chit man, I knew 'em better yesterday," Sonny said disgustedly.

"Well, we'll see. Guess we should 'ave studied more. I better get over to the chem lab."

Scooter hurried down the hall to the chemistry department and to the large room of the laboratory. He found some of the experiments interesting and generally went over directions before the class started, which helped to get the experiment done quicker. The instructor was getting some of the equipment out. Scooter said hello and put on his lab coat, opened his drawer and got out his protective glasses. He turned to the page in the lab manual and started to read the experiment, entitled "Williamson Ether Synthesis." He had at least looked through the lab manual at breakfast and thought the experiment would be interesting. He checked the list of equipment needed and went to the half door to the equipment room and checked out a special glass apparatus and a hot plate from Mr. Withers, the lab instructor.

A horse's anatomy came to Scooter's mind when he thought of Mr. Withers. The rumor was that Mr. Withers had been an officer in the Marine Corps during the Korean War. He had a white streak through the center of his hair that Scooter thought of as a mane. Scooter figured it had happened instantaneously during some horrific combat action. No one that Scooter knew had ever asked Mr. Withers how it might have happened, or even if he had been in horrific combat. He was tall and gangly, with a prominent nose and Adam's apple and eyebrows thick as shrub thickets. Mr. Withers was proficient in running the lab and in making sure that all the students finished the experiments. Scooter could see Mr. Withers as an army officer.

Some of the other students started to file into the room. Scooter's lab space was at the end of the long counter that was bisected lengthwise by a sink, spigots for water, and nozzles to attach Bunsen burners. The day's experiment was to distill naphthol and ido-ethane into ethyl ether using a distillation column. The end product was to be dried on filter paper and checked for purity as a part of the lab grade. The distillation used a complex set of glassware and included a glass cylinder with "angel hair" fibers in it, which Scooter had never seen before. *Interesting contraption.* He began putting the distillation tower of glassware together. The bell rang for the class period to start.

Scooter's concentration was broken by Orville, who occupied the area on the other side of the sink and spigots across from Scooter. Orville was a farm boy from an area north of Cortez, and was what Scooter called a "hayseed." He spoke as if he was from the backwoods and chemistry was not his forte. Scooter thought Orville was interesting, but he was always asking Scooter questions about the lab work. Scooter often thought: *Why don't you read the lab manual sometime,* but never said it aloud.

Scooter greeted Orville and several of the other guys in the class. It was composed primarily of boys, although several girls hung out together and even in the lab, congregated at the end of one lab counter. They were some of the better students. He continued to assemble the distillation column and measured out the reagents for the lower flask, swirled them, added boiling stones, and set it on a stand with clamps and placed a hot plate underneath, adjusting the height of the flask on the stand. It had taken over one-half hour to assemble the column and measure the reagents. The column of glassware for the distillation was nearly three feet tall. He turned the hot plate on high to heat the flask. He watched as condensate began to form and then turned the heat down. After a few minutes, a few amber-colored drops of material began to accumulate in the final test tube chamber.

He heard Orville say, "Hey, Mr. Withers, I ain't getting this here part." Mr. Withers came over, bent down and looked at where Orville was pointing in his lab manual. Scooter wondered why Orville was using a Bunsen burner instead of a hotplate. He was about to ask, but at that instant, a flash occurred, and fire ignited the distillation column, extending up the column of glassware nearly to the ceiling.

"Fire! Fire!" Mr. Withers shouted and ran out of the room.

Scooter stood back and then remembered the large fire extinguisher on the wall to the side of the lab counter. He unhooked the extinguisher from a bracket, aimed the nozzle at the fire, and squeezed the trigger. Nothing happened. He realized a pin needed to be pulled to make it work. This done, he aimed the large nozzle at the base of the fire, which by now was burning from the counter onto the ceiling of the lab. He aimed the nozzle and again squeezed. The force of the white chemical exploding out of the cone-like nozzle was much more violent than Scooter was expecting. It blew the distillation column apart and scattered glass pieces amid liquid across the counter, into the sink, and onto the floor. But, the fire was out. Scooter stood there surveying the carnage. He looked at the other students, who had been suspended in time by the event. Orville was against the wall, eyes very large, but apparently unscathed. The ceiling was scorched. Dr. Hardy, their chemistry professor, came into the lab and surveyed the scene. He told Orville to come with him. Scooter put the extinguisher back into the wall bracket.

"Do we have to finish this?" One of the students asked. No one knew. They didn't know if Mr. Withers was all right. Scooter took the crystals that had formed in the test tube and placed them on a filter paper in a funnel, rinsed them with ethanol, following the lab manual instructions, and left them to dry. He was hoping he could still get credit for the afternoon's work.

Dr. Hardy came in and said to Scooter, "I need you to come with me." He followed Dr. Hardy to the office where Mr. Withers and Orville were sitting. Orville looked scared. Mr. Withers was leaning forward in his chair, but Scooter could see that his eyebrows had been singed into a curly kind of mat, reminding Scooter of a "Brillo" pad for scrubbing pots and pans. Mr. Wither's forehead was red. It looked like he, or someone, had applied some greasy salve to it.

When asked, Scooter said, no, he hadn't noticed that Orville was using an open flame on the ether distillation until it was too late—right before the explosion. Orville took a side-ways glance at Scooter, perhaps hoping someone could help him out of this jam.

"You did the right thing. It's good you thought quickly." Dr. Hardy said to Scooter. Dr. Hardy was the antithesis of Mr. Withers, being short, nearly bald and somewhat round.

"It wasn't all that much really, the fire extinguisher was right there," Scooter said.

Mr. Withers looked sheepish and singed. Apparently, he had been partially blinded for a few seconds by the initial flash. Some of the other students in the lab wondered, after Scooter went back to dismantle his distillation column, if Mr. Withers had been mentally transported for a few seconds by the explosion back to some battlefield on the Korean peninsula.

CHAPTER SIXTEEN
PREPARATIONS

Scooter told Sonny about the fire at dinner, and several other students said they had already heard about it. After discarding their trays and dishes, Scooter walked back with Sonny toward his dorm and then veered toward the parking lot. He drove down the hill from the college and pulled in at a service station to have the oil and the filter in his car changed for the trip north. As he was waiting, he noticed a pharmacy across the street that was still open. He hurriedly walked over to it before he changed his mind and went inside.

It was a small store with a series of aisles between shelves of goods under long fluorescent lights, all leading back to an open portal that served as the pharmacy. He was going to buy a box of condoms, but a woman clerk stood behind the checkout counter and was waiting on a female customer. He dallied, not wanting to have a customer see what he was intending to purchase, nor have the woman cashier wait on him. He noticed an older man behind the pharmacy counter and walked to the back of the store. He grabbed a box that read *Sheiks* and took it to the pharmacist, hoping he could pay there. The man came over, and Scooter got out his wallet. The pharmacist asked, "Do you want all of those? It's twenty-four."

Scooter blinked. The box suddenly seemed quite large. He felt his face flush and said, "Yeah." His collar felt hot. It seemed the pharmacist was staring at him and Scooter looked around the store hoping no one else saw his plight.

"You have to pay for these at the cash register," the pharmacist said.

"Oh!" Scooter said. He contemplated putting them back, but then decided he had to go through with it. *I'm in the mix now. It's too late to put them back and run out of the store like some kid.* He glanced toward the front of the store and the cashier. She was studying a sheet of paper on the counter. He took a deep breath, walked to the front of the store and put the box on the counter.

The woman cashier looked up and picked up the box to check the price. "This is the large size, you know," she said.

He started to waver and then thought: *Are you a mouse or a bronc rider?* The woman looked to be in her thirties. She was married--well, at least she had a ring on her left hand.

"Yeah, I have a lot of girlfriends," he said.

"Or maybe an overactive imagination," the woman replied.

He felt his face flush, but said, "Yeah, that too. What time you get off work?"

She smiled at him and placed the box into a paper bag and gave him his change. "Get out of here before you get in trouble!"

"Trouble, huh?" He smiled but felt his face flush again. He noticed the woman giving him the once-over. Scooter took his package back to the service station, his face still feeling warm, but he was proud of following through and of his smart-ass quip. *Overactive imagination . . . sheesh!* He paid for the servicing of his car and drove back to his apartment, wondering: *What kind of trouble did she mean? I'm over eighteen.* He took one of the condom packages out and read the instructions, wondering if he could figure out how to use it, then stashed the box in the recess of his equipment bag, feeling as if he had committed a crime. He pulled a TV dinner out of the freezer compartment and lit the oven.

He placed the TV dinner into the oven and while it heated, he pulled his English essay out to finish recopying it, using his best penmanship. While eating dinner, he got out Charlene's telephone number. *I look forward to our talks. After my discussion with Katherine . . . complicated. Best anyway if we move on I guess. I wonder what Charlene's bringing to study . . . guess I'll ask. I'd like to get close to her again . . . smell her hair. Have her lean into me . . . put her fingers in my hair, on the back of my neck again. I better quit . . . I have a bareback horse to think about. I wonder what kind of a draw I'll have. Ridgeline Rodeo has some rank NFR horses . . .*

He finished his dinner and topped it off with a large glass of milk and bread with butter and jam, his desert. He dialed Charlene's number, and she answered after several rings.

"I was hoping you'd call!" she said. "Squirrel is coming over to do a study thing with me and I wanted to talk with you before."

"Yes, I said I would. Why do you want to talk before Squirrel is there?"

"Oh, I can talk to you more freely is all. Have you been good since Tuesday?"

"Well, no actually . . . I had to put out a fire in the chemistry lab and blew glassware all over the place with an extinguisher!"

"What? Are you kidding me?" Charlene exclaimed.

"No, you're talking to a real live hero . . . saved the whole college!"

"Scooter, you're so funny. What happened?"

Scooter regaled her with the details of the lab fire.

"You tell a good story," she said.

"What are we studying this weekend?" he asked.

"You're bringing something to study . . . right?"

"Yes, I got a big bad chemistry final next week and one in range management that could be tough, so guess I'll bring stuff on those!"

"Well, you can help me with an English paper, since you're such a hotshot," Charlene said.

"So, we're really studying? What a bummer. I had other ideas!"

"Like what?" she asked.

"Like us getting to know each other even better . . . you know, taking more chances, searching for some destiny."

Charlene didn't say anything for a few seconds, and Scooter wondered if he had overstepped a boundary. Finally, she said, "I think there will be plenty of time to know each other better. Do you know what I mean?" she softly asked.

Her words jolted him. "Yes. Like growing this larger?" he asked.

She didn't answer, finally saying, "Larger . . . oh, now I get it! Well, maybe it is, guess we'll have to see. You had my wheels turning there for a second." They both laughed at her comment. "Not to change the subject, but I'm bringing Star up on Saturday morning. It's not far for us here in Fort Collins, but I wanted her to get used to the arena before the afternoon."

"That's a good idea, then after the crowds get there, too," Scooter said. "We're driving through on Friday. Sonny and I can leave around two, so we shouldn't get there too late. I'll see you out at the arena probably on Saturday morning. Well, late morning. I like to get acclimated, too, before the excitement starts."

"Is your shoulder okay?" she asked.

"You told me to get it strong for you. It seems pretty good, actually."

"Well, that's good, you're a tough boy!"

"You think so, huh?"

"Uh-huh, I've seen the evidence. Well honey, I better let you go. Squirrel will be here soon."

"Listen, if you call me 'honey', what should I call you?"

"Well, you can call me daawlin'." She drawled as if from the South.

Scooter laughed and said, "Okay daawlin', I'll see you Saturday! Be careful out there!"

"You guys be careful driving up here . . . okay?" she said.

"Yeah, we're always careful!"

He said goodbye and hung up the phone. *She's the honey! Ah, what did she say about there being time to find what I'm looking for? . . . Judas Priest!*

She knows how to turn the heat up in me.

Scooter got out his duffle bag with his bareback rigging, boots, chaps, spurs and glove. He laid it all out to make sure everything was there. He then unrolled his chaps. They gave him a nice feeling—like seeing an old friend. He carefully folded and rolled them up again and put them into the duffle bag. One spur had a worn leather strap that went under the arch of his boot, and he replaced it, using a leather shoelace. He placed the spurs and the boots back in the bag, and then wrapped his glove around the handhold of the rigging and tied it there with a short strip of leather. The rolled ace bandage was on the dresser and he placed it in the corner of the bag . . . just in case. He zipped the bag shut.

Scooter got out another large overnight bag and folded several pairs of underwear and socks and placed these in the bottom, then carefully folded two shirts and two pair of Wranglers. The shaving kit could go in after his morning ritual.

Having packed, he thought about the two classes he had the next day and checked his English essay over one last time. Something was missing; he needed a clincher for a conclusion. He knew from other assignments that a conclusion was often the difference between a mediocre *C* and a higher grade. Mrs. Starmire looked for something from within—something insightful. He read his essay through and decided he needed to explain what it meant for him to compete.

He wrote: *Sporting events that require athleticism have one thing in common; they challenge participants to be their best, to train their bodies and minds to achieve the ultimate, to find that instance when everything comes together in perfect unison and the quest for perfection in movement is complete. Men and women have taken up this challenge since earliest times and we continue this to the present, with the Olympics as the showcase for this quest. Rodeo has these characteristics; it requires strength, agility, technique, mental focus, and being positive. But, it has an added dimension, and that is animals that are often unpredictable, and this adds to the challenge. It's true that rodeo "gets in your blood," which means after a person has started competing and sees progress in his or her ability, it is hard to quit. It might be that most sports are this way. There is another reason talked about in rodeo regarding an adrenaline rush that happens as a chute gate is opened for the resultant explosion of semi-controlled action or sometimes violence. I don't know if adrenaline levels have ever been measured or not, but that there's a rush seems likely, and it may be addictive. Another aspect is the human need to try to solve problems, and there are plenty of those to occupy a person's mind during an 8-second ride on a bareback horse. Of course, for everything that is worthwhile, there is risk. For people that decide to embark on the rodeo trail, they have to decide if the benefits are worth the risks. Those of us on the team here at Southwestern State have already answered this question. We love the journey!*

He read it over and thought: *Well, that's as good as it's going to get.* He took out clean sheets of paper and placed a ruled piece of paper underneath to keep the lines straight. He took out a fountain pen and dabbed it to make sure it didn't blot. He knew many of the students, including Katherine, typed their assignments, but he didn't have a typewriter and it wasn't required as long as a person wrote neatly. He had not identified anyone specifically in his story about traveling to a rodeo, having car trouble, the competition, injury, and meeting girls, but both Zeke and Sonny would be able to figure it out pretty quickly to whom he was referring. They might complain, but he wasn't sure they would ever read it. He fanned the last page to make sure the ink was dry and placed the essay into a plastic cover. He was thinking about going to bed, but looked in his animal science class notes, and realized he was supposed to read a chapter on "Feeds and Feeding." He had forgotten about this and forced himself to read, sometimes scanning parts of the chapter. As he did, he thought of the ranch and about feeding the cows when he was home. He thought his dad must know most of this stuff already—about supplementing with cottonseed cake or other protein-based feed before and after calving. Maybe it's just common sense. However, the text had a long discussion of how to calculate the amount of feed needed for different classes of cattle and ages to make sure they were getting the nutrients needed. He quickly scanned his notes from Range Management. A guy never knew when there might be a pop quiz. Fridays had a tendency for this it seemed.

Scooter glanced at his watch. It was after midnight. He finally put his textbook away along with his notes, brushed his teeth, washed his face, and then climbed into bed. He thought about the ranch; that he had a nice family that he missed, even though he and his older brother, Ron, didn't see eye-to-eye. Ron hadn't been very bookish in high school and there was no thought of him going to college. He didn't think it was necessary anyway—to go to college to learn to be a rancher or farmer—when a person could learn on the job or should know it by the time they grew up. He didn't mind getting on a rough-broke bronc once in a while though, and that's where Scooter and his brother were more aligned. Scooter expected Ron to get married soon, as he had been dating a neighbor girl since high school. The thought of them swirled Scooter's thoughts toward Charlene, and then Katherine. He had never met anyone like Charlene, but he liked the complex personality of

Katherine too. He could not figure her out. Charlene was more straightforward it seemed. Mature . . . maybe that was it. The persistent thought crept in though . . . *wonder if she's dating other guys.*

On Friday morning, Scooter asked Hank in English class how his essay had progressed. Hank presented his paper, which he had placed in a clear plastic cover. "Hey, it looks fine. You better not get a better grade than me on this," Scooter said.

"Now, that'd be somethin'!" Hank exclaimed.

The laboratory fire was a topic of conversation before the class started, some of the other students had heard about it. They asked how large the fire had been. Scooter mentioned that the fire had scorched the ceiling of the lab and that was maybe ten feet. "You should 'ave seen the mess after I let the fire extinguisher loose on it. There was broken glass and reagents all over the counter and the floor too! That thing had way more force than I was expectin'!" he grinned. The other students nodded.

Katherine walked into the classroom with Linda. "Hey, Mr. Fireman," Katherine said as she walked by, taking a seat next to her friend.

Mrs. Starmire came into class and asked that they pass their essays to the front of the room. She then started writing on the blackboard the different grammar subjects that were going to be on the next week's final exam. "Also, be prepared to write a paragraph on one of several designated topics," she said.

Scooter copied down the list of grammar subjects for the exam into his notebook. Mrs. Starmire then lectured on the flow of writing and using action verbs. Scooter liked this and wondered if he had used enough of these or those that are easier in his term paper. After class, Hank wished Scooter luck in Laramie, and said, "I'm hoping I can go to the last one over'n La Junta."

"This essay should help some, shouldn't it?" Scooter asked. He looked over at Katherine and Linda, who were gathering-up their books.

Katherine walked over to where he was sitting. See me before you leave, okay?" she said. "I'm working at noon."

He wondered what she wanted, but said, "I'll see you at the cafeteria, I guess."

"We better get to that other class," he told Hank.

Scooter found Animal Science class somewhat boring and had a hard time keeping his eyes off the clock. He and Sonny were going to meet Zeke for lunch in the cafeteria to make final plans, and then Sonny and he would head north after their Range Science lecture. Scooter wondered if Zeke and Molly were going to stay at the same motel as he and Sonny. *That would be interesting!* He heard his name being called, and automatically said, "Sir? Could you repeat the question?"

The instructor asked about high fiber feeds and how that needed to be balanced. Scooter's mind scrambled for an answer. "Either add some grain or green forage, I guess . . . for more protein," he said uncertainly. The answer seemed to be partially correct, but the instructor asked another student to expand on it.

"You better know this stuff . . . how to balance feed for certain objectives and the needs of the type of livestock by next Friday's final," The instructor warned.

After the class was over, Scooter walked to the cafeteria and saw that Sonny and Zeke were already sitting at a table. He looked for Katherine before he went to the serving line. She was bringing out plates of Jell-O on a tray. After putting the dishes out on the serving counter, she came over to him.

"Okay cowboy, I just wanted to wish you luck at the rodeo. Be careful . . . okay?"

"Always. I'll see you Monday. We need to study for Wednesday's test anyway, don't we? I could use some help!"

Katherine smiled. "Probably a good idea. I'll look for you." She grasped his hand as she said this, and her gesture led to a hug. Scooter remained rooted, looking after her as she walked back into the kitchen. *What the heck, hot and cold, hot and cold.*

He ambled along behind several students through the food line and then joined Sonny and Zeke at their table. They immediately started talking about the trip north.

"I'm going to Fort Collins for tonight, then I think Molly can come up after she gets off work on Saturday. I could only get some Podunk room near the edge of town," Zeke said.

"Well, we told you to find something earlier, and we're not trading! How do you know it's Podunk?" Scooter asked.

"Well, it's cheap. The guy said they had weekly rates. I ain't asking to trade you guys anyways. Is your new love going to be there?" Zeke asked.

"She's in the barrel racing. We said we're going to study together!"

"That's what you said, but I gotta ask for what course? Human anatomy?"

Scooter smiled at the jibe, didn't say anything, but Sonny finally put forth his opinion to Zeke. "I tell you something, from what I seen, that Charlene has set her sights on our pardner here, and fer whatever reason, he's allowing himself to be led along like a lamb to slaughter. Now that Katherine woman is after him too. He's buzzard bait."

Scooter was tired of the teasing and the undercurrent about him taking a fall. "It's old now, change the subject," he said gruffly.

Sonny and Zeke laughed at his reaction. They continued to eat and discuss what the competition might be like. "Some of those guys from Montana seem to specialize in saddle broncs," Zeke said.

"Well, Sonny's riding good too, so they better be ready," Scooter countered.

Sonny joined the conversation. "Zeke's right. Some a them come down to a rodeo in Utah last summer and could ride pretty good. But you guys know what I found out? Just doan worry about anyone else an' it works out better."

Scooter studied his friend for a few seconds. "That seems like good advice," he said.

With that, they carried their trays to the discard area and walked outside. Zeke headed to the parking lot and Scooter headed with Sonny to his dorm room to collect his gear. Scooter hollered to Zeke, "Be careful drivin' that truck o' yours."

"Eehaw, let's rodeo!" Zeke hollered as he sauntered down the sidewalk. He followed this outburst with several yodels and a rebel yell.

Two other students were walking by and looked toward Zeke as he ambled off across campus. "One of the crazy rodeo idiots," one said to the other.

Scooter and Sonny smiled at each other. "It's good to have Zeke on the team . . . fer the reputation y'know," Sonny said. Scooter nodded in agreement.

CHAPTER SEVENTEEN
HEADING NORTH

After their Range Management class, Scooter helped Sonny carry his gear to Scooter's car. They did the same at Scooter's apartment, throwing his two bags into the back seat. "We shoulda gone with Johnny and Will I guess, but they left mid-morning. I kind of got the impression they didn't want us to ask about hitching a ride," Scooter said.

"This uns better. We got more freedom, y'know . . . go to the arena whatever. Doan worry, I got gas money," Sonny said.

"Well," Scooter replied, "I wasn't worried too much about that."

They settled in for the similar, although longer trip to Laramie, and headed east toward Pagosa Springs and Wolf Creek Pass, essentially retracing their route of several weeks previously. Scooter commented near the bottom of the pass on the east side, "That's where Zeke about killed off all the vegetation last time." Sonny looked back toward the ravine but didn't say anything for a few minutes.

"That Zeke takes this rodeo life to the extreme, innit?" Sonny said.

Scooter looked over and asked, "What you mean, the extreme? He likes the women, that's for sure, and to party some."

"Did Hank tell youse about when they went down t' that bull sale in Farmington?"

"Well, I knew they both bucked off," said Scooter.

"Yeah, well it was mor'n that. Zeke 'n Hank went to a bar with some other guys, 'n according to Hank, he went back to the hotel room and left Zeke chattin' up some bar woman. Hank said that he figured buckin' off that bull musta screwed up Zeke's eyesight 'cause this woman was like old nuff t'be his mother."

Scooter looked over at Sonny and chuckled. "Sounds like him alright."

"That ain't the half of it though," Sonny continued, "he 'n her came back t'the room drunk and made all this noise an', hell, they got into bed. Hank said he had to take a blanket and pillow in the toilet fer a while . . . y'know, the head, t'get any sleep."

Scooter was puzzled why he hadn't heard about this from someone. "No kiddin'! No one said anything to me. So, what happened?"

"Yeah, Hank was telling the guys about it. They left in a hurry in the mornin', I guess.

"Why'd they have to get out?" Scooter asked.

"Well, the way Hank toll it, Zeke said he'd woken up with a thumpin' headache and some dream, like he was doing something at a . . . like a oil thing, or y'know pumper. He woke up staring at a set of huge teeth in a glass of water on the nightstand . . . damn neared couldn't figure out where he was. Told Hank his mouth tasted like the bottom of a birdcage, that he'd figured that was the cause of 'is bad dream. He couldn't even figure out who was in the bed with 'im!"

"So, is that it? They just made an escape?"

"Yeah, he told Hank that he had had t' take a leak sumthin' powerful an' said he nearly stepped on sumthin' seemed like a varmint, on the floor. Gave 'im a huge start. Checked, 'n it was a hair thing, y'know, fake hair!"

Scooter laughed. "A varmint? Musta thought it was a big rat!" Sonny laughed at Scooter's comment. He continued, "Serves him right. Jeez, I don't believe it! What happened to the woman?"

"Hank said he took a quick shower an' they got the hell outta Dodge . . . left her in the room, still snoring I guess. Hank said Zeke fell off'n his bull right outta the gate. They had to stop t'get 'im . . . somethin' fer his head and once at the border fer 'im to puke!"

"No wonder he never said anything . . . screwing around with some old gal like that! He better hang onto that Molly."

Scooter looked over at Sonny. That had been a pretty long speech for him. Sonny had pulled his hat down over his eyes, leaned his head back on the seat, having exhausted his verbal energies.

They filled the car with gas in Del Norte, and Scooter asked Sonny if he wanted to drive. Sonny said he would and added, "I'll be careful not to speed, 'cause I ain't gotta license."

"I thought you had one," Scooter said. "I never know when you're kidding sometimes. Well, anyway, take it easy." He lay back on the seat to snooze, as they headed north toward Saguache. *Wonder what Charlene's doing? She has to have other guys calling, asking her out. Be good to see her again. She sure is different than Katherine . . . not so complex, I guess. She seems like her mind is made up about us, though. It gives me pause . . . she better be straight . . . not jerking me around like that girl with Zeke at Christmas. What a bullshitter . . . twice with that girl . . . not sure I believed him. But Charlene . . . gives a guy pause, no matter if we said to hell with worrying about it . . . about taking chances with each other. Well, like a bronc, once yer out of the chute, too late to get off without getting stuck in the dirt.*

"I wonder if'n Zeke's truck can get past the place up here this time?" Sonny said, breaking into Scooter's thoughts about women.

"That'd be a hoot if he showed up on the bus again," Scooter said, his hat still pulled over his eyes. "I'd about die laughing! Course, we'd have to cough up some more money probably and help him out, but, couldn't you see him stepping off the bus with us waiting."

Sonny looked at Scooter and smiled, "Well it'd be pretty funny. I mean y'know what he'd say . . . swear words en all. What if'n we took this Molly out there t' meet 'im, and had our arms around 'er? He'd bust a gut!"

Scooter sat up. "You got an ornery streak in you." Sonny showed a wolfish grin. Scooter noticed he was still driving slowly, 45-50 miles per hour. Scooter relaxed again with his head back on the seat and the edge of the door.

They stopped at one of the service stations along the highway near Basin to top-off the gas and then went into town for dinner at the hotel. A few patrons at the bar turned to look at the newcomers. Scooter and Sonny sat at a table and ordered burgers and a tossed salad. They were both leery of bar patrons, as they knew some guys liked to think they were tough after knocking back a few drinks. Scooter realized that Sonny sometimes drew out the bully in people, who took him for being weak because he was small. *Another reason is people's prejudice against Indians . . . still! Well, they may be in for one big surprise, 'cause he's a lot tougher than he looks.*

Scooter assumed Sonny had been in some scuffles or fights before, based on their conversations. He had told Scooter that he knew his way around in a fight and had instructed him once when trouble looked imminent, "To aim for the soft spots!"

Scooter had wanted to make sure afterward which spots were included. Sonny told him matter-of-factly, "nuts, diaphragm, throat. Lots easier on yer fist. En now that I'm givin' away my secrets, carry a roll of nickels."

Scooter had been unable to see any relationship between hitting someone in a soft spot and nickels, so he had said, "Okay, I give up."

Sonny had explained, "A roll of nickels in your fist keeps you from depressing a knuckle. Not only that, but it feels like you're hit'n with a club."

After Sonny's explanation, Scooter had put a roll of nickels in his duffle bag with his gear, figuring he would most likely use the money for a payphone sometime, and then had nearly forgotten it.

After dinner, Scooter felt energized and took over the driving for their trip north through Denver. By now, it was after eight o'clock and it was still over two hours to Laramie. They again filled up with gas in Fort Collins and bought some snacks and filled their jug with water. "Remember what your Uncle John said, keep hydrated. I think that's good advice," Scooter said.

"Yeah, keeps a guy pissn' so that's good, I reckon."

Scooter looked over at Sonny to see if he was joking, but it didn't seem like it. "Why's it good t'keep pissn'?"

"Hell, I don't know, but isn't it good to keep things flowin'?"

"Well, guess it's better than not, that's for sure." He glanced at Sonny. Scooter thought the conversation had taken a strange turn.

Upon arriving in Laramie, Scooter and Sonny drove through the main street until they saw the green and blue neon sign shaped artistically like mountains for the Peak motel.

"Sign looks like a couple a boobs," Sonny observed.

Scooter checked to see if he could see the resemblance and grunted an affirmative.

They pulled into the driveway and both stiffly got out of the car. Scooter rang the night bell several times. Finally, a clerk came into the office in his robe and opened the front door.

"We got reservations," Scooter said.

The clerk had them fill out registration cards and asked for the first night's amount. Scooter asked for the rodeo contestant discount and paid in cash. The clerk gave him two keys and pointed down the way to the room. They parked the car in front of the room and carried their gear inside.

They each claimed a bed, and then Sonny said, "Let's go up the college and check the draw." Scooter wasn't too enthusiastic, but then thought it might be a good idea to know about the horses that had been drawn for them.

"We'll check Zeke's bull too," he said.

The two went back out to Scooter's car and drove into the middle of town to the college campus. They had to circle the campus to find the student union and noticed a few other contestants on the steps near the front doors. They parked and went in, saying hello. The rodeo staff was still doing business, so they checked in and received their numbers. As they had heard, there was only one go-round in bareback and bulls. They went over to the bulletin board to check the lists.

"Jeez! I'm up tomorrow and have that Popcorn horse!" Scooter said.

Sonny came over to look at the list with Scooter. "Talk about yer luck. That there's a fine bareback horse . . . jumps high though."

"I saw it in a photo in *Rodeo Sports News*—the National Finals last year. I think someone won a go-round on it!" Scooter exclaimed. "Sure, lots of contestants . . . Montana, too, and look, a guy from North Dakota."

"Be some tough competition I reckon," Sonny observed.

They looked at the list for the saddle bronc event. Sonny had drawn a horse called Hard Lemonade in the first go-round. Neither had heard of it before. They then checked the long list of bull riders and bulls. Zeke was up on Sunday and had drawn a bull called 04 Neoprene.

"That's a weird name," Sonny said.

"Yes, I think that one has been around some, may have been in the NFR before . . . not sure," Scooter replied.

The woman coordinating the registration said, "Hey guys, we're shutting this down until eight tomorrow morning. Only a few contestants, along with Scooter and Sonny, were still looking at the lists.

"Well, been a long day anyhow, innit?" said Sonny.

"I reckon," Scooter responded.

They walked back through the student union and then outside to Scooter's car and drove back to the motel. Scooter moved his duffle bag off the bed and sat on its edge. He was psyched about his draw for the next day, but was feeling the long drive, and it looked like Sonny was as well, as he pulled his boots off and lay back on the bed.

"You got it going right now pard. The gods are smiling on ya . . . good grades, girls fallin all over themselves, good bareback horses," Sonny said.

"It's mostly hard work and a little luck here'n there," Scooter replied.

"Yeah!" Sonny said, "Luck."

"A little luck never hurts in rodeo, but we been over this before. Hard work helps make it happen though."

Sonny nodded in agreement. "What about those girls though? Luck or hard work?"

"Well, you tell me," Scooter responded, "that Lisal and the girls on the rez who are all in love with you?"

"Well, maybe it's hard work 'cause they see that a guy kin do things, but hey, it don't hurt to be good-lookin' like me, neither."

"Judas Priest! Good looking? Guess I hadn't thought of that. I think they like getting hold of your long hair." Sonny laughed at this. "Well," Scooter continued, "I need to get rid of some road grime in the shower."

When he came out of the bathroom, the TV was on showing a snowy screen, and Sonny was asleep, rolled up in the bedspread. His feet were sticking out and one of his toes had pushed through a hole in his sock. Scooter just shook his head as he thought about Sonny's indifference to such things.

I reckon, though, we could travel like this to rodeos all summer . . . well, except that I have to help at home, especially during haying and some during harvest. But otherwise, be good. Wonder if Sonny does have a driver's license or needs to get one. He sure drives slow . . . needs some lessons. Sure hope I have a good go at that Popcorn. I better be ready to ride . . . no sucky stuff. Scooter made a fist and clenched his jaw with determination. Finally, he lay back on the bed, threw a blanket over himself, and went to sleep seeing himself riding Popcorn, simulating the picture he has seen in the *Rodeo Sports News*.

CHAPTER EIGHTEEN
LARAMIE

Scooter finally climbed out of bed and checked his image in the mirror. The view was not encouraging; his eyes were red, and a thick strand of hair was sticking up as if testing the wind. He shaved and opened the small bottle of motel-furnished shampoo to shower. He wanted to be presentable--just in case. Wonder if Charlene is out at the arena and is looking forward to seeing me? Well, I shouldn't dwell on this too much . . . just in case she isn't.

He checked on Sonny, who was still in bed, but at least moving. He had, at some point during the night, shed his pants, which were lying in a heap along with his shirt on the floor. One foot was sticking out from the blanket, and Scooter realized Sonny had not removed at least one sock, as usual.

"You alive over there?" Scooter asked.

Sonny's black eyes peered out from the edge of the blanket. "What? What time's it, anyways?" he asked.

"Sun's been up a while."

After showering, Scooter removed a dark blue shirt out of his luggage and snapped it to remove the wrinkles and any debris. Sonny grumbled something and headed into the bathroom. Scooter heard the shower running.

"Let's go get some chow, then I wanna go out to the arena early to just check it out. Okay?" Scooter said, after Sonny came out of the bathroom.

"S'okay." Sonny replied, never talkative in the morning. His long hair was wet, and he tried to fluff it up with a towel.

I want to check out that Popcorn horse, and maybe we can have a look at the saddle broncs too," Scooter continued.

Sonny nodded and pulled his dark hair back into a ponytail, wrapping it with a thin leather tie. He picked up his shirt from the floor and snapped it a few times as Scooter had, and then shrugged it over both arms. Scooter grinned at his friend's nonchalance toward personal appearance. Sonny did, however, take pride in his hair and black, high-crowned hat, carefully placing it above his ponytail, indicating he was ready to go.

Scooter drove his '59 Chevy along the main street of Laramie until Sonny spotted a restaurant. The waitress automatically poured coffee and Scooter asked for water, as well. After they had eaten, they circled the town, not knowing where the arena was located. They finally stopped at a service station and were told it was on the west side of town.

Scooter parked his car among a few trucks and horse trailers. He noticed Charlene's rig, but didn't see her. The arena was older than the one in Fort Collins but had been refurbished with new boards on the fence in a few places. The main arena fence was of hog wire but had a horizontal middle and top braces between the posts. Scooter stood on one of the wooden braces and looked over the arena. The history of the place seemed to be evident. *A lot of great bronc riders have come through here . . . probably Casey Tibbs, Jim Shoulders, maybe Jack Buschbom, last year's Bareback Champion.* The view to the west and north provided a vista of mountains. Scooter took a deep breath of the fresh air, with the slight smell of horses. He smiled to himself, liking the rodeo atmosphere.

"Let's check out the broncs," Sonny said and slipped through a small gate behind the chutes to an alleyway. Scooter jumped down from the fence, and they walked back to the stock pens. The bareback horses and saddle broncs had been separated. Scooter knew that Popcorn was a good-looking black.

"These must be the bareback horses here." He was looking at the pen closest to the chutes. The horses were munching on hay that had been thrown into the pen. Scooter felt a pulse of nervousness go through him. He shrugged it off.

Sonny ambled over to a second pen to spend more time trying to sort out the saddle broncs. "There's some big horses here fer the bronc ridin'," he called over.

Scooter joined Sonny and climbed up on the fence of the pen, "You may have to lengthen your stirrups just to get a mark-out." He was referring to Sonny's short stature, which could be a detriment to marking-out large horses as they came out of the chute.

"That ain't too funny right now," Sonny replied as he viewed the herd.

Scooter noticed a rider near the back of the parking lot and thought it could be Charlene. He took a harder look. The woman was talking to a guy who was standing near her horse. It looked like he had a hand on the horse's neck. A thread of jealousy coursed through Scooter, as he realized it was Charlene. She turned the horse and rode toward the arena. Scooter continued to watch and finally, she saw him and waved. He half-heartedly waved back, then got down off the fence and walked partway to meet her. He tried to force the jealous feeling out, thinking he was being ridiculous. He told himself: *You don't own her. Guess she can talk to anyone she wants.*

"Hey cowboy, you made it up okay," Charlene flashed a wide smile.

Scooter was aware again of her features that so attracted him; her dark hair and turquoise eyes, her lithe figure that sat a horse so naturally. "Yeah, no problems really. We got in around eleven 'n checked in at the rodeo office fer the draw, so it was late. How're you?"

"Good! I'm going to ride around the arena, hop on," she said, and emptied a stirrup for him.

He climbed on behind her saddle. "Your horse doesn't mind?" he asked.

"No, she's not like your bareback horses."

"Well, I knew that," he said, as she laughed. They started into the arena staying on the far side from a tractor and disc working the ground. Scooter noticed Sonny watching them from the horse pen and waved to him. Sonny continued to look but didn't wave back. He had his hat pulled low and it shadowed his face. Scooter figured he was glaring back at him and Charlene. He squinted back at Sonny's attitude.

"Sonny's over at the bronc pens trying to figure out which horse he might have . . . called Hard Lemonade but won't have a clue unless someone from Ridgeline comes over," Scooter said.

Charlene turned and waved at Sonny. "I'm glad you're here. I was hoping to see you. You know, Billy came over. He's doing something with his horse. Anyway, he wants to get back together." Scooter felt his stomach sink.

When she didn't continue, he tentatively asked, "Whaddya say?"

"Oh, I told him it's over. I don't want to go through all that again. I told him I was seeing someone. Is that okay?"

His spirits lifted. "Yeah, if that's what you want. I mean if that's how you feel."

"I told you I know what I want. I knew already when I saw you down at Alamosa."

"How'd you know that?" he asked.

"I have great intuition!" she laughed. "Do you?"

"I doubt it. I just know I like you. I think you are the most beautiful girl I have ever met. I like our talks."

"I want to know something . . . about those girls at Southwestern. Are you sure you don't have a girlfriend?"

"As I said, I have a friend in one of my classes. We've been on some dates. I like where I'm at right now though." Charlene turned in the saddle and looked at him. He continued. "You know what happened to me?"

When he didn't continue, Charlene turned slightly, and said, "Well, come on, I'm waiting!"

"Yeah well, I was just going along, minding my own business being into rodeo, college course work, when this goddess came up to me one night at a dance and hit me with lightning. I haven't been the same since."

Charlene realized he was talking about her and laughed. "You sweet boy! Lightning, huh? You're such a bullshitter. I like it though . . . I am seeing someone." She squeezed his leg. He laughed with her at his joke and their conversation. The day suddenly seemed amazingly sunny.

They circled back toward the chutes and Sonny, who was leaning against the arena gate, watched them. It was obvious to Scooter that Sonny had his back up and was stiff, still glaring out through the shadow of his hat. Scooter knew that Sonny didn't like the complication of Charlene being in the way before competing and was silently sending Scooter that message.

"You wanna get some chow with us before it gets too close to the rodeo?" Scooter asked. "Before I get too revved-up . . . y'know, nervous."

"I have to take care of my horse, so if you can wait . . . Is Sonny okay with me? He looks put out," Charlene said.

"Oh, he likes things to be simple . . . straight forward into the competition. Sort of like no diversions from the mission, if you know what I mean. I don't want to let you go, though. I mean that Billy may come back and take you away."

She turned to look at him and saw that he was smiling and smiled back. "You don't need to worry about him."

They approached Sonny, and Charlene said, "Hello!" Sonny grunted a reply.

Scooter thought he better change things up, as Sonny's attitude was starting to perturb him. "Sonny, meet a good quarter horse, Star. Star this is a bronc rider from New Mexico." His comments seemed to soften Sonny some and he pushed his hat back and leaned against the fence. Scooter continued, "Come on, we're going to take care of this pony and get a little lunch."

"Okay, I'll meet youse at the car," Sonny said.

Charlene angled Star over to her truck and horse trailer, where they dismounted.

"Well, I'm sorry I've upset Sonny's plans. I hope I haven't yours."

Scooter snorted a laugh. "I've been thinking about seeing you since last time. How about if I admit it? As we headed north yesterday, I thought of you more and more."

Charlene directed a bright smile toward him. "Like I said, I think you're starting to develop a pretty good line. But that's okay, I like it so far."

Scooter smiled at her comment and helped her take off the saddle. Charlene switched out the bridle with a halter and tied the horse to the trailer. She brushed Star down and asked Scooter, "Can you get some hay out from the front?"

He went to the front of the horse trailer and opened the compartment. He found a large net of hay and hung it on the back of the trailer for Star. There was a large plastic pail of water wired to the trailer. Charlene asked if he would top it off from another container. After he had complied, Charlene said, "Thanks!" and continued to brush Star. She moved to the front of the trailer to put the brush away and then grasped his arm. "Okay, here's for thinking of me so much." He turned, wondering and then knew. He pulled her the rest of the way to him into a kiss. Her lips and mouth were soft, and she smelled good.

"You are such a honey," he murmured. They continued to embrace, and he moved his hand down from her waist into the pocket of her jeans. He kissed her hair. She felt nice—firm and didn't seem to mind his hand being where it was. He felt her fingers on the back of his neck, then caressing his ear.

"Listen, I wanted to let you know . . . well, how I feel about you," she said, "but, I mean, both of us need to think about what we have to do today, 'cause I know Sonny's right. We need to get our minds on this competition."

Scooter pulled back slightly and took a good look at her. "Okay, okay I know . . . majority rules. I'm focused, really. Let's get some lunch."

Charlene and Scooter walked over to his car where Sonny was waiting. He climbed into the passenger side, and Scooter threw some gear into the trunk from the back seat to make room for Charlene. He was becoming miffed at Sonny's attitude toward her.

Charlene directed them to a restaurant that she knew. They were shown to a booth and Scooter ordered a toasted cheese sandwich. He was starting to get edgy as the time closed in toward the start of the rodeo. Charlene was trying to draw Sonny out a little and asked him about the country he was from and his family. Scooter told her about Sonny and their range plant lab test, about seeing some of the plants at Sonny's ranch.

"He had all these weird ways t' remember the names, the Latin ones especially," Sonny said, "But I couldn't 'member the clues, so, was kinda clueless." His pun caused them to laugh.

"But those clues were good when I came up to a mental blockage all of a sudden in the exam—like a horse being pulled up short, y'know?" Sonny just shook his head and Charlene laughed.

As they left the restaurant, Scooter said he needed to get something at the motel, and went into the room for a few minutes, but it was to use the toilet. No doubt, he was getting nervous. He tried to focus his mind on the bareback horse—to visualize the ride he would make. He would try to do this more frequently as time for the event came closer.

Scooter hurried from the room to the car, and they backtracked to the other side of town and the arena. After parking the car among the pickup trucks and horse trailers, Sonny gathered his gear and saddle from the trunk. I'll see youse over at the chutes." Scooter nodded and then walked with Charlene over to her horse as Sonny trudged toward the chutes.

"Well, I reckon it's time to bear down. Let's kick ass today, okay?" he said to Charlene.

"Okay, cowboy. Good luck! I'll see you after and before I run." she squeezed his arm.

CHAPTER NINETEEN
POPCORN

Scooter pulled his older, scuffed riding boots from his duffle bag and switched with what he called, "going-to-town" boots. He then removed his bareback rigging and took the glove from the handhold. He put the glove on and flexed his hand. Some of the other bareback riders were filing in behind the chutes. He said hello to those he knew. People had started to file into the stands, and riders were walking their horses around the arena. He saw Charlene was among this group, and another rider, a guy, was riding alongside her and they seemed to be chatting. Scooter turned away, not wanting to have this vision in his head.

He started his routine of exercises and stretches. His arms and shoulders felt strong, or compact. He couldn't quite define it. He had felt this way since the sweat lodge ceremony at Sonny's place, and he didn't know if it was mind over matter—*what was it the college trainer said—psychosomatic?* Whatever it is, he believed in it. He did a series of pushups and the oft-injured shoulder felt great. Maybe he would get off on the right side to protect it though. He reached up and grabbed a wooden brace that spanned the alley to the holding pen fence and did a series of pull-ups, and then finished using only his riding arm. He was breathing hard and figured he had raised his heart rate.

Sonny came over and said, "Chit, that Hard Lemonade horse is big. He still has on a winter coat. Bet he never sheds all summer, innit. What a ratty lookin' bronc."

Scooter chuckled at Sonny's analysis, "Wear your long spurs, huh?" Sonny grunted a response. Scooter pulled his chaps out, unfurled them and then draped them over the top board of the fence. He fished his spurs out from the bottom of the equipment bag and began to buckle them on. He checked that they were solidly anchored onto his boots. "Y'seen Zeke yet?" he asked. Sonny said he hadn't. Scooter put his chaps on and stared at the pen of horses, visualizing his ride. He had his mind made up to spur like Emmett Fox had admonished the high school kids at the jackpot rodeo on the reservation. He saw himself reared back, nearly on the horse's rear and spurring in time with every jump. He knew of the rank, athletic reputation of his draw, Popcorn, and knew he had to stay up close to the rigging. He set his jaw and continued to stretch his legs out on the boards of the fence along the alleyway behind the chutes. He transitioned into another set of pull-ups on the two-by-six brace.

"Doan overdo it," Sonny said.

The rodeo contractor's staff was starting to sort the horses in the holding pens and the activity brought Scooter back to the present. He asked the chute boss if there was an order. The man, who held a large, partly chewed cigar in the side of his mouth, let him look at the list. He was number six and therefore would be the last of the first batch.

As the horses were channeled into the chutes, the chute boss said to him, "Hey lucky, this uns yourn." Scooter had been right. Popcorn was a sleek, well-muscled, black mare. He thought she looked as if she could be someone's roping or steer-wrestling horse, but obviously, she liked to buck.

Sonny came over to the chute and they set the rigging. The horse stood quietly, and they relaxed standing on the back of the chute while the grand entry of mounted cowboys and cowgirls made their way into the arena. Then two rodeo queens raced their mounts around the arena and posted the American flag and Wyoming State flag on separate sides of the arena. The announcer asked for silence and offered a short prayer that all contestants would be safe and to be thankful they lived in a country where people could be free. The spectators and contestants stood and took off their hats, as a young woman in a dress and high heels laboriously trudged through the soft, disked-up arena surface to an area in front of the chutes. Someone handed her a microphone on a cord extending from the announcer's booth for her to sing the National Anthem. Sonny looked at Scooter and snickered. Scooter knew what he was thinking and hit him in the ribs with an elbow, as the woman began to sing to an instrumental recording. Both had removed their hats.

"Did y'see how she pegged 'erself into the dirt there in them shoes!" Sonny wondered afterward. Scooter smiled and shook his head.

"Let's rodeo!" the announcer exclaimed and mentioned the first rider and the college.

With that, the chute gate was flung open, followed by an explosion of horse and rider. The bareback horse quickly ducked back under the contestant, which flung him to the ground in a violent summersault. Scooter winced. The young cowboy got up, seemingly dazed, and slowly walked back to the chutes. Scooter tried to concentrate on his horse, as other riders performed. He gently shook its mane and talked to it quietly. There were several qualified rides of the contestants before Scooter.

Finally, the chute boss said, "You're the one."

Scooter stood over the horse, his feet inside the chute on the second slats. He carefully threaded his gloved hand into the handhold and pulled the extended ends of the glove's fingers around and underneath the palm of his

hand in a bind. The rosin that he had worked into the glove and handhold helped the grip. He sat down on the horse and positioned his butt tight to the rigging and then carefully slid his feet forward on the slats of the chute to be in front of the horse. The normal pre-ride nerves or tight, nearly humming, stretched-cable feeling in his core,
 had formed a backdrop during his warmup. But now, he was uncharacteristically calm, completely focused on his task. He pulled his chaps back away from his boots and tugged his hat down and said, "Let's go!"

The horse sprang out of the chute in a high arc, and Scooter clamped his spurs into its shoulders as it headed back to earth for the mark out. The horse then began to try to dislodge Scooter with more arching jumps as if on springs and circled near the chutes. It sometimes sprang straight up into the air and then twisted slightly with a whiplash motion. As he had envisioned, Scooter reared back and spurred up toward his rigging when Popcorn sprang into the air and then down into the horse's shoulders as its front feet landed. He became disoriented once, as all he saw was sky, but it didn't seem to matter. He realized his hat was gone. He felt the horse's hindquarters graze his head several times as he reared back in spurring. The strain on his arm became almost unbearable, his hand burned from the hard leather of the handhold, but he continued. At one point, he quickly adjusted to follow the horse as it changed direction slightly, but he spurred up again toward his rigging and out wide, flaring out his chaps, his head again snapping the horse's rear. He felt pieces of arena dirt hit his neck and head as if someone had flung it at him. He was aware of the height and swift movement and of Popcorn emitting throaty grunts as their struggle continued. He again lifted off with the horse and brought his spurring motion up and out with the upward force, now a completely natural action, his head again feeling the muscular buttocks as he reared back, seeing only sky.

Finally, when he thought he could hang on no longer, a loud horn sounded to signal the end of the eight-second ride. He then realized he had heard no noise other than his and popcorn's grunts during the ride; it was as if they had been transported into a vacuum. He became aware of a groundswell of noise from the crowd, which became increasingly louder as it surrounded him. He double grabbed the handhold, as Popcorn loped toward the fence. A pickup man tried to ride close enough for Scooter to grab and dismount, but the horse doubled back, nearly throwing him, although the man was able to trip the flank strap. It ran back along the fence, still bucking slightly, near the bleachers at the edge of the chutes, and Scooter grabbed the top pole as they went by in a violent dismount. One of his feet went through a square in the wire fence and he spun a little toward it before his momentum stopped. A large wooden splinter lodged in his arm. He was breathing hard and had to thread his boot and spur back out through the wire mesh. An older man, sitting in the bleachers with his family said, "Now that was a helluva ride, boy. You keep it up!"

Scooter nodded and said, "Thanks." He started back toward the chutes but stopped after a few steps and pulled the splinter out. It left some blood on the inside of his arm and he shook it several times as if that would erase the sting.

He jogged the rest of the way across part of the arena and on the way retrieved his hat. Scooter heard the announcer say something about a rider receiving a score of eighty-five, and he then heard loud applause from the crowd. *It must be a mistake. I bet they announce a correction.*

He climbed back onto the chutes and the stock contractor gave him a pat on the back, and said, "Way to use a horse, kid!" Scooter mutely nodded.

Sonny came and hit Scooter on the shoulder. "Somnabitch, man!" Scooter had never heard Sonny say many swear words and asked, "What?" He was in shock about what was going on.

"I never seen y'ride like that. Y'might as well go pro!" Sonny added.

"I dunno what happened. I just got in time or something. I tried to do what Emmett told those kids down on the reservation . . . at the jackpot," Scooter explained.

He went back into the alleyway, and some of the other bareback riders came over to give him "high-fives." He took his chaps off and then his spurs. He carefully folded and rolled his chaps and stowed them in his duffle bag. Sonny had gone over to the unsaddling chute and retrieved Scooter's rigging and brought it over.

"What was the score? Did they say eighty-five?" Scooter asked.

"Yeah! That's what I'm tryin' to tell youse. That Popcorn was on springs man. I see why the name. Y'knocked holes in the horse. Proud a ya out there!"

Scooter took a second look at Sonny. "Thanks, pard," he replied.

He watched some of the other rides and noted that one of the better riders from Central Wyoming College, named Jack, scored a 78. Johnny from his team had a dog of a horse and scored 65, although he had not used the horse very well either.

After he walked across part of the arena and back to the chutes, Scooter told him, "They should give you a re-ride." Johnny thought so too and checked with the judges. Scooter saw them shake their heads, indicating that the score stood.

In the final group, a rider from Montana State then scored an eighty-two and one from Wyoming, an eighty. So, his score was safe, at least until the next day. He smiled in relief. *Wow, so far, so good!* He pushed his glove into the handhold of the rigging and reverently tied it in place with a leather thong. He stuck it into the bag with the rest of his gear and cinched the bag shut.

Charlene joined him as he came out of the aisle behind the chutes with his duffle bag as he headed for his car. She put her arm through his but didn't say anything for a while. "So, you think you're a cowboy!"

He looked at her and noticed her eyes were sparkling. He then started to laugh, and she started to as well. They had to stop walking while laughter rolled over them.

Finally, after he had caught his breath, he said, "You're somethin'!" and they continued toward his car.

She continued, as they smiled at each other. "I'm quite amazed. "That was some ride!"

"Well, that's a really good horse, and felt great on her . . . just trying to do . . . well, what I'm supposed to, huh? I saw you riding Star out in the grand entry . . . I mean that should help settle her down, yes?"

"That's what I'm hoping," she said.

"The thing is, I'm hoping you do really well. You can you know."

"You have faith in me, huh?"

"Absolutely!" Let's both go for it!"

Charlene smiled her pleasure at him and nodded. "Okay cowboy, it's a deal!" After he had stowed his gear in the trunk, they went over to check on her horse. It was calmly standing, tied to her horse trailer. On the way back to the arena, Scooter spotted Zeke and Molly.

"Let's go over," Scooter said. "I'm assuming he's with Molly, the woman he met in Fort Collins. Guess he an' I are going to have to move up here."

Charlene looked at him and smiled. "Yeah, why don't you?"

"Yeah, maybe we will." He smiled back.

Scooter hollered at the couple. Zeke and Molly stopped to wait for them to approach. Molly had her auburn hair fixed into a single short braid and had on a crisp white blouse and jeans that showed off the flair of her hips. She had applied orange-colored lipstick and was wearing similarly colored earrings. Scooter thought she was more attractive than when he had viewed her at the house in Fort Collins as she came downstairs from a night with Zeke or earlier at the bus depot café while she had waited on them. He took a second glance at her almond-shaped brown eyes. He could see why she had

Zeke's attention

    Hey, dude, where y'been? Y' missed half the rodeo," Scooter said to Zeke.

    Zeke took in Scooter's comments, but said, "I want you both to meet Molly. Molly, this is Charlene . . . she's on the Colorado A&M rodeo team, and this is my sometimes pard, when he not snarky, Scooter, also from Southwestern."

    "We've met before, y'know," Scooter said to Molly.

    Molly didn't acknowledge this and instead said hello to both of them.

    "Have you been up yet?" Zeke asked.

    "Well, yeah. I had a pretty good horse, so did okay."

    "Like what?"

    "Like eighty-five."

    Zeke squinted at Scooter. "Eighty-five my ass! You mean fifty-eight, don't you?"

    "No, the judges went berserk and, well, maybe they're dyslexic. You know, I think someone scored a ninety-something on this horse at the National Finals, which for bareback is somethin'."

    Charlene smiled at their exchange. Scooter could see that Zeke didn't know what to think. "You better not be screwin' with me on this. Give me some details," he said.

    "Well," Scooter said, "I had that 'Popcorn' horse of Ridgeline's. And it's a very sweet horse, so I just reared back and spurred best I could." Zeke looked at Charlene, silently asking for corroboration.

    "He did too! I mean put on a great ride. It was amazing!" she said.

    "Foaming dogshit! No one's likely to touch that score. Wished I'd seen it! Give me five, my man," Zeke said. He and Scooter struck palms. "We'll have to bow down to you all week!"

    "Damn right!" Scooter said.

    "Does that mean you won?" Molly asked.

    "Well, there's some more good bareback riders tomorrow, 'cause there's only a single go-round, so we'll see," Scooter said.

    "I hope you win it. We'll put it in the college paper . . . front page. We never get much recognition down there at Southwestern," Zeke said.

    Zeke's enthusiasm was embarrassing Scooter, and he looked at Charlene and shrugged his shoulders. She was smiling and seemed amused by his discomfort.

    They continued toward the arena. "You know you're not up until tomorrow," Scooter said.

"Yeah. We're going over to the stands, then I'll be over to the chutes to help Sonny," Zeke said.

"Okay, I'm going over there now," Scooter said.

"Eighty-five! I can't get over it. We should all get together for dinner. You guys wanna?" Zeke asked.

"Sounds fine with me." Scooter said and looked at Charlene.

"I was supposed to get together with some of the other girls from my team, but I'm okay with it," and to Molly, she said, "nice to meet you."

Molly smiled at Charlene and said, "Same here."

As Charlene walked back to the chutes with Scooter, she said, "So, I thought they just met at the last rodeo. They act like a married couple."

Scooter thought she was quite perceptive. "They practically are, if you know what I mean.

"Oh! Well, she's quite attractive and seems nice," Charlene said.

"Yeah," Scooter said. "When we clumped into the bus depot that day in Fort Collins . . . I mean like five in the morning . . . Zeke didn't waste any time flirting with her and getting her phone number! I couldn't believe it . . . Sonny neither."

Charlene laughed at his explanation. "Well, honey, when you know, you know!"

Scooter nodded that he understood. "Yeah, I reckon so." He studied her, and they searched each other's eyes. "I better go find Sonny and make sure he's getting ready. Are you okay with your horse and everything?" he asked.

"Yeah, barrel racing isn't for a while yet, but I want to ride her around some and then warm her up. I'll see you after?" she asked.

"Okay, I'll help you take care of her after the rodeo or whenever. But, give 'em hell today."

Charlene smiled and nodded He walked over to the chutes and looked at the list of bareback scores that had been tacked on the side of the stairs leading to the announcer's booth. He tried to imprint the list in his mind with the top score by his name. While he was looking at the list, Jack, the contestant from Central Wyoming, looked over Scooter's shoulder. "You got lucky!" Jack said.

Scooter wasn't sure what he meant, and replied, "Yeah, I guess."

Jack continued, "They gifted you."

Scooter thought for a few seconds and felt a flash of temper. "So, take it up with the judges. Don't tell me about it!" The other rider started to walk away, and Scooter said, "What an asshole!"

Jack turned back and asked, "What'd you say?"

"I said, you're deaf and an asshole! What's wrong with you, anyway? If you have a gripe on the score, take it up with the judges."

"I should kick your ass for that remark."

The flash of anger surged again through Scooter and he was suddenly thinking about a roll of nickels in his fist. He then thought *diaphragm or throat*, as he and Sonny had discussed. "Let's go . . . right here!" He felt a hotness course through his veins, as he turned sideways and spread his feet for balance.

Jack gave Scooter a shove and Scooter grabbed onto one of Jack's arms to keep from landing against the holding pen fence. He found he could snake his other arm through and grabbed the back of Jack's neck. They pushed against each other, grunting. Scooter found there was no opportunity to throw a punch as he had envisioned. They wheeled around in a circle trying to find an advantage. Scooter repositioned his hand from the back of Jack's neck to his throat and pushed him against a board of the fence, trying to squeeze off his air. Scooter noticed Jack's breathing had become ragged, but then felt Jack's strength as he tried to lift Scooter off the ground. Scooter countered, and they again scuffled in a circle. Scooter planted a fist into Jack's ribs with his free arm but was rewarded with one from Jack in return. He grunted with the punch, then realized Jack was against the holding pen fence again and Scooter put as much pressure as he could against Jack's throat, causing his hat to mash against the fence. It fell to the ground. Scooter was aware of his head being close to Jack's ear and noticed a bead of sweat running down from his hair onto his cheek. Scooter realized that he had leverage and lifted Jack off the ground with his forearm on his throat. Jack's breathing was audible, gurgling. Scooter envisioned Jack turning blue, but he then tried to kick Scooter; his breath was sour. It seemed to Scooter they were locked in a stalemate, but having Jack against the fence, cutting off his air, was satisfying. Jack then tried to knee him, but Scooter turned slightly, and Jack's knee hit him on the outside of his thigh. He lunged harder against Jack's throat with his forearm.

Several contestants had sauntered over to see what was transpiring, but nobody intervened. Finally, another member of the Central Wyoming team pushed between them slightly. "Come on Jack, let it go, you'll get your butt thrown out of here." He placed a hand between them and on Scooter's shoulder. They slowly untangled and stood apart slightly, panting. Scooter eyed Jack to see if there was going to be any follow-up. Jack's face was flushed, and a string of snot hung above his lip.

"We'll run into each other again," Jack hoarsely said to Scooter.

"You can count on it!" Scooter said hotly. He felt like putting a knot on the side of Jack's red face with a fist. Jack turned away to retrieve his hat and Scooter finally relaxed. Jack looked back once, as he retreated down the aisle with his teammate. Scooter was still glaring at him.

"Jeez, what was that all about?" one of the other contestants asked.

"Oh, he has a problem with the scores. Guess his was too low." Scooter smiled as he said this.

"What an idiot," the other guy said.

Scooter walked down the alleyway behind the chutes, the adrenaline still coursing through his body. *What a knucklehead. He might not get in the money, depending on what happens tomorrow. That's the problem.* He worked his way back to the alleyway behind the chutes and found Sonny prepping his saddle.

"I just had a run-in with that Jack guy from Central Wyoming," Scooter said. "Claimed I got gifted on that horse. So, I told him to take it up with the judges. We started to fight right over by the holding pens, pushing on each other. I would've thrown a punch if I could've, but we just wrestled around. Anyway, turns out he's a big prick!"

Sonny stopped rubbing rosin on the swells of his saddle. "You shoulda called me. I'm a better fighter than you." He said it so matter-of-factly that Scooter had to laugh.

"You have no data on that," he said. "Well, if we run into him and his buddies we might have to see. Zeke's coming over in a minute. He had to escort that Molly woman to the stands."

Sonny just nodded and continued to get ready. Scooter knew Sonny was getting into his concentration mode. He watched for a few minutes trying to calm down. He felt sweaty from the tussle so he pulled a handkerchief out of a side-pocket of his vest and wiped the back of his neck and the inside of his hat. *This has been a day 'n a half already.*

CHAPTER TWENTY
HARD LEMONADE

Scooter sat on the top board of the fence, casually watching the timed events, but it wasn't long before saddle broncs were loaded into the chutes. He climbed down and checked the list of horses with the chute boss. "Looks like you're up in the second batch," he told Sonny.

Sonny, in what had become a common preamble before his ride, was sitting on the ground in his saddle as if they had been flung off together from some unmanageable bronc. He was diligently applying rosin between the leather of his chaps and the swells of the saddle. Scooter liked to watch Sonny's meticulous preparations; he spent a lot of time at it. After a few minutes of working the rosin, the friction between the leather increased until it squeaked. Satisfied, Sonny stiffly stood up, stretched and started warming up, first working on his quadriceps by pulling his foot back up toward his hip.

Zeke sauntered over behind the chutes and grabbed Sonny's hand to shake it, nearly tipping him over, and he hurriedly let loose of his foot.

"How 'bout this guy here in bareback? I can't get over it. I shoulda been here t' believe it," Zeke said.

"A pretty ride. That horse weren't no slouch neither . . . spring-loaded," Sonny said. By now, he had his feet wide apart and was attempting to touch the ground between them, his palms flat.

Scooter accepted this exchange with silent pride. He was glad his buds were proud of him. The three casually watched some of the team roping, but their attention was soon diverted as the saddle bronc event began. Several in the first group of riders scored in the high seventies.

"See I toll y'all, those northern boys can ride 'em," Zeke said. Scooter frowned as he absorbed Zeke's comment, as a rider from Wyoming was leading the event.

More horses were loaded into the bucking chutes, and Sonny watched for his mount; a large buckskin. He pointed to a chute and said, "This here's that Hard Lemonade, innit?" Zeke attached the thick cotton-woven rein to the horse's halter, and Scooter helped Sonny place the saddle and pull the cinches.

"This uns wooly, better t'ave named it Mammoth," Zeke observed.

"You should get the fur to fly off this one okay," Scooter added.

Sonny smiled. "Well, wish I'd seen it afore . . . how it goes." He plucked some hair out of the horse's dark mane and, after measuring back to the swells of the saddle, threaded the hair through the soft fibers of the hack-rein to mark the place for his grip. They watched the rider ahead of Sonny, but after several jumps out of the chute, the horse ducked back underneath him, slapping the rider lengthwise onto the ground. Scooter winced.

The chute hands came over to Sonny and he gently crouched down into the saddle and carefully placed his feet into the stirrups in his usual right-foot, left-foot sequence. He pulled himself down into the saddle using the swells, pulled his chaps away from his boots and spurs, and then positioned his hand with the rein out in front of him.

"Outside!" he said as he nodded.

The chute gate was flung open, and after the first jump, the horse took a hard left, which nearly unseated Sonny. He recovered and started to find his spurring rhythm when the horse feinted by dropping a shoulder. Sonny lost the swell of the saddle on one side, but recovered, only to have the horse duck the other way. Sonny lost a stirrup, was spun across the saddle in the opposite direction and came off the horse backwards. He landed on his feet, but his momentum caused him to do a complete backward somersault. He landed back on his feet as if concluding a gymnastic maneuver.

"Give 'im a ten!" someone at the chutes said loudly.

"Sheeit! That there was a nasty bronc," Zeke said.

"Very tricky," Scooter agreed. "Did you see those feints? He would drop a shoulder to get Sonny's momentum to go kind of sideways."

Sonny nonchalantly walked back to the chutes but cast several glances at the horse as it was being ushered out of the arena by the pick-up men.

"Helluva dismount, pard. You tryin' t' set a new standard?" Zeke asked, attempting to ease the disappointment of the buck-off.

Sonny just shook his head, "I never got with that horse at all . . . nothin'. If'n I could, I'd get back on en see what it is."

Zeke and Scooter helped Sonny retrieve his equipment. He stowed his chaps and rein in his duffle bag, wrapped the cinches and stirrups across the seat of the saddle, and tied them down to make a compact package.

"Let's stow this stuff." He and Scooter threw the gear onto their shoulders and then pushed their way through the other competitors toward the gate to the alleyway.

"I better go check in with Molly. I'll meet you guys here for the bull riding," Zeke said.

After placing Sonny's equipment into the car, Sonny said to Scooter, "Well, y'can't ride em all. That there's some a that reality, uh?"

"That bronc ducked a shoulder on ya and then would do the other one . . . zigzagging, y'know. Strong too. Well, you have tomorrow anyway," Scooter agreed.

"Yeah, I reckon," Sonny replied. They wandered back through the vehicles and horse trailers.

"Let's get a burger over at the concession stand. I'm famished," Scooter said.

They sat on the end of a bleacher munching their food. Scooter was turning over his confrontation with Jack; the thought about being gifted by the judges bothered him.

"That Jack bastard. I'm still ticked off about him. He thinks he is so friggin' good. It's the arrogance that ticks me off . . . that's it. It'd serve him right if he doesn't get in the money," Scooter said.

"Those other guys had, y'know, eighty, eighty-two fer good rides, but not the horse . . . yers weren't no gift. Quit stewin' about it," Sonny said. "You tol' 'im where to get off. You'd just get inta trouble, more fight'n. I'm still tryin' to figure how I can ride that wooly bastard horse. I never asked about the draw fer tomorrow but guess I should see what I got. I hope it's one that goes somewhat straight."

Scooter nodded and smiled at Sonny's comments, liking his pronunciation of the swear word. "Yeah, I guess. Straight's always good." Sonny chuckled at their conclusion. They went over to sit against the fence by the chutes in time for the barrel racing. Scooter was wondering if Charlene was nervous. He hoped she had a good run today, and then everything would be perfect. They watched the last of the calf roping and then the barrels were brought into the arena and placed in a triangular pattern for the event. This and goat tying were the only two girl's events. Scooter thought barrel racing was slightly dangerous. Not the part where the horse and rider went around the barrels, although a rider could go down under a horse if it slipped, but when they went racing out of the arena through the gate. He often wondered if anyone had ever been run over before the contestants could rein-in their horses.

One after another, the girls rode the figure-eight patterns in the arena. A few knocked over a barrel—a five-second penalty—in an attempt to shave off a few milliseconds. Scooter patiently waited, observing the other contestants, as one after the other raced through the arena. The best score early in the contest was posted at 16.2 seconds. Scooter stood up from crouching as Charlene's name was announced and then Star thundered into the arena with Charlene riding low and forward, as they raced hard for the first barrel. The dirt of the arena sprayed out from Star's hooves in a wake. Scooter moved forward a few steps to have a clearer view. They made another quick turn on the second barrel. Charlene seemed to be riding as if possessed. He watched, holding his breath as they made a final quick turn. They were close and hit the barrel slightly, but it stayed upright. Charlene again rode bent forward and low; her face nearly in Star's mane as she spurred the horse, looking for speed. Scooter observed her lithe figure. *She can ride! Looks really good on a horse. Some cowgirl.* He was relieved that Charlene and Star hadn't knocked over the last barrel and received a time penalty.

Her time was just under 16.3 seconds and good enough for third place. Scooter hoped it would hold up through several of the last competitors for the first go-round.

He looked over at Sonny. "Wow! She ran good today."

Sonny just nodded, but after a few seconds said, "She ain't too bad a rider." Scooter figured this was a strong compliment, coming from Sonny.

The last competitor's run was near seventeen seconds. Scooter nodded to himself in satisfaction. The barrels were removed from the arena, and Zeke came over to sit with them for the bull riding. However, instead of sitting inside the arena along the fence, they and the other contestant spectators moved on top of it or on the other side for safety.

Scooter noticed that the low, throaty clank of the bells grew more persistent as the ropes were being prepped with rosin and then set on the bulls that had been pushed forward into the chutes

"That clankin' seems like a harbinger to a bad storm," Scooter observed.

"I don't know about that, but it gets me to itchin'. My riding hand starts to flex all by itself. It's a-lookin' fer the glove y'know," Zeke said.

Sonny laughed at Zeke's comment, "Y'kin itch all y'want on that '04' bull tomorrow!"

Scooter liked Zeke's attitude about rodeo—to be somewhat happy-go-lucky, even though he became very nervous before a ride. Guess most bull riders do though. The bulls seemed to Scooter to be quite rank, quickly dispatching the contestants. One of the riders was thrown under his bull and was stepped on in the process of the bull trying to put a horn into him. The rider rolled into a ball to try to protect himself, and then hurriedly limped out of the arena, as the bullfighters took the bull away. Scooter had been on a few bulls in his early days of rodeo but didn't miss the event now. There were other things on his mind now though, and it wasn't the bull riding competition.

"I'm going to help Charlene take care of her horse. She can give me a ride back to the motel from there." He handed Sonny his car keys.

Sonny gave Scooter a hard look and then put the car keys in his pocket. "Be careful out there."

"We're still goin' to meet later for dinner, right?" Zeke asked.

"Yeah, we wanna get to know this Molly woman, to warn her away from you," Scooter said. "She doesn't know what she's getting into. So, give our motel, The Peak, a call and we can link up."

CHAPTER TWENTY-ONE
CHARLENE AND SCOOTER

Charlene was walking Star in the area behind the chutes and stock pens when Scooter ambled over to her. "Okay, you cowgirl . . . a helluva a run," he said, as he approached her.

She smiled at him, "Finally we had a pretty good go! I'm very proud of my girl here!"

"Well, don't give her all the credit! You rode really well . . . you look great on a horse is what I was thinking. Besides, you're in the money today so that's good! You want some help in taking care of her?" he asked.

Charlene smiled at the compliment. "I think she's cooled plenty, let's go over to the trailer."

Scooter followed alongside the horse and helped Charlene remove the saddle and blanket. Charlene brushed Star to help dry the sweat and then loaded her into the trailer.

"You and I have had a pretty good day; don't you think so?" she said.

"I do. I mean absolutely a very good day!" he said, smiling at her.

"I want you to know something . . . when you did that bareback ride, you stunned me. I had like tears in my throat when I saw you do it! You're going places. I hope you take me with you." He took her hand and stopped. Her words brought out sudden, strong emotions in him. He looked away, afraid she might see his soft side. A few seconds went by before he could talk.

"Thanks. That means a lot to me." Charlene squeezed his hand and they looked at each other. She rose up on her toes and kissed him gently on the lips.

"Such a cowboy," she murmured.

He returned the compliment. "Such a cowgirl and you're going places too, y'know."

"Well, I hope so."

"Yeah, the ability to compete at the highest level, huh?"

Charlene stopped what she was doing and turned to him. "Single-minded Scooter . . . I see how it is with you and I see that's a great way to look at it!" He nodded, and they smiled at each other with their understanding of the quest. "Come on," said Charlene, "let's take care of my horse." They unloaded Star from the trailer at stables west of the rodeo grounds and put her into a stall. Scooter placed hay in the feeder and ran fresh water to fill a large plastic barrel wired to the corner of the stall. Charlene brought out a small bucket of oats and poured them into a trough. She stood patting Star's neck and talking to her, while the horse munched on the grain. Scooter liked how Charlene felt about her horse. She looked over at him and saw that he was gazing at them.

"What are you thinking?" she asked.

"Well, I like this . . . you with your horse," Scooter said.

"So, when are we studying?" she asked.

"I guess we can right now if you want. I gave Sonny my car keys."

Charlene studied Scooter for a few seconds. He wondered what she was thinking.

"Come on, help me unhitch the trailer," she said.

They took her pickup back to town, bypassing the rodeo arena.

"Are we going to the library?" Scooter smiled at his question.

"Yes, you could call it that." She gave him a mischievous smile.

He wasn't sure what she meant, but said, "Stop by my room a minute." Charlene slowed her truck, angled it over to the driveway, and turned into the Peak parking lot. Scooter hustled into his motel room and into the bathroom to pee, and then picked through the notebooks on the desk and pulled out the one for chemistry. He was nearly to the door when he pulled up short. He paused and then turned around, going over to his overnight bag and fished around inside for the box of condoms. He opened it up and took out several packages and put them into his pocket, telling himself: *Just be prepared.* Yet, wondered if he should stop everything and back up. *She would think I'm the biggest chicken there ever was.* He jumped into the passenger side of Charlene's truck and they drove another several blocks to the Palomino Motel.

He lagged behind by the door of her truck. "Come on, cowboy . . . don't get shy on me now," she said.

"Well, this is a weird library. But naw, it's too late for gettin' shy," he said, and then followed her into the room. She placed a bag of gear in a corner of the room underneath a rack of hangers where she had hung some clothes.

"Are you still ready to take some chances?" she asked.

The room was more lavish than his and Sonny's at The Peak. The bed was large and had a shiny, gold spread. It dominated the room. The carpet felt thick. "Well, I've thought about you a lot since we met down in Fort Collins. I mean we've been going along pretty fast . . . taking chances. Don't you think so?" He sat down on a chair near a small desk.

She came over, around the bed. "Yes, we've been taking a few, but it hasn't seemed like it's been too risky yet, does it? I mean it hasn't felt forced or strange to me. Has it for you?"

"No . . . well, I don't know how to express it exactly. I mean it seems like we mesh or something. I can just be myself with you."

Charlene kissed his neck and ear. "That reminds me, you said you had written a love note and didn't have enough nerve to send it."

He looked up at her and thought for a minute whether he wanted to tell her. Suddenly, it seemed quite mushy. "Yeah, well, not sure if I want to now."

"Well, you trapped yourself by telling me about it," she smiled.

"Yeah, I know . . . I'll tell you what, maybe I can write it for you."

Charlene had closed the curtains, so Scooter switched on the desk lamp. He got out a piece of motel stationery from the drawer and found a pen. "I have to think exactly how it went. You know, when we were riding back to Saguache that Monday, one of the guys on our team had said that someone here was mad at me for trying to horn in on him, that he was sweet on you. It bothered me. I was working on an English essay, so started writing this . . . desperate, I guess."

Charlene laughed at his explanation. "Well, I need to see it now. You have me very curious about you writing a poem!"

"You might be disappointed in my ability," he told her.

"Hmm, I doubt it"

He wrote in rounded cursive:

I know someone,
Who has shining, raven-black hair,
Magical eyes that ignite my soul,
Dusky rose lips, my heart's desire.
Taking chances opens destiny's door.
He signed it: *To my Daawlin' Charlene, Scooter*

Charlene had been standing behind him with her hands on his shoulders as he wrote. She took the paper from him and read what he had written, then looked at him and smiled through shining eyes.

"You're multi-dimensional, aren't you?"

"You bring out a softer, sentimental side of me."

She came closer again and started to massage his shoulders. She again kissed the lobe of his ear and then moved to his neck. It felt nice; she tickled his ear with her lips.

"Dusky rose lips, huh?" I like how you said it. Come on, I'll give you the red-carpet treatment." She turned off the desk lamp and then led him over to the bed. With some effort, he pulled off his boots and then lay down on his stomach.

"I can't give you the red-carpet treatment this way. Take off your shirt!"

He turned to look at her and then complied as she helped him. "It feels good to get that sweaty thing off," he said and threw it over the chair by the desk.

Charlene straddled him across his buttocks and started working on his shoulders and back with her hands. "Oh wow . . . that feels so good," he murmured.

"You been lifting weights or what? You're thick through here." She kneaded his shoulders and triceps.

"Yeah, lifting weights . . . you're hired," he said absently as he relaxed under her touch.

He nearly fell asleep as she massaged his shoulders, neck, and back, but finally roused himself. "Okay, your turn." He rolled over onto his back and pulled her down to him for a kiss. Her hair tickled his face. He kissed her eyes and then their lips met again. He thought her's were so soft, so compliant. They opened for him.

"You smell nice, where do you get that fresh smell from?" he asked. "You bring it in from the country somewhere?"

"Yes, I go get it just for you," she laughed.

"Funny girl." He lifted out from under her and traded places. He began to massage her neck and shoulders.

She stopped him and said, "Just a moment," and removed her shirt. She lay down on the bed in her bra. He began to gently massage her shoulders, then moved his hands down along her back. Scooter noticed that Charlene had a ridge of muscle that extended from her shoulder to her upper back and there was some muscle definition on her triceps. He was enthralled with her form.

"You've been lifting weights too . . . or something!"

"Buckets of oats," she said absently. Scooter thought her answer was hilarious and had to stop his massage to laugh. Charlene turned her head to look at him.

"You're funny!" She smiled and lay back down again so he could continue the massage, and he worked on her shoulders, gently kneading the muscles there.

"Does it feel nice?" he asked.

She had her eyes closed and just said, "Ummm."

He couldn't get enough of the essence of her—the fresh smell that he liked. It reminded him of freshly cut cucumbers. He kissed her hair, took a breath through it, and then kissed her neck, the area behind her ear.

After a few minutes of gently working any tightness out of her shoulders and neck and running his hand under the strap of her bra several times, he unfastened the clasp.

That got her attention and she turned toward him slightly "Do you have anything?" she asked.

"Well . . . um, do you mean what I'm thinking, like from before up at Horsetooth?"

"Yes."

"Okay . . . well, I have a lot." He continued to rub her back where her bra strap had been.

She twisted her head farther to look at him and teased, "Scooter! You're very ambitious."

He felt his face redden. "Shoot, I didn't know how many. I mean . . . well, hell, I might make love to you everywhere." He laughed at his attempt to lighten the moment.

Charlene laughed, too, and kissed him. "You sweet boy." She got up from the bed and went into the bathroom. He was wondering what was next.

"Come in here for a minute," she called out.

He got up from the bed and walked over to the bathroom door where there was more light from a small window. She had turned the shower on and had stripped down to her panties. They were pale blue with darker lace around the edges and looked silky. Scooter was struck dumb for a second. He studied her form, as it made a magical impression on him; her pert breasts with their erect nipples, and then his eyes swept her length. She had seemed willowy to him, although he already had been conscious of her rounded, firm butt. Her curves were more than he had anticipated though--the long, gentle curve of thighs and reverse curve of calves.

"Wow!" he finally said.

"Come on, I'll help you," she said.

He peeled off his socks and she helped him unbuckle his belt and he pushed his jeans down. He threw them out the bathroom door. He was aroused; there was no hiding the fact—the front of his underwear had been transformed into a small tent.

"What a cowboy!" Charlene said.

"Yeah . . . well," he shrugged self-consciously and smiled.

As the water warmed, she pushed her panties down and stepped in. "Come on, the water's fine," she said.

He threw off his underwear and stepped in behind the plastic curtain to be with her. They embraced and kissed with the water running over them. She took the soap and washed his chest then turned him to wash his back. She then turned him around and moved down. "Scooter, you bad boy, you!" she teased.

He looked at her and smiled. "It's like steel today, but you did it— you're doing it." She embraced him again and he could feel it against her thigh and then her pubic mound.

Charlene felt for him, and he flinched. His reaction to her touched was involuntary and immediate.

"Oh hell!" He recovered slightly and looked at her. "Sorry. I told you before, it's like it has a hair-trigger with you."

"It's okay, big boy, we'll get it back! Now it's your turn." She gave him the washcloth and soap. He gently washed her back, working down over her buttocks and the backs of her legs. He had to come up for air, as the stream of water was on his face. He turned her, washed her neck, and slowly worked gently over her breasts.

Her erect nipples enticed him. It seemed that her upturned breasts were sending him a silent invitation of, "Take me!" He leaned down and took one of her nipples into his mouth. She placed her hand on the back of his head, increasing the pressure. He needed air, so moved to resume kissing her ear and then her lips. But his siege wasn't over, and he again washed her breasts and then stomach. "You . . . need to . . . stop for a minute!" He did as she asked, noticing that she was breathing hard. He was aroused again. She touched him. "See, I told you so."

"Yes, you have me like a stallion."

She smiled at his comment. "Stallion, huh? Isn't that good?" They got out to dry.

"I think the answer to that is, 'very,' now that I think of it." Charlene laughed. He took her towel and dried her back and front. "You're very beautiful," he said.

"Thank you. I'm glad you think so! I want to be for you." She smiled at him and then used a blow dryer on her hair, while he finished drying himself.

"I wasn't going to get my hair wet, but forgot," she said.

He laughed. "Yeah, I forgot everything but you."

She led him over to the bed. His towel dropped off part way there beside the clump of his jeans and socks, and he left it. She pulled back the spread and the blankets and threw them off into a heap at the foot of the bed, then left her towel on the floor and lay down. Her nakedness mesmerized him in the half-light. She wasn't shy with him, showing her full length. He joined her, and she pulled him to her for a kiss. He could feel her curves and edges. The sheets felt satiny to his nakedness, she felt satiny.

"You know, you told me how that bareback ride made you feel? I liked that you said that to me . . . that you let me see inside. But, you know . . . I want you to know how your ride was awesome too! Did you know that? That you were so . . . so capable, so cowgirl!"

Charlene looked at him, waiting. It seemed to him that she was turning something over in her mind. She pulled his head toward her and kissed him. "Do you know that I'm in love with you? It becomes more all the time?"

"No, I didn't know, but think it's become mutual. I reckon now we have to say it's getting pretty big." Remembering her previous comment that it was love, but they didn't know how large it was.

Charlene laughed and pulled him to her, kissing him more intensely with her lips, then her open mouth and her tongue. He moved against her length and noticed her smoothness, but also her breast against him, the curve of her thighs, the point of a hip.

He said, "Just a moment, I have to get something." He retrieved his jeans and dug in one of the pockets for a package.

Charlene watched him and then said, "Come here with that."

They kissed, and he felt her full lips and then her tongue again. A chill of excitement ran through him. She pulled him further onto her and wrapped her legs around him. He felt them merge into a single being and then felt her fingernails on his back. He needed no further urging, as if he was a horse responding to the spur. Charlene murmured, "Oh honey!" Then louder, exclaimed, "God damn, Scooter . . . what you're doing!" He liked what he was doing, what they were doing.

Afterward, she asked, "Did you like it?"

He laughed. "What do you think? 'Like' is an understatement! I wanted to last longer, though. I've never done this before."

"I figured," she said. "You know, I wanted to tell you . . . well, I thought I was in love once. I thought someone loved me."

"It's okay. Your past doesn't matter to me about that." She turned her head and kissed him.

"Do you know what love is?" she asked.

Scooter didn't say anything for a few seconds, pondering the question He looked at her in the half-light of the room. "I wondered about it with you. You were giving me clues, but I need a lot of data. I wondered how a person would know about love, like you and me. I mean to be sure. How do you know?"

Charlene mulled his question over, and then said, "You make me happy . . . to see you, to talk with you. Something blossomed. Like I said, you stirred me, and I knew I had found something special."

"When did I stir you?" he asked.

"I don't know if I should tell you that," she teased, "you'll know too much about me."

"I need to know," he said. "Come on, I bared my soul with that poem."

She laughed at his comment. "Well, you know it was gradual, but I liked it when you helped me with my horse in Fort Collins. I thought you were so funny. And, well . . . for another thing, you didn't feel sorry for yourself after getting injured. You didn't make it a big deal. Then when you kissed me at the stable and again up at Horsetooth. All those things," she said.

Keep talking," he said, "I like it."

"Your eyes stir me too. I like the light in them for me . . . your smile sparks me! I think you're handsome . . . kind of a hunk," she said. "But that's enough for now. I don't want to give you the big head." He chuckled and then kissed her, as she kissed him back.

"Talk about a big head, but it ain't where you think," he teased.

"You've become a bad boy," she smiled. "But making love is part of it too, that we love each other that way!" They kissed again, and he started moving down her neck again and then to her breasts. "You know, honey, you're going to start something again," she said. He stopped and came up for air.

"Yeah, I want to, but I better get back over to the motel. It's getting late. Sonny's going to be wondering about me . . . us." He got up and started to round up his clothes.

Charlene watched him and said, "I like you naked."

He looked back at her lying on the bed. "It's mutual. You don't know how damn good-looking you are!" After getting dressed, he came back over to the bed and bent down over her, gently placing his hand on her cheek. She had thrown a blanket over herself. Her dark hair was splayed out on the pillow; her lips curved into a smile.

He gazed at her and said, "This ain't over, y'know."

"My, as I said before, such an ambitious boy." They both laughed.

CHAPTER TWENTY-TWO
CAMARADERIE

Scooter used his key to open the door to the room. Sonny was reclining on the bed with an open notebook on his lap.

He studied Scooter. "Hey pard, I thought maybe y'fell in a trap."

"Well, yeah, something like that. Has Zeke phoned yet?"

"Naw, I haven't heard from 'im. I've been tryin' to get a leg up on you with this range management stuff."

"I better get some studying done as well, but I need a shower and change of clothes first."

Scooter pulled off his boots, then pulled off his shirt and jeans and went into the bathroom. Scooter was feeling a little guilty about leaving Sonny at the rodeo. The lovemaking with Charlene was a new feeling and, like he had felt with Katherine after their heavy make-out session, it seemed he had gone past a point of no return in his life—a loss of innocence. He had a slight feeling of regret, but on the other hand, the sexuality of Charlene excited him, He liked getting between her long legs. Well, it had to happen sometime. Cripes, I'm not a high schooler. Sonny would just have to cope with the situation. He came out of the bathroom and pulled clean underwear out of his duffle bag.

"Did you check what horse you drew?" he asked.

"Yeah, it's a big black called North Country. I asked some a them stock contractor guys 'bout it. Sposed t' be a pretty good trip."

"Well, that sounds good." Scooter pulled on a pair of fresh jeans and started to thread his belt through the loops. He opened his chemistry notes and a final exam study sheet and then sat down on his bed. He watched Sonny for a few minutes. He was propped against a pillow and the headboard of his bed. His lips moved slightly as he read.

"You know, we're good buds, right?" Scooter asked. Sonny looked up from his notes, waiting for Scooter to continue. "You ever had a girlfriend? I mean a steady one?"

"Why y'want'n t'know that?"

"Well, Charlene and I . . . it just changes things some, like how we've been hanging out together . . . y'know, traveling to the different rodeos, concentrating on our events and not much else. But I really like her. So, I just was wonderin'."

Sonny didn't say anything for a while, and Scooter saw that he was thinking about something. Finally, Sonny said, "I knew it was happening with youse. But, y'know that place we went up to on the rez, the big pine trees and the crick?"

"Yeah?"

"I used to take a girl there. We were in high school together t'start with. Her name was Noreen Doeskin."

"Where is she now?"

"Um . . . she was kilt in a car wreck. Her uncle was drivin'. They said he'd been drinkin'. He en one of his kids survived it. "Scooter suddenly noticed a scuff mark on one of his boots and wondered how it had gotten there. He didn't know how to respond to Sonny's revelation.

Finally, he said, "Sonuvabitch! You never said . . . I'm sorry, man."

"Well, it's been a while now. I'm tryin' to forget, but never will."

"Would you and she have married?"

"I don't know . . . we thought we would, maybe someday." They both returned to their notes. After a few minutes, Sonny said, "I never took anyone there since, till we went up the other day."

Scooter was touched by Sonny's admission and realized he had been given a gift. "I like that you took me," he said. "I felt it was a special place . . . thanks!" Sonny didn't say anything, and Scooter continued. "You know, a buddy or pardner is one thing, but a girl—a special girl—that's a whole 'nother matter. You know that."

"I know it," Sonny replied, "well, she's hot for ya, so guess I'm okay with it. Nothin' a guy kin do anyways bout it! Y'know?" Scooter nodded and both of them went back to their notes.

After several minutes, Sonny said, "You know that girl at the rez . . . Lisal?"

"Yeah?"

"She's Noreen's cousin. Our families want us to hook up. We been out a few times, y'know . . . well, more'n that."

"I was right. She has feelings for you," Scooter said. Sonny just shrugged.

They continued to study for a while. "Wonder where that Zeke is. My belly thinks my throat's been cut," Scooter said.

Sonny looked up and laughed at Scooter's remark. They continued to read through their class notes."

"Let's go over this stuff like we usually do this evenin'. Huh?" Sonny suggested.

"Be a good idea, we'll quiz each other, 'cause that always lets me know what I don't!" Scooter said.

Sonny chuckled at this. "Yeah, what a guy don't is about right."

The telephone rang. It was Zeke. He and Molly were on their way.

Scooter then called Charlene, "Hey, you hungry?"

"Famished!"

"Must be all the exercise you been doing."

"As I said, you're a bad boy," she teased.

"I know . . . see what you've done? You heard from Squirrel?"

"She's coming up tomorrow for the rodeo. I told her to get here for lunch and we would have a little reunion. Okay?" she said.

"Yeah, that'd be nice for the four of us. Is that what you meant?"

"Uh-huh! Well, get over here."

After he had hung up, he said, "We'll follow Zeke in my car. He's just got that truck and I don't want to ride in the back."

Zeke honked for them, and they went out to the parking lot. Scooter told him to follow. Molly was sitting close to Zeke.

"Looks like a two-headed driver in there," Sonny noted, "We coulda all fit!"

Sonny and Scooter clambered into his car, and Zeke followed in his truck as they drove down the street to the "Palomino." Scooter parked out in front of Charlene's room and got out. He knocked on her door.

She opened it and said, "Come in for a second." Scooter noticed her dark-red lipstick and she had added bluish eyeshadow, which enhanced the bluish color of her eyes. She blended the effect with a sparkly blue-green blouse. Scooter stopped mid-stride to view her.

"Judas Priest, Charlene, you look fantastic," he said.

She smiled her thanks, and said, "Come here! Let's do this for ourselves. Then we don't need to worry about it when we're with the others!"

She placed her arms around his neck and they kissed.

"Love is sweet, isn't it?" he said.

"Yes . . . very," she replied.

He felt her completely against his length, as if they had melted together. He ran his thumb down the length of her back and onto her buttocks. Their closeness and feeling her against him caused an immediate, striking reaction.

"Jeez, it doesn't take much!" he said.

She smiled and said, "I know. I think we're good for each other that way. But here's what I wanted to ask you. There's a rodeo dance at the college tonight. Have you thought about going?"

"I haven't. Do you want to go?"

"Well, I could teach you a little two-step. I mean we could go for a little while. I know we're supposed to study some too."

"There's some issues you need to know about. I mean besides my terrible dancing. I had a run-in with a guy from Central Wyoming . . . another bareback rider, Jack. Do you know him?"

"I don't think so," she said.

"He accused me of getting a gift in the bareback riding and we had some strong words and pushed each other around some. Just so you know. And what if that blockhead Billy's there and wants to dance with you . . . I mean I'm just thinking ahead."

Charlene laughed. "Blockhead . . . huh? "I guess nothing's ever simple. Look, I can take care of Billy, but if that Jack person is there can you be diplomatic?"

He laughed. "It's kind of late for that, but maybe I can defer things."

"Well, that's what I want you to do."

A car horn honked. "That's Zeke. Guess he's hungry! Okay, daawlin', as you wish." She smiled and kissed him again.

Sonny had gotten into the back seat of the car, so Scooter opened the passenger door for Charlene.

She said hello to Sonny. He responded "*Dahnzo!* It means hello," he explained.

"Don't believe him, he's always teaching me Apache swear words and claiming it's all nice stuff, like 'how are you,' see you later' stuff like that," Scooter said.

Charlene laughed. "You guys are a pair."

They left the parking area, with Zeke and Molly following. The restaurant was busy. They waited a while, talking in the foyer. Scooter observed Molly, trying to get a feeling of what she was like. She was attractive, as he already knew, with her blonde hair and brown eyes, but seemed reserved. She held Zeke's hand, and he was attentive to her. When they weren't holding hands, his hand was on her shoulders.

They talked some about bull riding. Zeke was hoping he could get an eight-second ride in, as it had been a few rodeos since he had. "Bull ridin's a hoot, but sometimes a tough way to get excitement," he observed.

Molly commented that it seemed risky and that there must be another way to get excitement in a person's life.

Sonny gave his short opinion that riding saddle broncs was a safer way to get excitement. Molly thought this was also dangerous.

"I can think of one thing that's ridin' and is pretty exciting, and it ain't bull ridin' either," Zeke teased.

Molly hit him on the shoulder, as the others chuckled.

Charlene asked Molly what she did. Molly mentioned she did wait-ressing and took night-classes in the business department at the college. They talked about some of the courses.

Finally, the hostess told them that they had a small booth if they wanted to squeeze into that.

"We better take it, or we'll be here all night," said Scooter.

Scooter, Charlene, and Sonny squeezed into one side, and Molly and Zeke got in on the other. Scooter quipped, "We'll just eat small meals, but lots of courses,"

"We can all share," Charlene said and laid her hand gently on the inside of Scooter's leg. He looked at her and she smiled at him. "Zeke said you're from the Jicarilla Reservation. What's it like?" Molly asked Sonny.

Sonny paused and then said, "Well, it's pretty wild out there yet. Our runnin' water's a crick, en we routinely go out on weekends en raid the white eyes, you know, the farms and small towns, take some prisoners, 'specially the better lookin' women. We're doing this to integrate ourselves into society!"

Molly looked at Zeke. "They do, too, I heard about it," he said.

Scooter came to the rescue. "These guys are such bullshitters, don't believe it." Everyone laughed. He continued, "I was there a couple of weeks ago. It's nice country and nice people, large valleys and mountains."

"I think I had this kidnap story spun on me several weeks ago," Char-lene observed.

"I've never been in that part of the country," Molly said to Sonny.

"Well, y'all are welcome to visit, en I'll give youse a tour," he said.

They continued to talk as they ate. Scooter and Charlene shared some of their food.

Scooter asked Zeke and Molly, "Are you guys going to the dance at the college?"

"We thought we would for somethin' to do . . . maybe for a while. Are you guys going?" Zeke answered.

"Maybe. What do you think?" he asked Sonny.

"I ain't too interested."

"Come on, go with all of us for a while. It'll do you good to get your mind off the feeds and range courses and that saddle bronc, or whatever. We won't stay long. I still have to study too."

"I'll think about it," Sonny said, which meant to Scooter that he likely wouldn't.

"I offered to teach Scooter the two-step. My offer is good for you also," Charlene said.

"Good luck on that one," Zeke said. "These guys both have two left feet."

"I'll go just to see, not fer long though," Sonny said to Charlene. "Scooter's right, I gotta get some fresh air in my mind."

"Just so y'all know, I had a tussle with that Jack guy from Central Wyoming, who thought I got gifted from the judges on that ride," Scooter said. "So, if he and his cronies are there . . . well, just so you're all aware."

"Let's not have trouble," Charlene said. "It just puts a pall on the whole thing." She squeezed Scooter's leg.

"Yeah, maybe I can defer it, so we don't get put on suspension. Well, I may be worrying for nothing," he said.

"Make sure I know 'im," Zeke said.

"He's a little runt of a guy, like t' blow over in a stiff breeze," Sonny offered.

Both Zeke and Scooter laughed at Sonny's description and the girls smiled, not understanding the joke.

"Yeah, runt is right. He didn't feel so runty this afternoon," Scooter said. He again was conscious of Charlene's hand on his thigh and he laced his fingers with hers. "Well, let's get doin' something."

The boys settled the bill between them and Molly and Charlene thanked them for dinner. Scooter said to Zeke and Molly, as they walked to the separate vehicles, "We'll probably see y'all over there."

Scooter could hear the Western music as they approached the ballroom door. He paid, and they received a red stamp on their hands as a receipt.

Charlene grabbed Scooter's hand. "Come on you guys, I said I would." She showed them how to step to the beat of the music and then slide into a step, and that a person could zigzag across the entire dance floor that way. She took Scooter out on the floor and he thought he was kind of getting it.

They came back to where Sonny stood, and she offered to take him out as well. He declined, but Charlene grabbed his arm and pulled him out onto the dance floor anyway. Scooter thought this was amusing. Sonny looked quite stiff as he held his arms out as an offering to Charlene. But then, as Scooter was standing at the edge of the crowd, he noticed Jack with a group on the other side of the dancers. Jack had already seen him, so Scooter just nodded at him. Jack glared back, but then turned to the group of people. *I better stay alert. I don't want that guy blind-siding me.*

Charlene and Sonny came back to where Scooter was standing. He told Sonny about the group and which one was Jack.

"Act like they aren't here," Charlene said and grabbed Scooter's hand. "Come on!" She and Scooter danced to another song. He liked her easy movements.

"I saw Billy over there, but he has a date, I think, so we don't have to worry about him coming over," she said.

"Yeah, I hope he marries her," Scooter said.

His comment brought out peals of laughter from Charlene, and then he joined her. They had to stop dancing to recover.

Zeke and Molly came over and they talked for a few minutes. However, when the music started up again, they swung away. Scooter envied how they smoothly glided over the floor. He told Charlene, "If they can, we can . . . well, with more practice I reckon."

"Hey, you're getting it."

As promised, they left after about an hour. Scooter was trying to figure out how, and if, he could go back to Charlene's room with her, but Sonny said, "Let's quiz each other on that range management stuff so's tomorrow I kin concentrate on bronc ridin.'"

Scooter reluctantly said, "Okay," and to Charlene said, "I'll go out with you in the morning to help with your horse if you want. We should do some more studying sometime."

"We can go over to the student union after for some breakfast and study there. Sonny can join us if he wants," she said. Sonny didn't respond. Scooter thought it was getting too complicated for him. Scooter absorbed this information and, in the process, didn't see any possibilities of being alone with Charlene. They approached her motel and he maneuvered his car into the driveway. She got out saying she would see them tomorrow. Scooter sat rooted in the driver's seat of the car.

Finally, he said out the window, "Hey, see you later." She waved back at him.

CHAPTER TWENTY-THREE
EARLY IN THE MORNING

Sonny and Scooter opened their range management chapter summaries that had been provided by the instructor for the final exam. Scooter asked Sonny questions, and then they reversed roles for the next chapter.

After several hours, Sonny said, "My brain's fried on this, an' it's late."

"Well, it might be good to let this vegetate some. Fried brain ain't too good at this stage of our lives."

"Ya well, I need to keep it unfried."

Scooter laughed at Sonny's comment. "You can hit it some tomorrow too. I gotta hit chemistry, and Charlene wants me to do something with her on an essay. I'm glad I don't have a bareback horse tomorrow. There're still some good riders, so guess I'll see if my score holds up."

"That score should, but guess y'never know," Sonny replied. "Be nice ifn y'could win it. With this many riders, it'll pay good. By the way, doan let it go to your head, but yer woman, that Charlene, she's okay. I might'a learned to dance a little."

"Yeah, good teacher," Scooter smiled.

It was near midnight, and they both got ready for bed, stripping down to their underwear.

Scooter woke up, not knowing what time it was. He went into the bathroom to pee and looked at his watch. It was nearly three o'clock. He went back to bed, thinking about Charlene. Once he started reviewing their love-making and how nice it had felt he was wide-awake. *Taking chances . . . the destiny thing, huh?* He quietly got out of bed and took the note with the phone number of her motel from his wallet. He hesitated, remembering that it wasn't a direct line. He decided he would have to go for it and walk over. Scooter went into the bathroom, shaved and brushed his teeth. He ran a comb through his hair, but the flip that curled upwards near his ear was stubborn. He took several condom packages out of his duffle bag. He hesitated, as it seemed he was planning to commit a crime. He stuffed them into his pants pocket.

He slowly opened the motel room door, trying to see if Sonny was awake. A long mound on Sonny's bed was evident in the light from the street. *He wouldn't make a very good scout, at least in the old days.* Scooter softly closed the door and started walking along the street. It was very quiet, and cooler than he had anticipated. He felt like running, then thought *a good way to get arrested, and thinking of which, I hope no cops come by.*

Scooter tapped on Charlene's door. He didn't hear her inside, so rapped louder, but was cautious about making too much noise. Finally, he saw her open the curtain slightly. He heard her take off the security chain and she opened the door.

"Scooter, you nut. It's like the middle of the night!" she said.

"I know, but I got to thinking about you. I think we need to . . . well, do some studying."

"You're something!" Charlene said. "But I wondered what you were going to do. I could nearly see the wheels turning in that head of yours when you left me off tonight, I mean last night. You stud you . . . not enough, huh?"

"You started me now, so it's your fault," he said.

She laughed. "You're cold, so get undressed and into bed. I have to take care of you."

He complied, and she took her nightgown off and got into bed in just her panties. She snuggled against him.

"This is sweet," he said. They kissed, and he felt her under the blanket. "I liked it tonight at dinner. I liked the undercurrent of knowing how you feel about us, and that you know how I feel about you, yet we don't need to express it. I mean we can in small things. I see your glances, your smiles, and I feel your hand on my leg."

"I know," she said and hushed him with a kiss. She bit his lip and then put her tongue into his mouth. They latched onto each other that way until they had to recover.

Charlene looked at him, pushed against him, and he felt her thigh touch him. "You are a stud, a studly boy," she said softly. She pulled him to her. It seemed he now knew what to do, what she wanted. He tried to be good to her.

Later, she said, "Jeeze honey, you learn quickly!"

I have a pretty good teacher," he replied.

But, aren't we learning together?" she asked.

"Yeah, that's good . . . the quest to be perfect."

"You know, we have to be careful, but I think I need to get something for us."

"You mean like . . . so something doesn't happen?"

"Yes, but so we can also be more natural."

"I don't know much about that."

"You don't mind if I tell you these things, do you?"

"No, I like that you do. You're teaching me stuff!"

Charlene smiled and then kissed him. He slowly rolled over onto his back to be beside her. Her eyes were closed, so he lightly stroked her face and hair.

"Can I ask you something?"

"I guess so," he said, wondering what else it might be.

"I assume Scooter is a nickname. Tell me your given name."

Scooter didn't reply right away. "That's quite confidential," he said. "Only a few people know—like my family."

"But don't you think I should know?" Charlene pleaded.

"Hmmm . . . I guess you should know, but you can't tell anyone."

She laughed. "I know, honey, but now you have me curious. It can't be that bad."

"Naw," he said, "but my uncle Jake started calling me 'Scooter' when I was a little shaver, running around the ranch, and it stuck ever since! I don't use my given name much . . . nearly forgot about it."

Charlene waited for Scooter to continue and when he didn't, exclaimed,   "Come on, you're being ornery!"

"Okay, okay . . . it's Llewellyn," he said, "after my granddad . . . Mom's side."

Charlene let out a peal of laughter. Scooter smiled and grabbed her in a hug. "You can't laugh about it," he said. This made her laugh even harder and he laughed with her. "Now you know why Scooter seems preferable?"

"Oh, I don't know," Charlene said, "Llewellyn though, who'd a thought it. Llewellyn Henry!" she turned the thought of it over. "I like it fine. It seems quite . . . well, sophisticated. And I'm glad you told me." She kissed him again and started to snuggle against him.

"Well, just call me Scooter, okay?" Charlene put her hand on his chest, twirling the sparse hair there. He stilled her hand, "Just a second, I'm going to get rid of this." He went into the bathroom. He washed up and went back to be with her. He got into bed and rubbed her neck and back.

"I love you, so much," she said.

"I never knew this was possible," he replied.

Scooter continued to stroke her back and neck as she sighed and murmured, "I'm so sleepy now."

Scooter woke and looked at Charlene. It was light outside and he tried to see his watch. It looked like it was seven o'clock. He straightened out, stretching, and then curled up against her again. She stirred. He kissed the back of her neck and then her ear.

She looked at him, smiled and said, "Morning!"

"Morning, sunshine!"

She turned toward him. "I better go to the potty." He watched her, as she walked naked to the bathroom. After a few minutes, she opened the bathroom door and asked. "You need anything?"

He thought about it and asked, "Well, I don't know . . . I don't have a toothbrush . . . you got any mouthwash? As Zeke says, my mouth tastes like the bottom of a birdcage".

Charlene laughed. "Well, that's bad. Come here." They stood naked together in the bathroom while he swished some mouthwash and then spit it out.

"It's interesting to see how we look . . . naked together," he said.

"I see you aren't very bashful with me."

"No, I mean why would I be now? You've seen all my imperfections and now I have nothing to hide."

She put her arms around him and they began to kiss and rub against each other. She looked down at him and said, "Let's get back in bed before it gets too late." She took his hand and led him toward the bed. After they lay down, he kissed her lips and they parted for his tongue. He moved down to kiss her neck and then her breasts. He stretched his arm toward his jeans lying on the floor and searched the pockets.

"See what I mean if we keep this up, it gets too inconvenient," she said.

"I don't mind, really," he said.

Yes, but I'm going to want you to go without soon. You're going to want to."

"You think so, huh?"

"I know so, but we'll see about this."

"What are you going to do, get something?"

"Uh-huh." She was on her stomach and said, "Like this!"

"Show me," he said, but he soon got the idea.

He felt like a stallion, as her comment about him being one earlier fired his imagination. She began to make sounds in her throat again, and he liked it. He kissed her neck and ears again, then reached around to kiss the side of her lips.

He heard her say, "Scooter, keep doing things to me!" He did his best but didn't know what else he could do. He pulled her hair to him and breathed through it—the essence of her. He felt her shudder and she suddenly and loudly exclaimed, "Dammit, Scooter honey!" Scooter could no longer hold back, and the nearly unconscious ecstasy overtook him.

Charlene put her head on his chest. He put his arm around her as she snuggled against him. "I was so right about you," she said.

"About what?"

"I just knew you would be good for me, that's all."

"I want to be good for you," he said. "I want to be perfect." He was thinking about in bed.

She lifted up partially and turned, looking at him. "Well, about that. You were very good to me tonight . . . this morning! Not only that, but being the kind of person I need," she said.

They kissed and caressed each other. Finally, Charlene said, "We better get out and take care of Star. Come on, I'll wash your back . . . and front."

He smiled. "I could get used to this."

Scooter hurried down the street to The Peak Motel and opened the door. Sonny was still in bed—a lump under the blankets. He stuck his head out and blinked his eyes. "You been out early," he said.

"Yeah, I've been up and at it awhile. Charlene's coming by to go out to her horse, and then we're going to the Student Union to get some breakfast and to study. Bring the car and join us."

Sonny yawned and said, "I might. I saw y'headin' out into the night. What were y'doin', goin' fer a run?"

Well, no . . . exercising though."

"Once the fuckin' starts, yer done!"

Scooter had started to head for the bathroom but stopped. He laughed self-consciously at Sonny's statement and then said, "Here we go again. Don't tell me that you haven't. That girl at the rez, she had her hands all over you."

"Yeah, but I move around some en don't linger too long in one place, en when I do, it's selective."

"Shit, I'm very selective," Scooter replied.

"She's yer girlfriend though innit, en fuckin' just makes it so when she snaps her fingers and says jump, you ask 'er, 'how high honey'?"

Scooter smiled at Sonny's comments but felt his face flush. He shook his head and moved back closer to Sonny's bed. "I'm going to win Regionals and maybe Nationals before I get out of college and go pro, so you'll see. And, if Charlene and I get married or whatever, then that happens. Or maybe we don't, who knows about that."

Sonny sat up. "Yeah, who knows? I'm just trying to give y'all my perspective, y'know . . . as yer bud."

"I know, but y'see, I still have the vision . . . the rodeo vision," Scooter emphatically said.

"Okay, I know. Hell, can't I give ya a hard time 'bout it?"

Scooter went into the bathroom to shower. He came back out toweling his hair and then pulled a shirt off a hanger and energetically snapped the wrinkles out it and slipped it on. He glanced at Sonny to see if there was going to be any more fallout regarding his relationship.

"We should be up at the student union in maybe an hour. I'm famished anyway, so see you there?"

"I'm thinking 'bout it. I'm kinda hungry too."

The phone on the desk rang and Scooter answered it. Charlene said she would be by in a few minutes.

Scooter sorted through his class notes and set aside the chemistry and range management notebooks. He put on clean socks. Sonny was lazily watching him, still propped up against the headboard of the bed.

"So, tell me again, what's up?"

"Charlene and I are going out to feed her horse, then to the student union for some grub and to study. So, bring the car and meet us."

Sonny sat up on the edge of the bed and flung his hair forward and then pulled it back behind his ears. "You mean at that there student union place. I hate studyin' on a rodeo day. I like t' do one thing at a time. Guess I'll bring them range management notes. Let's go by the arena though. I gotta see that horse afore I get on it."

"I know . . . that's how I am too."

Scooter climbed into the passenger side of Charlene's truck, and they drove out to the stables. "How's my cowboy feel?"

"You'd think I'd be tired, but I'm okay. I'm glad I don't have to ride, though. How're you feeling? I hope you're okay to run the barrels," he said.

"Oh, I know I've been loved, but I'm okay too," she said.

"You've been loved alright," he replied. She smiled at him and reached over to take his hand. He continued, "A lot has happened this weekend . . . more than I was thinking!"

"You're not sorry, are you?" she asked.

"Naw, nothing like that. After the night in Fort Collins . . . up at Horsetooth y'know, I couldn't wait to see you again."

"I hate to see you head back south this afternoon."

"Yeah, it's going to be a long trip, and we're going to stay till the end. Well, to see Zeke on his bull and I'm hoping you and I both are in the money for some awards."

"I do need to talk to you about something before you leave."

Scooter studied her. "Are you remorseful?"

"Oh, nothing like that. I haven't told you everything about myself . . . about some baggage. I just need to clear the air."

Scooter took a deep breath, trying to figure out what it might be. "Let's see, you said there's no boyfriends . . . you can tell me now."

"No, it may take a while and I don't want to before the rodeo."

He took a hard look at her to try to see if her eyes might give him a clue, but nodded and said, "Okay."

After feeding and brushing Star, Charlene and Scooter stopped at the student union and walked into the cafeteria. Only a few people were there for an early breakfast. "I think I'll have about a dozen scrambled eggs, maybe a loaf of toast," he said.

"Yes, you've been doing a lot of exercising the last couple of days," she laughed.

He kidded her back, and said, "One of the best routines I've ever been exposed to!" She leaned back into him as they went along the serving area.

After they had eaten, Charlene pulled out a notebook and an essay she had partially written for an education course.

"What do you want me to do?" Scooter asked.

"Just see if it flows, if it's organized in a logical way. That would help. You can write on it."

In reading her essay, Scooter realized Charlene was a fair writer. He made notes in the margin about the subject of each paragraph to see if that would help identify any logical flow issues. She looked on with him, and he liked that they were working on something together.

Sonny walked into the cafeteria and stood searching for them for a few seconds. He worked his way over to them, and after saying hello to Charlene, put a book and notebook on the table. "I'm a starvin' wolf." He went over to the stack of trays and got in line with some other students.

"I'm glad to see you guys are serious about college," Charlene said. "I know it's an eligibility thing, but a lot of the guys here are just doing enough to get by."

"Well, we sometimes don't do enough either, but we have finals next week . . . kinda sucks to have to study at a rodeo, but that's how it is, isn't it?"

They continued to work on the essay while Sonny ate. Finally, Charlene said, "Squirrel should be here soon, so I better get my studying done before."

Scooter gave Charlene back her essay. "I didn't do much. I think it's good. Those arrows mean to move a sentence if you want to," he said.

Charlene looked at Scooter's comments. "You do know a few things about composition apparently."

"I have a class in it . . . tougher than I thought, but interesting."

Sonny was writing out summaries of his range management notes. Finally, he looked up. "He's like the Einstein of our team. Y'got a weird guy here." Charlene laughed, and Scooter felt his face flush. "I gotta check out the saddle broncs before too long. I like t' get things kinda settled in my mind," he said, "I can only stand this whatever fer so long y'know."

"Yeah, it's an incongruity," said Scooter.

"That's what I meant. See, y'got yourself stuck with big words," Sonny said to Charlene.

She laughed. "That is a pretty big word for a rodeo cowboy. But look, if you guys need to leave before Squirrel gets here, go ahead and we'll catch up," Charlene said.

We'll go out in a few," Scooter replied. "To be congruent, huh?" Sonny shook his head.

Scooter got up and walked across the cafeteria to the large urns on the counter to refill their coffees. He nearly ran into Squirrel on his way back.

"Oh! Hey, Squirrel. We were just talking about you, that we need some tutoring on these courses."

"Well, it'll cost you," she replied. "How're you doing? I got something to show you if you haven't seen it yet." She followed him back to Charlene and Sonny.

Sonny stood up and Squirrel gave Charlene a hug, saying "Hey Char!" and then hugged Sonny.

Cozy, Scooter thought, and then asked, "Where's mine?" Squirrel turned and gave Scooter a hug after he set the coffees down.

"Have you guys seen this?" Squirrel asked. She opened a newspaper and turned to the sports section. Scooter was straining to see over the others but could only catch a glimpse.

"Well, what we got here is a movie star!" Charlene said.

"Criminy somnabitch! When they take that?" Sonny exclaimed.

Scooter crowded in more closely and saw a large photo of himself on Popcorn at Saturday's rodeo. He gazed at it, quite amazed. He looked at the front of the paper. It had a banner across the top that read, Laramie Tribune. He turned to the page with the photo again. There was a caption underneath the photo that read *Scooter Henry of the Southwestern State College Rodeo*

Team from Durango scores 85 points on Ridgeline Rodeo's "Popcorn" at yesterday's college rodeo. Scooter liked the photo. Popcorn had all four feet off the ground.

"Gettin' some air she was, pard!" Sonny said.

In the photo, Scooter was reared back; his head was nearly on the horse's rump. He had spurred out from his rigging, his legs wide, chaps flying, and toes turned outwards. An article under and to the side of the photo mentioned the college rodeo and had the top scores in the different events.

"Wow! Where did you get this? I need one for my folks," he said.

"There's a newspaper dispenser outside . . . takes a quarter," Squirrel said.

"Wow is right . . . a star among us," Charlene said. "Come on, I'll buy you some. I'm getting one for myself too and you have to autograph it."

"Come on now, don't get carried away. You're in here too," he said, "in the standings." He liked it though, being in the spotlight.

Charlene grabbed the paper and looked at it closer. "Let me see this! Well, that's nice. This is turning out to be quite a weekend."

"Wait till Zeke sees this. He'll have a foaming fit." Scooter said, "He's always trying to get the team publicity in the school rag." They opened the newspaper dispenser with a quarter and took out a stack of papers.

"Just a second." Scooter dug four quarters out of his jean's pocket. "Let's not bring on any bad luck." The two girls laughed.

Charlene opened a paper to the page with the photo, retrieved a pen from the spiral binding of her notebook. "I wasn't kidding. Write something nice," and put it in front of Scooter. He wrote; *To my Daawlin' Charlene,* then paused for a few seconds to think what else. He continued *a great barrel racer, Your buckaroo, Scooter.* He gave the newspaper back to her and she looked at what he had written. "Sweet . . . sweet boy . . . well, buckaroo apparently," she said and smiled her pleasure at him.

"Keep going, you celebrity!" Squirrel said and put another copy in front of him. Scooter wrote; *To Squirrel, Best to you in all things! Friends, always! Scooter.* She looked at it and said, "Nice!"

Charlene and Squirrel both looked at Sonny to see if he was going to do the same. "Hell no," he said, "he's got a big 'nough head already. I gotta go down the road with 'im!"

The girls laughed, and Squirrel said, "Funny. More than our team guys, I think."

Sonny and Scooter looked at each other and smiled. "I hate to break up this nice party," Sonny said, "but I gotta horse to ride yet and I want to check out what it looks like." To Scooter, he said, "Let's go! I wanna get my stuff ready, then let's go out t' the arena."

"I guess we better then," Scooter said.

"Yes, I better get ready for the big day too," Charlene said. "Some of us still have work to do, and can't loaf like some people, not to mention any names," she said and smiled at Scooter. As they walked toward the parking lot, she held Scooter back and said, "Don't forget, we need to talk before you guys leave today, okay?"

He wondered what it could be, as this was the second time she had brought it up. "Okay. Tell you what . . . we're going to get something to eat before we hit the road. Can you?"

Yes, I think we better too. Are you guys going to drive all the way to Durango tonight?" Scooter found their fingers intertwined. "I'm going to miss you," she continued.

He looked at her, as it sounded so final. "Good, 'cause I am, too. Won't we meet down at Baca Junior College? It's next weekend and on my mind."

"I know, but I'm still going to miss you!"

"Well, I reckon I'll miss you too, but we'll talk like we've been."

"I know, but I'm selfish now!" she replied.

"You have me anyways." He headed toward the driver's side of his car. "Run hard today!" he said across the car.

Sonny viewed the exchange as he was getting into the passenger side of the car and mumbled to Scooter, "True love, so sweet!"

Scooter smiled at Sonny's pronunciation.

"We'll see you guys later," Squirrel called out. "Good luck today on that horse."

"Thanks, I need some after that first un," Sonny replied. They drove back through town toward their motel room.

"Guess we better phone Zeke to see what he's doing." Scooter mentioned. "Well, you know 'im. He's doing as much as possible with that Molly. Hope he saves some energy fer that bull," Sonny said.

CHAPTER TWENTY-FOUR
SONNY AND ZEKE

"**W**hich'er the saddle broncs?" Sonny asked, "I'm looking fer that North Country."

The stock contractor told him to look in the second pen for a large black with a Roman nose. Scooter and Sonny walked over to the second pen and climbed on the fence. The horses snorted at them. "The only black is that there big 'un. Chit, another horse, could pull a plow!" Sonny said.

"Yeah, you better not have too short a rein on this un, it'll pull you over the front-end," Scooter observed. As they were talking, Zeke came over and climbed on the fence with them.

"Hey boys."

"Hey! Just checking out that North Country horse, the black un there," Scooter said.

"I came over to rub shoulders with a celebrity. I figured after the spread in the local rag you'd not even be talkin' to us," Zeke said.

"Who told you about it?" Scooter asked.

"That honey of yours. Molly and me seen her when we parked. She and that short girl were getting her horse ready. She thinks you're hot stuff now. You better strike while the iron's hot afore you cool off into a burnt-out cinder."

If you only knew what we've been doing, Scooter thought, but instead said, "Yeah whatever."

"I think the iron's done been struck," Sonny chimed in.

Scooter glanced at Sonny and felt his face flush.

Zeke didn't seem to catch the comment and continued, "I'm calling that reporter here about sending the article to the Durango rag, like a press thing, whatever you call it."

"Jeez man, what are you, my agent?" Scooter asked.

"Yeah, you need someone to boost you. You're too meek. I think I'll see about the bull a mine. Make friends before we have a close relationship."

Scooter turned and said, "Feed 'im some hay. You know, bribe him a little!'

Sonny snorted a laugh and they walked over with Zeke to another holding pen to see what kind of bull he had drawn.

The bulls were lazily munching hay or chewing their cud. "The contractor said he was a large spotted Brahma. That might be him over in the corner there," Zeke observed.

"Pretty large dude," Sonny said. "Why'd they call it Neoprene, anyways?"

Scooter knew that none of them had a clue, but said, "It's 'cause he's really slick, or feels that way when you're on him."

"He better not be too slick, or I'll rosin my pants. Course I think that's illegal anyway."

"You should put a rosin bag in yer underwear. I reckon that'd work," Sonny offered.

"Sheeit!" Zeke grinned, thinking about it.

Scooter chuckled at the thought of amber dust drifting up behind Zeke as he bounced across the arena.

They climbed down from the holding pen fence, crossed over to the side of the chutes, and sat against the fence where they could take in the activities. Scooter noticed that the first group of bareback horses being sorted, and said, "Just a minute. I want to see what the good draw is today." He ambled over to the stock contractor who was directing the sorting in the holding pens. He had a list of the horses and the riders on a sheet of paper in his hand.

Scooter watched the activities for a while and finally, the contractor asked, "You ready for another ride on that Popcorn horse?"

"Maybe. Or maybe two days in a row would be one too many," Scooter said.

The man chuckled. "Y'know, I knew your uncle Jake. We were at the National Finals . . . same year."

"Really!" Scooter said. "He's been gone for a few years now."

"Yeah, I heard. He could ride the rank ones. You put on a good ride yesterday."

"Thanks! What are the good draws today?" Scooter asked.

"Well there's one a lot of guys like to have and a couple most don't. The first one is a little brother to the one you had . . . another black, Random Logic. Be in the last group with Carl Kessler from Montana State. The last ones are a big black stud, One-to-Midnight, and a roan we call Calamity J . . . both in this first group."

Scooter thanked the man for the information and went back to where Zeke and Sonny were perched and climbed up beside them. He told them what the contractor had said.

"Kessler, you know from MSU, has a good horse, brother to Popcorn . . . Random Logic. Guess he could win it. Couple of outlaws in this first bunch." No one said anything for a few minutes.

"I like the name, Random Logic. Conjures up a bad trip!" Zeke said.

"Well, he's goin' t'have t'put on some show t'score eighty-five er better. Y'know that Carl guy?" Sonny asked.

"I know of him. He's good. He's high in the standings in the Northern Region," Scooter said.

"Well, don't worry none. I predict you're in the money in any case. Why sheeit, I'd eat my hat if anyone scored better'n eighty-five today," Zeke said.

"Well, hope you don't have to chew on that felt. That'd be one for the chronicles . . . to score an eighty-five after all these years and to end up like third. Be tough to take, actually."

"You know they're paying ten deep anyways. Course ten would about get your entry fee back and maybe a tank o' gas," Zeke observed.

"Ain't nobody touching ol' Scooter here," Sonny said.

He said it so matter-of-fact that Scooter decided to believe him.

The activity in the arena was increasing as people in the timed events were warming up their horses, and people started to file into the bleachers. The first group of bareback horses was loaded, and the three watched, as contestants started to find their mounts and attach their riggings. Scooter noticed the large black that the stock contractor had mentioned and wondered what it would be like, thinking it would be hard on a person's arm just to stay up on the rigging.

"I think that's the One-to-Midnight horse in the second chute. Be interesting, how it bucks," Scooter said.

As he sat on the top of the fence taking in the activities, Scooter wondered about Charlene and if she was ready to run in the barrels. He had seen her briefly with others, probably from the team, but now they were clearing the area for the grand entry and the National Anthem. He thought he would go see if she needed help after saddle broncs, and then wondered what she wanted to tell him, but was reluctant to approach the subject. Must be something serious. She had said that she was in love with him. This weekend was their second real date, but as he had told her, they had compressed time in their relationship. Her statement had unsettled him. *But love . . . being in love . . . guess this is new territory for me. She's on my mind . . . a lot! And I really, really like being with her . . . and well, jeez making love . . . I know that's brought us so close . . . a couple is what we are.*

Zeke was saying something and broke Scooter's reverie. "What?" he asked.

"I might stay over in Fort Collins tonight and leave early tomorrow. I don't have that first final till Tuesday, it's that P.E. course. I gotta know stuff about golf, though, for one thing."

Scooter laughed and said, "Golf! How tough can that be? Just hit the ball toward the hole. Anyway, we know what you're figuring on doing tonight . . . it's driving alright, but not your pickup or a golf ball either! Sonny and I gotta get back. I got the last English class before the final in the morning."

"Well, you can laugh all you want, I don't care. I know what I'm doing, not like someone I know. You guys would both flunk a test on golf."

"Yeah, and we wouldn't even care!" Scooter retorted. He and Sonny laughed.

Their attention was brought back to the rodeo when the announcer welcomed the crowd to the second day of the University of Wyoming Rodeo and the introduction of the grand entry. Scooter saw Charlene and Star lope into the arena with the other riders. After the flags were posted, the three friends climbed down off the fence and took off their hats for the national anthem. Afterwards, they again climbed up onto their perch, along with some of the other contestants. The announcer said, "Okay, ladies and gentlemen, let's rodeo!"

The first bareback rider came out of the chute, but the horse didn't buck very well, and the judges had thrown a flag on the ground indicating the rider had missed the mark-out on the first jump out of the chute. Another rider made a qualified ride but scored in the 60s. Finally, the big black came out with a rider from Central College in Alamosa. Scooter had talked to him before and thought he was a good rider. The big black jumped and kicked, and suddenly the rider's legs whipped back, and he somersaulted off onto the ground. Scooter winced.

"Just too much power, a lot of drop, and he zig-zags, you see that?" he asked.

"It'd be better for that horse to be in saddles where some of his force could be used better," Sonny said.

"Tough either way I think. Should put him on a plow; be better 'n a tractor!" Zeke said.

The rider on Calamity J only lasted several jumps, as the horse continued to athletically duck and dive across the arena after throwing the rider.

"Looks similar to the Pieface horse to me . . . the one I had in Fort Collins—nasty!" Scooter said. At the end of the first group, the top score was in the mid-70s.

"Well, you're safe so far," Zeke said.

More horses were moved through the alley into the chutes as the first section concluded. Scooter watched Carl Kessler thread his gloved hand into the rigging handhold and then he carefully scooted up to the rigging and squeezed his hat onto his head. Scooter thought this could be it; when all the hopes of winning the event would go down the drain.

Random Logic came out of the chute in a high arcing jump, but it looked like Kessler had anticipated this and made a successful mark-out. The horse sprang into the air in a large circle and the rider was spurring artistically, falling farther and farther back onto the horse's rear. Scooter had a vision of his own score sinking downward as the ride continued. Suddenly, the rider was thrown forward from the impact with the horse's rear and he was pitched across his riding hand and off the horse. It seemed that all this had happened before the horn had sounded, signaling the end of the ride, but Scooter wasn't sure. Being thrown back across his hand had locked the rider's hand into the handhold, and he flailed like a ragdoll alongside the horse as it continued to buck. The pick-up men undid the flank strap and tried to corner the horse, but it ducked away from them and the rider continued to bounce along as if a puppet controlled by a mad puppeteer.

Scooter found himself on the ground of the arena and heard himself say, "Sonavabitch, get him out of there!" Finally, one of the pick-up men roped the horse and then the other did the same from a different angle. The horse was caught and stood with front legs apart, breathing heavily. Control of the horse enabled Carl to elevate himself, releasing the bind of his glove from the rigging. He went down on his knees and medical staff attended to him. The horse, docile now, was led away from the rider and he was helped out, holding his arm.

"What a wreck! I hate to see that," Scooter told Zeke and Sonny.

"No shit!" Zeke said. "Did he make it? I wasn't sure. He rode good till the last second."

Sonny had gone to the front of the chutes and came back saying, "They said he slapped the horse anyways, so didn't mark 'im."

They squeezed back up against the fence, as several more contestants still had to ride. Scooter watched, wondering if more good riders were yet to compete. The next rider bucked off, but the last contestant was from Central Wyoming, and Scooter realized he was the one who had broken-up his tussle with Jack. The cowboy made a good ride, and Scooter found himself again being quite pessimistic, figuring his score would be bettered, but the judges awarded the rider an *82*. Zeke and Sonny slapped Scooter on the back with congratulations.

"Well, what a deal! I'm going back to check on that Kessler. He's a good rider," Scooter said.

He climbed over the arena fence and walked down the alleyway behind the chutes to find the injured rider, but saw him already putting his gear away.

"Tough luck on that horse. You had it, I think."

Carl looked up. "Thanks. You rode good this weekend. Those two horses are the draw here. I couldn't believe it when I got slammed forward . . . tricky."

"Yeah, I think a guy has to ride that un more upright, but it has a lot of drop, too. I think it sucked back under you. Your arm okay?"

"It's going to be sore as hell for a few days. I don't wanna do that again. See you at regionals, I reckon."

"Sounds good. See you there." Scooter said.

Scooter continued walking through the pickups and horse trailers in the parking area, thinking about Charlene and thinking he would get some sodas and take them back to the guys. He wandered over toward her truck but didn't see her although her saddled horse was tied to the trailer. He went to the concession stand and bought three colas. He wasn't sure if Sonny would drink anything but water before his ride. He had just started back toward the arena when Charlene came up to him and said, "Been looking for you, you hot-shot cowboy. They said you won it!"

"Yeah, been lucky this weekend, that's for sure. I was looking for you too." She took one of the colas out of his hand and drank some. He smiled at her thinking: *Guess this is love. The warm feeling had returned.*

"Well, you deserved it, believe me. No one rode as good by far. I watched."

"You think so, huh? You might be biased though," he said.

"Well, absolutely!" She smiled back at him and gave back the soda.

"You can have it if you want." He took a sip of it

She smiled. "No, I need to get on Star and make sure we're ready."

"I know. I want you to win this today. You can you know."

"Well, we're going to do our best. Come over to the trailer with me a minute!" She linked her arm in his as they walked. He was hoping not to drop one of the cans.

"I would help you after your run, but I have to help Zeke with his bull," he said.

"I know. I'll see you after anyway," Charlene said. They approached her trailer and Star and stopped near her truck. "I should give you a big congratulation kiss but guess it will have to wait until after."

"What? Just a kiss for a ride like that? I was thinking something else!"

he teased.

"Well, cowboy, keep on thinking. You already had everything else. Surely you haven't forgotten already."

He laughed and said, "You're the one said I'm ambitious . . . guess it's true."

She laughed with him and untied Star's reins. "You are pretty ambitious. Watch out for those buckle chasers now. They're going to be after you, stars in their eyes from all that silver and gold."

"You're funny. I'm sure I'll have to get a club to keep 'em off me. Isn't that spot taken?" he asked.

"Yeah cowboy, it is." She smiled at him, her eyes sparkling. She mounted her horse and they walked back toward the arena.

"Get some!" he told her and headed back toward the chutes to help Sonny with his saddle bronc.

Scooter's attention was brought back to the chutes by saddle broncs being loaded. "Here we go pard. I'll check the list." He had to find the stock contractor and climbed onto the fence to the side of the chutes. "When's the North Country horse up?" he asked.

The stock contractor said, "He'll be in this first group." Scooter went back to where Sonny was sitting on the ground working rosin into the swells of his saddle and chaps. "Be up in this group, so we gotta watch for it!'

Sonny's horse went into the third chute. "This uns it," he said.

They cinched down the saddle after Sonny meticulously placed it, and then he measured his hack rein several times and marked it. They then waited for the competition to start. One of the riders ahead of Sonny made a successful ride but was unable to spur much.

Sonny climbed down into the saddle as the chute crew came over to the gate. Scooter watched in case he was needed, but the horse stood quietly, although Scooter noticed its ears twitched as Sonny settled in. As usual, Scooter said, "Get the mark-out."

Sonny nodded his head and said, "Out!" Scooter had never heard him just say, "Out" before to signal he was ready. Maybe bucking off of Hard Lemonade had made him change his routine.

The horse took a short run out of the chute, but then exploded into classic jumping and kicking while turning a lazy circle back toward a side fence. Sonny spurred in time with the horse and Scooter held his breath that he would keep spurring and not buck off. The horse bucked up to the fence by the bleachers but weakened there as it slowed for a split second to change directions. After the horn sounded, Sonny double-grabbed the rein as the horse turned and jerkily ran along the fence, still bucking slightly. Scooter could hear Zeke's piercing whistle as Sonny was taken off the horse by a pick-up man.

Sonny trotted back across the arena to a small gate at the end of the last chute and Scooter met him there. "Nice job! You used him!"

"Felt okay on 'im!" Sonny said.

The announcer indicated a score of 76.

"It'd been a lot higher, but the horse slowed and weakened at the fence there," Scooter said.

"I felt it."

They angled over to the unsaddle chutes and retrieved Sonny's saddle and rein.

"Guess we'll see where this ends up fer the go-round. Lotsa good riders here." Sonny said, "But I'm glad t' get a score." They stowed his equipment and watched the rest of the competition.

The Wyoming rider, who had won the first go-round, scored a 78 and was in position to win the second go-round, but his score was eclipsed by a rider from Montana University, who scored an 82. Scooter was amazed by the ride and even thought it was marked low.

"Jeez, man, that cat can ride," Scooter said.

"Davis . . . from up there. He's leadin' the region. I got some work to do t'ride like that," Sonny said.

"You do ride like that! He had a classy horse."

The last contestant double grabbed to save himself before the eight seconds were up. Satisfied with the results, they carried Sonny's equipment out to Scooter's car.

"Third in the go-round should pay okay, en the points're good, innit," Sonny said. "If'n Zeke weren't up, we could get our checks 'n head out . . . be a long trip anyways."

"Yeah, that's rodeo. We might do this over the Fourth y'know, the long weekend with a bunch of rodeos, so we gotta get in practice. You better have a driver's license, 'cause you're driving part of the way."

"Hell, I doan need practice t' stay up all night goin' down the road somewheres. We practly done it gettin' here," Sonny exclaimed.

Scooter laughed at his reply.

Several of the other saddle bronc riders came over to Sonny and discussed how they were doing in the go-round and how things were shaping up for the regional finals. Scooter, at a slight distance, waited for Sonny and realized how the other contestants considered him a peer; part of the top echelon in this event. Finally, Sonny walked to where Scooter stood. "We all had the ave in mind, y'know, winning it," Sonny explained. "But only one kin, uh?" Scooter laughed at Sonny's explanation.

"Yeah, consistent is what," Scooter noted. Sonny grunted something in agreement. They walked beyond the chutes to sit along the arena fence and watched the calf roping.

Finally, the grounds crew came into the arena in a pickup and dropped off the barrels for barrel racing. A judge made sure they were set up in the right spots. Scooter had thought about checking to see if Charlene was ready but thought he might be a distraction. He waited for her to make a run, hoping she would do okay.

Zeke had come over with his equipment and said, "Let's get ready to spur something boys!" He went behind the chutes to warm-up.

"Guess we need to watch for his bull here pretty soon," Scooter said.

"Well, I'll watch the bull, you watch yer honey," Sonny replied.

Scooter noticed that several of the first few competitors were in the low 16-second range. He thought it might be hard to beat them. Finally, Charlene's name was announced, and she came thundering into the arena on Star. They seemed to be quick and wheeled around the barrels, the dirt of the arena spraying out from Star's hooves. Charlene was hanging low over Star's neck as they raced out of the arena, as she had the day before. Scooter said to no one in particular, "Wow! Another good ride!" He was proud of her.

Sonny had been watching also and said, "Yeah, not bad."

Charlene's time placed her in third. Scooter had been hoping she had been a few tenths quicker, as this would have placed her in first. Several more girls made their runs, but none moved ahead of Charlene. Well, third place and third in the average. Everything seems to be coming together for us this weekend. *She's a cowgirl—can really ride.*

The pickup came back into the arena and the rodeo grounds crew retrieved the barrels.

"Zeke's bull ain't in yet," Sonny said, breaking Scooter's reverie.

They walked over to the fence along the chutes by Zeke and waited. He was hanging by his arms from a two-by-six brace and did several slow pull-ups.

"Testing the lumber?" Scooter asked.

"Smartass," Zeke replied.

The three watched the action as the bull riding started. One of the riders was hurt after being thrown under the bull that then stepped on his leg. It looked bad to Scooter, as EMTs helped the rider out of the arena being careful of the injured leg. Scooter wondered what Zeke thought. Another group of bulls was loaded into the chutes. The large speckled bull was brought up into the third chute, and they checked to make sure it was the right one.

"This is Eckhardt's . . . Neoprene," the stock contractor said.

Sonny and Scooter helped Zeke place his bull rope.

"This uns round. Lot's t'get hold of," Sonny said.

Scooter thought the large size of the bull might fit Zeke's long legs. The three waited for Zeke's turn. There was only one successful ride ahead of him. The announcer commented that the bulls were rank and way ahead of the riders.

Zeke was keeping limber, swinging his arms and occasionally squatting while waiting. The stock contractor sidled around Scooter and Zeke on the narrow platform on the back of the chute and said, "Yer up!"

Scooter and Sonny helped pull Zeke's rope and he tied it off. He scooted up to his hand and pulled the lower part of his chaps back out of the way of his rope.

"Concentrate on him!" Scooter admonished.

Zeke pulled his hat down until it bent his ears out and said, "Outside, boys!"

The chute gate opened, and the bull immediately thundered out into high jumps and a spin, but it was slow. Zeke weathered the start of the spin, and the first three or four revolutions, but then the bull reversed and spun the other way. Zeke compensated, throwing his free arm in that direction, but started to slide off-center toward the inside. His position became more and more precarious as the ride continued until Zeke was still riding, but on the bull's side. The horns were near. Zeke angled his body up with his free arm, trying to keep off the ground. Scooter was hardly breathing.

"He's down 'n the well!" Sonny noted.

Finally, when it looked like Zeke would have to let go, the horn sounded, but he was nearly under the bull, just barely able to keep his free arm off the arena surface. He rolled to get away from its hooves, but the bull stepped on Zeke's upper leg and then turned and butted him several times, finally flinging Zeke away from further damage, as the bullfighters lured the bull away. Zeke scrambled to his feet and sprinted for the fence as if the bull was hot on his tail. One leg of his chaps had been torn loose and it flapped as he ran.

"Somnabitch, two bulls 'n two wrecks," Sonny said.

"He made it . . . I think. Although weren't pretty," Scooter observed.

After the bull had left the arena, Zeke climbed down from the fence and collected his bull rope and hat from one of the bullfighters, who patted him on the back.

"Nice job!" Scooter said. Both he and Sonny gave Zeke high fives.

"Well, I didn't know what to do once I got on the side of 'im. I seen them horns staring at me every jump so just kept thinking how I was getting away from 'em!" Zeke said.

Scooter and Sonny laughed at Zeke's analysis.

"He do any damage?" Scooter asked.

Zeke unbuckled the remaining portion of his chaps, took them off and said, "Well, look at these. He dinged my leg some, but it ain't broken."

"Yer good fer the crowd. They like the wrecks," Sonny chimed in.

"Mark one down in the cowboy column folks, we have a sixty-six for Zeke Eckhardt from Southwestern!" The announcer said over the PA system.

"I'm just glad you got out from under him. Must weigh a ton. If guys keep bucking off maybe you'll get some green today," Scooter said. They climbed over one of the empty chutes. Scooter noticed Zeke was favoring a leg. He asked, as Zeke began rolling up his bull rope and chaps, "You need to see the medics?"

"Nah, it's okay . . . just a bruise. I doan wanna mess with those guys again," Zeke said.

They watched the remainder of the bull riding. One rider from Colorado A&M scored a 78 and was leading the day's activities. Scooter commented, "Hell, pard, you're sitting third today after all the buck-offs. We better see how you stack up. I think you're in the money,"

"Should be. They're payin' deep," Sonny said.

"Well, they should have the results finalized soon. I'm gonna stow this stuff 'n see where this ends," Zeke said. I gotta drive Molly back to her place as soon as I can today."

Scooter took the opportunity to get back at Zeke and said, "Let her know that nothing vital was damaged . . . you know, your love-making equipment."

"Yeah, yeah!" Zeke retorted.

Scooter said to Sonny, "I'm going to see what Charlene's doing. You want to?"

"I'm goin' t'stay and see if'n me en Zeke get any money from that rodeo secretary here, so's will be here," Sonny said.

"Yeah, let's all get some green here. I'll be back in a few."

CHAPTER TWENTY-FIVE
CEREMONIES

Scooter pushed through the small gate out of the alleyway behind the chutes and walked toward the parking lot. He noticed several guys lingering at one of the pickups near his car and Scooter nodded to them as he walked by, realizing one of them was Billy Hall.

"Hey hotshot, you the one been going out with Charlene ain't you?" Billy commented as Scooter went by.

Scooter slowed and then stopped. The tone of the question angered him. "Who wants to know?"

"We don't take kindly for some hayseeds from Podunk college to come in here and mess with our girls on the team," Billy continued.

Scooter sized-up Billy and his companion, who stood casually to one side. If it came to a fight, Scooter wasn't sure if he should worry about Billy. The other guy looked tough--calm. He wished that Sonny had come along. *Then we'd see. They think the girls are property.*

"Here's what we do down at Podunk college," he said, "you know, when guys from another team come to town . . . we rent the girls out to 'em. You ought t'think about it."

"Fuckin' smart-ass," Billy snarled.

"You see, if the girls are property you can do that," Scooter continued, "maybe make a little money that way."

"You're about to get your ass kicked!"

Scooter continued to direct his conversation to Billy, ignoring his companion. "Not today. And you know that's a good way for someone to get hurt or kicked out. Maybe me, maybe you."

"Yeah, probably you!" retorted Billy.

Scooter continued on to his car, wondering if they were going to follow him. He decided he would open the trunk if they did and at least get out the jack handle. He looked back toward where they had been, but they were walking the other way, toward the arena. His blood was up, he was shaking some. *Must be adrenaline. That thug would have been a problem.*

He unlocked his car and sat in the driver's seat to calm down. *First, that Jack bastard from Central and now this guy.* He hadn't said anything to Jack today. *Wonder if he's still looking for a fight. He should get a small check at least. Maybe he'll be down at La Junta next weekend.*

Scooter took a deep breath and got out of his car. He checked the area again for Billy and his companion and then locked the door. He wanted to find Charlene and tell her how great her run had been. He ambled over to her pickup and horse-trailer. Star was already in the trailer. He decided he better get back to the arena and walked back the way he had come.

Zeke saw him as he neared the arena gate and said, "Hey man, they called for you a minute ago!"

"What for?" he asked.

"They're doing awards soon."

"You know if you placed?"

"Yeah, they got me in eighth. I already picked this up!" He showed Scooter a check for $120.00.

"That's pretty damn good! They paid well here." He shook Zeke's hand. "Have you seen Charlene?"

"Yeah, she was just here a minute ago looking for you, actually."

Scooter went in through the main gate of the arena and saw Sonny and Squirrel, and then Charlene. He walked over to them.

"Where y'been, dude? We 'bout sent a posse fer ya," Sonny said.

"I think I'm lost!" Scooter said. He suddenly felt like it.

"You okay?" Charlene asked.

"Yeah, I was looking for you. I loved your run today. You can flat ride a horse you know. You're going places too!"

Charlene smiled. "Well, I like that you think so . . . thanks! It's finally coming around. Guess practice helps," she said.

"She's third in the average and they're doing the top three awards too!" Squirrel exclaimed.

"Yeah, by less than one-tenth of a second, can you believe it?" Charlene said with a big grin.

"Well, now it's my turn for an autograph," Scooter said. Charlene pushed against him with her hip.

The announcer said over the loudspeaker, "Gather around for the awards people. We're going to do the top three in each event in the order they were run. We have, starting in bareback, a tie for second and third," and mentioned the rider from Central Wyoming College and one from Montana State. Scooter and the others clapped as the contestants received their awards. "Folks, we have a cowboy from Southwestern State College in first, with an outstanding ride on Ridgeline Rodeo's Popcorn. Let's hear it for Scooter Henry." Scooter could hear Zeke's piercing whistle among the applause.

Scooter shook hands with the other two bareback riders, and then they stood together as the checks were presented to them by the rodeo association president. Then a university rodeo queen presented Scooter with a flat box containing a large silver buckle with gold trim. He noticed it was engraved with the name of the rodeo and the year. A gold figure of a bareback horse and rider was in the center. It felt heavy. She shook his hand and then representatives of the college rodeo team presented him with a new bareback rigging, which had been stamped *University of Wyoming, 1960 Bareback Champion.* He felt like a robot and continued to say, "Thank you, thank you."

Scooter's face had a perpetual grin and it felt hot. All the attention was embarrassing him yet excelling in their rodeo craft--what he and Sonny, and Zeke too, had been striving toward all spring. He felt proud of himself and proud of his heritage, of his Uncle Jake and his father, and even his brother Ron, who wouldn't believe that his little brother had won an event at one of the largest college rodeos on the circuit. He looked over at Sonny and smiled, then at Charlene, who was standing beside Squirrel. *This is real isn't it? I've dreamed of what it might be like so many times . . . what a feeling to be up here with these other guys!*

He was about to turn and go back into the crowd of contestants to where Charlene and Sonny were standing, but someone said, "Just a minute, we need photos." The three bareback riders were asked to get closer together, and a man in rumpled slacks, a suit jacket, and street shoes took their picture with a large camera and flash.

Scooter walked back to the Charlene, Squirrel, and Sonny. They checked out the awards, and Sonny rubbed the buckle on his shirt and said, "I gotta get some a this here shine on me!" Scooter and the girls laughed. Zeke and Molly joined the group.

Charlene linked hands with him. He had noticed Billy in the crowd and wondered what he was thinking.

"Like you said, we have had a great weekend, don't you think?" Charlene asked.

"The best . . . well, even better if you had won it too, but I'm very proud of you," he said.

"I'm happy. We did our best. I still want to talk to you before you head out." He looked at her with a question, and she continued, "In private . . . it's something I need to do." Scooter viewed Charlene's earnest expression and wondered what it could be and again mentally reviewed their times together but couldn't think of anything he might have done wrong. The announcer called for the barrel racers and Charlene went to receive her award.

Scooter was contemplating the scene when another contestant came over to him and said, "Hi, I'm Bob Newell, President of the Colorado A&M Rodeo Team. Congratulations. But, I want you to know that not all of us are dick-heads like Hall. He can be a prick sometimes"

"How'd you know?" Scooter asked, thinking about the confrontation.

"Oh, he has a big mouth." Scooter grinned at the comment.

Charlene was receiving her award and he clapped for her and the other barrel racers in the first two spots. "I appreciate you coming over. You know, I need to transfer somewhere to finish the last two years of an ag major. Is there any room on the team here?"

"There likely could be," Bob said, "let's stay in touch." He handed Scooter a card with his name and phone number on it. Scooter decided that the team here was a lot more organized than they were at Southwestern.

Charlene came back to where he was standing. "I need one of those pictures . . . of you," he said.

Squirrel overheard him. "I'll see if I can get pictures for all of us . . . of both of you from the university here. This is a monumental day."

"Look at this . . . a gift certificate to a western store. My dad is going to be glad I earned a little money finally. Maybe I'll even make a payment on my truck," Charlene said.

Scooter laughed and said, "Yeah, rodeo can get expensive."

"I hate to break this t'ya, but we gotta get on the road," Sonny said.

"Well, we do too. Can we meet at that burger place on the south end of town? It's on the way." Charlene said.

Zeke had come over with Molly in tow and heard the question. "We can't. We gotta get back to Fort Collins . . . duties. I just wanna say it's been a blast here. We'll see you girls again somewheres down the road. Again, watch out for these guys. They can be a little wild, although it don't come out too often . . . 'bout once every five years."

"Yeah, yeah, we're hell on wheels," Scooter said. His and Zeke's comments got laughs from the girls.

"I really enjoyed meeting you all," Molly said.

"Likewise," Charlene said. She and Molly hugged.

Scooter thought that was an interesting gesture, but said to Zeke and Molly, "It's been fun. Be careful out there."

As they were leaving Zeke called back, "See you guys down at Southwestern. Don't get in any trouble now, 'cause I won't be along to clean yer noses fer you!"

Scooter just shook his head, but Charlene said, "He's a funny guy."

"He's the wild one we have t'watch fer to get him outta trouble," Sonny said.

They stopped at a drive-in and waited for Charlene and Squirrel, then went inside.

"I'm paying for this cuz I'm flush right now," Scooter said, as he Charlene, Squirrel, and Sonny stood waiting for their order.

"Let 'im. He don't pay fer anythin' normally," Sonny said.

"Right! I had to buy him all his clothes when he came to college," Scooter countered, "came to register in a breechclout and moccasins." This caused the two girls to laugh. Sonny observed the comment with a grin.

Charlene hugged Scooter's arm and said, "You guys are a pair and Zeke too! Guys up here are so dour."

"Dour," Scooter echoed. "That's quite a descriptive word. I gotta remember not to be that way."

Charlene smiled. "I don't think you have to worry."

They carried their order of burgers and milkshakes to a booth where they continued to talk about the rodeo. Squirrel thought she would compete in the rodeo the next weekend. She mentioned they still had three weeks of school after that.

"That's too bad." Scooter said, "'cause we're out after Friday and we're going to throw a big party down there in La Junta. We were going to invite you girls, but if you have to study . . . well, I don't know. We don't want to be a bad influence."

Charlene put her hand on his leg and said, "Well, we'll see about this. Maybe we'll be all studied up."

Squirrel laughed. "Well, I don't know, after the way you guys threw the margaritas down in Fort Collins, it might be a real wild party."

The others laughed at her good-natured ribbing, and Sonny said, "Well there might be other things t'do besides. We often kin think a somethin'."

Squirrel took a hard look at him and said, "I'm thinking you likely can."

Sonny nodded and chuckled. He directed his comment to Scooter, saying, "We ain't done any moonlight bronc riding fer awhile. These girls might be missin' out on some excitement."

"I think they have," said Scooter, "you haven't lived till you feel the horizon and stars wheel around your head on a bronc and you're hoping not to get throwed into some cacti."

Squirrel and Charlene laughed at this. "Cacti!" Charlene exclaimed. "You guys . . . you haven't done any of that, either."

Sonny and Scooter laughed at her comment. He noticed that Charlene had linked her arm in his and had nestled into his shoulder. He was conscious of her hair and the fresh scent he liked.

They finished their meals and started to leave the table.

"Don't leave without saying goodbye," Charlene said. She and Squirrel went into the bathroom.

"I gotta go, too," Scooter said.

Sonny followed him in and said, "Guess we better now," and went over to the urinal.

The two washed up and Scooter checked his hair under his hat. It was squashed down where his hat had been and then flared out. He ran his hand through it, but as usual, it didn't help. He put his hat back on and they went outside to wait by his car.

Charlene and Squirrel came out of the restaurant with fresh faces and they had fixed their hair. Scooter thought Charlene had put on lipstick.

"Come over here for a minute," she said, and led him to the side of her pickup. He noticed Squirrel had gone over to her car.

"You've had me really curious about this talk. You know, I met Billy today, before the awards," he said.

"Oh yeah? What'd he want?" Charlene asked.

"Oh, he and some thug wanted trouble, said you and the other girls on the team were property and didn't want someone from a Podunk college messing with y'all."

"I know who the thug is . . . bad news. What happened?"

"For once in my life, I was cool instead of letting my temper get me into trouble. I suggested that since you all were property, maybe the guys could rent you out. I told him that's what we did down south at Podunk college!"

Charlene laughed. "I bet he didn't like that!"

"No, he was spoiling for a fight, but I just walked off."

"Now you see why I had to get away from him . . . well, even before I met you." She paused as if steeling herself. Scooter waited. There's something I need to get off my chest. I mean . . . well, I don't know how to do this. I need to tell you about me . . . about my past. I wasn't worried about it at first, but after we met and then . . . now I have to let you know something. This is risky for me. I thought about telling you yesterday when we were together but chickened out. I'm not . . . I mean there're things you need to know about me before this goes any further. I have a past that you need to know about!"

Scooter thought: *Any further? Like, we've been making love for two days!* He then saw tears in her eyes. "What? You robbed a bank?" She didn't say anything but shook her head. He continued, "What could be so bad? Don't tell me you're married!"

"Was," she softly said.

He contemplated her statement: *Married. Judas Priest!* He didn't say anything for a while, and realized it was up to him to break the silence.

"It can't be too bad," he said. "I mean it's past tense, right?" He had taken Charlene's hand, and then looked at her and saw more tears.

"That's only part of it," she continued. "Have you ever wished you could leave part of your life behind, that it wasn't really you? That you could leave a mistake and be fresh? That's what I wanted to do since we met but can't. So, you see I have this past . . . I was going to tell you before but couldn't because it's very risky for me to lose you."

He was wondering what else there could be and said, "You have to trust me some I guess, that I won't stampede out of here . . . from us."

"I met a guy the year after high school. I thought he was God's gift to me. We decided to elope. My parents found out and did an annulment. Then later I found out I was pregnant, so they . . . well, I decided it best not to go through with it!"

"Judas Priest!" Scooter exclaimed, this time out loud. He noticed that Sonny had gone over to Squirrel's car and was leaning against the front fender; they were talking, but Squirrel gave Charlene and him a glance. He was thinking that maybe he should somehow put things in reverse, as if Charlene's and his relationship was like Squirrel's car, and the whole thing could back-up. He had told her that her past didn't matter, but now the past had gotten larger than he had envisioned.

"See, I knew this would be bad! I'm sorry. I wanted you to know though . . . from me."

"No, it's not bad for me. It's a surprise though. I have to absorb it all. What happened? I mean, an abortion! Were you sorry about it? I mean . . . do you have regrets? What happened to you and the guy? Sorry about all the questions."

Charlene smiled slightly through her tears. "No, I finally realized I had made a big mistake. The guy . . . well, he decided maybe married life wasn't so great. I guess about a week was enough for him. It took a while for me. I couldn't wait to start college, to get away from everything."

Scooter knew that Charlene was maybe a year older than he was and had about a lifetime's worth more experience. Zeke's mention of him being a greenhorn with women crossed his mind. Scooter suddenly felt like he might still be in junior high. He looked over at Sonny and Squirrel, who were still talking; they both laughed at something. Scooter had fallen for the beautiful cowgirl image of Charlene and now part of the image had eroded slightly, to where it wasn't quite perfect anymore; *like a sugar cube slowly dissolving in water. She should have told me before. Before we made love . . . maybe . . . or does it matter?*

Charlene had backed off from him. "Look, I know you may not want to be with me now. I didn't look for someone naïve and say, 'Okay there's an easy mark. I'll just grab him, and we'll go down the road.' I have to admit though I was infatuated with you . . . curious. I know. I pushed myself on you, but not because of this . . . in fact, maybe in spite of it." Her eyes pled with him. She looked away.

"I know that. Charlene . . . hey, look at me." She didn't. "Charlene, come on, look at me."

She finally lifted her eyes to him. He again absorbed the bright blue-green hue of them and then took the handkerchief from her and dabbed at her tears. "Just give me a few moments to absorb this. I am naïve, I have to admit it. But you said you had good intuition. Do you think I'm shallow?" he asked.

She answered softly, "No."

"Do you think I would let something like that run me off?"

"This has been hanging over my head, so it's become a big deal now . . . you know, the stakes got higher and higher. Do you understand that?"

"Well, maybe! How 'bout if I won't let go of you? What about that? Do you think that this past makes a difference to how you are to me, how I think of you after we've made love?" In saying this, Scooter was trying to convince himself that his feelings hadn't changed. "When you said you thought someone loved you, I thought you meant Billy Hall." He left it hanging like a question.

"No, I'd been bitten and was pretty cautious by then." He had to bend down closer to hear. He smelled her hair. Warmth spread through him, as if from her. "Well, until now with you. Now I've thrown all the chips on the table. I wished I had told you the first night . . . up at Horsetooth. I thought about it."

"Well, that might 'ave scared me off, that early in us knowing each other, I don't know. I doubt it though. You know what I worried about? That as beautiful as you are, I wouldn't be able to hold onto you . . . that I would continually have competition for you."

"Well, you can zero that out. Do you know why? Because I'm in love with you. It doesn't matter who's interested in me and I hope the same is true for you. I'm just sorry now that I'm damaged goods."

Scooter chuckled at the thought. "Damaged? Look, nobody's perfect. If they think they are, they're lying."

She hugged him hard. He put his face into her hair again and twirled it with his fingers. "This is what love is, understanding each other, making allowances for each other. I know that from my mom and dad. When you love someone, I realize now it doesn't matter. I'm glad you told me . . . that we had this talk! Anyway, that stuff is past tense for you . . . for us." Charlene looked at him and smiled through the last of her tears. "Look, don't worry about your past. Let's go forward with this . . . take a few chances. There's a reason we met! I mean, if it's destiny, how else are we going to see what's over the ridge, around the next corner. Weren't you the one that said it . . . that told me we need to take some chances? So, let's!"

Charlene searched his face and smiled. "You are my honey, so okay, if that's what you want." She kissed him lightly on his cheek and then his lips. "I mean it when I say it; I'm in love with you and there's nothing I can do about it. I worry about such a strong feeling because it's come so suddenly."

He searched her turquoise, luminous eyes and her curved lips. "Yeah, strong feelings . . . look, I want you to come with me to the ranch after the rodeo next weekend," he said. "Can you stay over into Monday? I want you to. I want you to meet my family and I want them to meet you. They'll like you. They'll like you because you're the one. They might be surprised that I have a girlfriend . . . well, more than that. Can you?"

"I'll see. I mean . . . if you want me to, I guess," she said.

He looked over toward his car. Sonny had gotten inside. "You know, things can happen sometimes in spite of our good intentions, or how we feel. Take Zeke and Molly for one. You know she has a kid from an earlier marriage, yet he's with her . . . her guy. He's had a record of playing around, so it's surprising to Sonny and me that he's suddenly lassoed. Like you said, when it's the one, it's the one."

"That's right. It's called being in love, honey. Look, I know you guys have to go. Sonny's over there chomping at the bit. Say you love me!" Her eyes burned into him. He felt their magnetic pull and again observed her features that so attracted him, her dark hair, slightly upturned nose and wide, expressive mouth with the full lips.

"Yeah, that's what it is. My intuition is to be careful with this, but I don't want to think we're that fragile when we talk about destiny!"

"I know! We both been talking it up about taking chances. Neither of us will walk around like we're on eggshells. It isn't in us rodeo people to do that."

"I know that," he said, "us rodeo people." They searched each other's eyes.

"Say you love me!" she said again.

"Okay daawlin', I'm in love with you and it's getting pretty damn big." He tipped her head back and they kissed. He felt her arm around his neck, her closeness.

They broke apart slightly and again searched each other's eyes. He smiled at her.

"Look, Charlene, don't worry about this. I'm glad you had the courage to tell me. I hate to go, but we better hit the road. I love you though, so there it is."

"Okay honey, I'll see you next weekend. I'm glad we talked. This has been burning a hole in my mind!" Scooter snorted a short laugh and smiled. "Call me! And be good and please be careful driving," she said.

"You too. Take it easy with that horse-trailer."

They kissed again, and he felt her lean into him. He kissed her hair and throat. She murmured, "Scooter honey!" The warmth and melting flared out from his center again—a feeling she so easily ignited in him.

"Honey is right! Charlene, what are we going to do about this?"

"I know!"

They then reluctantly broke apart and he walked toward his car, then suddenly changed directions and went over to Squirrel's car. She was still leaning against the fender.

"Hey Squirrel, take good care of yourself. See you next weekend. I invited Charlene out to the ranch after the rodeo, see if you can as well."

Squirrel studied him and finally asked, "Are you and Charlene okay?" Scooter again noticed the hard edge in her voice. He understood now that Squirrel knew about Charlene's past and about her rough relationships— about getting hurt.

"Yeah, didn't you warn me to do right by her?"

She smiled and said, "I'll see about next weekend. Thanks!"

Scooter walked over to his car and got in. He slid the key into the ignition. *Well, this has been some weekend. Seems like a whole bunch of time has been compressed into it. So, strong feelings that we both have had for each other from the first. Guess they were real. I wasn't expecting this much of a past, though. I am naïve!*

He started the car, and Sonny said to Charlene and Squirrel as they pulled past them, "See y'all down the road! Remember, midnight bronc ridin' next weekend!" Squirrel smiled and waved to him.

Sonny's parting comment brought Scooter out of his thoughts. "Midnight bronc ridin'? Talk about getting yerself in quicksand," he exclaimed.

"Yeah, but I'm better'n y'think about gettin' out, whereas yer not." He bent over and looked closer at Scooter and then broke into a wolfish grin. "She got lipstick all over yer mouth!"

Scooter stretched his neck out to look in the rear-view mirror and wiped at his mouth with the back of his hand.

CHAPTER TWENTY-SIX
HARD TRAVELIN'

They turned south onto the highway for the long trip back to Durango. "What a weekend!" Scooter said. It was nearly seven o'clock.

"Yep, talkin' 'bout quicksand. You might as well buy the ring," Sonny said

"Yeah, it's serious. I doubt if I want to get out though."

"Well, you can buy her a ring with all that money you're a carryin' now. Whad they pay you?" Sonny asked.

"Just over seven hundred. What'd you get?"

"Man! I knew it was going to pay well, but there musta been stuff added. I made bout one-eighty and that was fer one go-round. That riggin' they gave youse . . . nice too! I like Laramie. We should come back up here this summer to the pro rodeo, innit. If 'n you ain't married by then."

Scooter didn't say anything, wondering if he was about to get married. Well, not right now, but if his relationship with Charlene kept going at the same fast pace, he'd be married, and they'd have a bunch of kids before he was out of college.

He looked over at Sonny. "She told me she'd been married before . . . went off with a guy after high school. Her folks came down on them and then she had to have an abortion. Heavy stuff."

"Hell! I knew somethin' bad was goin' on over there. It's okay with you?"

Scooter looked over. "Well, it's unsettled me some. It's like I stepped into something beyond me . . . like some greenhorn. I mean, I never thought about it being in her past, and then . . . well, I figured as good lookin' as she is, she's bound t'have lots of boyfriends. So, I was leery 'bout that. "But, what if I knew upfront like Zeke did about Molly, guess I wouldn't care. She says she's in love, and guess I believe her. Hell, I don't know. So yeah, I guess! I got to thinking how vulnerable she looked back there, and what if it was me instead of her. I mean about havin' been married, had a kid, or whatever. Maybe been in prison or somethin' . . . how would I feel?"

Sonny nodded his understanding, but then shook his head slightly at his friend's plight. "Man, yer snagged."

Scooter continued. "I had a run-in with Billy Hall, her ex, the steer wrestler, and a tough he hangs with . . . just before the awards ceremony in the parking area . . . thought I was going to have to go at it!"

"I can't leave you by yourself anymore," Sonny said, "if 'n it ain't the girls wanting t' fuck ya, it's guys wantin' t' beat yer head-in. Yer a mess!"

Scooter laughed at his friend's comment, "You're a funny guy some-times." They continued driving south.

"We better stop for a little something to eat . . . maybe some coffee, huh? It's getting late. Might be our last chance." Scooter said.

They first topped off Scooter's car at a service station in Basin at the intersection of the highway with the main street. "I hope some stations are open in Del Norte or South Park later, or we may be screwed," he said.

"This car a yourn uses a lotta gas," Sonny observed.

Scooter knew that, but replied. "It's a V-8 y'know. Zeke's truck uses more."

"Yeah, If'n I had horses like 'em, I'd have t' get a barn full a hay . . . oats too." Scooter smiled at Sonny's analogy.

They followed the main street for several blocks into town and parked near the sidewalk in front of the Basin Hotel. The lobby was deserted; they walked through it into the restaurant. There was only one couple in the restaurant, but the adjoining bar had activity. At least there was music com-ing into the restaurant through an open doorway.

Sonny and Scooter sat down at a table and a middle-aged waitress came over with two menus. "We shut the grill off at nine," she said, "so it's just cold stuff now." Scooter gave her a questioning look, and she continued, "Sandwiches, but we can still do French fries."

"I'll have that chicken salad. Do you have any soup?" he asked.

"I'll have to see if there's any left. Chicken-noodle."

"Okay," he said.

The waitress looked at Sonny. "What he said. Add fries too."

"Me too," Scooter said.

She wrote on a pad and asked, "What to drink?"

Scooter thought about it and finally said, "Milk would be okay."

"Sounds good. We need coffee uh," Sonny said.

Scooter seconded the coffee.

"You boys were here the other evening I believe. Are you from around here now?" the waitress asked.

"Naw, we're from Southwestern State College . . . were up to Laramie at a college rodeo," Scooter said.

"You do any good?"

"Yeah, we did okay."

"Well, congratulations." The waitress walked back to the cash register to settle-up with the other couple.

Scooter noticed Sonny glaring at him and asked, "What?"

"Doan tell anyone, y'doan know who she knows," Sonny said.

Scooter was puzzled and asked, "What you mean, who she knows?"

"Someone may get the idea we're carrying some cash."

"Oh! I never had to worry much about it before. It's a check, anyways, and hidden in the car," Scooter said.

"Let's see who's in the bar fer a minute. I gotta use the head," Sonny said.

They walked across the room to the door leading to the bar. The level of the jukebox music increased. Scooter noticed several guys at the bar drinking beer. They turned to look at him. A couple was at a table in the corner. Scooter turned, and Sonny followed. They walked back out through the restaurant to the bathrooms.

"Pretty quiet. Sunday night, though," Scooter said.

When they came back to their table, they found that the bowls of soup had been brought out. Scooter realized he was hungry. They ate mostly in silence, the fatigue of the day settling on them. The waitress brought out their sandwiches and a plate of French fries. They continued to eat in silence. Scooter was in a hurry to get back on the road, and Sonny seemed to know this.

"Let's see . . . we got about four hours yet. Might get in about two. I got that English class at eight. Be a short night," Scooter said.

"Yeah, me too. Let's take turns driving . . . catch some Zs," Sonny said.

Scooter looked up as the two guys came out of the bar. One of them seemed to be unsteady. He stopped by Sonny's chair. Scooter tensed.

"You Indians going somewheres?" the man asked gruffly.

"Yeah, we're going somewheres," Scooter said.

The man continued while his companion stayed back to the side, "Drinkin' yer milk, huh? Doin' what mommy told ya?"

Scooter noticed that Sonny had pushed his chair back slightly and had coiled.

Scooter felt the heat of anger flare. "Get lost before you get in trouble!" he said. The guy was lanky and had long arms.

"You boys better get outta town afore ya git yer asses kicked!" the man said.

Scooter felt his face flush. "We'd kick your ass but wouldn't know where to start. It's all the same!"

The man turned to his companion and said, "Oh, a funny one." He flicked Sonny's hat onto the floor.

Both Scooter and Sonny scrambled to their feet.

"Pick it up!" Scooter said.

"Go fuck yerself, sonny." The man replied and started to walk off. Scooter cut the man's route off to the door.

"I said pick it up!" Before he realized he was going to do something, Scooter had grabbed the man's wrist and locked his elbow with his other hand. He bent the arm upwards. Their sudden struggle against each other took them across the floor. Scooter drove the man in the direction they seemed to be going. The man staggered with the force Scooter put on his arm and hit his head on an empty table as he went down. They knocked a chair over, making a terrible racket.

"Hey, cut it out before we call the cops!" someone hollered.

Scooter looked over and saw that the bartender had come into the room. The waitress and cook came through the kitchen door. Both looked concerned. Sonny was standing by the troublemaker's companion.

"Wally you and Bill get out of here and don't come back," the waitress said. "Go home and sleep it off!" She and the bartender escorted them out.

Wally looked back at Scooter and said, "You better watch it, kid."

Sonny picked up his hat and brushed it off. The waitress came back in and said, "Sorry about that. Those guys are trouble-makers."

Scooter took a long drink of milk and said, "Yeah, we could tell. Let's settle-up." He went to the cash register and got out his wallet. Their partially eaten meals were left on the table.

As she made change, the woman said, "Don't think too badly of us here. It's normally quiet."

"Naw, it's okay," Scooter said.

They went back out through the lobby and through the front door of the hotel. Scooter noticed someone sitting on the fender of his car.

"Hey!" he hollered.

Suddenly, a flash went off in his head. He thought the ground was floating up, but the impact snapped his head back. He slid part-way down the steps and felt a sharp blow to his ribs and another to the side of his face. He had a fresh, salty something in his mouth and tried to spit. He looked up and saw that Sonny was involved with two guys by his car. He started toward them, but found his legs were heavy as if filled with cement. He finally pushed up to his feet and staggered to find his balance. One of the men was hitting at Sonny while the other held him. Sonny seemed to be weaving—ducking and bobbing.

The man doing the swinging had his legs spread for balance. Scooter remembered about the "soft spots." He aimed a kick between the guy's legs and felt his boot hit something. He wasn't sure if his aim had been true, but the guy went down, bent over, making "huha, huha" sounds. Scooter aimed another kick at his ribs; the man feebly tried to grab Scooter's foot but rolled over onto his side. Scooter had a better angle with his other foot and kicked the man twice in the head. He thought he might have broken his toe with the last kick. He looked over and saw that Sonny had the other guy against the fender of the car and was whaling on him with his fists. Sonny seemed to be spewing expletives of some kind with every hit. *Must be Apache.* The guy was ducking back and forth, and Scooter realized that Sonny's fists were making dull "thunking" sounds as if a drum. Scooter wasn't sure if it was from the guy's head or the hood of his car. His head felt as if it had been filled with cotton, but he turned to look at his assailant, who had gotten up onto his hands and knees. Scooter aimed another kick at his head, with his uninjured foot, and then realized that a pulsing red light had come into the picture.

A loud voice said, "That's enough. Back up against the steps. Now!" Scooter backed up a few paces.

It seemed that Sonny was unaware of anything but his target and continued to hit the man. Scooter hollered at him and Sonny finally quit hitting and then turned to see what was happening. He stepped a few paces toward Scooter. A policeman shined a flashlight on them. Scooter blinked. The side of his head throbbed. He picked his hat up from near the steps and brushed it off. It looked like it had been run over by a truck.

"Sit down on the steps there," The police officer said. The bartender was looking out from the door of the hotel. Scooter and Sonny sat down. The police officer went back to his squad car that was idling on the street to use the radio.

"You okay?" Sonny asked.

"I ain't feeling too perky. You?"

"Guess I'm alright. Sonsabitches!" They sat there for a while.

"Well, what we got here is a real mess," the policeman said. "I got a paramedic coming up to look at y'all, and then we're going to the station and sort this out."

"Mike," the bartender said, "these two were in the restaurant and Wally and Bill decided to cause trouble. We had to ask 'em to leave . . . too much booze."

"Yeah, I know those two," the policeman said.

The guy that Scooter had kicked was sitting up, not saying anything.

Suddenly he leaned over and vomited on the sidewalk. Scooter noticed a two by four, maybe two feet long lying near the sidewalk in the shadow of the building. A van with red lights flashing came slowly up the street and stopped behind the police car. Another police car came from the other direction and stopped as well. More people came out onto the steps of the hotel and a few had gathered across the street to see about the excitement.

Two paramedics clambered out of the ambulance and came over; one carrying a small suitcase-like box. The first asked the police officer, "What we got here?"

"A regular fight, but the guy by the car seems to be out," the police officer said. The paramedics went over to check him.

After a few minutes, one of them said, "We better transport him. His head's beat-up pretty bad. Let's see what else." The second paramedic opened the back door of the ambulance. The first, who seemed to be in charge, shined a flashlight on the other fellow sitting on the ground. "He's bleeding from the nose!" He put thick gauze over the man's nose and told him to hold it with his head tipped back. The paramedic then came over to Scooter. The paramedic said to his companion, as he came over, "Take care of this. Butterfly should close it."

He asked Sonny, "Any problems?"

"No. Bad hand though," Sonny said.

The paramedic looked at Sonny's hand and asked him to flex it. "We'll scrub it for now. You might have it x-rayed. You have a cut over your eye." The paramedic dabbed it and continued to look at it. "This might need a couple of stitches."

The other paramedic walked over to Sonny and looked at his injury for several seconds. "It's marginal." the first paramedic said. "Squeeze it together and stick it." Scooter didn't know what that meant, but the second paramedic worked on the cut and some white material was put across Sonny's eyebrow. One of them shined a light in his eyes.

The paramedic working on Sonny said, "You need to get this looked at by a doc, 'cause this is temporary."

The first paramedic checked Scooter's assailant, handed him some gauze, and told to put pressure on it. The second paramedic pulled a gurney out of the ambulance. Scooter thought: *These guys know how to do stuff.* The first paramedic then came over to Scooter and said, "Tilt your head." He dabbed and then scrubbed the side of Scooter's head and it stung. He felt something being put across the side of his face on his cheekbone and then near his eyebrow. His face was numb. He spit out some more blood and the paramedic asked to look in his mouth. He shined a flashlight into Scooter's mouth and eyes again. "You have a cut inside your mouth. You'll need to rinse it with warm saltwater. You show signs of a concussion too, so I'm thinking you should see a doc about it."

"Well, we need to keep going. I gotta elbow." Scooter said. The paramedic looked at Scooter's elbow as he bent it up upwards. He took out some additional materials from the kit and scrubbed the large skinned spot, then put on stinging liquid. Scooter said to no one in particular, "I think that bastard hit me with that two by four there!"

The first policeman, Mike, came over and moved it slightly with his foot. "Maybe," he said.

"Well, don't put off seeing a doc and don't do anything strenuous." The first paramedic advised. "These guys should be okay, let's get that one to the hospital."

The second paramedic and second policeman loaded the man onto a gurney near Scooter's car. *Bill, if I remember right,* Scooter thought. He was hoping Sonny hadn't killed him. They could be in real trouble then.

After the ambulance left, Mike told them, "I'm going to take this guy to the station in my car. You boys follow me in yours. Don't think anything else. You won't get far!"

Sonny and Scooter went across the sidewalk to Scooter's car. He limped on the foot he had hurt. They carefully skirted around the pool of vomit.

"You better drive. I'm punky," Scooter said. His head felt thick.

Scooter climbed into the car on the passenger side, and as he did, saw Sonny take a roll of nickels out of his back pocket and put it under the seat.

"Yeah, don't let anyone see that. I wondered what was going on there," Scooter said.

"Damn guys had it comin' innit?"

"Yeah," Scooter said. He was wondering if Sonny would have killed the man if the police hadn't shown up, but said, "I might'a broke my toe on that guy's head!"

He wondered what he would have done as well if the police hadn't shown up . . . if he would have stopped kicking. He realized he had been out of control, in a kind of white-hot rage. They followed the police car for several blocks to a large wooden building.

They sat in the car until Mike, the police officer, pulled Wally out of the back. He had been cuffed. Sonny and Scooter got out and followed them inside. Mike told them to go into a room and sit down. He pushed Wally ahead of him. Scooter noticed Wally's cheek had a red mark and his face was swollen on one side, pumpkin-like. One of his ears was bloody. Scooter followed Sonny into the room and sat down, waiting.

After about ten minutes, Mike came back in and pulled up a chair, then sat in it facing its back.

"Okay, tell me your version," he said.

Scooter retold what happened until the police car had shown up.

Mike then asked Sonny "Is that right? Anything you want to add?" Sonny shook his head.

"Is that what happened?" Mike asked more emphatically.

"What he said, that's what happened," Sonny said gruffly.

After studying Sonny for a few seconds, Mike said, "Come with me." They followed him into a hall. Scooter was wondering if they were going to be placed in a cell. Mike took them into an office where another policeman was sitting at a desk.

"Jim here is going to take down some information. You both have IDs?" They nodded their heads. "I don't know if there are going to be charges on this yet, but there might be." He left them with the desk officer.

The desk officer asked them for IDs, and Scooter gave him his driver's license. Sonny passed over his student ID. The desk officer asked what they did, and they mentioned they were college students. He looked at Sonny.

"You have a college ID?" he asked Scooter.

Scooter fished it out of his wallet and put it on the desk. The desk officer looked at the information and began typing on a form. He asked them again to state what happened and slowly typed as they spoke. Scooter had an urge to reach across the desk and push some of the keys, to hurry his progress.

Finally, the officer gave the IDs back to them and pushed an intercom button. "Mike, we're done in here."

After another few minutes, Mike came in and scanned the report. "We don't like trouble here. We'll be talking to someone at the college, just so they know," he said.

"We just stopped in to get somethin' to eat," Scooter said.

Mike studied Scooter for a few seconds and then continued, "Put some ice on those knots. If you need to come back, we'll let you know."

"I reckon we won't be coming back," Scooter said.

Mike studied Scooter for a longer period. "Look, if there's a warrant for you to appear, you will be back!"

"Okay, we get it." Scooter said gruffly. He and Sonny walked out of the room into the hallway. They stopped at a drinking fountain and took several turns at it. Scooter rinsed his mouth and saw that what he spit out had a pink tint. He noticed the door to the men's toilet and Sonny followed him in. They hadn't said anything to each other.

Scooter finished urinating and finally said, "If that cop had been any slower on the typewriter I would 'ave had to piss on the floor." He went over to the sink and was going to put water on his face but stopped. He looked at himself in the mirror. The left side of his face was puffed out and swollen around his eye had the beginnings of being compressed into a slit. There was already a purple-black mark under it and an abrasion on the side of his face above his cheek.

"Shit!" he said, "that guy got me good." He looked at Sonny and said, "You got some blood yet on the side of your head near your ear. The medics missed it." Sonny looked in the mirror and turned his head to see the area Scooter mentioned.

"Doan even know how it happened," he said and bent over the sink to rinse the side of his head while Scooter watched.

Both went out into the hall and took another drink. Sonny asked, "Y'want me t'drive?"

They walked out through the front door. Scooter was hoping they wouldn't run into Mike again.

"Yeah, for a little while," he said. "Stop at that gas station on the way out of town, because I wanna get some ice and water for us . . . shit, it's eleven-thirty."

After stopping at the service station and weathering the questioning looks of the lone clerk, they continued south toward Salida. There were only a few cars on the road. Scooter leaned back in the seat and tried to relax. He put the bag of ice against the side of his face, wedging it against the door, and asked Sonny, "Where'd you learn to fight like that?"

Sonny didn't answer right away. Finally, he said, "You know the guys doing the sweat ceremony and Emmet Fox on the rez?" Scooter nodded his head. "They've been trying to teach the younger guys some of the old ways, the warrior way."

Scooter asked, "Like raiding, or hunting?"

"Nah . . . well, it's more complicated en that," Sonny said." A lot of what we're taught is to be good fer the people . . . our tribe . . . t' take care of each other, especially the young and the old, but the traditions too. But there's another side to this. The teachers know we're going out to where there's . . . evil or that there're evil people and we have to be ready, uh."

This interested Scooter and he asked, "Do you learn martial arts or boxing?"

"Yeah, something like that . . . judo fer one. Supposed learn not to be afraid to deal with a problem when it needs to be, but also not to look fer it, to know when force ain't needed. Guess I'm still learnin' huh? But, chit . . . just used my fists. I coulda twisted the guy around by an arm en kicked his ass if'n I did what we're taught in some a them training things." Sonny looked over at Scooter with a slight grin.

"You mean control?"

"Yeah, takes a lot of training see?"

I don't have it. You know my temper sometimes," Scooter said. "We couldn't avoid a confrontation . . . y'know fighting tonight. I mean, if we would have crawled for those guys I wouldn't have been able to look myself in the mirror . . . uhh, even if it ain't too pretty now what I'm seein'. That's what I think."

"Yeah, that's what it is. But, it's more en what yer thinkin' . . . I mean what we're sposed to learn . . . It's for the benefit of the people . . . innit, to stand up fer the old people, the kids. But, y'gotta be ready to kick ass if'n you have t' . . . like in a corner. They try to teach us the tools . . . y'know, mental and physical."

"Mental. I guess I understand it. Sounds like martial arts stuff."

"Now yer gettin' close."

"Yeah, like tonight . . . I'm seein' it. That was funny when that cop . . . Mike or whatever, asked you what happened, and you said, 'What he said.'"

"I don't trust cops, especially white-eye cops. But yeah, the warrior way is what. I kinda got in trouble on the rez when some kids were bein' mean to a little guy at the store there. I tol 'em if they didn't leave 'im alone, I was going to take their hair. There ran like rabbits with their tails lit!"

Scooter chuckled. "How'd you get in trouble?"

"Ah . . . one a the kid's dad was with the agency—a white eye. They had a meeting with my dad and mom, an' me a course, with the police in the guy's office. He asked me about what I'd said t' those kids—his kid. I tol him I'd take his hair, too, if I saw his kid doin' it again."

Scooter laughed even though it hurt his face. "So, what happened then?"

"Oh, the tribal police came and told me to tone it down. My dad didn't mind though . . . was a little proud a me."

"I didn't know you were such a badass!"

"Yeah, throughout, innit!" They both chuckled at Sonny's comment.

They lapsed into silence.

Scooter thought about what Sonny had disclosed and if he would do the same. He put his head back on the seat and started to doze. He woke later with a start and realized Sonny was talking to him. "Where's a gas station y'think?"

Scooter sat up. The ice bag had slipped onto his lap and his pants were wet from it. He placed the bag on the floor.

"Turn west, 'cause I think there's a truck stop near the edge of town." His face felt tight. He had to concentrate to speak clearly. They slowly drove through town.

"Shit, it's closed. What time is it?" Scooter asked. Sonny didn't know. Scooter turned on the dome light and checked his watch. "It's one-thirty. Isn't there a service station in South Fork?"

Sonny didn't know, but asked, "Kin y' drive? I gotta whiz."

He pulled the car over and they both got out and stood on the side of the road and urinated toward the borrow ditch. Scooter slid into the driver's side and waited for Sonny. His face was numb, and one side felt heavy. They headed west.

South Fork looked deserted. None of the service stations was open. Scooter looked at the gas gauge. *Dang, maybe an eighth.* "We may not make it," he said.

"I'm sure that truck stop in Pagosa's open twenty-four," Sonny said. "It's where the road branches t' the rez."

"What if we drained the hoses here?" Scooter asked. He pulled into the darkened service station to the first pump and shut off the car's lights.

"We better watch fer cops here too," Sonny said.

Scooter opened the filler cap to the car, stuck the nozzle in and lifted the hose to drain it.

"I think I got some," he said. He moved the car up and repeated the procedure at each pump. He got back into the car and looked at the gauge. It didn't look like it had made any difference.

"C'mon, we can coast down from the top a the Wolf," Sonny said.

"Yeah, that'll help." Scooter started the car and they headed west toward the top of the pass. They caught up with a semi-truck. It slowed them down. Scooter couldn't figure if this was saving gas or not. About halfway up they were able to pass the truck and then coasted down the other side, having to brake hard several times for curves.

"Y' need them gloves a Zeke's," Sonny observed.

"Can you believe that guy?" Scooter asked.

He held his breath as they got on the rolling hills below the pass. The gas gauge needle sat on the "E". Finally, they could see the lights of the town in the distance. Scooter thought they were going to make it, but suddenly the car hic-upped several times and they coasted over to the side of the road.

"Shit, what else?" Scooter said. "We just wanna get home."

Sonny got out and went around to the back, placing his hands on the trunk of the car, ready to push. Scooter got out by the driver's door but left it open, pushing on the frame. The car began to move, but the activity caused his head to throb. They worked up a slight incline and progress became slow until they were barely moving. Scooter pushed harder, grunting with the effort. They finally made some progress. He could feel when Sonny was pushing. Scooter pushed harder to keep the momentum, but the effort caused a pounding in his head. They finally reached the apex of the hill, and the car began picking up speed. Scooter hurriedly hopped in as the car left Sonny behind. Scooter continued to coast the car down the highway and stopped at the entrance road to the service station. The semi-truck they had passed on the other side of Wolf Creek came roaring by. Scooter was relieved the car was off the road and said to himself, "Lucky."

He wondered though if Sonny had gotten out of the way. He looked back up the highway into the dark but didn't see him and started to worry. Finally, he could see Sonny's slim silhouette jogging along the shoulder.

"Sorry, I couldn't stop," Scooter said.

"I needed the workout," Sonny replied.

Scooter grinned but felt the tug on his stiff face.

They pushed the car the rest of the way to one of the pumps and filled it up.

Scooter went inside and paid the lone attendant. He looked at Scooter and said, "Hard traveling, huh"?

"If you only knew the half of it," Scooter said. He went back out and tried to start the car. It didn't catch.

"Pump the pedal some. She's dry," Sonny said.

Scooter turned the key. It still didn't start. They got out and opened the hood. Sonny continued, "I know how t'do this . . . gas in the carburetor." He took the air cleaner off and said, "See if'n that guy has a funnel, bottle, or somethin'."

Scooter went back into the station and the clerk gave him an old plastic Clorox bottle that had part of the top cut out. They slowly squeezed gas out of the pump into the bottle and Sonny poured some into the carburetor. He told Scooter to pump the gas and then try it. The engine tried to start and then quit.

"Do 'er again!"

Much to Scooter's relief, the engine caught and kept running.

Sonny reattached the air cleaner. "I'll take this back'n settle with im." He took the bottle back into the clerk, came jogging back out and hopped into the car. "Let's get the fuck outta Dodge!"

Scooter looked at his watch. It was three o'clock. "Man, what a night!"

The rest of their trip to Durango was uneventful, with only a few other vehicles on the road. They arrived at Sonny's dorm at four, and Scooter helped him retrieve his equipment out of the car and then started to go with him to the dorm. Sonny stopped and said, "Naw, I can get it." He took his duffle bag and started to head out.

Scooter said, "Hey wait a minute. Here." He put out his fist. Sonny hit it with his uninjured hand. Scooter continued, "Been a helluva journey you bronc rider."

"Yer face looks like chit, y'bronc rider!" Sonny replied. *"Ikeego manana!"*

Scooter watched as Sonny slowly walked up the sidewalk with his duffle bag in one hand and his saddle slung over the other shoulder.

CHAPTER TWENTY-SEVEN
IT'S COMPLICATED

Scooter opened the door to his apartment. The tiredness had settled. *Bone tired. Now I know what that means.* He thought about taking a shower, but instead went into the bathroom and washed his face as best he could. He looked at himself in the mirror. *Yeah, a bad boxing match.* There was dried blood in his hair. He washed the area with cold water. The swollen side of his face with the closed eye and myriad of purple, green, and yellow was tender.

He ambled out to the kitchen and opened the refrigerator, took a carton of orange juice, shook it and poured a glass full. It seemed like he had been gone for a week. *Wow, a lot happened in three days. Wonder what that cop is going to do.*

He looked at his hat. It needed to be reformed where something had put a crease on one side. *Needs to be steamed I guess. Hope it can be fixed . . . expensive.* He found his alarm clock and set it for seven-thirty. As an after-thought, he pulled a shallow pan from the drawer under the oven and took some silverware from a drawer on the counter near the sink. He set the alarm and the silverware in the pan by his bed, as he had seen Sonny do. He was careful pulling off the boot from the foot he had hurt. He took off his sock from that foot and noticed several purple lines on the swollen big toe. He flexed all his toes several times; they didn't feel too bad. He pulled off the other boot and his jeans and then turned off the light. He went to sleep thinking about Charlene, Popcorn, and how long the guy's arms were as he had come into the hotel restaurant.

It took Scooter several seconds to figure out where he was and what was making such a racket when the alarm went off. He felt like he had been drug through a knothole. He gradually sat up. His head ached. He limped over to the bathroom to pee and looked for the super aspirin that he still had from the Fort Collins trip, took the last two, and went back into the kitchen to chase them with orange juice. He placed two pieces of bread into the toaster and left them while he went back into the bathroom to shave. He had to be careful with the injured side of his face. His eye was a slit and under the eye, the black and purple mark with a greenish tinge between had become more pronounced. He quietly said, "Sonofabitch!" He finished shaving and turned on the shower water. After it was hot, he stepped in and took a longer-than-normal shower. The shampoo stung the skinned spots on his face. He carefully dried around the Band-Aids and then realized he needed to be careful drying his skinned elbow too. He ran a comb through his hair and then hunted up a clean pair of jeans and took a shirt out of the closet. He looked at his watch. He realized he had to hurry and put on a pair of shoes instead of boots. It seemed he could walk okay, but it hurt. He grabbed the toast and slapped some jam on one piece to make a sandwich, and then grabbed his English class notebook and a pen.

By the time he parked in the college lot, he had five minutes before his class started. He hurriedly limped across the campus lawn to the lecture building and scurried down the hall and into the classroom. He hustled toward the back of the room, hoping to be inconspicuous. He saw that Katherine was sitting in her usual chair. He didn't think she had noticed him.

Hank, however, said, "Hells bells man, what happened to you?"

"It's a long story . . . complicated," Scooter said.

Katherine turned to look back and the shock was evident on her face. Mrs. Starmire had come into the classroom, so Katherine mouthed, "What happened?"

"After!" Scooter mouthed back.

"I have your essays to pass out," Mrs. Starmire said. "Then we'll go through some of the things you need to study for the final exam on Wednesday. If you concentrate on these, you won't have too much difficulty. First, however, I want to commend most of you on your essays—much improved from the first of the year. Maybe there's hope for you yet." Some of the students looked around smiling at each other. She continued, "When I call your name, come up and receive your paper."

Scooter waited, thinking about what else he could have added—if he had done enough on it. He waited and wondered if it was alphabetical or by descending grades, as more and more people received their essays. He watched as Hank received his. Hank smiled as he looked at his grade and went back to his seat.

Finally, Mrs. Starmire said, "Mr. Henry." She looked up as he limped to the front of the class and said, "Oh my!" as she saw his face. She continued, "You boys and rodeo . . . I don't know. By the way, I enjoyed your explanation of what it is."

"Thank you," he said and looked at his paper. It had some writing on it and a grade of *88* written in red. *That's better than I thought, but I wish it was a 90.* As Scooter sat down, Hank showed him his paper. It had, *78, C+!* written on it. He grinned and nodded his head at Scooter, who gave Hank the "okay" sign. Scooter wondered what Katherine had received. It would be great if he had surpassed her. He rifled through his paper, glancing at a few comments, written in red. He had spelled rigging as "riggin" which, if spelled that way, needed an apostrophe. He knew that. Dang! There were a few other comments, including praise of his explanation of what it means to compete and of the attraction of rodeo.

He got out his notebook as Mrs. Starmire started putting highlights on the board. She was interrupted by a rap on the door. She walked over to open it and came back in with a note. She said, "Mr. Henry!" He went to the front and took the note. It said: *Mr. Hennessey wants to see you at the college newspaper office at your earliest convenience.* The other students had turned to look at Scooter. He shrugged. He had hoped the knock wasn't a summons for that incident in Basin.

After they were dismissed, Hank came over and said, "Jeez you must've been on a rank one!"

"Huh, wish it had been actually," Scooter said, "Sonny and I got in a fight with some guys in Basin on the way back. Between that and sitting in the police station and running out gas, we had a blast! I'll tell you more later. I gotta check on something. By the way, you did it . . . the essay!"

"Well, I guess we did it," Hanks said.

Scooter noticed that Katherine was waiting for her friend, Linda, who was talking to Mrs. Starmire. Scooter went over to where Katherine was standing. "So, how'd you do?" he asked.

She looked at him, scanning his face. "I thought you were going to be careful. You look like a train wreck!" He smiled at her remark.

"We tried to be careful but had some problems. We got in around four. Do you have time for a coffee at the student union? I'm whacked."

Katherine seemed undecided. "Linda and I were going over that way, so come on," she said.

"So, did you ace the essay?" Scooter asked. "I wanna know if you beat me again. Maybe I beat you this time!"

"Mrs. Starmire liked yours. I did okay," she said, and showed Scooter her paper and it had a 95 written on it along with, *Excellent!*

"Wow! You're a natural, apparently. Why don't you become a writer?" he asked.

"Maybe I will," she smiled.

Linda chimed in and said, "I never beat her either . . . in this class or others! By the way, your face gives me the willies."

Scooter laughed at her remark, which hurt the injured side of his face.

"Not that it's any of my business, but we don't often get notes from administration during class," Katherine said, "we're both curious!"

"You guys know Hennessey from the college newspaper? The guy wants to see me I guess," Scooter replied.

"No, what do you have to do at the school newspaper?" Katherine asked.

"Well, I'm not sure. Maybe it's something about the rodeo. The rodeo was fine, but Sonny and I ran into trouble in Basin. Couple of drunks. There might be trouble yet. A cop there said he was going to call the college."

"Were you fighting? " Katherine asked. Her voice went up an octave.

"Yeah, we had to." He noticed she was scrutinizing him with an intense look and he hurriedly explained, "Believe me, we had to. We didn't go looking for it. We were just trying to get some dinner! Were at the police station there 'til nearly midnight!"

They got coffee at the counter and went to a table. He continued, "Then cuz it was so late, we ran out of gas near Pagosa. Had to push the car . . . seemed like a mile. There was nothing open in Del Norte and not in South Fork either. We coasted off Wolf Creek. It was a long night!"

Katherine was studying him as he told the story. "You should go to the Dean's office and tell them about that incident before that policeman calls."

"Yes, if they don't know and the police call, that's worse," Linda agreed.

"I was hoping he wouldn't call, y'know?"

"Your face gives you away. The whole college will soon know." She had her hand on his arm. "What about your buddy, Sonny?" she asked.

"He's supposed to see about having an eyebrow stitched and he did something to his hand from pounding on a guy's head."

"You guys! Come on, we'll go with you to the office before the next class."

"I have to get back to the dorm or I would," Linda said, "I'll see you later." To Scooter, she said, "Good luck over there. You should have your face looked at." He nodded.

Katherine and Scooter walked across campus toward the administration building. Will was walking across from the other direction and called over, "Hey you, hotshot. You giving out autographs yet?"

"Yeah, all day!" Scooter called back.

"What's he mean . . . not about fighting I hope," Katherine said.

"Oh, it's about the rodeo."

"Okay, Mr. Modesty, what is it?"

"I had a really good horse. A National Finals horse and it didn't buck me off. So, won the bareback event."

Katherine had stopped. "Oh, that's why the newspaper wants you. I'm walking with a celebrity!" she exclaimed.

He smiled. "Damn right! One that might be in trouble though."

Katherine took his hand, "Well, congratulations! Come on, we'll get you out."

"I wanted to ask, how're things at home . . . your mom?" he asked.

"Mom should get out of the hospital this week. The doctor is optimistic. She will have to do chemotherapy, though."

"That's tough," Scooter said. "I know . . . well, my Uncle Jake." He didn't finish, and they went through the doors of the administration building and to the Dean of Students' office. The secretary looked up and then did a double-take when she saw Scooter's face.

She came over to the counter. "What do we have here?" she asked.

"Is the Dean in?" he asked. "We had a little trouble, um . . . had a run-in with some guys traveling from the rodeo in Laramie and the cop there said he was going to phone."

"The Laramie Police Department was going to phone?"

"No, it was in Basin . . . Colorado." Katherine squeezed his hand.

"Just a minute," the secretary said, and walked back to an office.

After a few minutes, she came out with Mr. Walters, the Dean. "What's the problem now?" He scrutinized Scooter's face.

Scooter reiterated what he had told the secretary. The Dean asked, "When you say 'we' who do you mean? I suppose Eckhardt was involved?" Scooter noticed the Dean was studying his face.

"No, it was Sonny and me, Sonny Valverde."

"We haven't had a phone call that I know of yet. Apparently, it was a serious confrontation. Were there charges?" the Dean asked.

"No. Two guys jumped us." Scooter said.

The Dean asked his secretary, "What's my schedule like this afternoon?"

"A meeting at one, but otherwise your afternoon is open."

"I want you and Valverde to meet with us at three. We need to sort this out. What was the policeman's name?" he asked.

"Okay. It was Mike something," Scooter said.

"Okay then. Be back here at three and bring Valverde with you."

"Okay." He and Katherine walked out of the office and then back out of the administration building. He stopped and checked his watch. "Thanks for coming with me," he said. "I have a few minutes before animal science class. Let's go over to the newspaper office. I'll see what they want."

"You go," Katherine said, "I need to get ready for class and then have work."

"Okay, maybe see you at lunch. I'm starving."

"Do you still want to study later? I mean are you going to want to?" she asked.

"If you still want to. I could use help from Miss A-Plus. What about after that meeting I have with the Dean? Of course, I won't have to study anymore if they kick Sonny and me out."

Katherine smiled at his anxiety. "They're not going to kick you out. You're the school hero now. See you later."

He watched her as she walked across campus.

Scooter retraced his route back into the administration building and scanned the directory in the hall for the location of the *High Desert News* office. It was in the basement. He walked into the office, but didn't see anyone, so rang a small bell that was on the counter. It took a few minutes, but finally, a slight man with thick glasses came out and asked, "Can I help you?"

"I'm supposed to see Mr. Hennessey. I'm Scooter Henry."

The man blinked a few times as if trying to place Scooter, and then said, "Oh, the rodeo rider." He extended his hand. "Congratulations are in order." Scooter shook the extended hand. Mr. Hennessey continued, as he viewed Scooter's face. "I guess injury is part of the sport."

"Uhm . . . well, guess so," Scooter said.

"Here's what I'd like to do. One of your teammates informed us, so we had the *Tribune* from Laramie wire a photo . . . one of their photographers took it of you on a bucking horse."

"I saw it."

"Well, the deal is we can run it with a credit to the photographer and paper there, but I want to do a press release to go with it. Then I want to release it to the local paper here. The college doesn't have an issue out until the end of the week, but we'll run it in that also. Does that sound okay?"

Scooter wasn't sure where this was going, but said, "Yeah, I guess."

"We'll send the release out to your home-town area too. It's our normal procedure."

"Okay. Guess that'd be Bunting . . . the *Plainsmen*." Scooter said, not sure if he had to do anything.

"Anyway, we need to do an interview. Do you have a few minutes?"

Scooter paused and said, "I have a class I have to get to. What about this afternoon, say two-thirty?"

Hennessey took a small notebook out of his shirt pocket and looked at it. He said, "That's going to be tight, but let's do it." He put out his hand and Scooter shook it again.

"I'll see you then," He hustled as fast as his limp allowed to his animal science class and realized he had left his class notebook in his apartment. Guess I'll use my English notebook.

The class had already started, so Scooter slid into the first available chair amid curious stares from the other students. He concentrated on the lecture, as he realized it was critical to have this review for the final. After the class was over, Hank and several other students came over and wanted to know what had happened. Scooter retold the Basin story.

"Yeah, but I heard you did great in Laramie," Hank said.

"Well, that was the good part of the trip," Scooter said, "had that Popcorn horse . . . you know, it's been to the NFR. Tough, yet sweet if a guy can stay on fer the eight . . . y'know what I mean?" He noticed that Hank was nodding. "So, scored an eighty-five, if you can believe it?"

One of the listeners said, "Wow! You won the event?"

"Yeah, they're going to do some kind of a press release I guess."

"Well, you been ridin' better 'n better all spring," Hank said.

"Have you seen Sonny?" Scooter asked. "I think he was supposed to see the nurse about a cut and have his hand x-rayed."

"I haven't. You should have 'em look at yer mug, too . . . yer eye's swollen shut!" Hank said.

"Yeah, but I gotta get some lunch first," Scooter said.

He walked across campus to the cafeteria, figuring that Sonny might be there. He wondered about phoning his parents. His mom might be in, and maybe his dad for lunch. *Guess I better wait though until after that meeting to see what they say.*

He checked the dining area for Sonny and then for Johnny or Will. None was evident. He went over to the serving area and grabbed a tray. He decided he would eat a full course. It had been a lean two days.

The full-time staff was mostly older women who were familiar to Scooter. He held out his student ID to be checked as he started through the line. "Now what happened to you?" the first woman asked. "Don't tell me you wrecked your car!"

"No, just rodeo stuff," he replied. She looked at one of the other women and they both shook their heads.

Katherine came out from the kitchen to help serve.

"Hey, put on a big steak and a gob of mashed potatoes," he said. "Well, actually just the mashed potatoes. Hold the steak for later."

The first woman asked Katherine. "Isn't this wild boy one of your friends?"

Katherine blushed. "I know, he looks terrible," to Scooter she said, "You better have that looked at."

Scooter tried to make light of the situation, "Y'know, it's not as bad as it looks . . . only hurts when I laugh!" This got a few smiles out of everyone.

"Did you go over to the newspaper guy?" Katherine asked.

"Yeah, they want to do a press release. There's a photo from the Laramie newspaper they're going to use here too. It's cool."

"I'm happy for you. I'm sure the Basin thing will be okay. I mean it wasn't your fault."

"Yeah. Have you seen Sonny? I've been looking for him."

"I haven't yet. He usually comes in for lunch. Here!" She put two small plates of Jell-O on his plate. "So, you don't starve."

He carried his tray into the dining room and sat with some of the guys that had come over from the animal science class. They continued to ask Scooter about the rodeo and he told them that Sonny, Zeke, and Will had also placed, so it had been a good trip. They wanted more details about the fight. He told them they had held their own, but that a guy had hit him with a two-by-four when they had come out of the restaurant. He mentioned that Sonny was like a . . . he was trying to find an analogy. "He might've been like a wolverine out there . . . a wild man. It was bad!"

"That's sucks they jumped y'all. I mean we should all go over there and clean out the town!" One of the students said.

Scooter chuckled at the thought. "No, the cop would just arrest everyone. He wasn't too pleased there was trouble anyway," Scooter said. "One of the guys . . . um, Sonny knocked him unconscious . . . had to be taken to the hospital in an ambulance. It was serious!" He hadn't noticed him coming over, but Sonny slid into one of the chairs at their table.

"*Daahnzo!*" he said.

Scooter knew it was "hello," but said, "I hope that's 'howdy' and not some swear word like usual."

One of the others at the table said, "We been hearing about your weekend adventures."

"Yeah, bout 'nough fer a day er two," Sonny said.

"We're sposed to meet with Walters at three . . . you know, Dean of Students," Scooter said.

Sonny looked up from eating and said, "I ain't. You can if'n you want."

"They just want to know what happened."

"I doan trust 'em. If that cop says so, they'll kick us out. That there's how it works, innit." Sonny said.

"Naw, I'll tell them. You don't have to say anything," Scooter said. "Just say, 'What he said,' like to that cop. Finish up. We need to go over to the infirmary after class. You need that cut looked at and I need some big-assed aspirins."

"I doan know if I need to 'bout that cut. But I should 'ave this hand looked at. It's sore'n hell 'n it's my ridin' hand." He stuck out his hand to show Scooter. It was swollen to the point that there was no knuckle definition.

"You were thumpin' the guy's head and my car with it."

"Could be broken," one of the other students observed.

Scooter waited for Sonny to finish eating and then turned in their trays and stacked the dirty dishes.

After their range management class, they walked across campus to a small building across the road from the administration offices. Several students were sitting in the waiting room. They went up to a window and waited for a receptionist to recognize them. Scooter was hoping this wasn't going to take too long, but with two students ahead of them, it could. He thought the receptionist was likely a student. She looked up and he could tell she was checking out his face and then Sonny's.

"We were supposed to come over and see someone. He has a cut that might need stitches and it's been since last night," he said. The receptionist looked at Sonny again.

"I need your student IDs first," she said. She took the cards they placed on the counter and went back to a photocopy machine. She came back and then gave them clipboards with forms to fill-out. They went back to the row of chairs and started working on the forms. Scooter had his done first. He looked at Sonny, who was slowly reading through the questions and writing.

"Give me that!" Scooter said. He took the clipboard and wrote where the form had "Details of Incident": *What he said!*

Sonny grabbed it back and looked at what Scooter had put and laughed, "You like that, doan you?" He continued to write about his injury, and then asked, "What should I put about who or what?"

"Just put unknown third-party," Scooter said.

Sonny nodded and then asked, "Shouldn't I put down 'unknown fourth party', too?"

Scooter looked at him and said, "Judas Priest! It's complicated enough!" He noticed that Sonny was laughing silently at his own joke. He finished and signed the bottom of the form. They handed the forms into the receptionist, and she checked them over and then told Scooter and Sonny to sit back down. They waited for a while.

Finally, as Scooter was wondering if they were going to be all day, the nurse came out and said, "Mr. Valverde? Come with me." She held a door open for him.

One of the other students in the waiting room asked Scooter, "What happened to you guys?"

"Ah, had a fight, up'n Basin . . . coming back from a rodeo," Scooter said.

The second student sitting on the other side of the first was a girl. "They shouldn't have that here," she said. "This isn't the Wild West." The boy sitting between her and Scooter looked uncomfortable.

Scooter talked over him, "Who says it isn't the Wild West? We think it is!"

"Society doesn't need you," she said. "You can herd cows with those four-wheelers, or whatever they are."

Scooter felt the first flare of anger, but swallowed it and said, "Oh really? Then why am I taking 'Manual Cow Herding 101' here? Anyway, it's a moooot point, we're getting vaccinated for it . . . to get it out of our systems. That's why we're here. My friend's getting his now."

The girl's face turned red. Scooter noticed the receptionist was laughing silently. He felt proud of himself; that he had thought of a good response for a change.

Silence returned to the waiting room. After what seemed like an hour, Sonny came out and the nurse asked the girl that Scooter had the discussion with to come with her. She glared at Scooter as she left the room.

Sonny said, "She put in three." He pointed to a Band-Aid over his eyebrow. His hand was in an elastic bandage over a splint.

Scooter pointed to it and asked, "What's the deal?"

"Um . . . they had to clip some dead skin from the cut since it shoulda been stitched last night, she said. It's tight there, innit! This hand though . . . broken, cracked a bone on that dude's head! Chit . . . I gotta put ice on it and then keep it wrapped." He looked sorrowful.

"What're you going to do this weekend?" Scooter asked.

"Guess I'll see if I can hold on t' anything by then. I already figured on if'n I could ride lefty . . . never done it."

"Shit, man, that's no good. I couldn't ride very well with my other. I tried it once."

"I'm going back to the dorm. Guess I might as well study somthin."

"You comin' over to the Dean's office at three?"

Sonny didn't respond right away, and Scooter waited. Finally, Sonny replied, "I guess. If'n I don't, be more trouble, innit? You do the talkin' though." Scooter nodded. He noticed the other guy was called into the back by the nurse. Maybe he would get out of here sometime.

"Okay, I'll see you there," he said.

Sonny had seemed down. Scooter knew not being able to ride was a big deal for him. It was for all of them. He decided he better open his notebook. He turned to the notes he had taken during animal science. The English stuff he could study later in the library with Katherine. He wondered: *I should mention something to her that there's someone else I'm seeing. Not sure how to do that. She might not like it. Well, we're just studying. Term is out at the end of the week and I may not be back here, so we're not going anywhere anyhow.* He shook off the thoughts and started reviewing his notes. *There was a chemistry study session on Tuesday evening. Guess I better go. That might help more than anything. Wonder if Mr. Withers is going to lead it? Sometimes he does.*

His reverie was broken by a girl and boy that he knew from his chemistry class coming in through the front door. Scooter and the boy nodded to each other. The boy said, "Wow, what happened, you get thrown?"

"No, aah . . . problems with some drunks in Basin."

The girl was looking at him with interest too. The nurse called his name, saving him more explanations. He walked through the door that she held open for him and followed her into an examination room. She asked him some questions about where it hurt and shone a light into his eyes. "You may have had a slight concussion," she said.

"I had a dull, kind of throbbing headache last night . . . today also," he said.

She looked at his eyes again with the light. "Do you have a physician here that you go to?"

"No."

The nurse went over to a drawer and pulled out a sheet of paper. She circled several names on it.

"You should see one of these doctors. I'm going to give you something for pain and for inflammation, also a cold pack. Do you have a refrigerator you can use?"

"Yes."

"You should put the cold pack on those contusions, on your face. Five minutes on, fifteen minutes off. I know you have classes, but at least do this in the evening and mornings for the next several days. The contusions, the skinned spots, are closing. I'm going to give you a small bottle of antiseptic soap. Use it on your face and elbow when you shower."

He nodded that he understood. She went to a cabinet and after several minutes wrote instructions on two envelopes, then handed them to him. "These are for pain, headaches included, and the second is to reduce inflammation. Take these with food or milk. Have Susie out front contact either of the doctors on that list." He nodded. "And like I told your teammate, it's a good idea to stay out of bars."

"But, we weren't . . ." Scooter started to protest. "Well, yeah. Thanks."

He went back out to the lobby and stopped by the receptionist's counter. He said, "I'm supposed to see you about making an appointment with one of these doctors . . . about a concussion."

She looked at the list. "Which do you want?"

"The closest to the college," he said.

She looked at the list and dialed a number. Scooter heard her talking to someone. She said, "They want to see you now!"

"I can't till tomorrow morning. I have classes."

She shook her head at him and continued to talk on the phone. If you can't see him now, he wants you to check back with the nurse here, so just a minute," she told Scooter

The nurse came out and checked with Susie. "A concussion is nothing to be nonchalant about. You should rest and if the headaches continue into tomorrow, come back and see us." Scooter indicated that he understood. He started to head out the door.

"Just a second, I forgot to give you and Mr. Valverde your IDs." Susie said. He went back over to the counter to retrieve them. She continued, "Oh, did the vaccinations work?"

It took him a few seconds to catch on, but then he said, "Oh yeah. Well, guess we're immune to that vaccine." They both chuckled. He took a second look at the receptionist. Susie, the nurse said. She had fixed her light brown hair into two short ponytails and had a pert nose with freckles scattered across her cheeks as if she had gotten too close to a paint job. Her eyes were lively, and she smiled through them at him.

He looked at his watch. He had half an hour before the interview with the newspaper guy. He asked her, "Is it alright if I study here for a while? I have a meeting in the admin building at two-thirty, and . . ." he shrugged.

"No, doesn't matter to me as long as there are plenty of chairs." He turned to look at the waiting room. Except for the fellow from his chemistry class, it was empty. He turned toward her and realized she had made a joke. He smiled and said, "Funny!"

"One good joke deserves another," she said.

"I'll agree with that." He was curious and asked, "Are you a student here?"

"Yes, but I thought I'd skip all the boring class stuff and become a doctor."

He exploded in a loud guffaw. He glanced at his chemistry class compatriot, who was smiling from across the room, likely wondering what was so funny. After he had recovered from his laughter, he said, "You should forget about medicine and be a comedian!"

Susie smiled back at him. "Good advice, but I like to give shots to rodeo cowboys is what!"

Scooter suddenly realized she was boldly flirting with him and he liked it. He smiled back at her and had an urge to find something out about her; if she had a boyfriend.

Their conversation was interrupted by the nurse that came into the reception area and asked Susie for some records.

"See you later," he said, but observed her as she got up and turned to access a large file cabinet. Not bad . . . a little thin maybe, but nice. She smiled back at him and said, "Yeah, later!"

He walked over to the chairs along the wall, where he had sat before and opened a notebook. *I'm Zeke all of a sudden. This is kind of like going to a rodeo and drawing all the best stock . . . just fall into it suddenly with all these girls . . . women.* This trend was perplexing, and he shook his head slightly as he thought about it.

As time for the interview approached, Scooter walked to his car to stash all the items the nurse had given him. He took the envelope of pain pills and stuffed them into the pocket of his jeans. His toe still hurt some, especially when he tried to walk fast.

He angled across the campus to the admin building and into the newspaper office, wanting to get the interview out of the way. A woman in a denim apron led him into a cluttered office and told him to have a chair.

She left and said to someone, "Cam, he's here for that interview."

In a few minutes, Mr. Hennessey appeared. "You're prompt," he said. "Let's see, I'll just go through the standard questions of your hometown, family, and other achievements."

Mr. Hennessey looked rumpled, as if he had slept in his clothes. His thick glasses magnified his eyes and he had ink stains on his off-white shirt.

He reminded Scooter of a seedy Clark Kent.

Scooter told him about Popcorn and that it had been at the National Finals Rodeo last December, where the stock has to be good—proven, and is selected by the rodeo committee and contestants from all the rodeo stock contractors approved by the pro rodeo association.

"It's one of the great draws in rodeo—a horse that is hard to ride—but if you do, you can score well."

"Okay, I'll write the release up this afternoon for the *Chronicle,* so we can get it out. So, that has to happen pronto. However, I'll do a write-up for the college paper, the *High Desert News* today. Can you proof it early tomorrow?"

"I have a class at eight. I could after," Scooter said.

"Okay then. Thanks!" Scooter got up from the chair and Hennessey shook his hand.

CHAPTER TWENTY-EIGHT
EGG-SUCKIN' DOGS

Both of the Deans wore white shirts and ties. Dean Mills of Intercollegiate Affairs had a full head of gray hair and smiling eyes. Scooter thought that both Deans looked distinguished. He felt a little intimidated. His eyes narrowed: *Be tough now, don't be sucky.*

"Let's go over this incident," Dean Walters said. "I talked to the Chief of Police in Basin. He indicated there will be no charges. You boys have a couple of friends there at that restaurant. But, I want you to tell me what happened. Why you were there, that sort of thing."

Scooter retold the episode. He mentioned that they had stayed at the rodeo in Laramie to receive awards and left late, so wanted to get something to eat before everything closed and had been to the restaurant before. He told about the two guys coming out of the bar and being abrasive and knocking Sonny's hat off.

"We want you to know that every time you travel somewhere for a competition that you represent Southwestern State College," the Dean said. "You need to keep that in mind."

Scooter felt his ire rise slightly. "We know that, but sometimes you have to do what you have to do. I mean, we could've hunched our backs up and tucked our tails between our legs like yellow, egg-sucking dogs and slunk out of town."

Dean Mills seemed to be suppressing a smile. Dean Walters looked at Scooter for a while as if contemplating the explanation and then asked Sonny, "Do you want to add anything?"

Sonny didn't say anything for several seconds. Finally, he shook his head and said, "What he said." Scooter looked over at Sonny and had to smile. *If we get kicked out, we're just going to go rodeo together . . . hit the trail . . . that's it.*

Dean Mills chimed in, "Well, you're both good students and I gather good at riding bucking horses. I think what Dean Walters is saying is that you have to be careful of the situations you might get into, especially traveling around the country."

Scooter nodded in agreement. Dean Walters said, "The one man was injured pretty badly, and is still in the hospital. That's one of the consequences of something like this. Something you need to be aware of. Someone can be severely hurt or even killed in these kinds of things."

"We're very aware of what can happen and didn't want it to happen to us," Scooter said. "In fact, we had to become physical to try and prevent it!"

"Remember to try and talk your way out of a confrontation, not into one. They tell me you both have likely qualified for the regional rodeo in Central Wyoming. We both wish you well and know you will represent Southwestern State College to the best of your abilities." Dean Walters stood up, indicating the meeting was over.

Dr. Mills told Sonny, "If you have any problems let me know. We're here to help you."

"Okay," Sonny mumbled.

Scooter and Sonny left the office together and went through the front doors to stand on the steps. A light breeze was blowing across the campus and it felt good. Scooter was relieved that the meeting had not been as bad as he had envisioned. He looked across the campus grounds, at the students walking toward the lecture hall and thought that maybe Southwestern State was a pretty good college.

He smiled at Sonny. "I'm going to put a banner on your riding vest that says, 'What he said.' That's twice and I liked it both times," he chuckled.

"I liked your yeller egg-suckin' dog speech . . . was true. We ain't never slinking outa town, you bronc rider."

Scooter laughed, "Yeah, I hope not. There's something else about this that I didn't want to get into in there . . . that I've been thinking about."

"What's that?" Sonny asked.

"Well, it's like those guys thought they could push us around. I think they thought we were Indian—Native American . . . I mean, me too. I thought they had a shitty attitude about it . . . needed an enema of the mind . . . something like that."

"Hell, good luck on that un . . . changin' people's minds . . . people like them. It ain't going t'work. Might as well piss inta the wind. Trust an Indian on that un!"

Scooter chuckled at Sonny's explanation. "Yeah, I guess . . . I better get. I have a study session with Katherine coming up in the Library. You wanna join us?" Scooter asked.

"Maybe later. I might take a snooze first. Pushin' yer car last night tired me out."

"Yeah, not to mention everything else. If not, maybe meet you at the cafeteria later."

Katherine looked up as Scooter approached and sat down in the chair beside her. "So, have you been expelled?" she asked.

Scooter caught her up on the events. "No, but they want us to go out for the wrestling team and maybe a boxing team too." She smiled at his comment, and he continued, "The nurse said I have a mild concussion, so have to rest some.

He saw that she had her notes opened, so he opened his notebook.

"Concussion! Shouldn't you be in bed? Isn't that dangerous?" she asked.

He shrugged. "The nurse never said . . . well, said not to exert myself." He noticed the concerned look on Katherine's face. "Naw, I'm okay!'

One of the librarians came by their table and shhhed them. Scooter scooted his chair closer to Katherine and whispered, "Let's hit it for a while, then I'll treat you to a coffee. I'm needin' some."

"Maybe," she said. They went over the notes together; sentence structure and noun-verb agreement. Scooter thought that some of these were tricky. They went over indefinite pronouns. Some were variable and the verb-noun agreement depended on real verbs.

"If a person inserts the real verb, then it's easy, huh? I mean the tense of the verb."

"Yes. Let's quiz each other," Katherine said. He moved closer to her still, so they could whisper and ask each other questions.

He noticed the nice fresh smell of her again—a light citrus-like perfume scent perhaps. "You smell nice."

"Keep your mind on your studies, cowboy!" She smiled, though, as she said this.

"Well, just sayin'."

After more than an hour of going over sentence structure and rules for grammar, Scooter thought they had done enough. His head was aching.

"Come on, my mind's full," he said, "let's go over to the student union. I'm buying . . . celebrating not getting kicked out."

They folded-up their notebooks, and headed out of the library, walking beside each other across the campus toward the student union center. Scooter suddenly stopped, and Katherine turned toward him.

"This has been a long day. I'm thinking I've had enough. Do you mind?" he asked.

Katherine studied him. "I'm worried about you. Come on, I think you need some TLC."

"TLC?"

"Yeah, I'm providing it."

"You don't have to."

"Come on, Scooter, you need some help!"

They walked across the parking lot to Scooter's car and drove down the hill to his complex. "Stop in at the office. We better tell your landlady what's up," Katherine said.

"What's up? You better tell me."

"Yes, you'll know in a minute."

Katherine took the plastic bag of medical items, and they went into the office and stood in the small lobby for a few minutes, not seeing anyone. Finally, Mrs. Warner came in through the door from the outside, and said, "Oh, I saw you stop. My gosh! What happened?"

"Rodeo sometimes gets dangerous," Scooter said. Mrs. Warner continued to study Scooter's face.

"I'm from the college and want to make sure he's doing what he needs to," Katherine said. "He's not supposed to drive because of a concussion, so I'll be driving him." Scooter looked at her in amusement.

"Does he need to be in the hospital?" the Mrs. Warner asked, still observing Scooter's face.

"No. He just got out of the infirmary," Katherine said.

"Oh! Do you need me to do anything?"

"I think we have most everything. He needs to get some sleep now. Do you have a plastic bag? We need some ice until I can get a cold pack ready."

"Just a minute," Mrs. Warner said, and walked around the corner of the room and out of sight.

Scooter had observed the conversation as Katherine and Mrs. Warner talked across him, as if he was mute. Mrs. Warner was a divorcee and lived alone and had been nice to Scooter. He figured she was in her mid-forties or possibly fifty, and often came out in the mornings in her robe and house slippers to pick-up the morning paper, her hair in a mass of curlers. She frequently had a cigarette hanging out of her mouth, and a near-baritone voice, one of the hazards of the vice, he figured. The room reeked of smoke.

Scooter could hear her opening doors and knocking something into the sink. She came back out and gave Katherine a bag of ice cubes.

"Let me know if you need more."

"This should be enough for now. Thank you!" Katherine said.

They went outside, and Scooter told Katherine, "You're quick."

"Where should I park your car?" she asked.

He met her at the door to his apartment and unlocked the door. "It's a mess. I haven't even unpacked yet."

"That's the least of my worries," she said.

"You don't have to do this. You're being very nice."

"You let me worry about how nice."

He studied her for several seconds, but said, "I'm supposed to put this cold pack on my head and take these pills with milk or something." Katherine took the cold pack and stuffed it into the small freezer compartment.

"Let's see the pills," she said.

He gave her the envelopes, including the one he had stuffed into his pocket. She read the instructions and said, "Take your clothes off and get into bed."

He looked at her. "My clothes?"

"Well, leave your pants on if you're bashful.

She smiled at him, as he took off his shoes and shirt. She brought him a glass of milk and two each of the pills. He took what she offered and swallowed the pills, then washed them down and said, "Thanks."

He lay back on the bed and Katherine put the bag with ice cubes on his head and said, "I'm going to take your car in a while and go back up to the college. I'll be back later to check on you. Is this your apartment key?"

"Yes," he said, and watched her, as she started washing the dishes that he had stacked in the sink.

CHAPTER TWENTY-NINE
TLC

Scooter woke and struggled to sit up. His head felt fuzzy, thick. He turned on the bedside lamp and checked his watch. It was after midnight. He limped to the kitchen sink to get some water. There was a note on the counter. *Don't forget the cold-pack. There's a sandwich in the frig. See you in a while. K.* He opened the refrigerator and noticed a sandwich on a plate and wondered where she had gotten the lettuce and tomato. Then he realized she had apparently bought groceries. He took the sandwich out, poured a glass of milk and slowly ate while pondering why Katherine was doing all this. *I should have taken her out earlier in the semester, or at least asked her. Now it's near the end of the year, and I've already been with Charlene . . . I need some distance.*

He took the cold pack out and placed it on the nightstand. There were two more pills and another note not to forget to take them. He took off his jeans, then grabbed the pills and went into the bathroom to use it. He swallowed the pills, chasing them with water, and then went back into the bedroom and lay back, again placing the cold pack on his head.

He woke to the sound of someone unlocking his door. He sat up slightly and waited. He looked at his watch in the half-light. It looked like it was six o'clock. Katherine came in and shut the door.

"I wondered if it was my nice nurse. I owe you for this . . . for the groceries," he said. She came over to him.

"Yeah, you're paying alright. How're you doing?"

"Much better. I did what you said . . . mostly slept."

"That's what the doctor . . . well, the nurse ordered," she said.

He started to get up and realized he was only in his underwear. He pulled the bedspread around him and went into the bathroom. His mouth tasted bad: *Yeah, it is the bottom of a birdcage.* He used the toilet and then took a swig from his mouthwash bottle and swished it around. It nearly choked him, and he hacked it up.

Katherine asked from the kitchen, "You okay in there?"

"Yeah, trying to drown myself." He came out trailing the bedspread.

"I got some eggs, you like scrambled?"

"Yeah, but you don't have to," he said.

She pointed to a loaf of bread and said, "Here, make some toast while I do these."

He went back into the bedroom and pulled on his jeans and then shuffled into the kitchen. He said, "You're very nice to me. I don't know if you should be."

"Well, I thought about our last date and it wasn't like I envisioned. But I want you to understand . . . how I feel," Katherine said.

"This is nice, and I appreciate it, but I've dated another girl some . . . a girl from Colorado A&M . . . a barrel racer on the rodeo team, just so you know," Scooter said.

Katherine studied him with her dark eyes. "I know. I thought you might run into others. You're getting too famous. Too many women want you. Linda and Ellen from English class think you're cute. Even Mrs. Starmire wants you; she wants to take you home with her."

Scooter laughed and stammered, "Mrs. Starmire? Sheesh! You were giving me the big head, till you said that!"

"You can laugh, but it's true. That's what I was talking to you about the other night . . . at the restaurant."

Scooter couldn't remember that there was a connection. They sat at the counter and ate together. He spread margarine and then jam on two pieces of toast and offered Katherine one. "Okay, tell me why again . . . what you mean exactly?"

"Do you need it written down? Don't you get it?" she asked.

"I must need it written down. I'm thick about some things," he said.

Scooter thought she looked very attractive. The domestic scene appealed to him; of her cooking breakfast--well, not entirely domestic. Sitting on the barstool had caused her skirt to ride up on her thigh, and he noticed her angular knee. Scooter tried not to look too much.

After they finished eating, she put the dishes into the sink and ran some water, "You are thick," she said. "Come with me." She pulled his hand and led him into his bedroom. "You need the rest of the treatment!"

She began unbuttoning her blouse and shrugged it off. Then unzipped her skirt and let it fall. He stood still, as if a statue, watching her. She had a nice shape, *lithe* came to mind. He wondered how far this was going. She stood for him in her bra and panties and smiled mischievously. She unhooked her bra and let it drop.

"Judas Priest!" he exclaimed.

Her breasts, although small were rounded, yet upturned, with large, darker aureoles. They mesmerized him, and he thought of exclamation points. She hooked her thumbs in the waistband of her panties and pushed them down. They dropped onto the floor and she stepped out of them. He took her in, enthralled by her slender waist that was offset by curves, her shapely legs. She had nicely rounded buttocks and brazenly turned for him.

He heard himself say, "Hell!"

She came over to him and kissed him gently on the lips and then on the uninjured side of his face. "Well, cowboy, you just going to stand there?" she asked.

He noticed her dark, luminous eyes and long lashes. They seemed to be smiling at him—enticing him. He looked at her full, pursed lips. He felt a silent message of promises from them. He continued to absorb as much of her image as he could on such short notice. Her honeyed color: *She's darker than Charlene, those dark eyes, probably her heritage . . . a little more compact too . . . I've always liked her legs. I knew they were good—curvy, but those round buns and pointed breasts . . .* "Jeez, Katherine!"

She unbuttoned his jeans and forced the zipper down, and he helped her push them over his hips. It was as if his hands had a mind of their own—no willpower—he was completely in Katherine's spell. She pushed his underwear down and he let her. She gently touched him, and then took his hand, guiding him toward the bed and then pushed him down onto it.

He looked at her again. "I told you that I liked your legs, but I like all of you!"

"I think it's mutual."

She lay down beside him and kissed the uninjured side of his face. He could feel her silkiness, her curves, her breasts as they pushed into him. Katherine placed a leg across him and centered herself on him.

"Wait! Is this okay? I mean isn't this dangerous?"

"We're okay. I mean, it's alright."

"You better be sure, 'cause we can't have . . . um, y'know, complications!" He felt himself wilt slightly.

"Scooter, honey, do you trust me? Do you trust me that I know myself?" She kissed him again and then placed her tongue in his ear. He kissed her back and found he had plenty of renewed desire for her. She bit his neck and brought him to her. He jerked away from her teeth.

"Sorry, but Scooter, you're doing it!" She grabbed his back with her fingernails and dug-in. This drove him to be hard on her, to be in the center of some sweet pain and take her with him. He concentrated on her eyes, which were shrouded by her lashes. They kissed and then she put her tongue in his ear and said, "Sweet Scooter honey!" He could hold back no longer.

"Wow!" he panted. "See what you did to me? You're a very good nurse!"

"I felt you. You're a good lover. Been practicing?" she asked.

"Yeah, all my life."

She laughed at his answer. They remained joined and nuzzled each other. After a few minutes, he felt himself become interested again and started to move in her.

"Again?" Katherine asked.

"You started something. Now you're the one going to pay for it."

"You're an athletic boy, aren't you?"

"Yeah, and you're an athletic girl."

She smiled and nipped at his lips.

Scooter lasted longer. He concentrated on being good to her, what he thought she liked. He liked to hear her moaning under him—on top of him too. He heard her say, "Oh God . . . do it!" He wasn't sure what else he could do. She bit his neck again. He thought she might have drawn blood. She scratched his back again and that hurt too. He thought of her as a wildcat.

"Judas Priest! You're some girl!" he said. She pulled him to her and they kissed. She put her tongue into his mouth—pushed his teeth apart.

"And you're a sweet boy." He looked into her dark eyes with their long lashes. She continued, "I wondered about you some. What it might be like. It's better than that." She relaxed on top of him.

He stroked her back. Her words drew a smile from him. "What a confession! I never have, y'know."

"Liar! I saw you looking . . . in class."

Scooter laughed as they disengaged and sat up on the side of the bed. He looked at Katherine, at the naked length of her. "Yeah, I like to look at you," he said, and ran his hand down the length of her and then leaned over and kissed her again.

He sat back up. "We better get going though." He looked at his watch. "Judas Priest! It's nearly eight! I gotta be in class soon."

Katherine jumped upright. "Oh, me too! Come on!"

She hurried into the bathroom and turned on the shower. Scooter followed her. He came up behind her, circled his arms around her and cupped her breasts while he nuzzled her neck. "Maybe we should skip them."

Katherine let him fondle her but said, "You couldn't do it again if you had to."

"I think I could . . . maybe soon, too," he said.

"Yeah, right! Come on, we can make it. You've become a naughty boy."

As they pulled on their clothes, Scooter said, "Just a minute." He quickly shaved but had to be careful of the injured side of his face and just skipped that part. He noticed a reddened mark on the side of his neck and rubbed the spot. He took two more of the super-aspirin tablets, washing them down with water, not worrying about taking them with milk or food. He had to paw through his books and notes to find the ones for chemistry and range management lab. Katherine watched him from near the door. Finally, he was ready.

"I nearly forgot. I have to see the nurse up there if these headaches continue. You have me thinking about other things," he said.

She took his car keys. "I mean to . . . to get you thinking less about others and more of me."

He looked at Katherine from the passenger seat in his car, as she drove them up the hill to the college. He was turning a question over in his mind, but thought: *I know this shouldn't have happened, but I liked it anyway.* "Okay, tell me, why this is happening, because I thought we had like broken up last time. Is it love or what, because I'm confused?"

She smiled at him and said, "Of course! It's part of it. Maybe the dessert. You like it, don't you."

He suddenly felt a piece of his shyness come to the surface, like ice forming around the edge of a pond. He suppressed the feeling, not wanting it to control him in thinking about their relationship and how he felt.

"Well, yeah . . . when we were making love, I wanted to have a part in making you more beautiful than you already are. That's what I thought . . . that I had a purpose with you. I think you're very beautiful, more than I thought all the time I looked, as you say, during class."

She shook her head slightly and wouldn't look at him. Scooter thought maybe he had said something wrong or hurt her feelings. "Hey, it's okay. I just wanted you to know . . . to know me a little."

She finally looked at him. It seemed to him that her eyes were glistening. "You better be careful. You're going to trap yourself."

"Well, I just want to know about it . . . the rest, you know, the non-dessert part.

She parked the car and they both got out. "The non-dessert part takes time. Do you have it? I think I would always be second fiddle to rodeo." She handed him the keys and said matter-of-factly, "Come to the cafeteria for lunch. I'm working then."

"Okay, I'll see you then," he said uncertainly. It seemed as if their relationship had reverted to its confusing state. Her staid attitude seemed to indicate it was back to friendship. He realized Katherine had hit upon a truth about him. He was slightly disappointed that she had so easily seen this characteristic, but also relieved. She turned back toward him and reached up to him for a kiss. He returned it and they melded together for a few seconds.

"Don't worry about it . . . just the way it is," she said. He watched her walk across campus.

Scooter hurried to make it to class on time. *Well, going to be a few minutes late. What am I doing? I'm as bad as Zeke! What did he say? Something about the dam breaking? Man, I'm going to drown . . . Charlene would shoot me. Maybe I'm one a those Mormons, wanting to have two wives! Shit, I don't really want even one right now. I have to rethink this whole thing. Katherine is sweet. So is Charlene. Yeah, two wives what it is. Ten kids running around on a farm out there somewhere . . . Well, maybe not with Katherine now . . . Don't worry about it she said. What does that even mean?*

Scooter quickly moved down the hall to the lecture room, limping slightly. Walking fast still hurt his big toe. He hurried through the door and skidded into an empty chair, hoping he wouldn't be noticed. Dr. Hart continued to lecture, but then stopped when he noticed Scooter.

As others had told him, "The rodeo circuit can be a rough life, apparently," Dr. Hart observed. Students at the front of the room turned to look at Scooter. He felt his face redden. Dr. Hart continued, "We're just starting the review. Class, you need to concentrate on the last part of the term, on heterocyclic compounds. We'll go over the main classes of those today. Mr. Withers is conducting a review session tonight and tomorrow night at seven, this room."

Scooter continued to take notes. He was suddenly worried about the exam. *I better bear down . . . this morning and tonight. Could maybe this afternoon, but there are the other classes too. Shit! I've been dinkin' around too much!* After class, a few of the other students asked what had happened. He kept the explanation short. The guy he had seen in the infirmary was standing with the others, obviously by now curious about the incident.

Scooter walked through the main doors and the short distance to the library to try to jump-start a study mode. He gazed at the other students and found a vacant table near the science stacks, making a clatter as he slid out a chair.

After studying for a short time, he suddenly realized he was supposed to go over the press release with Mr. Hennessey. He jumped up and folded up his notebook and textbook and again tried to hurry. He was almost at the door to go outside when he nearly ran into Zeke.

"Hey man, y'going to another fire?" Zeke asked. "I wanted to see that ugly mug a yours. I saw Sonny at breakfast. He said y'got yer ass kicked."

"Hey, good to see you, too," Scooter responded. "I got to see a guy over at the college newspaper. You know, they're doing a press thing. How's yer trip?"

"Well, a whole hell of a lot better'n yers, apparently. It was okay. Long. I got in late last night. Yeah, I called that Cam yesterday . . . left a message about your fame. You doin' lunch at the cafeteria?"

"Yeah, I guess. I'll see y'there," Scooter said.

He limped across the campus to the administration building and hustled downstairs to the *High Desert News* office. The same girl was there and told him that Mr. Hennessey had to leave but showed Scooter a draft of the press release. He went through it and made some corrections. Hennessey had written "bronc riding," so Scooter changed it to "bareback riding," and put a note in the margin that bronc riding indicated the saddle bronc event. His dad's name was spelled "Ethan" and he spelled out "Evan."

He gave the page back to the girl and said, "Should do it, thanks."

His head still seemed thick, but the headache wasn't as bad as the day before. *I bet I just needed some sleep.* It seemed he would make a speedy recovery and be able to ride at La Junta with no problems. He paused suddenly. He realized he had not sent his entry in. *Shit! I better talk to Sonny and Zeke. We're going to have to wire the money. Too much has been going on here. I better call my folks too . . . catch them up on all the events.*

He had to find change for the call, so he walked through the hall. The cafeteria wasn't open yet, so he backtracked and asked several students to change some bills. He dialed his home number and then waited for the amount to be indicated. He fed a series of quarters into the change slot.

It rang several times and finally, his mother answered. She said she was glad to hear from him and wanted to know how school was going. He told her about winning the bareback riding and that an article was going to be in the local paper—the *Plainsmen.*

"I'm quite amazed," she said. "Can you call back this evening when your dad is home? He'll want to talk to you about it. Rachel wants to talk with you also." He said he would. She continued, "Ron will also. He envies you, you know, and he's quietly proud of you." He was going to tell her about the fight and getting injured but decided not to. She asked him if he was doing well in classes. He said he was trying to, and his first final was Wednesday. He asked if they were going to the rodeo in La Junta. His mother said that they had talked about it. Maybe they would on Sunday. He thought about mentioning that he'd asked a girl out to the ranch, but decided it was too complicated. He told her he'd better go and said he would call back in the evening.

Scooter hung up and walked back toward the bookstore and snack bar. He decided he better continue studying until the cafeteria opened. He needed to continue with chemistry, but the range management final was also on Thursday. He and Sonny had not finished studying that either. He had to check in with the physical education instructor too after lunch. He opened up his range management notes and started to read through them, hoping none of the other students would stop by to chat.

After going through several lectures, he was aware that students were starting to come through the snack bar on their way to the cafeteria. He closed up his notes and followed a group down the hall, getting in line. He wondered if he would see Katherine; if she would be hot or cold to him, he never knew which it would be. She had quite amazed him, possibly had taken charge of him, perhaps claimed him. He didn't know what to think about what had happened to him in such a short time. Or, did he let it happen to him? *It's like they've both taken advantage of me. Now that's a twist on roles. Wait a minute . . . maybe I'm playing them in a new way that Zeke has no knowledge of--a kind of style that has to do with being shy, letting them mother me. Wow, some weird thoughts. Must be that head injury!*

He closed in on the stack of trays, lifted one off and slid it along the grill-like shelf of the serving area. He didn't see Katherine at first, but then she came out from the kitchen carrying a pan. She had on mitten-like potholders and a white apron. She noticed him after she had set the pan into the serving area. It looked like scalloped potatoes. She smiled and mouthed something. He said, "What?" She just shook her head.

She came over closer and softly said, "See me before you leave."

He nodded, "Okay."

He looked over the offerings and asked for the potatoes and some meatloaf. He took a salad and some pudding and then filled a glass with milk. He realized it had been a long time since he'd eaten the eggs Katherine had scrambled. He took his tray to an empty table, but Hank, and then Will, soon joined him. They wanted to talk about the rodeo and the Basin fight again. Finally, Zeke and then Sonny joined them. Zeke asked Scooter to fill him in on the details.

"Sonny don't do himself justice," Zeke said. "He's terse! How's that for a word for you?" Wanna know about the meeting with the Dean too. I knew you guys were in trouble. Without me, you're like babes in the woods."

Scooter retold about the fight. Hank and Will crowded in closer, as they apparently wanted to hear it all again too. Scooter told Zeke, "You should have seen Sonny. He was like a wild man. The guy he hit had to be taken to the hospital! Was knocked out cold!" The three listeners looked over at Sonny who was quietly eating. He looked at the others and just shrugged. Scooter continued, "I ain't kidding . . . a wild man!"

"Yer bareback rider here busted the dude's balls. Guy heaved right there on the sidewalk front a the cop 'n medics too!" Sonny put in. "I think it best t' avoid that place fer a while, innit?"

Zeke looked doubtful, but said, "Guess y'never know. Still waters are deep."

"Run deep," Scooter corrected. "Anyway, the Dean thing wasn't so bad. Told us we're ambassadors of the college though . . . are supposed to think about that or something . . . not to go in bars or whatever."

Here's somethin' fer youse t'know," Sonny said. "He tol' 'em we weren't goin' t'get run outta town like some egg-suckin', yeller dogs with our tails tucked. Y'd a been proud of 'im!"

Zeke and the others laughed, "You said that?" asked Zeke. "Hell, I am proud of you! I think there might be hope for you guys yet." They all laughed again.

Scooter continued, "Our bronc rider there said it best though. When the cop asked him about what happened, he said 'What he said, that's what happened,' and he told the Dean that too. I nearly choked tryin' not to laugh."

"You two are a becomin' a regular couple of outlaws," Zeke said.

"Not to change the subject, but any of you entered in La Junta yet?" Scooter asked. Zeke gave him a blank look.

"I did last week, 'cause I was thinking I'd be eligible by now. Got a room at the headquarters place too," Hank said.

"What is it . . . the headquarters?" Scooter asked.

Hank said he couldn't remember the name exactly, "Maybe the La Junta Motor something. Maybe Inn." Will didn't think he was going.

"The thing is," said Scooter, "we need to get our entries in pronto. We should wire the money and our association numbers in today, this afternoon! The Registrar has to send in the mid-term eligibility grade report, so we need to have that done too."

"I'm not sure yet. I mean if'n I can ride with this hand." Sonny said.

"I got that P.E. test at two, so I can't," Zeke said.

"I gotta check in with the trainer and the P.E. guy," Scooter said, "but then I'm going downtown. How 'bout you give me your association numbers and I'll take 'em with me to Western Union? Oh, hell! I need where to send it!"

"I have it . . . in the room. I'll go with ya. Guess I'll enter and see if'n I can ride by then," Sonny said.

Zeke took his intercollegiate rodeo card out of his wallet and wrote the number of it on a napkin. He gave it to Scooter, stood up and said, "This was a hell of a lot easier when Susie was the team secretary. We should kick Johnny's ass for screwing that up."

"Yeah, I second that. Come on we gotta get," Scooter said. He and Sonny took their trays to the discard area. "I got to do something, come on." They walked back to the serving area. Scooter saw that Katherine was still working, so waited for her to notice him. She came around the counter and said hello to Sonny.

"I heard about your adventures and that you rode well at the rodeo," she said.

Sonny nodded and said, "Yeah, thanks, was okay!"

Scooter wondered if Sonny meant everything, the whole trip.

"I just wondered how you were doing?" she said to Scooter.

"I think I'm recovering. Thanks to some TLC, as you said, and some sleep."

She placed her hand on his arm. "Call me this evening, okay?"

Now does she want to kind of make up? "Well, we have to go to the gym and then downtown to send some entries in before our range class at three. But, I can call later this evening."

"Okay. I'll be in my room studying."

Scooter and Sonny headed back through the cafeteria and through the main doors and then toward Sonny's dorm. "You in big trouble man," he said. "Two women is big, big trouble!"

"Yeah, tell me about it. I may become Mormon," he said. Sonny grunted. Scooter continued, "Seriously though. I don't know what's going on with me. Katherine said I'm going to trap myself. I think I got each leg in one! But then . . . well, she said she wouldn't be second fiddle to rodeo, so I thought that was it. Now she wants to talk. Hot and cold, hot and cold!"

"Well, traps 're bad for a rodeo guy. I hope y'don't have to gnaw yer legs off to get out! I tell ya, make up yer mind. If you had to marry un of 'em, which would it be?"

Scooter nodded and said, "Yeah . . . well, marrying! Hell, don't say it, 'cause that's way down the road over the hill somewhere. I don't know, Katherine is too complex for me."

"She just wants y'all to herself I reckon. Anyway, just tryin' to help y'out of a jam, y'know? So y'doan start gnawing on yer legs," Sonny said.

Scooter grinned at Sonny's descriptive analysis. "Yeah, me neither." They stopped by Sonny's dorm room and he found the information about the Baca Junior College Rodeo. Scooter looked it over and said, "Heck, we have two go-rounds. It'll cost us thirty bucks."

Sonny looked at it as well. "Must be too many bull riders again . . . one go-round and a short-go of finals." He stuck the notice in with his books.

"Maybe the thing to do is to enter and if you can't ride, phone them later. I hope you can though."

Sonny got into the passenger side and said, "Me too, but we gotta think 'bout regionals. I'm qualified there anyways."

"You mean heal-up before regionals?"

"Yeah, t'make sure."

They drove through town to the railway depot near the downtown area where Scooter knew there was a Western Union office. They had the agent send a message to the rodeo secretary with their association numbers and the events they wanted to enter and then wired money for the three entries.

As he and Sonny headed back to his car, Scooter said, "Guess we better get on the range management stuff some before class. Wonder how we did on the lab test. Guess we'll get that back today."

"I'm dread'n that un. I fucked it like a bronc stuck my head in the dirt!" Sonny said.

Scooter looked over at Sonny surprised at his words, "You said that last time, too."

They stopped at a bank, so Scooter could deposit the Laramie check. "You can have yer bank cash mine too. I don't have one . . . just keep cash mostly." Scooter looked over at Sonny and wondered how he had sent entries in before.

"You mean a bank?"

"Yeah, doan trust 'em."

CHAPTER THIRTY
LATIN

They took their seats in the range management class for the final exam review. Scooter and Sonny again explained to some of the other students what had happened in Basin. Word had apparently gotten around campus about the guys on the rodeo team, not only doing well in the arena but starting fights as well. Scooter realized what really had happened was being supplanted by rumor. He explained that they had been set upon. It seemed like the other students wanted to believe the worst—that they were badasses. Mr. Dunn, the instructor, came into class, ending the discussion.

"I'm passing out the lab exams first and then we'll go over the material you need to know on the final exam. By the way, you will have a range improvement problem, an essay question," Mr. Dunn said. "I can tell you that right now. Also, many of you were not up to par on the lab exam. Here's what I'm going to do. Look at your grades and see if you want to retake it. The retake will be at four on Thursday. But here's the deal . . . if you retake it, that's your score, so the bet is that you will improve."

He began to come around the room with a sheaf of exam papers. Scooter waited for his. He saw that Sonny had received his test paper and was staring at it. Scooter took his and looked at the first page. It had a large 78 written in red. He then rifled through the paper, viewing those he had missed. He had made some bone-headed mistakes—had been over-confident. The grade was not what he had envisioned.

Scooter looked over at Sonny, but knew from his expression that the verdict was not good, but asked, "What is it?" Sonny just shook his head. He had turned his paper facedown.

The instructor finished passing out the graded exams, "I'll leave the specimens out in the lab, and it will be open each day and until ten each evening. Here's what you need to know for the exam on Thursday." He started writing on the blackboard.

Scooter was doing some math to see if he should retake the lab test, or how high a score he would need to get to raise his grade. He had a solid *B* and a 78 wouldn't bring it down much. He might talk to the instructor and see. He began to copy down what Mr. Dunn was writing on the board. Much of the material was what he and Sonny had studied in Laramie. Scooter was encouraged.

After class dismissed, he waited to see Mr. Dunn to find out if it would help to take the lab exam again, but asked Sonny, "So. Is it as bad as you thought?"

"Worse!" He showed Scooter his paper. It had 58 marked on it.

Scooter gritted his teeth and said, "Jeeze! Well, there's no question whether you'll take it again. I have to see about it."

"Chit man . . . doan think it'll do any good," Sonny mumbled.

"How 'bout if we study together? I'll have some time after tomorrow morning."

Sonny dejectedly sat in his chair and didn't respond. Scooter went up to the front of the room and waited for Mr. Dunn to finish talking to a student. Finally, he was free, and Scooter asked the instructor about his grade, if he should take the lab test again.

Mr. Dunn looked through his grade book. "Let's see. You have to do some math for me—averaging. The lab exam counts ten percent of your grade. All right now, you have an eighty-four average. That's based on one hundred sixty-eight points out of two hundred possible. You got a seventy-eight on the test?"

"Yeah, seventy-eight."

"So, figure out how many points that is out of twenty and then see how you come out with a total possible of two hundred twenty up to the final. The most you can get on the lab test is twenty points. So, you could figure out your average going into the final, and you could see what it would be with all twenty points"

Scooter copied the information down onto his test paper and mumbled, "Thanks."

He walked back to where Sonny was waiting, still sitting in his chair. Scooter said, "Let's go get something at the snack bar and figure this out. I have to do a bunch of math. If we both study those specimens, I think we can ace it." Sonny was shaking his head. "Come on man, we can do it!" Scooter said.

"Yer goin' to have t'help me a lot . . . on that Latin crap," Sonny said.

"Aren't some of these plants important to the tribe? Let's start with those and memorize the Latin." They ordered milkshakes at the snack bar. Scooter tried to figure out if it would help him much even if he got all of the points available. He asked another student at a nearby table if he could borrow his calculator. He determined that even if he got all twenty points, it would only raise his average from 84 to almost 86. He was mired in a *B* unless he perhaps aced the final. It was worth one hundred points. It seemed that retaking the lab test didn't matter very much, but if he studied with Sonny he might as well take it.

"If you do well on the lab and then on the final, where will you stand?" Scooter asked.

"Well, I gotta make sure I don't slip into a *D* is what. Gotta get a *C* outta this course."

"Okay, let's plot this out. We can start going over it tomorrow after my English exam. I have a chemistry review tonight and tomorrow night. We need to go over the stuff for the range final tomorrow afternoon. I have to study for the animal science class sometime—like tomorrow. Well, wait . . . let's go over to the lab now and start with those plants that are important and the ones we missed. Come on, we have an hour. Then I need to go down to my place before that chemistry review."

"Well, if'n we got to."

They walked back to the academic building and down the main hallway to the lab. As Mr. Dunn had said, the room was open, and the plant specimens were stacked on the end of one of the tables. Several other students were also shuffling through the specimens. Scooter and Sonny greeted them and started working through the ones that the other students put aside. They wrote down the common names and the Latin names on the blackboard. Scooter said, "Do you know the ones that are important to your tribe . . . the people?'

"Maybe some a them. Big sagebrush is one . . . used for ceremonies."

"Let's put a mark by that one and any others that you figure."

They completed the list of the plants and went through the ones that they had gotten correct on the test. They set those aside and wrote the ones they had missed on the blackboard.

"I figure we keep writing these over 'n over, we're going to have it down cold." Scooter said. "And for the Latin, I don't know . . . big sagebrush is *Artemisia tridentata*. I see it as a girl's name and see the three lobes on the ends of the leaves? That's the tri-dent-ata . . . you know, like three teeth."

"Guess I see it."

Scooter realized that Sonny was grudgingly doing the review. "Look at this as a tough rodeo—a tough bronc, you can do it!"

"This is tougher 'en that fer me," Sonny responded.

They worked through the problem plant specimens until Scooter could not think of additional clues for the scientific names.

"This here's goin' t'take some time. These grasses all look alike to me. Let's go through those uns today and then the others tomorrow that'er tough," Sonny said.

Scooter looked at Sonny, wondering about his logic and then realized he was being sarcastic. "That's what I like about you . . . I gotta get to the pad soon and call my folks before the chem review. We'll hit this some tomorrow morning after class and we can study for the final in that room too."

They continued to study the plant specimens until a girl came into the laboratory and began talking quietly to Sonny. Scooter stopped studying, while still absently holding the specimen he had been reviewing and observed them. He had seen the girl occasionally on campus and with a group of Native American students that Sonny sometimes hung out with. He studied her, figuring they were talking about one of Sonny's other classes. Scooter thought that she was somewhat attractive and that she would be more so without her glasses that partially hid her thick, curved lashes. Scooter thought of a deer; *those big doe-like eyes.* She was several inches shorter than Sonny. Her dark hair had been cut in a kind of bob and was longer over her ears than in the back. It seemed their conversation was serious, and Sonny ushered her outside the room into the hall. Scooter could sometimes hear snippets of their conversation but thought they might be speaking Apache.

The conversation continued for some time and Scooter realized that Sonny's part of it was subdued, maybe he was mumbling, whereas the girl's side was more vocal and strident. Scooter picked up a different plant specimen and studied it for a while.

Sonny came back into the room and sat down. He put his head in his hands and said, "Chit! Dammit!"

Scooter became alarmed. "What's up now?" he asked.

"Oh, I doan know. Everythin's goin t'hell right now!"

"Who's that girl?"

Sonny didn't answer for a while. Scooter was wondering if he had heard his question. "Her name's Erin." After a minute or so, he continued. "Spottedgale. We're in the Native American Club. Were the Apache reps."

"Was she mad 'bout something?" Scooter asked.

"Might say that." Sonny left it at that but stared across the room into space.

"So, come on, tell me what you did or didn't do?"

Sonny turned his head and gave Scooter a vacant look. Finally, he said, "Somnabitch! It ain't goin' t'happen!"

Scooter waited to see what else Sonny was going to say, but when he didn't, he said, "So what's going to happen or not?"

"Well, y'might as well know. She thinks she's going t' have a kid!"

Scooter waited to see if Sonny was going to say more, but another conversational gap ensued. He looked at Sonny, trying to decipher his emotions and figure out why he would care if this girl, Erin, was going to have a kid—unless it was Sonny's. This connection finally dawned on him.

"Judas Priest! You mean she's going to have your kid?" Scooter reviewed his image of the girl. She hadn't looked pregnant.

"What she says," Sonny mumbled.

Their study intentions had suddenly gone by the wayside. Scooter observed Sonny, thinking suddenly of all those comments he had made about Scooter being in quicksand with Charlene and about rodeo not being the top priority. Scooter blinked a few times to bring this completely out-of-the-blue development into his understanding. He realized that there was a lot about Sonny that he didn't know; well, he knew Sonny had other classes and sometimes hung out with a group of Native American students. His and Sonny's friendship revolved around their ag classes and rodeo, and now Scooter realized it was not the center of their college life like he had been thinking, that Sonny had a whole other side to him that Scooter didn't know.

"Is she from Jicarilla . . . from the reservation?" He assumed that she was.

"Nah, she's from Ruidoso . . . Mescalero."

"Wow, this is heavy! Talk about quicksand . . . sorry, man."

Sonny grimaced and nodded as he looked at Scooter. "Well, it happens. I reckon all that grief I was puttin' on ya, came back t'roost on me."

"Yeah, you've been telling me how good you are about escaping quicksand. What y'going t'do?"

"I tol' her, she could be wrong . . . just late a couple months. Says she miscalculated . . . I mean . . . y'know."

"You never said. I mean, you never said about her."

"It started happenin' after some of our club advisory meetin's. We started hangin' out. Our families know each other . . . some way back thing between 'em."

Scooter wondered where they had made love, if they went to Sonny's room or what? They continued to sit in the lab. Scooter couldn't believe how something could suddenly change everything. He looked at a specimen of western wheatgrass that he had been studying. The label read *Agropyron smithii. Wonder if this Smith guy ever knocked up a girl, or even had an illicit relationship?* The lab and the exam now seemed so insignificant—the whole thing about the grades—suddenly not important. *Wonder what I'd do if Charlene or Katherine got pregnant. A guy's got to be more careful, like how Charlene and I've been. Katherine better be right about her . . . what did she say . . . biology?* The last thought—the "what if," unsettled him.

Scooter looked over at Sonny again. He continued to stare at a specimen on the lab table in front of him. "Come on, let's get out of here," Scooter said.

"I gotta study some fer my native history and cultural class too," Sonny said. They headed out of the building and across campus toward the dorms and the parking lot.

"Don't worry about it too much, y'know? She could be wrong about it." Scooter said. "I'll see you tomorrow. I should be over at the lab around ten." Sonny gave a wave over his shoulder. Scooter watched him slowly walk across campus. Sonny kicked a crumpled piece of paper that had been dropped onto the sidewalk.

Scooter had several free hours before the chemistry review. He headed down the hill to his apartment to get a few things done, including dinner. This had been an interesting day. He parked near his unit and hurried to the door. There was a note taped to it. It read, *Come see me when you get in! M. Warner.* It was from the motel manager. *Damn, I bet it's about Katherine being here this morning!* He unlocked the door and checked the kitchen and the bedroom. Everything looked like he, or they, had left it. He went back outside and walked across the courtyard to the office. He went inside and rang the bell on the counter. It smelled like Mrs. Warner was frying something—maybe pork chops. It made him hungry. She came out from the back rooms wiping her hands on a small towel.

"Oh, it's you. Just a second! Are you getting better?" she asked.

"Yeah, am on some pills."

"Well your face doesn't look any better to me. It's colored!" Scooter lightly felt his face.

She walked over to a stack of newspapers on the end of the counter. "Have you seen this . . . in the *Chronicle*?" She leafed through one of the newspapers and held out a page of it. Scooter saw the picture of him on Popcorn.

"Yeah, I saw this picture in Laramie." He read what it said. It was different than what Mr. Hennessey had written. It mentioned Southwestern State College and the rodeo team, and that Scooter was likely qualified for the Western States Regionals after winning the University of Wyoming Rodeo. He continued to read, that he was a sophomore and was from Bunting.

As he read, Mrs. Warner said, "I didn't know I had a rodeo star staying here. Congratulations! I know you're going to be checking out on Friday. I just wanted to say it's been nice having you. No trouble, like some of the students here."

"Thanks . . . I need some of these papers. This don't happen every day, y'know!"

"I'll buy you some," Mrs. Warner said. "Take however many you need." Scooter hesitated. Mrs. Warner lifted four off the top and gave them to him.

"Thanks! It's been nice staying here," he said. "I'll be heading out Friday afternoon, so will check with you then on stuff." He wanted his damage deposit back.

He carried the papers to his apartment and placed them on the counter. He checked the two TV dinners that were in the small freezer and selected the one with a picture of Salisbury steak covered with gravy. He set it on top of the stove. He took off his shirt and went into the bathroom to wash his face. The skinned places on his elbow were already starting to tighten, to itch slightly. He went outside to his car and retrieved the salve from the front seat. He walked back inside and to the bathroom. He held the elbow up to the mirror. It looked a lot better than the area around his eye. He scrubbed the elbow with the special soap. It stung, and he rinsed it with water, patted it dry, and then squeezed salve onto the area. It was cooling.

Scooter thought he better call home and finish telling his family all the news—good and bad. He could hear the phone ringing on the other end and was about to hang up when his sister, Rachel, answered. He hadn't talked to her for what seemed like ages.

"Scooter!' she exclaimed. "I was hoping you would call soon. Mom said you had won a rodeo. We're all pretty excited!"

He said it was really nice to win, to be a dark horse and to come out of the pack. He asked her how she was doing and how school was going. She said she was in a play and they were practicing because the performances were soon and said that maybe he could go to it if he was home next week. She said she had a part opposite of Ryan. Scooter didn't know who Ryan was and Rachel explained he was a boy she liked.

"You mean your boyfriend? You have a boyfriend?" he asked.

"Well, we've had a couple of dates. Do you have a girlfriend yet?"

"Yeah, I have two," he said.

"Oh, sure. I hope at least you've been on some dates by now," Rachel said.

"Well, actually I have. A girl from Colorado A&M—a barrel racer—may come to the ranch after the Baca rodeo. She and I have been on a few dates."

"Really? I'm a little surprised, I guess. I mean that she would be visiting, and we didn't know anything about her," Rachel said.

"Yeah, her name's Charlene—Charlene O'Brien. She's nice. You'll like her. Are you coming to the rodeo this weekend in La Junta? She's going to be there too."

"I don't know. Mom and Dad are going, I think," Rachel said. "Ron, too. I better holler at Mom. She was outside by the chickens. Just a minute."

Scooter could hear Rachel indicating that he was on the phone, and then someone talking in the background. His mother came on the line and said they had been wondering about him, and that Rachel had gone out to find his dad.

"Hold on," his mother said, "your father wants to talk to you."

His father got on the line and Scooter recounted the bareback ride on the Popcorn horse. "You know that horse, Dad . . . she's been to the NFR mor'n once. It was tough to hang on, but we been working out in the gym a lot too and I'm spurring better, as the rodeos have been going on this year, at least I think so. I told Mom there's supposed to be something about it in the Plainsmen whenever it comes out."

His dad asked again what his score had been and exclaimed, "That's up there!"

"The downside to the trip was this. We . . . Sonny, a saddle bronc rider on the team and me got into a tangle with two guys in Basin on the way back. I got whacked with a club, so got a black eye and stuff."

"What?" his father said, "Give me details!"

"We held our own. Sonny put the one guy in the hospital, but I wanted you to know, 'cause my face is still puffed some and my eye is black, so you can tell mom," Scooter said.

"You guys didn't start it did you?" his father asked.

"No, these guys were drunk. Thought we were both Indian I guess. We had a meeting with the police in Basin and one with the Dean of Students here."

"Judas Priest! You guys have to be careful out there," his father admonished.

Scooter realized where he had gotten one of his favorite near-swearing expressions.

"We'll be down to La Junta on Sunday, I believe. Your mother wants to talk to you again."

Scooter waited. This was turning into a long phone call. He stretched the cord across to the oven and stuck the TV dinner into it. He heard his mother ask if he was still there.

"Yeah, I'm here," he said.

He had to repeat what he told his dad about the fight and getting injured. His mother mentioned that she was very concerned about this, and they should be more careful. She asked if they had been in a bar. He convinced her that they had been in a restaurant eating dinner.

"Hey mom, ask dad too, is it okay if a girl stops by on Sunday after the rodeo? I mean at the ranch and what if she stayed over into Monday? I asked her to."

"A girl? Do you mean a girlfriend?" she asked. Her voice had gone up in pitch.

"Yeah, she's a girl from Colorado A&M . . . a barrel racer . . . Charlene. I asked her to visit and her friend too, a goat roper on their team."

"Well sure, if you want them to." Scooter could tell his mother was a little puzzled. She continued, "How long has this been going on? You never said anything."

"Well, a few weeks . . . since the A&M rodeo," he said. "She's nice, from Colorado Springs and is going to leave her horse there afterward. They still have several weeks of classes. I'm thinking you can meet her on Sunday anyways."

"You're full of news," she said. "Ron wanted to talk to you too, but he's out in the north pasture checking on the calves. But talking about news, he and Denise are going to announce their engagement."

"That's no surprise," he said. "They been going together for practically a century!" he heard his mom laugh. "What about that issue of them moving in together?"

"Well, you know how far that went with your dad and me."

"Yeah, I could 'ave told him how far that idea would get—like not even off the kitchen table." He heard his mom chuckle at his comment; he smiled that he could still make her laugh. "Look, Mom, I have t' get. I'll try to talk to Ron later in the week, okay?"

"We're both proud of you, although I have some reservations about spending so much energy on rodeo!"

"Yeah, I know. Look, Mom, I love you guys. I'll call later in the week." They said goodbye and he hung up the phone.

The dinner was starting to smell good. He checked his watch. I was six o'clock, and Charlene was on his mind. He picked up the telephone and wondered how she was doing. He dialed her number and waited while it rang. No one answered, so he put the phone back on the cradle.

I better straighten this thing out with Katherine. I think Sonny's right. He had to look up the number to Katherine's dorm. He dialed the number and asked for her. He waited a few minutes. He knew someone had to go to her room and tell her there was a phone call. Finally, Katherine said, "Hello?"

"Hey, it's me. Wondered what you were doing." Scooter said.

"Well, just studying. What are you doing?"

"I was cooking dinner and called my parents."

"Cooking? Like a pot roast or Peking duck?"

"Oh yeah, you know it. It's called Peking duck ala tin-foil."

Katherine laughed, "It sounds like you're feeling better."

Well, I had a good nurse! I have a chemistry review tonight . . . probably get out at eight-thirty. I was thinking of coming over. Do you want me to?"

Katherine didn't say anything for a while. Finally, she said, "I guess I could see you for a while . . . not too long, though. I have a final in the morning, remember?"

"One thing I was thinking about . . . well, do we know where we're going? Like this morning and then after . . . I mean, I'm just wallowing around wondering."

She didn't answer for a while. "Are you getting cold feet? I mean about what happened this morning?"

"No, not about what happened. To be honest, I liked what happened . . . our lovemaking. Like you said, the dessert, but the rest is murky. I just need to figure this out, okay?

"Come over to the dorm when you're through," she said and hung up.

Scooter could tell by the tone of her voice and how quickly the conversation ended that she was not pleased. The light, lilting quality of her voice—the teasing—had suddenly disappeared.

Shit! I've really screwed this up. I didn't want to hurt her. He called information and asked for the La Junta Motor Inn. He waited for the number and then dialed it.

A woman answered, and he asked for "reservations." The woman said, "This is reservations. How can I help you?"

"It's for the rodeo this coming weekend. Do you have any rooms left? I need one with two double beds," he said.

"We're nearly out," the woman said, "let me look." He waited. She came back on and said, "We don't have any doubles left. There's one room—a single, and that's it!"

"Do you know of any other motels or whatever that might have rooms?"

"Well, the Lamplighter's just down the street from us and they're full because they referred people here!"

"Okay, I'll take that one!" and gave her his name and contact number.

Wow, lucky! Good thing I called. If we all go, going to be tight, but better than nothing. He took a dishcloth and used it to remove the TV dinner from the oven and then a fork to pry off the top. It smelled good. He set it onto the counter on an old newspaper and filled a glass of milk from a bottle he took from the refrigerator. He started with some of the mashed potatoes and mixed them with some gravy. Not too bad. He cut some of the steak and chewed on the uninjured side of his mouth. His telephone rang. He let it ring a few more times while he hurriedly chewed and then swallowed, thinking it might be his brother.

He answered and heard Charlene's voice with her familiar, "Hey, how's my cowboy?"

"Hi, Charlene! How's it going?" Scooter answered. "I just tried to call you 'bout an hour ago."

"Well, I just got home from a lab—education course, but hadn't heard from you and was wondering about you . . . If you had gotten back okay, you know?"

"You won't believe it when I tell you . . . we kind of had a trip from hell. He filled her in on the details.

"Scooter!" she exclaimed. "Did you say police station? What did you guys do?"

He retold the story about the fight and what had happened. That he had received a slight concussion, a black eye, and a scraped elbow. "Oh, and Sonny and I had to meet with the Dean of Students about the Basin thing and were kind of given a lecture about, you know, representing the college."

"Wow! You guys live adventurous lives. I'm sorry for you about the fight. You said concussion. Are you okay?" she asked.

"Yeah, well, I have a puffed-out face, black eye . . . trying to look like Zeke I guess."

"I know you guys . . . I mean guys on the rodeo circuit have to walk the walk, I guess. Do you and Sonny?"

He didn't say anything for a while as he contemplated her question. This conversation wasn't going like he'd planned. Finally, he chuckled at the thought. "Oh yeah, we're tough as hell! Honest, we weren't looking for trouble; it just seemed to find us. You know what it is. It's what Sonny and people from his tribe run into sometimes . . . why he's cautious. He looked in the bar before we sat down in the restaurant to see who was there. I think those dunces thought we were both Indians."

"Look," she said more softly. "I didn't mean to accuse you. I know sometimes it happens. We have to watch, too, I mean us girls traveling . . . even two of us together. I just don't want you to get hurt. I'm selfish. I want you in one piece."

"Yeah, me too, but sometimes you have to stick up for yourself . . . not tuck tail. Yet, we have to learn better to talk our way out of things without being yellow—you know, like with Hall . . . so . . . I know."

"Not to change the subject, but with all the stuff going on here and finals, we nearly forgot to enter the rodeo this weekend. We don't have anyone doing that for us here now, so we had to wire the money in. But you know, we made reservations at the La Junta Motor Inn . . . the last room and a single for us three, if Sonny goes."

"That'll be cozy. Squirrel and I are there too, but we're not trading, so don't even think of it."

"Hmm, I wasn't. Here's a better plan. You come with me, and Sonny and Zeke can bunk with Squirrel."

He heard Charlene laugh and it made him smile, "Yeah, you'd like that, wouldn't you," she said. "I might too, actually. Listen, what I wanted to tell you . . . I don't think I can stay over with you, I mean come visit at your ranch. Can I take a raincheck on it? It'd be better when the semester is over. My folks were getting strange about it—although I could withstand that I guess."

"Well, I want you to come out and visit—to show you my favorite places there, but if that's better for you . . . I think my family's coming to La Junta on Sunday to see the rodeo." He pushed his disappointment aside. "Would you like to meet them? I think they're curious about me having a girlfriend, you know. I mentioned that you might come out and I think they were surprised—kind of sudden."

"Well, me too, I mean I'm old enough, but my parents are wondering who you are. I guess we better get them all together, so we can get their blessings."

Scooter laughed and then could hear her laughing too. "Yeah, I'm going to kiss you right in front of all of them anyway," he said.

She laughed, and then said "That'd be a good way to introduce yourself. So, how're finals going?"

"Yeah, your dad would like me right away. Finals? I have a chem review in a few minutes and have to go over a few things for an English exam in the morning. Then Sonny and I didn't do as well as we had thought on a range plant test, so have the option of retaking it, if you can believe that! So, kind of hectic. How are your classes?"

"Oh, we're not into finals, so that's the good news. I'm starting to think about them though and that's another reason about not missing Monday. Okay, honey, I better let you get to your class. Call me Thursday night. Okay?"

"Okay, I'll talk to you later."

"Hey, another thing . . . good luck on your exams. I'll be thinking of you. Love?"

"Yeah, me too, and absolutely, it is!" He hung up the phone and went over to the TV dinner and started to wolf it down. It had cooled. He washed the bites down with the rest of the milk and gathered up his chemistry notes and a pen.

CHAPTER THIRTY-ONE
ESCAPE ROUTES

Scooter opened his chemistry notebook to the first clean page and began copying down what was already on the board. Most of the formulas were familiar, although Mr. Withers wrote out several that were new to Scooter and he found this disconcerting. Scooter noticed that Mr. Withers still had eyebrow damage from the laboratory fire and a red mark on his forehead. Scooter smiled as he thought of how the fire had transpired and how he had blown glassware all over the floor with the fire extinguisher, the force of the expulsion being much greater than he had anticipated. He still wondered, as those in the class had, about the rumor that Mr. Withers had been a Marine in the Korean War. Scooter's classmates had thought the explosion, which had happened nearly in Mr. Wither's face, had caused a sudden flash-back to an old battle—possibly the reason he had run from the lab.

Mr. Withers continued to diagram a reaction on the blackboard. The complexity of the review brought Scooter back to the present. Some of the formulas were long, with requirements for catalysts. Mr. Withers explained that in order to break bonds, especially double or triple bonds, energy and, or a catalyst, was needed and that when the bond broke a lot of energy could be released, sometimes resulting in explosions. Scooter had an urge to raise his hand and ask, "Like the lab fire?" but thought better of it. They had a round-table discussion regarding the reasons for the exchange of elements and how the equations needed to be balanced. Scooter liked the logic of it. Mr. Withers ended the session but said there would be another the next evening.

Scooter told the other students "So long," and headed out of the building and cut across the campus to the girl's dorms. He thought he might as well get this over with, although he didn't have the faintest idea what he was going to say. *If I hadn't of been so sucky earlier in the semester and asked her out and if we would have become girlfriend and boyfriend, in a relationship probably, then what? Then, if Charlene had come along, then what? Like Sonny says, a guy better not get into a trap . . . commitments with women—like we both have now. Course, he never said if he was committed . . . think he isn't actually. I know we shouldn't have . . . that I shouldn't have let her, but the way it happened . . . that would be a cold day in hell.*

He walked in through the main door to the lobby and asked the dorm monitor if Katherine Sandoval was in. The monitor told him to wait while she called the room. Scooter waited; it was taking a while. He then saw

Katherine walk briskly through the hallway doors and into the lobby. "Hey, how's it going? How was your review?" she asked.

He thought she looked really nice; clean, as if she had just scrubbed her face. She had put on a light application of blue eye shadow and pink lipstick. This was not going to be easy.

"Oh, pretty good. I'm glad I went. There's another one tomorrow night," he answered. "You want to go for a walk or over to the snack bar? I'll treat you."

"I need to walk. I've been sitting at my desk most of the afternoon. Are you ready for the exam tomorrow?"

"I could be better prepared. I'll review a little more later on tonight and then that's it," he said.

They walked along the plaza and a low rock wall that delineated its edge and headed toward the perimeter road of the campus and mesa where a chapel sat on the edge of the skyline. Katherine took his hand.

"Do you ever wonder why things happen like they do?" she asked. "There's an old saying that things happen for a reason; that they happen for the best. I don't know if I believe that."

They had stopped by the end of the retaining wall and he jumped up slightly and sat on the top of it. He didn't know how to answer her. "I believe in making your own destiny, working hard for something. What are you thinking?"

"I'm talking about us. Isn't that what you wanted?"

He didn't respond right away. "You know, early in the term, I finally was getting up enough nerve to see if you might want to go out. I mean, you seemed friendly in class and I thought you were nice—nice looking too. Then I saw you and that guy from the cross-country team on campus holding hands. I thought about how naïve I really was. But now I wish I had anyway, 'cause at least you would know that I was interested. I wasted a lot of time being shy. So, do things happen for the best? I'd say not always."

"Yes, you should have asked me. I knew you wanted to. That guy you mentioned, Tim, we broke up probably not long after that, so maybe you did waste a lot of time, I don't know. I dated a few other guys, but I have to admit, I was interested in you. I should have taken charge. Linda told me to grab you, because someone else was going to get you. Have they?"

He paused, thinking about what he wanted to say, "The girl from Colorado A&M, Charlene, we've been on several dates. I guess it's gotten serious, but we haven't been out very much, either. Look . . . well, I don't know."

"You want your cake and to eat it too. Well, that's not going to happen with me!"

He thought this might be true. "Maybe . . . maybe that's it, I don't know. I know I like you . . . to be with you. You're fun and witty . . . you know, interesting. So, what do you want to do?"

"I'm bummed that we just didn't keep going and not look back. We're looking back. There're complications to our journey and we've barely started."

They were still holding hands and Katherine was standing between his legs as he continued to sit on the wall. "When you asked me if I needed it to be written down, what did you mean exactly?" he asked. "I'm not good at reading signs maybe, at least women."

"Look, I don't know if I want to get into that now."

"Here's what I think, that there are lots of kinds of love. Do I love you? I do, because I want the best for you and I don't want to hurt you. So, if you don't want to see me anymore, I understand that!"

Katherine looked up at him and he thought there might be tears in her eyes, but it was hard to tell in the half-light from the walkway. "That's not going to help! What if I can't get over my strong feelings for you and you don't reciprocate. Then I get hurt. I can't help how I feel. I wish I could. I'd turn it off and not worry about you going off with your barrel racer," she said.

"Can't we be friends?"

"You're such a dummy! I'm not going to share you."

Katherine wouldn't look at him. He tipped her head up and said, "Come on, give me a hug!" She moved into him as he pulled her slightly and he smelled the light citrus-like scent of her hair. "This had so much promise, that's what I hate. We're breaking up before we really got started," she said.

"Well, we kind of got started, didn't we?" he kidded.

He saw her attempt a smile. "Well, I think I made a mistake," she said.

"I don't know about that . . . maybe. I'm still your friend, even if you don't want to be."

Katherine pulled his head down slightly and kissed him. "I don't know if it's possible to be friends—just friends . . . what if I want more than that? . . . If you want honesty, is that plain enough for you?"

"I know!"

"Come on, I have to get back. We better be fresh for tomorrow." They started back toward her dorm and he walked her into the lobby. "See you. Don't sit by me in class tomorrow," she said.

Scooter didn't say anything as he watched her walk back through the doors and down the hallway. He stared after her until she disappeared from sight, thinking how complicated life was.

Mrs. Starmire came into the classroom with a sheaf of papers in her hand and began passing them out. Scooter looked up as more students came in and noticed that Katherine and Linda had taken desks near the front. Katherine didn't look at him. Scooter took a copy of the exam and passed the others to the student next to him. He wrote his name on the line provided and looked through the questions. Many of them were what he had reviewed. *Maybe this wouldn't be too bad.* He turned to the first page and began. He worked through rearranging sentences to be less convoluted and finally completed everything but an essay question. There were four topics to choose from. One was "What is love?" *He couldn't believe it, as this topic had never come up in class. It's like Katherine had talked to Mrs. Starmire about him. Well, unlikely.* Another question was traveling to a favorite destination and why. That question seemed plausible, yet he stared at the one about love, continuing to think about his recent experiences with the girls in his life. He wrote about the strong emotions of love, whether it is love for a person's parents, or siblings and other members of a family or whether it's love that develops for a member of the opposite sex. He asked the question concerning this latter issue, about how love could be recognized. *How a person knew when they were in love with another person. What happens when the being of the other person merges into another; when their image, their smell, their voice, their thoughts sparked another's thoughts and imagination. When they inadvertently were in a person's mind, as if their silhouette had been placed inside a person's brain.* He thought of Katherine and he thought of Charlene and how they both had made such a large impression on him because they were interested in him as a possible partner in their lives.

He was aware that a few of the students were turning in their exams and he saw Katherine turn in hers. She looked across the room at him and their eyes met. He suddenly knew how to end the essay. He mentioned that with such strong emotions, with such feelings of ecstasy, there was another side to this if a relationship, which had such promise when it first blossomed, turned inward. That hearts could be broken, and feelings could be hurt. These two extremes are what poets and songwriters have been trying to capture since before David wrote Psalms. He looked at the clock and saw there were only five minutes left. He checked back through the exam and decided he had done okay. *Maybe even an "A!"*

He turned in his paper to Mrs. Starmire and checked back to see if

Hank was finishing as well. He still had his head down in concentration. Mrs. Starmire said, "Mr. Henry."

He turned back toward her. "Yes?"

"I've enjoyed having you in class, but I see that you have become famous this past week. Don't forget to use your imagination in this endeavor."

Scooter had no idea what she meant, and it must have shown. She continued, "Set your goals high."

"Thanks, Mrs. Starmire, I aim to. I've enjoyed your class," he replied.

Scooter thought he better go by the registrar's office and have the grade reports sent to Baca to verify their eligibility while he was thinking about it. He had done this before and told the secretary what was needed for Zeke, Sonny, and himself. Each request cost one dollar, and Scooter pulled out his wallet. She recorded the information and gave him a receipt. Scooter thanked her and walked back to the main entrance. He thought he would grab a coffee at the snack bar but waited to see if Hank wanted to go as well and thought he might see Zeke and Sonny. Hank finally came out of the English exam and shook his head at Scooter before he had time to ask how he'd done.

"Don't ask. I just hope I passed. I never finished that essay question . . . sheesh!"

"What'd you write about?"

"Well, that one if you could go anywhere where it would be and why. I decided I would try to 'wow' her and said I wanted to go to the moon, but then couldn't figure out a good reason why and got all balled up and then . . . shit, ran out of time!"

Scooter laughed at Hank's explanation, "Come on, I'll buy you a coffee."

They walked into the snack bar and Scooter ordered two coffees and they took them to a table. He noticed that Katherine, Linda, and another girl that he didn't know, were at another table.

"I gotta check something," he said and opened his English notes to double-check on a few things he wasn't sure about. It seemed that he had done alright. "I always second guess myself. Some things are tricky."

"There're a lot of tricky things . . . too many rules. If it wasn't a requirement I wouldn't take it . . . just do ag classes," Hank said.

"Well, this semester's about to be history. We have that Animal Science final, and then I'm heading for La Junta Friday as soon as I get things packed into the car."

They talked about the rodeo and if they knew any of the stock. Hank said, "That's Flying A . . . got some pretty rank stock. Some 'ave been to National Finals, too, so it'll be tough. I haven't ridden for a while, so I have to cock my hammer over there."

"Yeah, I hope I get as good a draw as in Laramie. We got two go-rounds in bareback, so that's good."

"As usual, we only got one to qualify for a final. I don't know if that's good or bad. Guess I'll see after the first ride whether I'd like to go again."

Scooter finished his coffee. "Well, I have range science on my mind. See you tomorrow at the big exam" He noted that Katherine turned away from him as he walked past her.

Scooter ambled back across campus to the administration building, into the science wing and the range management lab. He was still thinking about Katherine being angry with him; ignoring him. *So that's what the cold shoulder is . . . well, what do you expect?* He started to sort out the specimens that he had missed on the earlier lab exam. Many of them were grasses. He listed the Latin names of these on a piece of paper and then looked at each as he tried to recall both the common and scientific names. He liked the names of some . . . *Bouteloua gracilis* or blue grama, and *Bouteloua curtipendula*, side-oats grama. Both grew on parts of the ranch. He should know these. The inflorescence and seeds of side-oats grama were oriented to one side as if standing in an unseen wind, so that was easy. Blue grama reminded him of a curled toothbrush.

As he looked at some of the other specimens, Sonny came into the lab and they grunted greetings to each other. "You need to get that hand healed," Scooter said. "I had a great idea. How 'bout you and I go down the road before the regionals? You know, travel the circuit and end up at Central Wyoming."

Sonny took this in and bobbed his head, "Be a great way t'keep the edge. We should. I have enough money. I don't wanna hang around the rez with Erin waitin' t'spring on me!"

Scooter laughed. "You mean disappear and hope she ain't growing while you're off rodeoing?"

"Yeah, if'n I'm on the road, how will I know?"

"Interesting philosophy," Scooter said, "but here's what I'll do. I gotta work some, y'know, at home. Let me check the schedule with the Western States Association, and also if we could get a permit with the pros. I think that costs like fifty bucks, but we could maybe find a Wyoming rodeo."

"What'll we do in the middle of the week?"

"I dunno, maybe go up to Yellowstone . . . never been there, have you?"

Sonny grinned at the question. "Chit man, I never been north a Laramie. Hell, les go! I'll be well by then, fer sure!"

Scooter nodded, and they went over to the specimens. They broadened their study to others that they had known on the first test or that they seemed to know now. They wrote and rewrote the scientific names on the blackboard. Scooter realized that both he and Sonny were making progress. Several other students joined them, and they jointly went over the specimens, studying until near noon. By then, Scooter and Sonny decided they had enough and headed across campus to the cafeteria for lunch.

Scooter mentioned that he had asked the registrar's office to send grade reports, so they were set for the rodeo. Sonny flexed his hand, which was still wrapped in a splint with a thick, elastic bandage. He mentioned that it was still swollen and stiff. He still had a small Band-Aid covering the stitches above his eyebrow.

They stood in line at the cafeteria and several students told Scooter congratulations. His fame had spread with the article in the Durango newspaper. As they went through the serving line, Scooter observed Katherine, back in the kitchen area, but she didn't look out toward him. They took their trays to an empty table near Zeke and some of the other guys from the team.

Johnny looked over and said, "Hey, you hot-shot, giving autographs?"

"Yeah, get in line," Scooter said. "Are you going to La Junta? We nearly forgot to enter but wired it in yesterday."

"I gotta enter it, 'cause there's still a slim chance I could qualify for the regionals," Johnny said. "This is tough to have a rodeo and finals and the end of term and all that. By the way, yer face looks more normal today—ugly as ever!"

"Yeah, yeah! But, this week has been hell an' you haven't helped. We were taking your name in vain, about breaking up with Susie and having to do all our own stuff."

"Ah . . . she was spoiling you guys anyways."

Zeke came over to their table and Scooter told him that he had requested the grade reports be sent.

"Let's get together for dinner up here, you want to?" Zeke asked.

Scooter wasn't sure, but it sounded better than being alone in his apartment and he had the chemistry review anyway.

Scooter drove back to his apartment after the chemistry review and washed the breakfast dishes that had been stacked in the sink. He built a peanut butter and jelly sandwich and then set it on the kitchen counter. He pulled out his notes and the textbook on animal science and sat looking through them as he ate. He wondered what Katherine was doing . . . what Charlene was doing. He pushed the thoughts out of his mind and tried to concentrate on the lecture notes and what the instructor had told them to know. His concentration was broken by the phone ringing. Scooter wondered if it might be Charlene or maybe Katherine. No, wouldn't be Katherine. She doesn't want anything to do with me now.

He answered and realized it was his brother, Ron. "Hey, bud, what's up?" Scooter asked.

"Is this the champion bareback rider we been hearing about out here?" Ron asked.

"Well, been fortunate y'know. But, been riding pretty good part of the time all spring. I think I've qualified for the regional rodeo in Central Wyoming but will see."

"Well, I just wanted to say congratulations."

"Mom said congratulations are due to you as well. When's the big day?"

"Oh, yeah! Denise and I decided we might as well get hitched. Save on gas money and all that, you know?"

"So, is it soon?"

"She said it's in August, so it's coming up. You might be invited . . . Actually, I wanted you to be the Best Man. How 'bout that?"

"Be my pleasure. I can tell everyone about some of your worst qualities."

"Be careful with that. You're my little brother and I can still kick your butt!"

"Don't be too sure of that. I'm gettin' to be a street fighter!"

"Yeah, Dad told me. Be careful out there. I think we're all going to come down to La Junta on Sunday, so I will see you there. By the way, we need you here. We got a lot to do."

"I'm going to help, but there's one thing we need to talk about when I get home. You know I'm going to rodeo some, after regionals. Dad and us need to talk, because it's important for me to do this."

"That's what I'm talking about. We need you here. You can't just leave us saddled with all the work and go off running around all the time."

The old sinking feeling came over Scooter of when his brother decided to be the boss. "We'll have to figure this out, because this is something I need to do," he said more emphatically. "You better mention this to Dad, too. I mean I'll work my ass off while I'm there, but we need to all agree on this."

Neither of them said anything. Finally, Ron said, "I don't know, you can't have it your way all the time.

"Okay, I'll see you Sunday. You bringing your honey?" Scooter asked.

"Yeah, I'll see you Sunday. Good luck!"

Scooter hung up the phone and sat dejectedly looking at it. *I knew this was going to be a problem . . . we better get this lined out, 'cause I'm going if I keep improving. If I don't do any good, then that's different. I'll pack it in.* He took the belt buckle from the top of the dresser and looked at it. He hadn't put it on his belt yet. He rubbed the sheen of it with the sleeve of his shirt. It was a nice buckle and now it seemed like a dream that he had won. *Maybe rodeo is easier than the rest of life.* He put the buckle back on the dresser and went out to the kitchen where he riffled through his class notebooks for the animal science notes.

After studying for a while, Scooter checked his watch and decided he better get some sleep. The exam material, Charlene, Katherine, Ron, home, and rodeo swirled through his mind as he stared out at the darkened room. *Yeah, be good just to hit the road—the circuit.*

CHAPTER THIRTY-TWO
CRUTCHES AND SCIENCE

Scooter took a copy of the chemistry exam and passed the rest to the student behind him. He quickly checked the questions. Some looked immediately familiar, but others looked more problematic. He signed his name on the line at the top.

Dr. Hart said, "Begin. You have one hour."

The first set of questions was multiple choice, and after checking the rest of the exam, Scooter started on those. He thought it was a good way to warm-up for the harder equation problems. These took the most time, and as he started on them, he checked the clock. He drew the diagrams of the compounds that were listed, and as they had done in the reviews, included the catalysts and balanced the equations. The last question was an essay about an experiment they had done in the laboratory. This was a surprise to Scooter, but he remembered doing it. Diagrams of the apparatus used for the experiment, the reagents, and the resulting chemical compounds were to be included in the answer. Scooter struggled with this question and thought it was unfair, but thought he knew enough to answer it sufficiently. He went back over it several times checking his answers. He then checked the clock, realizing there was only five minutes left. He noticed the last two questions were bonuses worth two points each. The first asked to define "K9." Scooter stared at the question. *Potassium 9? What the heck!* The second was to define PbH2O. *Lead water . . . wait a minute. Heavy water! And K9. Maybe part of the dog family. Funny!* Scooter wrote these down and went back to the start, rechecking his answers. He went back to the lab question and made sure his reaction arrows were sufficiently indicated, and then double-checked several exam answers one more time. Dr. Hart said, "Okay class, hand your exams in. Results will be posted by tomorrow noon on the bulletin board by your initials."

Scooter gathered his notebook and handed in his exam paper along with of the other students. He didn't think that anyone had been able to finish early. He walked down the hallway to the range management lab and went through the specimens again. He had until two before the final in that class and the retake of the lab quiz was at four.

Near noon, Scooter decided he better grab lunch and headed toward the student union. He noticed Zeke and Johnny walking toward the cafeteria and hollered at them. They waited by the door and stood in line together. Zeke was talking about a math test he and Johnny had just completed, complaining that he should have studied more. Johnny noted that everyone always figured that way. "Unless a person was so smart that they got one hundred percent, of course."

"Well, that ain't happening to me in this lifetime," Zeke said.

As they were standing in line with their trays, Scooter saw that Katherine was working, and said to Zeke and Johnny, "Hold my place." and slid around the end of the serving counter.

"Hey, don't be mad at me. Can we talk? Maybe this evening?" he asked.

Katherine looked up and said, "What about? Haven't we said all there is to say? You're not supposed to be back here."

"Look, I'm going to come by this evening for a few minutes. Okay?"

Katherine shrugged and went back into the kitchen. Rebuffed, Scooter looked around to see if anyone noticed and hurriedly slid back into the serving line behind Zeke and Johnny.

"Someone's mad at you. I told you that you didn't know squat about women, and see?" Zeke said.

"You're right. I did just enough to get into trouble, now am trying to figure how to get out," Scooter said.

Johnny and Zeke both laughed. "Good luck on that one," Johnny said.

They finished eating, and Scooter walked back to the Range Management Lab, which was where the final was scheduled. He tried to tuck the last bits of information into his head that were likely to be on the exam—to polish it slightly so that it might be readily available. Some of the other students were starting to gather and Sonny slid into a chair beside Scooter's.

"*Daanzho!*" he said.

Scooter returned the greeting, "Jeez, where y'been man?" he asked.

"I have other class's y'know, but this is my last final, I mean except fer that plant thing. I'll look at those after this till they kick me out."

Scooter thought the exam was relatively easy, especially compared to the chemistry exam and even the one for English. He was done before the hour was over and whispered to Sonny as he left, "See you at four."

Mr. Dunn, the instructor, looked up at him as Scooter came to the front of the room and turned in his exam paper.

"How was it?" Mr. Dunn asked.

"Oh, it was okay . . . helps to study."

"That's for sure," Mr. Dunn replied.

Scooter walked across campus past the student union and then administration building to the physical education complex. He went to his locker and changed to his gym clothes. They reeked even worse than last time. He did a lightweight workout, wondering if his head would start throbbing. It seemed to be okay, and he continued to work on his shoulders and arms and then switched to lower his legs as the trainer had suggested.

He finished his workout and decided he better shower after exposure to the high stink of his clothes. He then turned in his lock and wet towel to the attendant in the main office and received a receipt. He threw all but his gym shoes into a trash bin near the main entrance. These he smashed into his large zippered notebook, causing it to bulge. He then hiked back across campus to the academic building for the range management lab retake.

Scooter felt confident, yet there was a temptation to cram as much information into his brain as it would stand. Sonny was in the lab when he got there and was looking through the plants.

"What were the crutches on these two?" he asked Scooter. "Looka here, *Sarcobatus vermiculatus*, that stickery one, and then that needle grass thing, *Stipa*."

Scooter took hold of the mounts and thought about it. "Look, this greasewood grows over in the valley on that bottomland. I'm not sure about the *Sarcobatus*, but the *vermiculatus* . . . I think of that soil needing vermiculite."

Sonny gave Scooter a blank stare. "Hell, that's no help. I knew these crutches wasn't something I got in the first place."

"Come on, think about it some," Scooter admonished. "This needle grass is the green one, *Stipa* means needle to me and *viridula* I think means green, like virden. So, think of that last term."

"Another not-so-good clue fer me," Sonny grumbled.

"Think of this . . . part of your last name, verde, means green."

Sonny replied, "I never thought of that. So, it should be *Stipa verde*, huh?"

Scooter stared at Sonny trying to figure if he was joking. "Okay, well, it isn't. So, write it down a few times as *viridula*. We have a few minutes yet. Hey, I forgot to ask, you want to ride over with me tomorrow? I'm going to try and check out by early afternoon. My last exam is at eleven."

Sonny flexed his hand. "I might hitch a ride to that station on the edge . . . where we got gas. I don't think I'm a going t'that un."

"Well, whatever you want to do," Scooter said. "I gotta know how to get hold of you to so we can connect fer the road trip and the Central Wyoming rodeo." He shut up while Sonny studied the plants.

Mr. Dunn came into the room with a student assistant and said, "You guys need to clear out now. The room will be locked until four."

Sonny had a last look at one of the specimens and then he and Scooter walked down the hall and out the main entrance and into the library. Sonny wanted to continue to recopy the scientific names and Scooter watched him from across the table. He felt confident that he could ace the test.

They retraced their earlier route at four and waited a few minutes in the hall with a handful of other students. Finally, the student assistant opened the door, and they filed into the room. As before, the plant specimens had been spread out on the lab tables with the labels covered with small pieces of paper held in place by a large paper clip. Each specimen was numbered. Mr. Dunn handed out sheets of paper with corresponding numbers and two rows of lines by each. There were twenty questions. Scooter looked around. There were approximately ten students taking the test. Scooter took a position at the station beside Sonny, and Mr. Dunn told them there were three points possible for each scientific name and two for each common name, that they had an hour and to begin. They all knew the drill. Scooter found himself cruising through the stations. He skipped some that were busy. He came to a specimen that he knew was not a grass, but it grew in the bottom-lands of the ranch along the creek—they called it wiregrass. He wrote that down and then, *Juncus balticus. So far, so good.* About halfway through, his progress suddenly halted. He starred at the specimen of a coarse grass. It had a spike inflorescence of thick seeds. He couldn't think of its name, so left it and went on to other stations. Not knowing the specimen bothered him, and he glanced back at it. He tried to recover among the others he did know. His strategy was to return to any problems after completing the other stations.

He was nearly to the end when he came to a specimen that he hadn't seen before. *What the hell . . . what's he doing throwing this in here?* Scooter felt his anger rise toward Mr. Dunn. It looked like a thistle. Scooter knew that much. It may have been on a test earlier in the term. He finally wrote down "Thistle" in the first line of the column and *"Cirsium"* in the second. He looked toward Mr. Dunn to see if he looked smug or was smiling. He didn't seem to be either. Scooter finished the rest of the stations and went back to the grass he couldn't remember. He stared at it for several minutes. He had to get out of the way of another student. Scooter shook his head to himself. He went back to check on several other specimens just to be sure.

He did a double take on one that he had labeled, "Big sagebrush." It wasn't right. It had the three clefts in the leaf, but it was silvery. He erased what he had written and put in "Silver wormwood" and then erased the species name and put in *"filifolia."* He looked at the clock. There was only five minutes left. He had to hustle to find the big sagebrush specimen to see what he had labeled it. He was starting to panic a little; he felt a trickle of sweat behind his ear. He found the specimen and realized he had marked it as black sagebrush. They did look alike to him. He made the corrections and then went back to the grass he didn't know and stared at it again. He was still in this position when Mr. Dunn said, "Okay everyone, turn in your test sheets. I'll have the scores up tomorrow on the bulletin board along with your final exam scores. Have a great summer."

As he handed in his paper, Scooter asked Mr. Dunn, "What was that rank grass on number thirteen?"

Mr. Dunn looked over toward it from the front of the room and said, "Think of bottomland, a swampy place and you'll have it!"

Scooter said, "And that thistle?"

Mr. Dunn said quietly, "That's musk. You don't want that started in your pasture, remember?"

"Okay . . . well it's been interesting." He waited by the door for Sonny, who was still trying to finish up.

Mr. Dunn said, "Come on students, time's up. Let's turn them in."

Scooter noticed Sonny furiously erasing and then writing. He finished and quickly came to the front of the room and turned in his paper. He and Scooter walked down the hall and to the main door before starting to talk.

Scooter looked around to make sure no one would hear and said, "That son-of-a-bitch put on some new plants, just to be sure no one—well, me—could get a hundred, or even close."

"Thanks for helping. I done better," Sonny said.

"Yeah, it's okay." Scooter was thinking about their study sessions.

"What I mean is I heard that grass thing when y'asked and wrote down, 'slough grass' that thing about the swamp tipped me. I didn't get the scientific though."

Scooter stopped and said, "That's it! You got more'n I did on it. *Beckmania 'sz'* something is what. Well, I missed all five points on it and only got part of the musk thistle. So, I may've improved some, but not much. I don't know."

"I know I improved, so was worth it. Would 'ave helped if you would'a said that thistle louder. I was listening."

Sonny was smiling, and Scooter laughed. "You cheater," he said, "let's get some grub, and then I gotta go and pack up. I gotta study yet for the last one. Let's figure on leaving as soon as we can tomorrow. We can check our grades and head out."

He walked back along the walkway of the student union toward the girl's dorms and into the lobby of Katherine's. No one was at the main desk, so he waited. He happened to see Ellen and Linda walk through from the outside and asked, "Hey, do you guys know if Katherine's in? I wanted to say 'hello.'"

"I'll check for you, but she may not want to see you," Linda said.

"Well, I know. I just wanted to say goodbye is all," Scooter said.

They went on back through the doors to the rooms and Scooter waited, not sure if Katherine would to see him. He sat down on one of the chairs and leafed through a magazine on home decorating. He heard someone and hoped it was Katherine, but it was the dorm monitor. She asked him what he wanted, and he said he was there to see Katherine and that Linda and Ellen had gone to check. After a few more minutes, he realized that it seemed unlikely Katherine was going to show up. He asked the monitor for a piece of paper and sat down to write a note.

Katherine,

Thanks for everything you did for me. Here's my home address and phone number:

P.O Box 1449
Bunting, CO 80821
743-5512

If you ever need anything, let me know. I wish you the best. Maybe I'll see you at the Cortez rodeo or at the Fiesta here in Durango!
I'm sorry I hurt you. You may look back on this time and realize that maybe some things do happen for the best and are glad that you didn't get hooked up with a "rodeo bum!" But, know also that love has many different forms.

Love,
Scooter

Scooter asked the monitor for a stapler and then folded his note over and stapled it shut. He wrote, Katherine Sandoval on the outside and asked if the monitor would give it to Katherine. The monitor took it and put it in one of the mailbox openings.

Scooter drove back down the hill and parked by his apartment. He saw that there was a note inserted into his door. He pulled it out and realized it was from the landlady, Mrs. Warner. It said *See me when you get in!* He wondered; now what? but went back to the office and rang the bell on the counter. Mrs. Warner came into the office from the living quarters.

"They delivered a letter for you . . . special delivery," she said. "Just a moment, I put it somewhere here." She rifled through a stack of mail and pulled out a long envelope and handed it to him.

Scooter looked at the envelope and saw that it was from the Inter-collegiate Rodeo Association and said, "Thanks. Could I borrow the vacuum tonight? I'll check out after my last exam tomorrow, just after lunch."

Mrs. Warner went over to a closet in the office and pulled out an up-right vacuum that Scooter had used before. "I'll need to inspect your apart-ment before you check out. I'll mail your final bill for the phone," she said.

Scooter nodded and told her thanks, but his mind was on the cor-respondence. He hastily opened the envelope. It was a typed sheet on letter-head. He scanned it and realized it was a notification that he had qualified in the top fifteen in the bareback event for the regional finals held the first weekend in June in Casper, Wyoming. He read the letter over more slowly. He had to commit to an entry by June 1 or forfeit his place. A form had been included with blanks to complete, and a place for him to sign with an address on the top. There was an envelope enclosed with a return address. The top five in the event would then qualify for the national finals. At the bottom, he noticed that copies had been sent to the college. He slowly folded the letter and placed it back in the envelope. The notification excited him. He felt a lit-tle of the current running through his system that he felt before a ride. *Well, all the work was worth it. All the stuff we did this year was worth it. Sonny should be getting one too . . . Bound to be tough horses I'll bet. No slouches.*

"Thanks Mrs. Warner, I'll bring the vacuum back later," he said.

Scooter began to clean his apartment, first placing all of his dirty clothes in a large garbage bag. He packed up the shirts and pants in his closet and then pulled out a drawer of the dresser and dumped his socks and un-derwear into a suitcase. He set the suitcase on the bed and began to vacuum. He barely heard the telephone ringing and had to hurry to shut the machine off and get to the phone. He answered, but whoever it was had hung up. He remembered he was supposed to call Charlene and decided he better before it got too late.

He dialed her number and waited while it rang. He was about to hang-up when she breathlessly answered. He always liked the sound of her voice.

"Hey good-lookin', did you just phone? 'Cause I was vacuuming and missed a call," he said.

"No, I was waiting for you to call me! How have you been? I mean how're finals and how are you doing with your injuries and all? I've been wondering about you."

"You have? I have too." He heard her laugh. "I floundered a little on Range Management. I only have Animal Science left. But I was cleaning house, you know, being domestic, vacuuming. I wondered about you, too."

"I'm glad you're wondering about me, or at least thinking about me once in a while. I like that you vacuum and all that. Maybe you'll make a good husband someday."

"Well, if that's all it takes, just to vacuum the house, hell, I'm prime real estate." He heard her laugh and it made him smile. He liked that she thought he was funny. They talked about courses for a while and he told her about retaking the range plant exam and how Sonny had gotten one he didn't because he had heard the instructor tell Scooter where it grew.

"You guys are always interesting. You make a good pair. I can see you traveling together on the circuit," she said.

They started talking about the upcoming rodeo.

"I'm going to be there sometime Friday night. We can't leave until around two, so be like seven maybe. You want to have dinner with us—Squirrel and me?" she asked.

"Why not? I'll probably be in at around the same time. Sonny's not going because of his hand, but I'm giving him a ride to Pagosa to meet up with someone. Zeke's supposed to come over, but I don't know when. I think you and I need to see each other."

"What do you mean, see each other? Do you miss me?"

"Yeah, I've missed you. You know what I need, don't you?" he asked.

"Well, I have a pretty good imagination about it . . . after last time. I've missed you too. Are you going to transfer here next year? It'd be nice if we were together."

"I've been thinking about it. I'll have to see. I have to sort out some stuff on the ranch with my brother and dad, too, about what I'm doing and what they want from me and what I'm willing to give them. My brother thinks he's the boss of the place already and that I'm going to be his hired man. If I keep riding well and improving, I want to do that while I can . . . you know what I mean?"

"I know. It's what we talked about . . . about defining our own destinies."

"Yeah, that's what I mean. About our destiny, I think we need to figure on it more, don't you?"

"You're puzzling me. If you want to know whether I love you or not, you can quit worrying about it!"

"Why, 'cause you're going to tell me you don't . . . I know," he said.

He heard peals of laughter from her. It made him laugh too at his own joke.

Finally, when she caught her breath she said, "Yes that must be it. You know . . . I need to squeeze you, so you better watch out tomorrow night."

"You're the one that's going to get squeezed and other things too. Well, daawlin, I better get. See you tomorrow."

"Okay honey, we'll see who does the squeezing. So long. Drive safely."

"Yeah, you too."

He hung up the phone and thought about how things always improved when he talked to her. Maybe we need each other. He finished the vacuuming and took the machine back to the office.

He rang the bell and hollered back into the living area. "Mrs. Warner, it's just me, Scooter. I'm returning the sweeper."

He heard a television blaring and she hollered back. "Just leave it out. I have others wanting it."

"Okay. See y'later," he said.

Scooter went back to his apartment and continued to pack. He got out his duffle bag with his rodeo equipment and sorted through it. He pulled out a plastic garbage bag from under the sink and started filling it up with old notes he didn't need anymore. After finishing this, he decided the rest of the cleaning could wait until the next day; that he better study for the animal science test.

CHAPTER THIRTY-THREE
LINGERING SENTIMENTS

Scooter was excited about it being Friday. The semester was nearly over. He was even more excited to be traveling to a rodeo and that he would see Charlene. He hustled to the library to go over the high points of animal science and reran the calculations on a feeding equation to balance the protein and carbohydrates. He looked up as someone approached and saw that it was Zeke.

"I figured y'd be over here," Zeke said. "I'm not headin' out until tomorrow, 'cause I called and ain't up until Sunday again. Then could get into the short-go of the finals . . . at least that's the plan, huh? That's good though 'cause Molly can meet me in Pueblo on Saturday night and we'll come over on Sunday morning. Just wanted you to know you're out on your own over there."

Scooter looked at Zeke, taking this all in and said, "You mean you're staying in Pueblo Saturday night?

"Well, what'd you think . . . we're staying with you and Sonny? There aren't any more rooms in that burg anyways."

"Yeah . . . well, I didn't know Molly was coming to it. Sonny and I are leaving after lunch, but he's just to Pagosa. Anyway, let's get together and see where we're all going to end up this summer. You want to hit the trail with us some? I mean we're going to hit a couple of rodeos somewhere's up north on the way to the regionals."

"Okay, I'd like that! See you in the cafeteria. If you guys weren't traveling, I'd buy you and Sonny a beer!"

"Yeah, see you at lunch," Scooter said.

He resumed studying. He checked his watch. He had about forty-five minutes. He was concentrating on cow-calf ratios for a pasture and was calculating production to determine animal-unit months and how many head could use an area and the length of time. Over-grazing was a big issue. A person sat down beside him, and a vision of Katherine brought him out of his notes.

He looked at her in surprise. "I know . . . I wasn't going to. Don't you ever answer your phone? I read your note," she said.

"I may have been out or was vacuuming. Packing up, you know . . . I just wanted to say goodbye before headin' out."

"I'm not really mad at you . . . well, that's not entirely true. It just didn't go how I had imagined . . . how I wished it would."

Scooter looked at her dark eyes and thought how pretty she was. "I know. You always had my interest, but things just happened. I think you're very pretty—always have—a beautiful person, that's what I think." This seemed to bother her, and she looked away. He continued, "Let's keep in touch, okay?"

"I liked your note." She looked past him as if there was someone standing above him and softly said. "If you come to the rodeos in Cortez and Durango too, the jewelry shop puts up a booth . . . a kiosk. I was going to say something hurtful about you buying something for someone, but after seeing you, decided not to."

"You don't need to do that with me. I haven't done this deliberately. You know that, don't you?" Scooter looked intently at her, wanting her to see the earnestness in him.

"Okay, I didn't think you are the love 'em, leave 'em type, or you don't seem like it. There's a hidden, latent wild side to you, but I didn't think that."

"Latent wild side? Katherine, do you think I took advantage of you?"

"No, I did it to myself. I just think you and I had a great future together . . . as you said, forming our own lives!"

"Yeah, forming our own lives, riding a new trail, I know. But I didn't want to take advantage of you."

They looked at each other. Her eyes softened him until he wanted to come over and clasp her to him—to take any hurt that he had made and pull it away from her.

Katherine finally smiled at him and placed her purse on the table. "Anyway, here's my phone number."

She handed him a slip of paper and he looked at it. She continued, "I nearly just let you go, but my better judgment overcame the temptation. Or maybe it was the other way around. I thought, 'Okay, he's right, we don't know what's going to happen, do we?'"

Scooter looked at her and nodded, "Yeah, anything can happen. I haven't looked at the rodeo schedules yet. Durango is in July. I don't know about Cortez."

"I think it's usually in June."

"Well, the first part of June is the regional college rodeo. I sure would like to do well there and go to nationals. Well, anyway . . . maybe we'll see each other out there. I got one more final and then Sonny and I are headed east. He's just going to Jicarilla, though, but we're hitting the road—the circuit—before going to regionals—together. Well, sorry I got sidetracked, just . . ."

"No, it's okay. I see the light in you when you think of going. I envy you. I liked to do that too, to go to other colleges for a cross-country race. I understand it. I'd like to go too," she smiled. "Just be careful. I know you have another exam, so I'll let you get back to studying. See you!"

She got out of her chair. He stood up. "Come here!" and gave her a hug. She returned it, and he again smelled her nice fresh scent. "Yeah, see you Katherine," he said.

"You know this is about love, don't you?"

He took a deep breath. "I do know that." They smiled at each other.

He watched her walk out past the stacks of books. *It never gets any easier. She's smart. She knows how to work me, just like a cutting horse on a green calf.* He went back to his notes, realizing he only had fifteen minutes before the exam was to start. He forced himself to concentrate on what he had left off with and finished calculating the animal unit months. He decided he'd done as much as he could before the exam.

Scooter grabbed his books and headed out of the library to the science wing and then waited in the hall with some of the other students. They asked Scooter about the regional rodeo and where it was held. He told them that Sonny and he were going on the circuit before that. *Well, two rodeos isn't really the circuit, but it's part of one.* Hank showed up and they stood together.

"I got a bull on Saturday, so am heading over there this afternoon too," Hank said. "Johnny and I are goin' over together." He started to say more, but the instructor, Dr. Miller, unlocked the class-room door and opened it. Scooter filed in with the rest of the students. Scooter glanced at Dr. Miller as he worked his way across the room to a yet-empty desk. He silently characterized Dr. Miller as "hatchet face," not necessarily in a bad way, unless Scooter hadn't received a very high score on an exam. The AKA described Dr. Miller's narrow face and pointed beak-like nose. He was mostly bald but pulled a few long strands of hair across from one ear to try to mask some of the exposed skin. Dr. Miller was knowledgeable though about animal science and showed some likely country roots by wearing fancy ostrich-skin boots.

The exam seemed similar to what Scooter expected. He had trouble with a question about cattle breeding and couldn't remember the number of bulls that were needed for a certain sized cow-calf operation. He figured one bull could service twenty cows, but this was based on what they used on the ranch. There was a question about hogs that he hadn't studied, and he had to think back to lectures from earlier in the term to try and develop an answer. He finished five minutes early and scanned back through his answers. He thought he had done okay, although it was likely not an "ace." He turned in his test paper, thanking Dr. Miller for a good class.

Dr. Miller said, "Best of luck out there. Grades will be mailed out."

Zeke, Scooter, and Sonny met in the cafeteria for lunch. This had become the best way for them to meet. Scooter hadn't seen Katherine and didn't know if she was working or had another exam. He tried to put her out of his mind as Zeke and Sonny discussed rodeo and possible summer plans. But, the image of Katherine and the hurt in her eyes stayed with him and he recalled her words about lost opportunities and things not working out. He was brought back to the present by Zeke saying he might go with Molly back to Fort Collins after the rodeo.

"You mean to move in with her?" Scooter asked.

"I dunno, man . . . maybe," Zeke said, "I met her mom after Laramie . . . dad too. I can rodeo from there some but will see if I kin find a job. But . . . what I'm saying if you guys head north on the way to Regionals, let me know. Maybe we can link-up."

"You two white-eyes are letting the wimmin lead y'around by yer peckers," Sonny said. "If'n we hit the circuit, y'shouldn't be having any skirts back home with a rope on yer neck. Not healthy!"

"Here we go again," Scooter said.

Zeke chimed in, "Sometime y'might find one you don't wanna forget so easy. That's what it is."

"That could happen to Sonny real easily is what I'm thinking," Scooter said. "All the girls on the rez are thinkin' he's prime y'know."

Sonny kicked Scooter's foot under the table.

"Yeah, I reckon he's a hot prospect with his bronc ridin' and being a college boy too. He'll have kids all over the place out there," Zeke chuckled.

Scooter nearly choked on a sip of water.

"Yeah, that's how it is fer sure," Sonny gruffly said. He gave Scooter a hard look and Scooter knew not to say any more.

Hank and Johnny joined them, and the subject changed to the up-coming rodeo. Scooter was getting itchy to get going. He still had to checkout of his apartment.

"Look, we gotta check some grades and I have to clean out my place some to try and get a deposit, so I gotta get," he said. "See you guys out there."

Sonny got up from the table as well and told the others, "*Ikeego!* Which means, so long you white-eyes. See you out there in the arena somewheres." The others touched fists with him. Scooter noticed Sonny used his left hand, keeping his other hand—his wrapped riding hand—protected.

Sonny and Scooter walked back across campus to the academic

building and went first to the science wing. "Look, I'm not trying to turn the screws on ya with yer woman thing, but you been walkin' tall on Zeke and me with this," he said.

"Yeah, but it ain't least bit funny if'n y'get one of them tuggin' on yer belt as yer head'n out to the arena!"

"Yeah, I know. These grades better be up, so we can get," Scooter said.

There were other students in front of the bulletin board in the hall across from the range management classroom. Scooter craned his neck to see over them, but he had to wait. Finally, a space opened up and he and Sonny checked the scores that were listed across from their initials.

Sonny said, "Okay man, a *C* on the lab and for the final. That's all I needed!"

Scooter continued to study the listing. He saw that he had received an *85* on the lab test and had a *B* for a final grade. "Jeez! I only improved seven points on the lab exam and a *B* on the final. An *89* on the final . . . shoot! Guess I'm a *B* student in this all the way through."

Sonny looked at the listing along with Scooter, "It's nearly an *A* minus. I doan know why they have t' split hairs some. Makes a difference in our grade points."

"It's comes down to a math thing," Scooter said.

They ambled down the hall to a bulletin board near the chemistry department. There were other students there as well, some of them copying down information. Scooter looked at the listing. He saw that he had received an *A* on the final and for the course. "Alright! That's better!"

Some of the other students looked at him and one said, "Must be nice."

Scooter checked through the list of grades and saw that there were only four *A*s listed. "Maybe I should go into chemistry, become a professor," he said to Sonny.

Sonny snorted a laugh and said, "Thad be a switch from cowboy to chemist. I better get. I hafta clean out some stuff still and check out."

"I should be back here in an hour, maybe an hour and a half, so will park as close as I can, and I'll help you load your stuff. Oh, call that number on the sheet about canceling out of that rodeo," Scooter said.

"Yeah, okay. What should I tell 'em?"

"That you got injured. They don't need to know how."

Scooter continued through the hall of the building and turned a corner toward the liberal arts area to see if the English grades were posted. If he had gotten an *A* in that course, he would likely be on the Dean's list, which required a 3.3 average on a four-point scale. He had a *B* going into the final but hoped he did enough on the final exam to pull it up. A *B* in English might screw things up.

He again waited until other students had read the verdicts and had turned away, some groaning or complaining. He ran his eyes down the list. The grades were posted by student numbers and he found he had received a 92 on the final and an *A* for a final grade. He smiled to himself, relieved and tried to figure out what Katherine had gotten, but had to speculate about which grade was hers. Someone had received a 96 on the final and had an *A* listed for the final grade. Scooter figured this was likely Katherine's grade. Some people just have the smarts . . . *make a great teacher I guess.*

Scooter backed his car close to his apartment. He packed all his clothes and carted them out to his car. He placed the boxes of his books and papers in the trunk and then put his duffle bag of rodeo tack there as well, but on top. He went back in and cleaned out the refrigerator and cupboards. At first, he was going to salvage some of the food, but decided to throw out everything but the bread and peanut butter. Maybe Sonny would want it. He wiped down the cabinets and the inside of the refrigerator. He took the bedding off the bed and placed it into another large garbage bag. He looked around and thought the place looked presentable. He checked the bathroom and wiped it down as well. He had to work on the soap scum on the sink and rinsed the shower out.

Scooter left the door of the apartment open and walked across the parking area to a dumpster in which he tossed the old food and old papers. He then headed past the other apartments to the office. Several other students whom he knew were also cleaning out their places. He rang the bell in the lobby and Mrs. Warner came out from her living quarters.

"Do you want to check the place?" he asked. "I'm ready to head out."

They walked back to his unit together, and she went inside with him. She went into the bathroom and then came back through the bedroom and looked inside the refrigerator. He was hoping she wasn't going to look inside the oven, because he had started to clean it and realized it would take a lot of work—maybe all day.

"I guess I can give you a passing grade," she said. "The owner is going to have these places painted anyway. Stop by and I'll give you your deposit back." They went back outside, and she locked the door with the room key and kept it.

He stopped by the office and waited for her to write out a check and said, "I've liked it here. You can send the phone bill to my home address and I'll send you a check."

Mrs. Warner stuck out her hand and Scooter shook it. "As I said, you weren't too much trouble. So, if you ever come through again . . . we rent by the day in the summer too."

"Okay, maybe during Fiesta Days."

He drove out of the complex, turned onto the main street again and headed up the hill to the college one last time. The parking lot was starting to empty. He parked in the first row and walked up the steps and sidewalk and into Sonny's dorm. The door to Sonny's room was open and a fellow Scooter didn't know was in Sonny's room with him.

"The thing is, you have to at least scoop up the dirt that has accumulated all year . . . like under your bed," the fellow said. Sonny looked around the room as if what the man was talking about was a foreign concept. The person, who Scooter assumed was the dorm monitor, continued, "You have a damage deposit and I have to sign a form for you to get a refund. Otherwise, we use it to pay someone to come in and clean this up. Let me know when you think it's ready and I'll check it again. I need you to leave the key with me."

Scooter moved out of the doorway slightly as the monitor walked past him. Clothes, saddle, and the rest of his rodeo tack were piled high on Sonny's bed.

"Hell, it looked good 'nough t'me. That damage deposit is a hunert bucks," he said.

Scooter was wondering how long this was going to take. "Well, let's hit it. It's a small room. Where's the mops 'n stuff?" he asked.

Sonny pointed over his shoulder, "Down the hall there in that closet . . . the head."

Scooter retraced his route back down the hall and opened a door where there was mop and pail, a broom, and dust mop. Sonny had followed Scooter and said, "Give me that broom. I might as well start."

Scooter ran water into the pail and wheeled it down the hall to the room. Sonny was sweeping out from under the bed and Scooter waited for him to finish scooping up the dirt and fuzz. Scooter watched as Sonny dumped piles of gunk into the trash can, and then he pushed the bucket to the area that had been swept and started to mop.

After they were finished with the floor, Sonny said, "Give me that." He took the mop from Scooter and used it to swab off the top of his desk.

Scooter laughed and said, "That's one way to do it!"

"Yeah, I'll swab everythin'," Sonny said. He rinsed the mop, squeezed the water out, and then opened his small closet and mopped out the base of it as well.

"You weren't kidding," Scooter smiled. He wondered where Sonny's roommate was. "Where's Billy?"

Sonny was concentrating and said, "Huh? Oh, he left earlier this morning. I ain't cleanin' his side too much. He was sposed to."

After they were finished cleaning, Scooter started to carry a box of books and Sonny's saddle out to his car, while Sonny went upstairs to find the monitor. Scooter wondered where the rest of Sonny's books were, but figured he had already sold what he could back to the bookstore. After having the room inspected again, Sonny also helped bring his clothes and riding tack out to Scooter's car.

"Did he sign it?" Scooter asked.

"Yeah, they're going t'send it out if'n there ain't any late book charges 'n stuff."

They finally drove down the road from the college. Scooter gave it a last look as they left. "It's been an interesting ride up here. May even miss the old place," he said.

Sonny looked back too and said, "I gotta come back some more. Won't be the same. Guess I'll have t'find another white-eyes to hassle."

Scooter looked over at Sonny and grinned. "We'll keep in touch."

Once onto the highway, they settled into the flow of traffic, but a cattle truck slowed their progress. The road curved and there was little opportunity to pass. They talked about rodeos they might enter during the summer. They figured they should do the Pagosa Springs Rodeo and the one in Durango.

"Fiesta Days is a pretty good rodeo and I think it pays good, but you have to come out east to the one at Bunting and maybe Eastgate too, 'cause you could stay with us out at the ranch."

"Yeah, you could stay with me an' my folks fer the Pagosa one . . . it's close 'nough," Sonny said.

Scooter wondered if Sonny's predicament would be a factor or not in the rooming arrangement. *What if Sonny's married by then?*

"What're y'going t'do if that Erin has you figured for a husband? You going to invite me to the ceremony?"

Sonny had been slouched in the car seat, but this question jolted him into an upright position. He wiggled to get comfortable and threw a glance toward Scooter. "Why'd y'bring that up fer? I didn't say I would. I mean marry her. She might 'ave other ideas, but I tol' her after we been screwin' some, it was just . . . wasn't fer permanent, y'know? I still hope she ain't is what!"

"You mean you never said the 'L' word during your throes of passion?"

Sonny studied Scooter and asked, "My what?"

"Y'know, when you were about to seduce her . . . you know." Scooter couldn't help needle Sonny after all the grief that he had given out about women and rodeo. "Anyway, I was just wondering, her with those sweet, doe eyes . . . kind of cute is what I thought. But you had me going about getting caught in traps and all, so just asking."

"Yeah, when she was a talkin' t'me I saw a steel leg-hold trap a tryin' t'grip one leg or the other. Hell, this were a big surprise is all. I thought she was being careful, so she better not 'ave set me up!"

"Yeah, gettin' set-up is bad for a guy with a woman. A guy's got to be careful so it can't happen."

Sonny took off his hat and pushed his hair back from his forehead. "Yeah, innit! What would ya do, though, if'n yer two women both told ya they're havin' yer kid?"

Scooter wiggled in his seat and the car swerved slightly. He took a glance ahead to see if he could pass a semi-truck of cattle. The manure smell wafted back into the car occasionally and seemed to be placing a pall on the whole subject. "Yeah, be a bad deal. Don't think it ain't crossed my mind . . . after the fact, though. We gotta be thinking in front of the fact, is what!"

Sonny carefully put his hat back on and nodded in agreement. "Yeah, after the fuckin' is too late. I'm already seein' how that goes. It ain't no . . . science problem, that one. I may be out there on the circuit and sending money back fer the kid."

Scooter looked over to his friend and grinned. "Yeah, rocket science. But, hey, if there's a ceremony, I don't want to miss it."

"Chit!" Sonny exclaimed. "Don't jinx me on that ceremony thing."

Scooter grinned at Sonny's words, thinking that now Sonny couldn't lecture him any more about women and rodeo not mixing.

They cruised through the curvy main street of Pagosa Springs and pulled into the service station at the junction of the highway with the road that headed south into New Mexico. This was the same station where they had filled the car with gas after running out.

"Looks different in the daytime, not such an oasis," Scooter said.

Sonny looked over and said, "Jest pull over side that red pick-up. To my dad."

Scooter pulled alongside of the truck and they both got out. Sonny's dad came over along with Sonny's younger siblings. His dad said hello to Scooter and shook his hand. Sonny came around from the other side of the car and his dad gave him and half hug. They greeted each other in Apache and it was more than just *daahnzho* that Scooter knew as "hello." The younger brother and sister were again somewhat shy, but it didn't take long for them to start hanging onto their older brother.

Sonny's dad asked about the incident and about Sonny's hand. He explained that they had to take a couple of drunks to task. "Scooter wanted to give 'em an enema of the mind, but y'know 'bout how much good that does fer drunks," he said.

Sonny's dad chuckled. "Yeah, hard to change people's minds that way." They began transferring Sonny's few boxes and his duffle bags to the back of the pickup,

"Well it seemed like a good idea at the time," Scooter said.

After they transferred Sonny's possessions, Scooter took out a small notebook and wrote his home address and phone number on a sheet of paper and gave it to Sonny. He asked for the same and Sonny gave him his address.

"Have to phone the store for us yet an' leave a message. Here's the number. Then I'll phone y'back as soon as I get it," he said.

"We might get a phone sometime but been reluctant I guess. Some of the people have 'em now," Sonny's dad explained.

Scooter nodded, "Well, this'll work. After this weekend, I'll see about us getting permits for the pro rodeos. We might as well . . . I'll send any stuff about it down to you. Guess I better hit it."

He and Sonny touched fists. "Good luck, you bronc rider, and *ikeego,*" Sonny said.

"Yeah, heal up you bronc rider, *ikeego*," Scooter said. To Sonny's dad and siblings, he said, "Nice seeing you again. I may be back out for the rodeo here."

Sonny's dad nodded, "So long and good luck this weekend."

Scooter drove toward the bottom of Wolf Creek Pass. The rolling hills were a reminder of the effort it had taken to push his car up the slight inclines.

CHAPTER THIRTY-FOUR
NOT SO FAST

It was nearly six o'clock. Scooter pressed on as fast as he dared, keeping the speed to within five miles per hour over the posted limit. He took a few chances on the descent of Wolf Creek Pass, and the tires squealed in protest to the curves in the road. It would be a late dinner if Charlene waited for him. He thought of her striking features; her thick dark hair and luminous, turquoise eyes and long legs. *Yeah, those long legs . . .* He thought about her physical features and smiled. He hoped she would be happy to see him. *Well, as happy as I am to see her . . . I don't care if she was married before an' all that.* The image of hurt in Katherine's eyes flickered in his thoughts. The images irritated him like a rock in his boot. He tried to push them away. *She's too complicated for me. Like walking the top of a fence in a gusty wind . . . interesting . . . tough choices, but Charlene and I mesh, she makes me feel happy, like someone opened a window for fresh air.*

He continued traveling east; through Del Norte and the service station where he and Sonny had stopped during the return trip from Laramie. He noticed that it was open, but, of course, it wasn't the middle of the night. He continued across the San Luis Valley and then through Alamosa, climbed out of the valley and through the old military post of Fort Garland, and over La Veta Pass then down its long flank and into Walsenburg.

Scooter stopped to fill the car with gas and to stretch and walk around some to get rid of a stiff butt. He paid inside and then used the toilet. Afterward, he bought a few snacks and a soda. He checked the road map and saw that the shorter Highway 10 route to La Junta was nonetheless a long stretch with no service stations and no towns, although out in such country, as where his family had settled, he knew there were scattered ranch headquarters.

The lights on his car stabbed through the twilight as he continued across this section, heading northeast. He suddenly noticed a few sprinkles of rain on the windshield and struggled to see while he pushed out some washer fluid onto the glass and used the wipers, which smeared everything for a few seconds. He slowed down a bit to make sure he could keep the white centerline of the road in view. There had been only a few cars. A huge jackrabbit gave him a start as it bobbed across the highway through the lights of his car. It had seemed as large as a kangaroo.

The rain quit, and he increased the speed, but resisted the temptation to ramp it up. He was cognizant that there could be a State Patrolman waiting out here somewhere. After more than an hour along this road, he saw the lights of a town ahead. They began to spread in front of him and he went through the small town of Hawley and knew he was close to his destination. The road turned east, and he traveled another 10 miles and cruised into La Junta. After the long, lonely stretch, it seemed like a metropolis. He slowly drove along the main street, finally spied the motor lodge and turned into the parking lot. It was crowded with cars and pickups as well as a few horse trailers. He parked near the office and went inside.

There were a few contestants in the lobby and he said hello to several he knew. He was hoping to see Charlene or possibly Hank and Johnny, but knew he was later than he had predicted. He walked up to the desk and a clerk came over to serve him. He gave her his name and filled out a registration card.

"Do you have a room number for Charlene O'Brien?" he asked.

"Let's see . . . I do." She gave Scooter the number and said, "I see there's a message for you."

She gave Scooter a folded piece of notepaper. It read: *Hey, where are you? We're in the restaurant! C*

The clerk slid him a room key and said, "You're on the second floor."

He thanked her and walked down the hall to the restaurant. He stopped near the door and looked around. He heard before he saw Charlene and Squirrel with several others. Charlene hollered and waved to him. He went over to the group, which was in a large corner booth. Charlene was sitting between two guys and Scooter found this disconcerting. He noticed Squirrel was also there sitting beside the second guy. *This looks cozy.* A third girl was in the booth with them and a third guy. It looked like three couples to Scooter.

"Hey, we nearly gave up on you. Pull up a chair," Charlene said.

One of the guys on the edge of the booth scooted over slightly, and Scooter grabbed a chair from an adjacent table, asking the people there if they needed it as he was already taking it away. He set it in the opening at the table while trying to decipher the situation and saw that there were several beers on the table.

"Well, it was a long ol' trip. I thought I might be in Australia in that desolate stretch from Walsenburg . . . might a seen a kangaroo out there," he said.

His comment caused some laughter among the group. "I'll introduce you," Charlene said, and mentioned the names of the others and that they were members of the rodeo team. He assumed the Colorado A&M team and was wondering if the guy sitting by Squirrel was her boyfriend, and who or what the situation was with the one sitting next to Charlene.

He shook everyone's hand and said, "Hey Squirrel, how's it going?"

"Good to see you. Where's that bronc rider partner of yours?" she asked.

"Oh well, that's a long story. I left him off in Pagosa. He's going home to heal a broken hand."

"Yeah, we heard about you guys street fighting. Your face looks like you got the worst end of a boxing match. Which do you like better?"

Scooter took a hard look at her, not knowing what she meant. He saw that she was smiling and softened slightly. "Rodeo might pay better, y'know? Might have similar results though, depending what a person runs into."

His comments resulted in a few uneasy laughs. The one fellow sitting on the outside by the new girl asked what happened, and Scooter told the story again as briefly as he could.

"It happens sometimes out there, around the sport," he said. The fellow nodded that he understood.

Scooter asked the boys what events they worked. He had forgotten the names of the two in the back part of the booth, but Ernie was the guy sitting beside Charlene. They said they were in roping. It seemed Ernie and one of the others was partners for team roping.

The server came over, and Scooter ordered a BLT, not waiting for a menu so he could catch up with the others. He glanced at Charlene. She looked angry or on edge about something; it didn't look like she was overly glad to see him. The whole situation was starting to chaff. They continued to talk about rodeo and how they had done over the season. The others already knew that Scooter had won the bareback riding in Laramie.

Charlene asked how final exams had been and Scooter said he might have squeaked through.

She chided him, "Squeaked? You probably got all *As.*"

"I wished," he said. "This has been a tough week, but we're done now. You know after the rodeo on Sunday? I believe there's going to be a big Southwestern State College blow-out. I told the girls here about it last week. Now normally this is open to all college students, but if they're still in school . . . well, we don't want to be a bad influence. In fact, were warned not to be a bad influence, since we're ambassadors of the college and all. I mean we were given a big lecture about that very thing just this past week."

Squirrel piped up, "You're being naughty now, twisting us for still being in classes. We can take it I imagine . . . in fact, as I've told you guys before, I know we can drink you Southwestern State cowboys under the table without even trying!" The others laughed.

Scooter smiled. "Unfortunately, that's probably true. We're pussycats when it comes right down to it. Well, guess we'll have to share the party favors then. You guys are all invited."

The waitress brought their meals and Scooter ate his sandwich while still trying to decipher the relationships of the boys and girls. The girl he hadn't met before was another barrel racer, and it seemed she and the one fellow who had asked him about the fight were a couple. He wasn't sure about the guy sitting with Squirrel, and he tried not to assume anything about Ernie and Charlene, warning himself not to be jealous. The group continued to talk about the rodeo and what the performance might be like here. The fellow in the back of the booth was talking about the colleges that were at this rodeo and that competition wouldn't be quite as tough as in Laramie, or for that matter, theirs at Colorado A&M. Scooter realized through the conversations that his name was Bill and the other barrel racer, his girlfriend probably, was Naomi.

"It's mostly colleges from Colorado, but someone said Eastern New Mexico is here and they have a tough team," she said.

"The bucking stock will be tough 'cause it's Flying A," Scooter said, "and they provide a lot to the NFR." The guys nodded without commenting and Scooter realized he was talking to a bunch of ropers and they likely had little understanding of bucking stock. He trailed off. *Wish Sonny had come to the rodeo, or that I'd see Hank or Johnny.*

The group finished their meals and Scooter pushed back his chair to go. "I still have t' get stuff in from my car," he said. "I got all my worldly possessions in it." He took his check and started to get up.

"Call my room when you get back. I want to talk to you," Charlene said. Her tone or attitude made him wonder what had happened. He looked again at Ernie, who seemed to be attentive of Charlene. *Frickin' hell, I wonder what's goin' on here.*

"Okay, be back in soon. Nice meeting y'all." He shook hands with all three of the guys and in the process, gave Ernie's hand an extra squeeze. He was tempted to see if he could crush it, but instead gave him a direct look.

Scooter walked back out through the lobby and ran into Johnny and Hank. They exchanged pleasantries and asked each other about the trip; about the stock they had drawn. Johnny mentioned that Scooter had drawn a horse called "Little Joe" for the next day but didn't know anything about it. He had drawn a nasty horse named "Gingerbread," at least some of the contestants from here thought it was rank.

Hank mentioned he likely had a rank bull, as nearly all of them were. "Here's a name fer ya, 'Ofadelimma.' Can you figure it out?" he asked. "It took me a while. We were pronouncing it, 'Ova deleema,' but the rodeo secretary said it's short for 'On the Horns of a Dilemma.' Weird, huh?"

Scooter smiled and nodded, "Sounds like you don't want to get on those horns to me! By the way, Zeke is hooking up with his honey in Pueblo. He's up on Sunday, so will come over then. I better get some stuff."

"Let's get together fer breakfast tomorrow," Johnny said and told Scooter their room number.

"Okay, I still have to check-in too with the rodeo secretary."

He walked outside and to his car. It was still parked near the entrance and it had a piece of paper under the windshield wiper. It had rained again while he was inside, and the paper was wet. He carefully opened it up and saw that he was asked to move his car to a parking space or it would be towed. The evening was not going quite how he had envisioned. *That guy with Charlene . . . that Ernie.*

He moved his car to a space near the street, as the parking lot was nearly full. He gathered several shirts and clean jeans from the clothes that he had thrown in from his closet and then his duffle bag of gear and another of his underwear and toiletries. He made his way back into the hotel and found his room on the second floor near the end of the hall. He went in and stowed the clothes and bag of equipment. The room smelled of old smoke. There was a phone on the small desk and he read the instructions and then dialed Charlene's room number. After a few rings she answered.

"Well, I'm settled in here. You want to get together?" he asked.

"Okay, what number? I'll be over shortly"

There was no lilting quality in her voice; no bantering. Whatever it was, Scooter thought it was like thunderheads before a bad storm. He shook his head at this turn of events, but opened the door so she could just come in. He went into the bathroom and got a small bottle of mouthwash, drank some out of the bottle and sloshed it around then spit it into the sink. While he waited, he opened up the duffle bag and got out his gear. He looked at his bareback rigging. It settled him somewhat as he thought about what his mission was here in La Junta. It was hard to get his mind off that group that had included Charlene and Squirrel and how he had felt like an unneeded fifth wheel.

Charlene knocked on the side of the door and Scooter said, "Hey, come on in." He pulled the chair out for her, but she leaned against the desk instead, half sitting on it. They looked at each other. Charlene glared at Scooter and had her arms folded across her chest.

"Okay, what is it? Is it something that I'm not going to like?" he asked.

"I think so," she said.

Scooter had a sinking feeling in his stomach. "So, what's happened? Do I have a rival . . . that Ernie guy?"

"I'm going to ask you the same question. Do I have a rival with your so-called friend from your English class?" Charlene asked.

Scooter continued to gaze at her, wondering what she knew. "I told you we'd been out a few times. I think we're just friends," he said.

She looked away, toward the window and said, "Don't lie to me! You know the girl from my high school . . . Marlene, the one I asked about you? She thought it was more than that. She knows this Katherine person from some class. I think they're in the same dorm. Marlene told me that Katherine's in love with you."

Scooter took a few seconds to digest what she had said. He thought how beautiful she was; her blue-green eyes that stirred him. *Or where they more greenish tonight?* Her arching eyebrows and angular nose that turned up slightly at the tip, her lips with their reverse curves at the edges that reminded him of birds in flight for some reason, and of course her thick, dark hair. Absorbing her features nearly brought tears to his eyes. She had a smoky, angry look about her now though; one he hadn't seen before.

"I told you about her . . . some. She and I have been on a few dates. If I hadn't met you, she and I would likely be going out . . . you know . . . a couple. We kind of broke up before we got started going out very much is what happened. I mean . . . I was interested earlier in the year, but she was on the cross-country team and with a guy from there. So, the timing was never right. Then, of course, I was way too shy to ask her out anyway. Finally, we started to have a few dates, but never . . . well, got going, really. I mean . . . if we hadn't met, I expect things would be different. But meeting you changed everything. She asked me about you . . . who you were, or what it was. I told her it was serious, that suddenly it had gotten serious. So, we broke up before we really ever got started too much. So, she's mad at me too . . . hurt I guess. Anyway, this is serious, or I thought it was, or is. What do you think about it?"

"Marlene called me earlier today about when I was going to be home and I mentioned you. She told me about this Katherine and you. I was pretty mad . . . hurt . . . all day. I thought we were serious too. I thought we loved each other."

"Yes, that's what it is. So, what are we doing to each other now? Tell me about my rival. I'm not surprised that other guys want to take you out. I just didn't know that I'd want to kill them."

He saw the ghost of a smile cross her face. "Oh, you don't have a rival. Ernie's been around all year. I mean part of the team. He's asked me out, and finally we went to a team function once last fall. I'm not interested in him. I told him I was seeing someone. He slid into the booth beside me tonight. Don't worry about him."

"Well, I was just trying to figure out the territory there, that's all. But a guy can see when another guy is interested in a woman. I know that you turn heads . . . guys look . . . just how it is!"

"Women have radar, too, and I don't want to lose you already . . . to this Katherine or anyone else!" Charlene said.

Scooter noticed that her eyes were glistening with tears. He didn't know what to do, but finally went over to her. He pulled her to him and she rested her head against his shoulder.

"Let's get this straight. If we say we love each other, that's what it means. There no second guessing. I don't want to feel like either one of us has to worry . . . like tonight. If we say that we do, then that's what we mean. It ain't any bullshit. Do you understand me?"

He heard her say, "Tell me you love me!"

"No, you first. You have to say you love me." he said.

She lifted her head up and looked at him, finally smiling through her tears, "You're still my ornery cowboy, aren't you?"

He kissed her eyes and lips. "I do love you. It's serious. No doubt about it."

"Well, it's mutual. Let's not give ourselves scares like this, okay?" She kissed him, and the intensity started to build. Scooter could feel the fire for her flare in him.

"Yeah, okay. I want you to stay with me tonight. Zeke isn't coming over until Sunday, 'cause he's waiting for Molly to join him in Pueblo."

"You mean you want me to sleep with you . . . all night?"

"Yeah . . . I need you."

"I don't know. I need to think about it. I'm rooming with Squirrel and Naomi. What will they think?"

"They'll think you're in love. That's what."

"I don't know . . . maybe."

He tipped her head toward him and kissed her again. He could feel her hand on his neck. He placed his hand in her hair. They broke apart for air.

"I need to take care of you. You have a nasty black eye . . . I hate that you were hurt." She gently touched the side of his face. He looked into her eyes as if to see inside her. The strong feelings for her intensified,

"You're so beautiful, do you know that?"

She smiled at him and said, "It's my duty to make you think so."

"It's my duty then to tell you, so you don't ever forget." He again saw that there were tears in her eyes, and she kissed him again and melted into him with enough pressure he could feel her curves. They again broke apart.

"I feel so much better," she said, "I was really mad at you. I couldn't believe that I could be that wrong about someone. I wanted you to be different than the others . . . all the other guys."

"Well, I really want to be different . . . to be what you need.

Scooter smiled at her and they kissed again. He had his hand on the small of her back and then rubbed her vertebrae with his thumb. As he moved back and forth across her back. It seemed that heat suddenly built and radiated between them. She pushed back away from him though.

"Scooter, honey, we better quit for now or you'll have to do me. You know what I mean?"

"Well, is that so bad? To do you? You know how I am with you."

"Yes, but I need to go back to the room for a while."

Her comment drew out a big sigh from Scooter. "I like being like this . . . making out, getting hot, getting you hot."

Charlene smiled and kissed him lightly. "Getting me hot . . . you're just a big tease, huh? No, really, I want to go back for a while."

Scooter nodded. "Okay, guess I can wait for a little while. She stepped back away from him. "Okay, I'll give you my room key. I can get another one if I need to. Just don't keep me waiting all night," he said, "I've been thinking about you all day."

He was still wondering about the pairing or lack of pairing, whatever the case, among the group from Charlene's team. "So, is that Squirrel's boyfriend she was with?" he asked.

"Oh, you mean Alvin?" Charlene laughed. "He's a funny little guy. Well they've been out some I guess, but more like friends. Do you catch on that she's always asking about Sonny . . . like 'where's that bronc rider friend of yours?' I asked her what's going on, but she won't admit anything. She likes adventure and new horizons. I think she wants to go meet up with him . . . you know on the reservation."

Scooter thought about such a meeting and decided that would be very interesting.

"He had a girlfriend there, but she was killed in a car wreck. He seems to have a girlfriend down there now, but it's hard to tell. When I was down on the rez with him, there was a girl that showed up at the rodeo . . . a tall, pretty girl . . . had her hands all over him. He was nonchalant about her, though. Comfortable is how I'd characterize it. When I tried to tease him about her, he just said that all the girls on the rez were in love with him, an' I reckon there's some truth in that. That's how he is . . . kind of close to the vest."

"Wow, that's so heavy, about the girl. So, do you think he's interested in Squirrel?"

"He's never said. I think he likes her as a friend. He said he thinks she's okay, whatever that means. Well, is she heading back to California after the semester is out?"

"She is for a while. We talked about getting together to rodeo some this summer. Why? Are you going to try to get them together?" Charlene asked.

"Naw, not me . . . that's up to them. We're going to hit the road together though and I know we need to go through Colorado Springs, just logistics, if you know what I mean. I think Squirrel perked his interest when she mentioned goats." They both laughed.

"What a funny guy," Charlene said.

Thinking of Sonny's dilemma with the girl from college, Scooter continued, "I think he's got enough going on with the girls on the rez and he and his dad are thinking about diversifying the livestock down there . . . lots of scrub for sheep and goats. Anyway, we're going to link up and head north a couple of weeks before the regional rodeo. But what if we stopped in at your place on the way? I mean, seems like a great plan. Be in a couple of weeks. I mean . . . Squirrel and Sonny are friends, so whatever."

"I'll mention it. You're right. It's up to them. Squirrel is a little strange sometimes. She's never had a steady boyfriend, just shops around. Well, honey, it's getting late and we have a big day tomorrow. I better get."

"We can sleep in some. Let's go shopping in the morning," he said.

"Shopping! What for?"

"Well, could be for a ring, huh?" he grinned.

"Don't tease about a ring. You'll get yourself in trouble!"

"Well, if it ever comes to that, you need one that's special anyway, not store-bought. Actually, I think I need a new hat. It's about time, and . . . mine got ruined in that incident. We can try on some fancy boots if you want. But before that, come back or I might get desperate!"

"What if I'm desperate? I was missing you so much, and then I was thinking about tanning your hide after talking to Marlene."

"Well, see, I got caught some in a transition. Katherine and I sort-of started to get interested in each other. I mean like maybe a real date and things started to become . . . well, more like girlfriend-boyfriend. Then I met you, so I had to figure out how to . . . where this whole thing was headed, then to backtrack some. But . . . well, I'm not good at this. I just know that you bring out strong feelings in me."

"Well that's kind of an explanation. I can see it with you. Were you ever in love with her? That's my bottom line. I mean . . . what I wondered about."

"Well, maybe . . . although our relationship was just getting started. I mean if you and I hadn't met, I guess we'd be a couple. But I'm not even sure about that. She was difficult . . . sometimes warm, sometimes cold. And then she was smart enough to see through me that she would always be second fiddle to rodeo. So, sometimes I thought we were in love or going to be, the next day not!"

Charlene laughed at his explanation. "Well, she had strong feelings for you apparently, based on what Marlene knew. Anyway, I don't want to think about it. Now that I have you."

"Yeah, let's get back to the basics here, huh?" He kissed her, and she returned it. He kissed her eyes, her throat, her ears.

Scooter heard her softly say, "Yes!" She opened his shirt and kissed his chest, his throat. She put her tongue into his mouth and then broke away from him.

He stood there disheveled. She took his key and said, "Strong feelings, huh? I might be back . . . hmm, I'm still thinking about it!"

"Now who's being mean and ornery? Don't make me come down and jerk you out of that room. Naughty girls can get spanked, you know!"

"Is that a promise?" He saw the sparkle in her eyes and her smile, as she walked out the door, closing it.

CHAPTER THIRTY-FIVE
SWEETNESS

Scooter gradually woke up. It was dark, except there was light leaking out through the edges of the bathroom door. He heard the water running and couldn't believe that he hadn't heard anything before. It could have been a burglar and he would've been cleaned out. He could have woken up in the morning to a bare room with nothing left but his underwear.

Charlene opened the door and turned out the light. He watched her shadow as she approached the bed. She stood beside it and said softly, "Hello sleepy head."

Scooter looked at her silhouette against the faint light of the window. It seemed that she was naked. "Hi, beautiful!" he said, and threw back the blanket and sheet, "Come on, don't be bashful."

"Since when am I the bashful one? I don't think so." She climbed in beside him and he felt the length of her against him. He ran his hand along her side and hip. She had a light, almost elusive scent and he tried to catch it. He thought it might be lilac. He was already aroused.

She felt him and said, "That's what I like to do to you!" She pushed his briefs down. He helped her and slung them onto the floor.

"Yeah, you do it easily to me. It must be your gift." She laughed at this and snuggled up beside him with her head against his neck. He felt her breasts and lightly touched one of her nipples. "Show me how to do this. I mean the way you like it."

"Here's how, so it isn't painful." She lightly stroked one of his nipples and he felt his chest muscles contract. It tickled.

"Let me try it." He did as she had and then moved down to take her in his mouth. He heard her moan softly. He used his tongue to stroke across her nipple and then kissed her stomach and continued downward. "I'll get something," he said.

"No, you don't need to. I . . . hmm, I told you what I was thinking. If we're going to be in love, we . . . I mean to be prudent without being like two kids behind the barn." He laughed at her words, and she then laughed as well. She continued, "So we don't have to worry about it. I just need to know when to use it."

"You mean an IUD?" he asked.

"Something like that. Kiss me! Make love to me."

"Not yet love, you're not hot enough."

Charlene grabbed his head and tried to pull him on top of her. He chuckled and resisted. "You can't have me yet. I think we need to wait. Let's wait until we're married!"

She laughed and said, "You bastard. Do your duty!"

"You can only have a little. We have to wait," he continued to tease.

She grabbed his head and kissed him. She must have forgotten about his sore face, and he gently removed her hand from that side. He felt her tongue thrusting his teeth apart and joining with his tongue. He felt as if he could stay wrapped in her forever; her legs around him, her whispering his name.

Charlene suddenly grabbed his back and loudly said, "Oh damn! Her exclamation startled him and brought him out of his nearly unconscious state. He kissed her lips, then her eyes and ears. He put his tongue through her lips as she had done. She grabbed his head and hair and pulled him to her to return the kiss. "What a sweet boy you are to me. You like it don't you?"

He smiled. "Naw, I'm faking it."

She laughed and kissed him again. "So, honey, do you want to hit a double?"

"Yeah, honey . . . let's do a double." He kissed her again, moved to one of her breasts and again teased her nipple with his tongue.

She suddenly moved out from under him and said, "Turn over. I'm doing some of the work!" They made love for a longer time and again he felt the sweet, yet nearly painful sensation, but gritted his teeth and held off as he heard her moaning again. This was like sweet music to him and drove him to try fulfilling her needs. He heard her cry out and felt her fingernails in his shoulder. He knew she was digging in, but the pain was incidental to everything he was feeling with her. They gradually slowed down, and she continued to lie on him as they snuggled.

She kissed him on the mouth and then in rapid succession, his eyes, nose, and throat. "Now that honey . . . that's love! What you did to me."

"Yeah, what you did to me too. I liked how it felt!"

They stayed together for a while, but finally disengaged and she rolled over to be beside him; nestled inside his arm. "I love you so much. This just makes it more so. I want to know you . . . all of you," she said and kissed him again. "Tell me about your family, your ranch out there in the 'sticks' as you say."

He thought about her question and asked, "Why do we have to think of my family now? I'd rather not . . . just wanna think of you."

"I want to know what it's like. What your family's like. More of who you are."

"I've told you some about my family. My dad's name is Evan. He took over the ranch by himself after my Uncle Jake passed away. My uncle Jake was my favorite growing up. He was a bronc rider when he was young and helped my brother Ron and me to learn how to ride the rough horses is how he put it. My dad and Uncle Jake rodeoed together some after high school, so you see, it's in my blood. My great grandfather started the ranch . . . long time ago. I have a sister Rachel. She's a junior this year in high school. She'll scout you out. Ron is a typical big brother . . . wants to be the boss all the time, and me as his hired man. My dad is okay, but you have to do your work and not cut any corners. He had us work pretty hard in the summers, well, winter too." He stroked her back and shoulders as he talked.

"Will your mom like me?" Charlene asked.

Scooter thought about it for several seconds, wondering if she would, knowing that his mom would be giving Charlene the once-over with a critical eye. "Hmm, she's going to be a little bristly at first. But, I think you guys will get along. Her name is Connie. She was the one that helped me go to college. Ron didn't see any use in it, but he was in a hurry to get out of high school with like a C average."

"Yeah, she'll like you. They were surprised that I have a girlfriend. If they only knew how much of a girlfriend, they would be speechless." He chuckled at the thought.

"Well, I think you'll be a big surprise to my family too. But tell me more . . . what's your ranch like?" Charlene asked.

It's way out there . . . about twenty-five miles southeast of Bunting. Boyero is closer—a dinky burg. Rush Creek goes right through the ranch. In some areas of the pastures there are cottonwoods and also box elder trees, peachleaf willows too. This area is like an oasis, especially on hot days. Those cottonwoods are tall, and breezes ripple through the leaves sometimes and there's a whispery sound, as if there's a conversation taking place. Then in the fall they turn so golden. It's like . . . a huge lantern out there in the pasture . . . on cloudy days, especially. There's a place that has a grove of cottonwoods and some peachleaf underneath, and it's thick enough that in the summer the light streams down to the ground in like . . . shafts, shafts of golden light. I see it as your special place, actually."

He felt her lift up and noticed that she was intently looking at him and then she kissed him. "I love your description of this place. When are you going to show it to me?"

"Well, let's see, I guess. I mean . . . let's say we follow the rodeo trail and keep it going, and are at the top of the pro ranks, and we're thinking ahead to the next step, huh?"

Charlene replied, "Oh, you're making me wait until then. You're being ornery now."

Scooter laughed and said, "Okay . . . I'll take you when you come out to the ranch. We'll take the horses and I'll give you a tour."

"You know, we keep dancing around that future step. I think we don't want to rush things or get ahead of ourselves, or to jinx what we want to achieve."

"You mean we shouldn't talk about too far into the future, like getting married?

Charlene continued to study him. "Yes, thinking too far ahead is risky in that each of us might have expectations that are ahead of our relationship." Scooter raised up to observe her, as he understood she was getting at something he had wondered about. "Yet, you know when we were saying goodbye in Laramie, and were hanging onto each other, you asked, 'What are we going to do about this?' The answer is that I want to be with you forever . . . in that moment I felt it, I knew it."

Scooter observed her features that so attracted him, as they continued to study each other. "I know, I felt it too, that we had moved on from just exploring a relationship to something more. It scared me some then, but now I understand it. That it's not so risky, and taking chances has been . . . well, fun, exciting! Eventually though, we'll have to do something about it . . . in this rodeo quest. I know you are right though, when the time is right."

Charlene smiled as she studied him, "Yes, it's just that this needs to evolve without rushing. I think I am way past being scared now too, and we talked it up big that us rodeo people are good at taking chances anyway . . . right?" Scooter laughed at her description of them being risk takers. "I just know I love you! Tell me more about where you grew up."

"Okay, I know . . . here's about the ol' ranch. We try to keep the cattle out of the creek now. They had trashed some areas of it," he droned on and on. "We irrigate about two hundred acres now . . . might do more . . . grain and hay, but also pastures. Haying is a big-time job, so won't be rodeoing then. We have a big old barn that I want to show you too . . . I mean when you visit. I'm going to tell my dad that I want to concentrate on the livestock part of the operation and Ron can do the crops and land stuff. We need to do some blooded stock; maybe more Angus or even Charolais. But, being more of a partner . . . well, that way I won't be a hired man to him. It has to be more of a partnership. Do you think that's a good idea?"

Charlene answered sleepily, "Uh-huh."

He realized she was nearly asleep and still cuddled into him. He must have nearly bored her to death. He gently pulled his arm out from under her and covered her with the sheet. He got up and padded softly to the bathroom to pee. *What a night.* He looked at his watch. It was two o'clock. He went back to the bed and climbed in beside her and stroked her hair and back. She murmured something.

Scooter woke and saw that it was light outside. He stretched and then realized that Charlene was gone. He could still smell her musky scent mixed with the fresh cucumber-like smell that he liked. He checked his watch and saw that it was after eight. He slowly got up and padded naked into the bathroom to use it. He then looked in the mirror and saw that his hair was nearly standing straight up, but it curled upwards in back as usual. He ran a hand through it, but that didn't help much. He walked back into the room and ransacked his duffle bag for a clean pair of briefs. He noticed that there was a note on the desk. Charlene had written: *Scooter, I had to get back, but don't forget, we're going shopping! I love you!! Char.* He smiled as he read it: *Yeah, shopping might be nice.*

He shaved and then showered. He noticed that at some point he had broken the scab on his elbow and it had bled a little. He used some of the antiseptic soap on it and it stung. He carefully dried the area of his elbow. His face was better than his arm and he thought the puffiness had substantially subsided. He noticed there was some blood on the sheets, so he must have hit his elbow making love to Charlene. He found the salve that the doctor had given him and squeezed a thin thread of it onto the skinned area.

He pulled his jeans from a hanger in the small closet and tugged them on. He took one of his clean shirts from there as well, shrugging it on, but rolled the sleeve up over the elbow to avoid the abrasion. He called Johnny and Hank's room, but no one answered. Scooter decided he should get his mind on the competition and that he better check in with the officials at the college and get his number.

Scooter noticed that Charlene had left his key on the desk with the note, and he took the keys and then walked down the hall and downstairs to the lobby. He thought the college was south of town, but then remembered someone had mentioned that the headquarters was in the hotel.

He checked the motel bulletin board in the lobby and noticed that the Pawnee Conference Room had been reserved for the Intercollegiate Rodeo Association.

Scooter walked down the hall. There was a sign that read *Rodeo*

Headquarters. He felt a thread of nervousness go through him. There were other contestants milling about and he went to a table where a woman was sitting and told her his name. He rifled through his wallet for his intercollegiate card and handed it over.

She looked through a list and said, "You're all checked in. We have you in bareback, you're riding both days—two go-rounds. The draws are up on the board." She handed him a large number, and he told her thanks. He started toward the bulletin board and then wondered about Sonny.

"Sonny Valverde entered, but got injured. He was going to phone," he commented.

"We never heard anything that I know of. I don't know if we can refund his money now. We'll put a note to the stock contractor," the woman said.

Scooter nodded and walked over to the bulletin board but had to look over and around several other people. He found the list of bareback riders and saw that there were 18 on the list. *Quite a few contestants. Thought this was supposed to be a small rodeo.* He read down through the list for the first go-round and saw Johnny's name and then his farther down the list across from "Little Joe." He looked over at the second list for Sunday's second go-round and saw he had drawn "Mucho Blanco." He said to no one in particular, "Holy hell! That's a horse!" Scooter had heard of the horse before; another one that had been to the NFR. *Seems I'm a lucky dude.* Among the bull riders, Zeke was listed on Sunday's roster. Scooter had no idea of the bulls. He turned to walk back out, thinking he better get some breakfast.

He wandered through the other contestants, and one of them asked, "Hey, are you Henry?"

He looked the fellow over and said, "Yeah!"

"I just wanted to introduce myself. I'm Vince Claypool from Eastern . . . Eastern New Mexico. I saw you had won the Wyoming rodeo, so wanted to say hello."

Scooter knew of him and said, "Glad to meet you." They shook hands. Scooter thought Vince looked tough. *Well, coiled energy with some powerful shoulders.* He was shorter than Scooter.

Vince continued, "I see y'got that Mucho horse on Sunday. I had it at our rodeo earlier this spring. Pretty damn rank is what I'd say."

"Oh yeah? I heard it was one to win it."

"Well, yeah," Vince countered, "if a guy can stay on! I had my hands full. Mean bastard is what, twisting and turning. After it tried to bite my foot in the chute!

Scooter studied Vince to see if he was just trying to put a scare into him or shake his confidence. He couldn't tell. "Well, I know it's been in the Finals before, so . . . Um, thanks for the tip. What do you have?" he asked.

"One named 'Sand Creek.' First Go. One of the guys from Flying A said it's okay."

"You're in the top ten in the Southwest Region, last I knew," Scooter said. "You goin' to regionals down here?"

"Yeah, I went last year too, but didn't fare too well," Vince smiled, "competition is tough!"

"Yeah, I figured that," said Scooter, "I'll see you later and good luck."

"Yeah, see ya out there. Luck to you."

Scooter walked back out into the lobby and used a phone at the desk to call Charlene's room. It rang a few times and a girl said, "Hello!" Scooter didn't recognize the voice.

"Hey, is Charlene there?" he asked.

"Just a minute," he heard the person say. "Charlene, I think it's your honey."

Scooter waited and finally Charlene answered, "Hello?"

"Hey, Charlene! It's your secret admirer. How 'bout some breakfast? Someone is starving."

He heard her laugh and she said, "Hi secret! I was wondering about you . . . if you had over-indulged . . . you know what I mean?"

"Yeah, well . . . no I'm okay I think, but I'm starving 'cause of all the indulgence. I'm down in the lobby."

"Okay, we'll be down in a few minutes."

Scooter leaned against the counter and then thought he better call Hank and Johnny again. As he was calling, he saw them come out of the restaurant, so hung up the phone and called out to them, "Hey, don't you guys ever answer your phone?"

They sauntered over. "We couldn't wait anymore. We phoned earlier. Where y'been?" Johnny asked.

"I had to check in and then ran into Claypool . . . from Eastern New Mexico. Said that 'Mucho Blanco' horse I have Sunday is rank. He had it at their rodeo, so guess I better get ready to rock 'n roll."

"Yeah," said Hank, "that 'Gingerbread' of Johnny's is no cookie either!" He snorted a kind of pig laugh at his own joke. "Both of you better crank one this weekend."

Scooter smiled and said, "Guess we all do, don't we?"

Hank and Johnny both nodded. As they were talking, Charlene, Squirrel, and Naomi came down the stairs to the lobby and approached them.

"Hi y'all! Guys, I want you to meet the best of the A&M rodeo team. This is Charlene, Squirrel, and Naomi. Girls, these two scroungy-looking dudes are Hank, a bull rider, and Johnny, another bareback rider, both my teammates," Scooter said.

Hank and Johnny seemed tongue-tied but shook hands with the girls. Finally, Johnny asked them what events they worked, and they talked a few minutes about the different rodeos they had been to on the college circuit.

Scooter broke the discussion up by saying, "Look we gotta eat before I faint. My belly thinks my throat's been cut!" Scooter didn't know when but realized Charlene had slipped her arm inside his.

"Jeez, Scooter, you're trying to ruin our appetites." Squirrel said.

The others laughed. "Where're the other guys?" he asked.

"They're sleeping apparently." Squirrel said, "They went out on the town some . . . without us, too!"

Scooter told Hank and Johnny, "I'll see you guys at the arena. Let's pull for each other."

"Sounds good. Be out there around noon," Johnny said.

Scooter and Charlene followed Squirrel and Naomi into the restaurant. He looked at Charlene and she smiled at him. "Really now, how's my cowboy this morning?" she asked.

"Your cowboy is fantastic. How's my cowgirl?"

"Oh yeah, she's really good."

"I been thinking, I think we should hit a triple soon," he said.

"Scooter!" she exclaimed.

"Yeah," he said, "I'm going to die happy makin' love to you."

His comment caused her to break out in peals of laughter. Squirrel and Naomi looked at each other as they approached a table. "What a couple of love-birds! Let us in on the joke," Squirrel said.

"Okay . . . so one frog said to the other as they sat on lily pads, 'Time sure is fun when you're having flies!'" Scooter said.

All three of the girls laughed. "Pretty good," Naomi said.

Charlene said softly to him, "Don't ever change, okay?"

After breakfast, Charlene asked Scooter, "Are you still up for it?" She saw his mischievous smile and continued, "I mean shopping. You're naughty."

She told Squirrel and Naomi, "We're going downtown for a little while. I'll meet you guys back here . . . what do you think, around eleven thirty?"

"Okay, but we have to take care of the horses," Squirrel said. Charlene handed Squirrel the keys to her pickup.

Charlene and Scooter walked out of the hotel and to his car. They slowly drove along Main Street looking for a Western clothing store. Charlene sat close to Scooter and kissed his neck and ear as he drove. She told him she hadn't wished him a proper good morning, but he said she was going to cause an accident.

They located a store and went inside. Scooter tried on several hats. He said that he wanted one like Casey Tibbs and tried on one that resembled what he thought it might be like, based on pictures he had seen in the small booklets on rodeo that came with Wrangler jeans. Charlene was looking at others, not being impressed with the "Casey Tibbs" look. She was twirling one that was tan and had a high crown. She thought it suited Scooter and convinced him to try it on. He noted it was more than what he had intended to spend.

He looked at his image in the store mirror and liked how the hat looked. He said, "We always wear black ones though . . . I mean Sonny and me . . . Zeke, too."

"I like it on you though. It matches your hair and you look like a real buckaroo in it," Charlene said.

Scooter looked at himself in the mirror again. He did think it made him look the buckaroo part. "Okay," he said.

He went with the store clerk to a small room in the back to a steamer and shaped the brim to curve up on the sides slightly and solidified the crease in the crown. The clerk told him not to steam it too much, as that would take the "starch" out of it.

He walked back into the main area of the store and noticed Charlene holding a western-cut blouse up against herself while looking in the mirror. "I think I better get this one. I really like it."

"Looks like it was made for you." Scooter noted. She turned toward him, and he realized the color brought out the blue-green of her eyes. "Yes, looks great! I can you know . . . how 'bout a birthday present?"

Charlene laughed. "You only missed it by a month. Anyway, I don't want to be a kept woman."

"Now, that's a thought!" Charlene hit him with an elbow as they angled to the front of the store to pay their bill.

Scooter checked his watch. "We better get going!" They walked back outside and to his car. Scooter was starting to think about "Little Joe," the bareback horse he had drawn for the first go-round, but Charlene had her hand on the inside of his thigh. It had started to rain again.

"I hope you do well today," he said. "If it keeps raining some, we'll have to see how it changes the arena; could get slick." He started to open the door of the car to get out, but Charlene grabbed his arm.

"Just a second." Scooter turned to see what is was. She continued, "You're not getting away without kissing me!"

"Yeah!" Scooter said and bent Charlene back into the seat and planted a passionate kiss on her. He caressed her ear with his hand and then twirled a finger in her hair and then cupped a breast. They finally broke apart for air, and he kissed her throat and her neck and then put his tongue in her ear.

"God almighty, Scooter, I just wanted a kiss!" Charlene said. "You're something else." She grabbed him by the neck though and kissed him back. "There, you get some from me, too."

CHAPTER THIRTY-SIX
THE LUCK OF THE DRAW

Scooter had to admit it. He missed not having Sonny and Zeke at the rodeo. It was nice having a room where he could rendezvous with Charlene and make love to her, but now he wished the three of them were kidding around while they set their minds to their upcoming rides as they had all spring at the different rodeos. *Well, guess Johnny and I can help each other.*

He parked his car among pickup trucks and horse trailers of the other contestants and retrieved his gear from the car's trunk. He threw the duffle bag over his shoulder and walked around contestants riding their horses and walked toward the area behind the chutes. Scooter saw Billy Hall riding his horse through the grounds. Hall hadn't seen him, and Scooter stopped and watched him until he rode behind several horse trailers. *Wonder if he'd be so ballsy without his thug partner?*

Scooter continued toward the chutes and angled through the walkway behind them. He took his rigging out and centered it on the top rail of the fence. He sat down, switched to his riding boots, and then put on his spurs. He was a little early, but he started to stretch out and then did his usual push-ups and pull-ups to warm up. He wiped mud off his hands with a small towel. Johnny and a few of the other bareback contestants were gathering. He said hello to those he knew. They asked him how it had been to ride the Popcorn horse, as most knew of the horse's reputation.

"Must be living right. Y'got that Mucho horse on Sunday," one of the contestants said.

"Yeah, a little luck never hurts," Scooter said. He asked, but no one seemed to know about the Little Joe horse. One of the contestants from Southeastern Junior College thought it was new. Someone knew the Gingerbread horse of Johnny's and indicated it was tough.

Scooter continued to go through his routine of exercises and then stretched again, placing a foot on the fence. He pulled his rigging off the fence and energetically rubbed rosin into the handhold with his leather glove. He noticed the horses being sorted and then the first batch was loaded into the chutes. He climbed onto the back of the second chute to see them better.

"We got Jones, Claypool, Snyder, Henry, Reynolds, and Rodriquez in that order," the chute boss said.

Scooter climbed down and carried his rigging and duffle bag to the fourth chute. He checked out the horse; a small buckskin. It spooked against the chute as he climbed up on the fence. He got down and talked to it softly through the slats of the chute, while putting on his chaps. Johnny came over and took Scooter's rigging, carefully centering it onto the horse's withers.

The chute boss approached them. "Hey, you're Evan Henry's boy?" It was more of a statement than a question. Scooter turned toward him. The man stuck out his hand and said, "I'm Bud Simmons. Used to rodeo with him and his brother . . . back in the old days. Looks like you ran into somethin' mean!"

"Yeah, a guy swinging a two-by-four. You mean with my dad and Uncle Jake?" Scooter asked.

Bud continued to gaze at Scooter's black eye and discolored face, but said, "Yeah, mostly saddle broncs, but bareback too. That was before any of us was married, so we hit the road most the summer fer a couple of years. Your Uncle Jake had the knack. Went to the finals couple of years . . . won some go-rounds there too."

Scooter reflected that this had happened in Laramie as well and re-alized these guys had been thick back in the old days. "Yes, we have some old clippings and photos," Scooter said. "I'm glad to meet you. My dad is coming down tomorrow. I'll tell him you're here. This is Johnny Archuleta a teammate from Southwestern."

Johnny and Bud shook hands and he said, "Good t'meet y'all." To Scooter he said, "I'd like to see yer dad . . . been a few years. You got a squirre-ly horse there. Sometimes bucks pretty good, but still getting used to coming out of a chute."

Another contestant was hollering at Bud, so Scooter said, "Thanks for the tip."

He and Johnny continued to set the rigging. The horse seemed ner-vous. Scooter again talked softly to it, hoping it would settle down before he got down into the chute. The grand entry started, and the chute crew came along and placed the flank straps on the horses. Scooter leaped down from the chute and again did some stretches and jumping jacks. It didn't feel like he was ready yet—like he was revved up. He got back onto the chute again in time for the National Anthem. The announcer went through an introduction about rodeo history that Scooter barely heard and then asked for silence as he said a prayer that the contestants would be safe and to be thankful that they all lived in a country where people could be free. He explained the bare-back event and announced the first Cowboy, who was from Rio Grande State. The announcement garnered Scooter's attention, as he realized another New Mexico college was represented. The chute gate opened, and Scooter watched as the cowboy spurred weakly until a horn sounded signaling the end of the ride, although he was on the side of the horse. Then it was announced that he had missed the mark-out.

Scooter and Johnny were more interested in Vince Claypool. He spurred in classic fashion, although in lying back away from his arm, he ended up slightly sideways, away from his handhold, and had trouble being taken off by the pickup men. Scooter heard the announcer indicate Vince had scored a 78. He and Johnny casually watched the rider named Snyder in front of Scooter, but the horse ducked back underneath the rider, flinging him forward and into the arena surface. After the horse had been ushered out of the area, Scooter carefully crouched down onto Little Joe. He heard the announcer broadcast his name, the college, and the horse.

Little Joe was shaking slightly, and Scooter said, "Hey Little Joe, it's just me. Let's go out and show these people some action. You listenin'?" He wedged his gloved hand into the handhold and slid up close to it, then slid his feet out in front of the horse's shoulders. He tugged his hat down and said, "Outside!"

The horse wheeled out hard as the chute gate opened, and Scooter had to hustle his feet to get a mark-out. Little Joe galloped out into the middle of the arena and Scooter leaned back, waiting for it to break into bucking. When it did, the sudden change in momentum nearly catapulted Scooter over the horse's front. He pushed against the rigging to counteract the force. The horse then whirled around in a circle while crow hopping. Scooter became slightly disoriented but tried to spur as best as he could with a horse that bucked so disjointedly. He was aware that a few small clods of mud that were kicked up by the horse hit him, some sticking to his face. He finally heard the loud horn that signaled the end of the ride and a thought crept in that he and the horse hadn't accomplished very much.

Little Joe finally slowed and one of the pickup men tripped the flank strap off it, and it loped to the perimeter of the fence. Scooter worked his hand out of the handhold and grabbed onto a pickup man as he caught up, aware of his bad shoulder, but was set down onto the ground with no mishaps. He had to trot halfway across the arena to the chutes and heard before he got back that he had scored a 65.

The announcer said, "Give that cowboy a hand folks, 'cause that might be all he's getting, and that cowboy won this event in Laramie!"

Scooter heard polite applause. *Well, with that score and a dollar, a guy could maybe buy a cup of coffee. That's the draw, I guess.* He checked with the judges about a re-ride, but one of the judges indicated the cutoff was 60 or less, and there already had been a similar score. Scooter climbed over an empty chute and took off his chaps and glove, then his spurs, and changed boots. Vince Claypool walked over and said, "What a dog of a horse. It mayn't stay in the string. They should'a given you a re-ride."

Scooter took a look at him and saw that he seemed serious and answered, "Yeah a re-ride woulda been nice. Guess they're not, though. You made a good ride . . . leading the go-round."

Vince said, "Thanks! We'll see how it goes tomorrow! Hey, what I wanted to ask . . . are you getting a card for this summer? I'm looking for a traveling partner."

Scooter studied Vince for a few seconds and said, "I have a buddy, a saddle bronc rider from Jicarilla, and we thought about it . . . figuring to hit a few before the regionals. But then we could maybe link up." He dug a piece of paper out of his duffle bag and searched out a pen. He wrote his phone number out and gave it to Vince. "It's at Bunting, but we could rendezvous wherever."

Vince wrote his phone number on a strip he tore from a paper cup he had retrieved off the ground. "I live out west of Wagon Mound." He gave the paper to Scooter. "It's better to partner up to try and break into the pro ranks. I went to a couple last summer, and it seemed tough to get a decent score. They didn't know me."

"Well, let's figure on it then." They shook hands. Scooter walked to the end of the alley way and through a gate to the unsaddling chute and retrieved his rigging.

Bud Simmons was walking through the alleyway and called over, "Well, win some, lose some I guess."

Scooter smiled wryly and said, "Yeah, that's rodeo."

He packed up his gear and stowed it out of the way, and then checked with Johnny to see when he was up. Johnny said he was down the list in the last group. He and Scooter continued to watch the competition and commented on several rides in the low *70s*, the best from a Colorado A&M student named Meyers, whom Scooter didn't know. However, no one topped Vince Claypool.

"You could still go on top with this Gingerbread," Scooter said.

"Yeah, I'd like to," Johnny responded.

Finally, the last few horses were loaded. Hank and Johnny placed the rigging on the large palomino, as it stood quietly with no sign that it was unbroken.

Johnny slowly climbed into the chute and threaded his glove into the handhold. Hank stood on the back of the chute near the horse's head. "Give 'im hell!" He told Johnny.

Johnny gave an exaggerated nod and, when the gate opened, the horse took a giant leap out of the chute, as if happy to gain its freedom. It continued to jump and kick. Scooter could tell from his vantage point that it was a powerful horse. Johnny kept spurring toward the front near the shoulders to try to keep his butt near the rigging. But because of the hard momentum of the horse as it leapt upward, Johnny kept sliding back. Scooter held his breath as the horse circled back toward the chutes.

Johnny missed spurring and making the position adjustment as the horn sounded and was flipped forward in a somersault, landing hard on his back. He didn't get up. Scooter bailed over the empty chute and, along with several of the chute crew, ran out to where Johnny was lying. He was on his back and gasping, as if a fish out of water. One of the EMTs also came out to see if he was needed, but one of the rodeo crew lifted up on Johnny's belt to help him breath. Scooter wasn't sure this was an effective method or not, but it had also been used as the occasion warranted on his high school football teammates. Finally, Johnny took a big breath and then several more. He looked a little pale around the mouth and eyes and spit some phlegm onto the ground. The EMT and Scooter helped him up and they all walked back with them toward the chutes.

He asked Scooter, "Did I make it?"

"Yeah, I heard a seventy-five, so that's damn good. Be in third, I think!"

"My arm feels a foot longer after that. What a horse!"

Scooter observed that Johnny's shirt and the back of his jeans were partly covered by a large smear of mud as if from a large paintbrush. "You did what you needed to. You rode good!" They touched fists and walked back through the alleyway to retrieve Johnny's gear.

"I'll hang around for Hank with that bull. I gotta see one with such a strange name," Scooter said.

"Okay, maybe we can get together after for a beer."

"Well, I'd like to, but have a date."

Johnny seemed to think about this for a few seconds and said, "She's got you roped and tied, looks like. Well, you could do lots worse."

"Yeah," Scooter said, "a lot worse I reckon. But hell, I'll have a beer with you guys anyway to celebrate you being in the money. I got time." He smiled and threaded his way through the other contestants. Several told him tough horse on which to get any points. He nodded and said, "Felt like possibly being on a helicopter blade." They chuckled at his analogy. He stowed his gear in the trunk of his car.

Scooter walked over to Charlene's pickup and horse trailer. He figured she must be somewhere on the grounds riding Star, so waited patiently. He thought about the bareback ride that with such a low score he likely had no chance to win or even place well in the average. *I better give it hell tomorrow and try to win the go-round . . . have the horse to do it, probably.* It had started to lightly rain again. He was glad he was wearing his old hat even if it did look ratty now, especially compared to the new one. He looked up and saw that Charlene was riding toward him. She had on a yellow rain jacket.

He waited for her and she said, "Hey you, buckaroo. Where'd they get that horse for you?"

He smiled, "Yeah, guess y'can't win 'em all."

"Well, you didn't buck off, so that's something!"

He laughed at her statement, "Yeah, at least that. I told that Little Joe to go out there and show the people some moves, but he just wasn't listening . . . was too nervous actually. I been there y'know, stage fright. Bud and those guys ought to give him a chance . . . take him to some junior rodeos."

Charlene smiled at Scooter's assessment. "You feel sorry for him, what a softy."

Scooter laughed and said, "Well, yeah guess I am. Bud, the chute boss, said the horse bucks good sometimes. Give me a ride over to my car. I gotta get a rain jacket."

Charlene emptied a stirrup for him and he swung up behind her and cozied up to her with his arms around her waist. She turned to look at him and said, "Hey lover, take it easy." She squeezed his leg and walked Star to where he directed to his car.

He swung down and said, "If it keeps raining, you might need to take some off in the corners. What y'think?"

"It must be getting muddy. You have some on your face and some chunks on your hat yet."

He looked up and saw that she was smiling. Grinning, he took off his hat and flicked them off. "Yeah, the little buckskin kicked up some dirt. It might be slick if this keeps up is what I'm saying."

"I know. You already told me, and I thought about it."

"Well, be careful, but get some. Okay?"

"Okay, cowboy. I'm going to warm her up."

He nodded. "I'll see you after."

Scooter watched her ride back toward an open area of the grounds and then walked back toward the arena to watch the saddle broncs. He was interested to see how Sonny might have done.

Scooter perched on the top of the fence beyond the chutes, and Johnny climbed up to sit beside him. There were several good rides in the first group, one by a tall cowboy from Pueblo Eastern College named Millner that Scooter had talked to a few times, and one from Baca Junior College, the host school. One of the Eastern New Mexico cowboys started a great ride and got their attention. Suddenly, he was jerked over the front end of the horse and hit the ground in a heap. He slowly got up, retrieved his hat and limped back toward the chutes.

"Ouch! He could've won it. Things can go south in a hurry," Johnny said.

"Saddle broncs seem like they would be fun, or maybe a challenge is more like it with all the paraphernalia . . . stirrups, a rein, and just the swells to hang onto." Scooter replied.

"Yeah, maybe when we get older and can't take the jerkin' of the bareback horses we'll do it." Scooter chuckled at Johnny's sarcasm.

Scooter thought that Sonny would likely have done okay, maybe even won it, depending on the draw. They stayed perched on the arena fence during the calf roping and Scooter observed that the fellow from Colorado A&M that he had met in the restaurant had a good run. He was trying to remember the guy's name . . . *Naomi's boyfriend.*

After the last calf roper, the three barrels were brought in and set up over short length of rope that had been tied to a buried stake to mark the correct locations. Scooter got down off the fence to see better. The announcer called out each of the contestant's name, and an official outside the arena had a list with the order and gave each of the contestants a sign when they could make their run. Scooter thought it might be better to go later in the group after some of the mud had been dug up but wasn't sure. Charlene was the second competitor though and he watched her, and Star make their run. It seemed Charlene was not holding back after all, and Star was throwing up clods of mud on each barrel. They hit the last one and it rocked some but stayed upright.

Scooter said to no one in particular, "Wow!"

There was a groundswell of noise from the bleachers as Charlene and Star thundered out of the arena. The announcer said, "That, ladies and gentlemen, might be the time to beat. Charlene O'Brien of Colorado A&M has set a tough standard!"

Scooter continued to watch, and Johnny came over to stand by him. He said, "That was a helluva ride . . . that girlfriend a yours."

Scooter smiled, "I was worried about the turns in the mud, but she and her horse apparently weren't."

"Yeah, mud 'n all. That's a good horse," Johnny said.

Scooter heard the commotion as the first batch of bulls was loaded in the chutes and followed Johnny to find Hank. He was behind the chutes working on his rope.

"Could you tell us when that Dilemma bull is in, so's we know. This is Hank, another teammate," Scooter said to Bud.

Bud nodded to Hank and looked at his list, "We got him in like number eight spot, so be after the first set. He spins right."

"Thanks!" At least it's into my hand. I seen 'im and he's got horns a mile long," Hank said.

Hank looked tight, so Scooter said, "Warm up good." He climbed back onto the chutes to watch more of the barrel racing; to see if Charlene's time was going to hold-up or not.

He watched as Squirrel and Naomi made their runs. Their times seemed to be in the thick of a group nearly half a second slower than Charlene's. Finally, the last rider, who was from Colorado College, thundered into the arena, but had trouble controlling her horse, and finally knocked over a barrel. None eclipsed Charlene's time. Wow, she's gotten better and better since I saw her first time . . . a real cowgirl.

"I'll be back in a few," he said. He jumped down from the chute and walked back out of the alleyway through the bull riders who were either placing their bull ropes and loosely tying them off or were still stretching and limbering up.

Scooter walked through the crowded parking area to Charlene's pickup and horse-trailer and waited for her. He was dismayed when he looked across to an open area and saw that Billy Hall was riding along side of her. Scooter thought about what they had talked about; that they were in love and weren't going to worry about these kinds of situations. This is a good test for my temper . . . my jealousy. He decided to see what was going to happen, but fairly confident that he could trust Charlene.

She had noticed him and waved, then angled her horse over toward him. He leaned back against the rear fender of the pickup. Billy followed her over and then veered off when he saw Scooter leaning against the truck. Scooter acknowledged Billy with a nod, but only received a glance. Scooter then noticed the big smile on Charlene's face and smiled back.

As she stopped Star near him, he exclaimed, "So, you think you're a cowgirl! That was a helluva run!"

"I'm so happy about it. Everything just came together. Star knew more about the mud than I did. Come on, I need you to ride with me!"

He swung up and said, "I'm very proud of you. I need you to take me back over to the chutes though, 'cause I gotta help Hank with his bull. Wait for me though. I'll help you take her over to the stables."

He didn't say anything about Billy Hall and Charlene said, "Okay. I'm going to ride her around for a while. I don't want to get off yet."

He swung down near the gate to the chutes and said, "I'll meet you back at your rig in a while."

"I know you're wondering, but I told you not to worry, didn't I? Billy won the first go-round of the steer wrestling, so thinks he's hot stuff now."

"I'm not, 'cause you told me. You can tell me about it later if you want to."

"Okay," she said, and pantomimed a kiss.

Scooter smiled at her and realized he hadn't even paid any attention to the steer wrestling and hadn't known that Hall had won. He walked behind the chutes to locate Johnny and Hank.

A few of the bulls and riders had been out already and Hank and Johnny were watching for the Dilemma bull. Bud came through and said, "It'll be in with the next two, but we want to slide 'em up into the empty chutes."

After the bull was brought into the chute, Scooter and Johnny helped snag the rope underneath the bull with a wire hook and gradually brought the tail up to where Hank could loosely tie it off. Scooter thought the techniques used around most of the bulls was like feeding lions at the zoo. Dilemma was a large, spotted Brahma with a hump of muscle across its shoulders, but the most notable feature were long, banana-like horns that swept upwards in an arc. They barely fit into the chute.

The three continued to watch the rides ahead of Hank.

"That first rider out made a good ride. The bull wasn't too tough . . . went straight down the chutes and then back, looking for the gate to go home," Johnny explained.

One of the competitors from Southern Colorado College made a qualified ride on a fairly rank bull and had the leading score. "Who's that?" Scooter asked.

"Yoder from Pueblo," Hank said. "He's had a card already . . . last summer I guess." They followed Dilemma as the chute crew moved it up to the last chute.

One of the crew told them, "Go ahead and pull."

Hank straddled the bull and placed his hand in the handhold of the rope. Johnny pulled on the tail of the rope while Hank tested the tension on the handhold.

"That's good," he said and took the tail of the rope, pulled it across the palm of his hand and then brought it back around and threaded it through several fingers. He hit his fist with his free hand as a signal for it to stay shut. He scooted up close to his hand and mashed his hat down hard over his ears. Scooter liked Hank's tough look; the hawk feather he had stuck in the band of his hat, his pant legs tucked into the tops of his boots. Their relationship had changed since they had worked on the term paper together.

"Bear down on 'im!" Johnny said.

Hank slapped his face several times. Scooter had seen other bull riders do this and thought it must be to make sure to be focused. He had asked Zeke about this, but Zeke had said to it was to make sure they didn't doze off. Scooter figured Zeke really didn't know why bull riders went through this strange ritual.

"Let's go!" Hank said,

The gate swung open and "Dilemma" took a high jump out of the chute and, as Bud had said, spun to the right. Hank adjusted with his feet and spurs each time the bull's front feet came down and was using his free arm to keep his momentum corrected with the bull's spin. Scooter thought Hank was going to make the eight seconds, but he started to slide to the outside. He was finally on the side and came off just before the horn signaled the end of the ride. His hand remained tied into the handhold of the rope though, and Hank was drug under the bull, but lurched to his feet and then was swung out as if tied onto a merry-go-round. The bull jumped out of the spin and hooked Hank with a horn to try and get rid of him. This allowed one of the bull fighters to reach the tail of the rope, which he pulled to release Hank's hand. Hank fell to the ground but was up in a flash and quickly sprinted to the safety of the fence.

After the bull was ushered out of the arena, Hank jumped back off the fence and retrieved his rope from one of the bullfighters. He walked over to where Scooter and Johnny were still standing on the side of the empty chute. Scooter noticed Hank had blood on the side of his head, about the same place where Scooter had been hit with the two-by-four.

I think it was close! Did he get a score?" Scooter asked Johnny.

"About a seven-point-nine ride, then, if not an eight. That was a helluva ride in any case . . . yer best of the year." Johnny said.

Hank climbed over the last part of the chute to where they were standing. He was still breathing hard. "Shit! What a bull! I thought I made it, but, guess not."

Scooter climbed back across the chute as more bulls were being brought in and asked one of the judges, "Did he get a score?"

The judge just looked at Scooter and shook his head. "Close, but no cigar." The announcer confirmed this, indicating that Hank had no score, but should get a round of applause for his effort.

He clambered back to where Hank was taking off his glove and his chaps. "Naw, the judges should've have given you a score just for the effort!" Scooter said.

"Yeah, I coulda used a score and a nice cash prize. Well, I'll just have to keep it going this summer."

Scooter then noticed that blood was trickling down Hank's face from the gash on his head. Johnny had noticed it too. "You better have that looked at. Seems to me it needs stitches."

Hank gingerly touched the area and checked his hand for blood. "I didn't even know he hit me there."

One of the sports medicine crew had already been looking for Hank to see if he was okay. "I need you to come with me and we'll get this fixed. Your buddy is right. You need some stitches," he said.

Hank followed the medic out through the other riders, some of whom told Hank, "Helluva try man!"

"He's a tough guy. Jeez, didn't even know he'd taken a lick," Scooter told Johnny. "Okay, I need to see about a horse. I'll see you guys later."

"I know about that horse. We'll meet you later in the hotel bar."

Scooter noticed that Charlene was brushing Star and that another horse was also tied onto the back of the horse trailer. He figured it was probably Squirrel's. "Hey Charlene, you better take good care of her after that run," he teased.

Charlene looked over toward him and said, "Hey cowboy. That's right. Us cowgirls gotta take care of our rides."

Squirrel emerged from the front of the horse trailer and Scooter told her hello and said, "I saw you make a pretty good run out there today."

"Yeah, but not as good as ol' Char there." She untied her horse, a little bay with a dark tale and mane. "This is Little Diablo, a name that suited him early in our career together."

Scooter rubbed the horse's nose and between its ears. It sniffed him. He said, "Seems nice now and it ran the barrels good."

"Yes, he's a sweetie now. Took a while though, typical man."

Scooter laughed and said, "Guess us broncs are hard to break that's all. We like the wide-open spaces . . . wind in our hair."

Charlene smiled at the exchange and said, "She's giving you ideas. We fillies like to run too . . . wind in your hair. What a bullshitter you are." Scooter laughed.

"See, I'm bringing out his true identity. He's going to bolt for the open corral gate as soon as you try and put a saddle on 'im." Squirrel said.

Scooter knew Squirrel was teasing, but had always thought she had a slight edge toward him. "Well, that's right. You hit it on the head, but I'm taking her with me. We're going to be wild and free together." Scooter noticed that Squirrel was smiling and yet, not really.

"Come on you two. Remember you're friends. And yes, wild and free like mustangs is how we already are . . . us rodeo people. Let's load these horses," Charlene said.

"I like that wild-free thought," Squirrel replied.

Scooter stepped out of the way and helped push the horses into the trailer. Squirrel's horse took some persuading.

"Do you want me to go with you guys and help out?" he asked Charlene.

She thought for a few seconds. "We don't have much to do. Tell me about later."

"Yeah, put on your glad rags, 'cause we're doing dinner and dancing. How 'bout seven?"

Charlene laughed, "Glad rags, huh? I'll see if I have any."

It made Scooter happy when he made her laugh. "I told Hank and Johnny I'd buy them a beer," he said. "Hank had to go get some stitches from taking a shot off'n that bull. Now Squirrel, if you want to tame a wild one, you should get hold of that guy."

Squirrel paused while closing the tailgate to the trailer. "He appears pretty raunchy . . . looks like a bull rider even. I like your bronc rider friend better. I still gotta get him out on a dance floor, y'know."

Scooter laughed and said, "That'd be a major accomplishment. Might be scuff marks on the wood! Well, stop by the hotel bar if you guys want. I'll buy you one to celebrate."

"We'll see. Our team is having a little gathering there, too. Maybe you guys could all come over."

"A social. I should say hello to Bob if he's there anyway—about next year. Maybe to Billy, too," Scooter said.

"No fighting! You been doing enough of that already. Your reputation is getting out of hand. The word is now that you're a tough," Charlene said. "If they only knew what a softy you are." She kissed him on the cheek. "So, be good or I'll tell on you."

"Come on! You can love him up later," Squirrel said.

CHAPTER THIRTY-SEVEN
ROMANCE

The desk clerk thought about Scooter's question regarding a good restaurant. "There's only one really good restaurant here. They have good steaks. By the way, there's a message for you." She pulled a slip of paper from a cubbyhole behind the counter.

"Thanks, on both accounts." Scooter said. He opened the paper, and it read: *Be there in the morning. Call us! Mom.* Scooter thought about this new development; if it was a good deal or not with the rodeo and all, and with what he had in mind or hoped with Charlene. But, it would be really nice to see the family again. It had been since the Easter break and that was a short visit. He asked the clerk if he could get change for the lobby pay phone.

"You should call that restaurant too for reservations. They get busy on Saturday nights. You can use the phone on the counter for that," she said.

Scooter looked at the phone book page again and dialed the number. The person that answered said they had an opening at 7:30 and took his name. He took a hand-full of change, walked across the lobby to the pay phone, and dialed his parent's number.

"Hey Mom, guess who?"

"Scooter, we were hoping you'd call. We decided to come down early and want to have breakfast with you or guess it would be brunch. Is that okay?"

"What time would you guys be here, 'cause I have to be at the arena near noon."

"We should be there around ten. We want to know how you did today."

"Oh, not so good. I marked a sixty-five . . . didn't have much of a horse. I have that Mucho Blanco horse tomorrow, so am hoping I can stay on!"

"Look, can you get a reservation there at the restaurant for ten? I'll ride herd on the others to make sure we leave when we're supposed to."

"I guess. How many?"

An operator broke into the conversation and told Scooter another fifty cents was required for three minutes. He slid additional money into the coin slot. Scooter asked again, "How many?"

"Well Ron is bringing Denise, so us five plus you."

"Hey Mom, I want to see if Charlene will join us. Okay?"

"You mean the girl you met?" she asked.

Scooter laughed at his mom's phrase, "Yeah, the girl I met . . . Mom, she's my girlfriend!"

"Well when you put it that way, I guess we had better meet her. Did you say she's a barrel racer?"

"Yeah, Mom." He was about ready to drop the subject, but needled his mom with, "She rides like the wind! Won today's go-round. You'll like her. I better go, I'm running out of quarters."

He heard his mom say, "Okay. We're looking forward to seeing you." It sounded to him like she was still trying to figure out this new development—the new person in his life.

"Yeah, me, too. Been a while. Tell everyone hello," he said.

He heard her say she would and hung up. He walked through the lobby and into the bar looking for Johnny and Hank. It was noisy, and people were milling around. He saw Bob Forsythe near the bar and they shook hands.

"We have a hospitality room opening up down the hall soon, so come down and say hello to some people."

Scooter said he would but had to find his teammates first. He didn't see Johnny or Hank, so went back into the lobby and up the stairs to his room. He decided he needed to grab a quick shower and quickly stripped off his clothes and turned on the hot water. He checked his face out in the bathroom mirror. It seemed his face was looking much better, except for the black and blue around his eye, along with some remaining yellow and the abrasions. But the swelling was down some. He stepped into the hot water, lathered his hair with shampoo and used soap to get rid of the arena mud. He quickly rinsed and then stepped out and dried. He ran a comb through his still damp hair and put on fresh underwear, a clean shirt and jeans. He threw his dirty clothes into a plastic bag, stuck it in the small closet and forced his still-moist feet into a clean pair of socks. He looked at the new hat he had set upside down on the desk and decided to see how it looked. He tried several angles. *Maybe Charlene was right, not too bad . . . a kind of buckaroo look.* He forced his feet back into his boots and grabbed his wallet and keys, then headed for the door, but stopped. He went back to the duffle bag with his clothes and took out the gold and silver buckle from Laramie. He started to switch-out his old one and then paused and put the new buckle back in the duffle bag, thinking it might be too ostentatious and the new hat was enough.

Scooter again walked through the busy bar. He found the guys slouched against the bar; they each were each holding a bottle of beer.

"Bout time man, we had to buy our own," Hank said.

Scooter inspected Hank's injury, but a Band-Aid covered an area over his eyebrow. Yellowish iodine residue was evident from where the doctor had scrubbed the area.

Hank noticed Scooter's inspection. "Only three stitches, so weren't as bad as it looked."

"Guess that's the good news," Scooter said.

"This place is a zoo. We couldn't get a table," Johnny said.

"Tell you what; finish your beers. We been invited to the A&M party . . . um, hospitality room. I'll buy you a beer down there—3.2 per usual. Might be some girls you guys could check out," Scooter said. "That Squirrel . . . she thought Hank was raunchy; a real bull rider. They might be hooked up, but y'never know."

"I'm supposed to be going with someone, but a visit can't hurt," Johnny said.

"Going with someone? You barely broke up with Susie, or did you get back together?" he asked.

"Yeah. Well, we decided to give it a chance during the summer to see if we still like each other or not."

Hank threw back his beer and set the bottle hard onto the bar. "Come-on, let's go check that big-school team!" Johnny drank several big gulps out of his bottle and they wound their way through the bar crowd, saying hello to some of the other contestants who they knew.

The three sauntered into a large banquet room and stopped inside the door to survey the crowd. Scooter first noticed Bob Forsythe, who had invited him and then while looking to see if Charlene was around, noticed Billy Hall.

Bob came over to them and said, "Come on in. We have three-two beer and sodas. No hard stuff."

Scooter said, "Bob, this is Johnny Archuleta and Hank McLeod. He took a hit in the bull riding."

"Well, that's a tough life out there on the bulls," Bob said. "Nice meeting you guys." To Scooter he said, "I noticed you had a rookie horse today. Maybe your luck will change tomorrow. Of course, our guys in that event were a little relieved." He chuckled at his comment, and Scooter smiled.

"I have that 'Mucho Blanco' horse tomorrow, so I'll try to make up some ground."

Scooter then noticed Charlene, as she quickly walked over from across the room. "Hey, you guys made it. Come on over to our table. Some of the others you met are there, too," she said.

Scooter told Bob, "Thanks for the invite. See you later." The three then followed Charlene to a table across the room. She introduced them to the three boys that Scooter had met at dinner, and they said hello to Squirrel and Naomi. The three crowded their way into chairs at the table.

"What do you guys want? I'll get it for you," Charlene said. They said beer and she told Scooter, "Come on, you can help me."

"He's sposed to buy but knows how to get out of it!" Johnny complained.

"Join the club. He was supposed to buy us a round, too!" Charlene said.

"Well, I am buying, but with my tax dollar working at a state college." The others laughed. "Okay, smarty, come on," said Charlene.

They wound their way through the crowd to the bar where she used tickets to order three beers. "I'm glad you stopped in. Are we still going out?"

"Absolutely. We're supposed to be somewhere around seven-thirty. We have an hour."

"By the way, you look . . . handsome in that hat and all. I think I have very good taste."

"You do. I mean about the hat," Scooter teased.

"I think I finally got it right in men too." She put her hand in his. They smiled at each other.

They grabbed the bottles of beer and went back to the others, who were already in a good-natured argument about the best event. Hank was making a case for bull riding; that it only took spurs, a glove and a bull rope.

"A guy could get to a rodeo easily on a Greyhound bus or even hitch-hiking with yer gear practically in yer back pocket," he said.

His argument was weakened by the obvious danger of the event, as emphasized by the damage to his face. Johnny thought the bareback event didn't quite have the danger and yet didn't require horse-trailers, a rig to pull it and all the expense of horses.

"Scooter told me it's artistic and now I see it. It's poetry in motion," Johnny said.

"Shit, give it up. Poetry . . . that's a stretch," Ernie said.

Everyone laughed at this. "But it is. Most all of our events are. Think of saddle broncs too, roping, and barrel racing," Scooter said. "I'm not so sure about bull riding or steer wrestling. They're more brute force. But when it's together, the spurring and the bucking, that's beauty in motion!"

"Wait a minute here," said Hank, "that's right! It's the best kind of poetry there is, spinning around in the middle of a kind a tornado! I'm just saying bull ridings' pure, no trappings t' speak of . . . light travelin'."

Squirrel couldn't keep out of it any longer. "You guys are a lonely sort, traveling around by yourselves on Greyhound buses, dragging your bull ropes along like little lost boys with their blankies."

They all laughed, and Scooter noticed that Hank had moved to sit beside her. He still had manure on his jeans. Scooter smiled at his teammate's verve. *He's a real bull rider now, looks like to me. Zeke would be proud of him.*

The group continued to talk about rodeo and course work at the two colleges. "You know Sonny, the bronc rider from the team. He broke his hand in that fight . . . on a dude's head, or he'd be here. He's Jicarilla Apache from New Mexico. So, we have a small team, but it's diverse—only one girl though and she hasn't been competing much. Anyway, Southwestern has a large contingent of Native American students. It's near a number of reservations," Scooter explained.

Bill and Naomi wanted to know more about the college and the area. They had heard of Mesa Verde. Johnny, whose family lived south of town on Florida Mesa, told them about the narrow-gauge train that ran between Durango and Silverton.

Squirrel asked Hank about his background, and he said he was a town kid from Montrose but had been exposed to rodeo early at his cousin's farm where they would ride calves. "We had to think up plausible excuses to why we had fresh manure all over our clothes from gettin' dumped. Now we often get the same stuff from the grown-up versions. My dad said I must be addicted to crap."

This caused everyone to laugh, although Squirrel said, "Yuck!"

After the laughter died down, Charlene said, "Well, it's been fun, but I better get ready for my big date!"

Scooter stood up to go out with her and asked, "Can I go, too? I mean on your big date?"

"I don't know yet. I'm thinking about it," she said and smiled at him. To the others she said, "We'll see you guys later at the dance."

They walked out through the room together and Scooter again noticed Billy Hall watching them, so Scooter nodded curtly to him. "Hall watches but doesn't say anything. What's the deal?" he asked Charlene.

"Oh, he doesn't like to lose control. He doesn't want anything to do with you now though. I told you that your reputation is preceding you. If they only knew what I know," Charlene smiled at him.

"What's that? That I'm strong as Superman, faster than a speeding bullet?"

"That you're a lover, not a fighter." They both laughed at her comment. "I know you're a softy—feeling sorry for your bareback horse—but they don't need to know that."

"That's right," said Scooter. "I gotta keep 'em guessing."

At the top of the stairs, Charlene said, "Okay, honey, come down to the room in about twenty."

Scooter and Charlene swung across the dance floor, missing the other couples, angling for open space. On the slow songs, she put her head against his and into his shoulder, sometimes kissing his neck. They would come apart slightly during music with a faster tempo, and then he would twirl and spin her. She showed him how they could skip to the beat side-by-side, arms linked. It was more fun than he had envisioned. He self-consciously showed her how to clog, which seemed to surprise her.

Squirrel and Hank skipped by. "Hey, what's up?" Hank fleetingly said.

Then later, Scooter noticed Squirrel and Ernie dancing and then also Naomi and Bill.

Suddenly, Scooter felt a tap on his shoulder. It was Ernie, wanting to cut in.

Scooter didn't want to, but shrugged. "Be my guest," he said.

Charlene telegraphed something to Scooter with a look, but Ernie was already leading her away to the music

Scooter walked through the other dancers to the sidelines and went out into the lobby to use the restroom and get a drink of water. He realized he was sweating slightly and the cooler air outside the auditorium felt refreshing. He went back into the dance to see if he could reclaim Charlene, but noticed she was now dancing with Billy Hall. Scooter was tempted to go over and claim her away but decided to wait and see what would transpire. He continued to lounge against the wall until Squirrel came by and grabbed his hand, "Come on, it's about time you danced with me," she said.

He followed her onto the floor and they danced at arm's length, as if kids in junior high.

"So, Charlene said something about you and Sonny coming by her place on the way to regionals," Squirrel said.

"Yeah, that's kind of the plan. I may have to go to Pagosa Springs to pick him up, but then I think we would make time to stop in. It's the second weekend in June, but we're going north to some rodeos on the way. Why don't you stay over for a couple of weeks after your semester is over and we'll double date," he said.

"I don't know if 'dating' is the right word, but he's interesting. Well, we're good friends, but who knows?"

"Yeah, who knows how things will work out? He's famous on the reservation . . . going to college and being good at saddle broncs."

The music stopped. "Well, it would be fun. I'll see if Charlene wants a house guest for a week or so. You better find her. Don't leave her with Billy too long. He's trouble," Squirrel said.

"What you mean trouble?"

"He doesn't seem to hear 'No' is what it is."

Scooter nodded and headed through the crowd to see if he could find Charlene. He said hello to Vince Claypool, and then Hank waylaid him and asked where he had been. Hank was reeking of beer. He was with a blonde girl who Scooter hadn't seen before and Hank introduced her as Gale; *or did he say, "Girl?"* Scooter wasn't sure, as Hank had slurred the word. They danced away when the music started up again.

Scooter meandered through the other dancers and spectators to the lobby. He looked one way and when he didn't see Charlene, turned in the other direction and saw her rushing toward him. He took several steps toward her and she took his hand as they met.

"I needed you to rescue me and couldn't find you," she said.
He noticed she was flushed. "Yeah, Squirrel grabbed me to dance, and then I ran into Hank." He noticed Billy Hall trailing along, but he stopped when he saw Scooter.

"Just a minute," Scooter said. "I better meet this guy for real," and he broke away from Charlene.

He stopped in front of Billy Hall. "I don't think we've been formally introduced. I'm Scooter Henry, you know the guy that rents college girls out." He looked Billy in the eyes and stuck out his hand. Billy uncertainly took Scooter's hand and Scooter squeezed with some strength and didn't let go immediately. He was aware that Billy was thick through the shoulders and the thickness extended downwards through his waist, giving him a linebacker physique. Scooter thought he better stay out of any clinches.

"I know who you are," Billy gruffly said.

Scooter continued, "Guess congratulations are in order for your win today."

"Yeah, thanks. Think you can hold onto Charlene?"

"Well, that's between her and me isn't it? You don't have anything to do with it, do you?"

Scooter had become wary at Billy's question and had turned his body slightly to be at an angle.

"I might have something to say about it," Billy said.

Scooter was wishing he had brought the roll of nickels from his duffle bag because his anger had flared, and he thought about planting a fist in the middle of Hall's face. Scooter had his arm down by his side and instead, figured he would bring his fist in a straight jab into Hall's diaphragm. He remembered Sonny's advice about hitting the soft spots.

"Why, are you her brother, her dad? I don't think so. You might have something to say about it, but it doesn't matter. It's up to her . . . who she wants. If you think you have something to say beyond that, maybe you and I should go outside. I think you need an enema of your mind!"

Billy snorted at the comment. "Maybe we ought to!"

Scooter thought Billy said this uncertainly and he was looking back and forth through the lobby toward the auditorium. "Just you and me. No one else." Scooter continued. *If anyone else is coming out, I'm going first and I'm hitting him before he gets through the door.*

Scooter moved toward the door and was nearly there but felt someone take hold of his unclenched hand. "Come on Scooter, he's not worth it!" To Billy, Charlene said, "Go find Audrey or one of your other so-called friends that appreciate your machoism. We have other things to do."

She pulled Scooter away from Billy. "Come on, we got some dancing to do!"

Scooter reluctantly followed her lead but was still looking back toward Billy. "You're like a dog on a leash, honey." Charlene said "Come on, he ain't going to do anything. He's breathing a sigh of relief that he didn't have to go outside with you! I told you, the guys from the team, you know Ernie and Alvin, were talking about the 'toughs' from Southwestern."

Scooter laughed. "Yeah, we're hell on wheels. Where'd they get that idea?"

"I think Squirrel was telling stories about you guys going crazy on the reservation and then the fight you had in Basin sealed it. Hank makes an impression that way too. Funny . . . you're such a pussy cat. I can make you purr until the cows come home. If those guys only knew."

"No honey, not till the cows come home. I only purr when my kitty purrs!"

They had gone back into the auditorium and she turned toward him as they glided into a two-step again.

"Yes, I know what you do to your kitty and your kitty likes it!" She nestled back into him as they slow-danced across the floor. He could feel her lips on his neck again and thought: *She's right. The hell with Billy!*

She put her lips near his ear. "I was frantic to find you. Don't leave me by myself again!"

Scooter leaned his head back slightly and looked into the turquoise depths of her eyes. She had her arms around his neck and he kissed her.

"You are such a fox! Don't worry. I'm never going to be very far away."

They swung into a fast step as the music changed and he swung her around him as he had before. They smiled at each other. He noticed that Hank was dancing with Squirrel again in a frantic kind of jitterbug. Charlene had noticed too, and they smiled at each other at this wild dance step.

"Maybe they're going to dance their way right onto that Greyhound bus after all," Charlene said.

Scooter laughed at her comment. Her eyes shined their pleasure back at him.

Finally, after another slow dance where they had melded into each other again, Scooter said, "I think we better go soon, we have other things to do."

"Yes, we better get a lot of sleep, so we'll be fresh," Charlene said.

"Sleep? That's not what I had I mind."

"Oh, that's right, my ambitious boyfriend . . . I know what you want. I don't know, you've had your way with me so much. What if I want a vacation?"

Scooter stopped and turned her toward him. He figured she was kidding, but said, "Is that what you want, a little vacation from me? I think you need concentrated lovin'!"

She nestled her head onto his shoulder and kissed his neck again, as they again stepped to the music. "You know I'm kidding. You're my lover. You can do with me what you want. Come on," she said.

She pulled him with her and he walked to where she was leading him; to where Squirrel and Hank were still gyrating.

"We're going. Don't wait up for me. Oh, we're invited to brunch at ten," Charlene told Squirrel.

Squirrel gave them a blank look. Her eyes were glazed, but she nodded. Scooter looked at Hank and thought he looked quite wild with his patched eyebrow. One of his pant legs was stuck inside the top of his boot and he still had on the same jeans he had worn for the bull riding. They whirled away with the music.

Scooter laughed. "Judas Priest, what a pair! They both look kind of wild,"

Charlene and Scooter walked toward the lobby. "She can be a wild girl. I had to watch that she wasn't a bad influence on me. She doesn't mind drinking occasionally."

"You know when we were dancing? She wanted to know about Sonny. Like you said, I think she wants to experience him."

"I know she does . . . typical," Charlene said.

"I told her to hang around after your finals and we would stop in for a few days in Colorado Springs on our way north. I mean if you don't mind."

"No, you better stop. I'd be disappointed if you didn't."

"Yeah, I need to meet your family and make love to you again!"

"Scooter! You're so single-minded."

Scooter smiled back as they proceeded to walk through the lobby, "Yeah, you did it, now you're paying for it. I know you like it though."

She smiled at him. "Think so, huh?" She pulled him toward her and whispered in his ear, "Yeah, I like you to love me . . . like you've been doing!"

He grinned at her mischievous look. "Yeah, honey. Me, too." They approached the door and suddenly he stopped, remembering the exit at Basin.

"Just a second here. I need to scout this out." He cautiously peered out the doors. There were a few other couples and several clusters of guys on the steps. Scooter didn't see Billy Hall and didn't see anyone in the parking lot near his car. "Come on, let's get," he said. They stepped out into the night. It had started to rain again, and they ran for Scooter's car.

CHAPTER THIRTY-EIGHT
PLAYING HOUSE

Charlene walked up the stairs in the hotel with Scooter. She had stuck a hand into one of his back pockets, having him pull her up the stairs. He had to pull upwards on his pants to keep them in place.

"You're feeling frisky," he said.

"Uh-huh! I liked tonight."

He unlocked the door to his room and went inside. She continued, "I love you more all the time, if that's possible."

"I know, me too. I figure I've really been lucky . . . y'know."

They grabbed onto each other, barely waiting to be inside the door. She unsnapped his shirt and he shrugged it off. He then did the same to hers and helped her out of it. He grunted as he pulled off his boots, throwing them out of the way.

She held a foot up and said, "Help me." He bent down and pulled first one boot off and then the other. He unbuttoned her pants in a kind-of assault toward clothing removal. He then stood up and pulled her to him again, feeling her bra against his chest as he kissed her lips and throat, and then her ear. He noticed a faint fresh-cut cucumber smell as she returned his kisses.

"I love how you smell . . . always have," he said.

"I'm glad you do. It's mutual, you know. That's part of falling in love we don't even know about. Did you know that?"

"What, the smell of the other person? Well, I never thought about it I guess. Where'd you find that information, in a woman's magazine?"

Charlene smiled at his teasing. "No, honey in one of my courses. It's scientific."

"Yeah, guess it wouldn't be too good to try and fall in love with someone that turned your stomach."

Charlene laughed at his comment. "You are so funny sometimes!"

They looked at each other, searching eyes, looking for feelings. They then started kissing, and he again caressed her eyes and ears with his lips and she reciprocated.

He unsnapped her bra and she helped get rid of it. She tugged at his belt buckle and he helped her. He moved down to her breasts and ran his tongue over her nipples, first one and then the other.

She moaned something and then said, "Just do 'em honey!"

Charlene placed her hands on the back of his head and pulled him to her. He still had his hat on, and it had tilted onto the back of his head. He thought she might be squashing the crown of it, but didn't care.

He thought about carrying her to the bed but lifted her. She placed her arms around his neck to help him and then put her legs around his waist. They banged into the door, creating a loud, incessant pounding, as if carpenters had suddenly started work. He heard her say, "Sweet cowboy!" She kissed his neck, and then he felt her nip him there. He realized they were both breathing heavily, but they gradually slowed and then disengaged.

"Are you okay?" he asked. "I didn't know we were going to be like that!"

"It's okay. Are you?" She then started to laugh. "Sweetie, you still have your hat and socks on. What a cowboy!"

He laughed in response and said, "Yeah, that's a first, I reckon." She leaned into him and they kissed. The light was still on; he liked to look at her, trying to imprint her form into his mind.

"Excuse me for a minute, I have to use the potty," she said.

She walked into the bathroom and shut the door. He went over to the bed and turned it down and took off his socks then placed his new hat crown-side down on the desk. He had to use the bathroom too but decided he could wait a few more minutes.

He lay down on the bed to wait for her and rubbed the spot on his neck where Charlene had bit him. He thought it might be the same place where Katherine had nipped him, which he had tried to hide with his shirt collar. He rubbed the spot. *This lovemaking is dangerous.*

He left the nightstand light on, and as she came out from the bathroom, she paused by the door and posed with one arm behind her head and with one knee bent. She then turned and smiled. Charlene had loosened her hair and it was long and wavy. Scooter lifted himself off the bed, sitting partway up to immerse the image of her into his vision—to take a visual picture.

"So, do you still like me?" Charlene liltingly asked.

Scooter took a few seconds to answer. "Judas Priest! What do you think? Not much, you know. You have the nicest legs and ass . . . among other things."

Charlene smiled at his comments and slowly slunk her way across the room to him as if modeling. He threw back the blanket and she snuggled in beside him, nestling inside his arm.

"You lover, you. A real buckaroo, my buckaroo. " He kissed her, and she returned it. He kissed her eyes and nose, and then lips again. He turned to be above her and began caressing her face and hairline and down the side of her face to her ear with his fingertips.

He stopped and said, "I gotta go, so don't go away." He looked into the mirror and ran a hand through his hair and then drank several glasses of water.

Scooter opened the door and stood by it as she had done. Charlene looked and then started laughing. "I need to give you some lessons in posing. You're studly, though. I like your thick shoulders . . . I see why the girls think you're cute."

He smiled back at her and said, "Just shoulders, huh? Move over, sweetie. What girls? You're pulling my leg. Like, if we keep doing this . . . well, I just want to do it more . . . to make love to you. When we're apart that's all I might think about. Maybe we should get married like we said."

"Now you're pulling my leg. As soon as I'm out of sight, you're thinking about rodeo. Well, you better not be thinking about anyone else. Marriage though? Seriously, that's a big step . . . we already said, right? Like, we'll see. There's no rush . . . right? Anyway, it'll have to be in the springtime for me. That's been in my mind as the time for some reason, even as a girl."

He kissed her, and she smiled up at him. "So, next spring or the spring after, or the one after that. Easy!"

Charlene let out her musical laugh, "Easy, huh? You're so funny!" She pulled his head down to her and kissed him.

"I need to get you a ring though before that. I better win some money, 'cause it's going to be special. You need something extraordinary, like an heirloom."

"I love you so much. When I used to say, 'How's my cowboy?' I really meant it," Charlene softly said. "Did you know that? I didn't even know how much I meant it. I think it was more a question that you needed to answer, and you have."

"I heard you when you would ask me. It made my heart soar like a big hawk on thermals. Then Squirrel would say, 'Here's your woman.' I was in love with you then, but was shy about it, skirting it, sliding, like a colt on ice."

"What about now, are you still like a colt?" she asked.

"No honey, now I'm like a stallion with a fine filly!" He kissed her lips and then moved down in succession to her throat, breasts, and stomach. He smelled the musk of her and thought of making love to her again. After a few minutes, Charlene pulled him toward her.

"You are a stallion! Are you going to do me like one?"

He understood her question to mean that he should and said, "Absolutely. Do you like me to?"

"Uh-huh. I like you a lot of ways," she said.

He was starting to be highly aroused again; being against her smooth legs and looking at her curved lips and her eyes that so enchanted him, her dark, Gypsy hair splayed out on the pillow. He moved down again to tease her nipples with his tongue.

"Are you sure you're okay?"

"You're making me okay."

"This love is sweet, "she mused, "I love how you do me . . . bring me up to the crash."

"Yeah, the crash," he chuckled. "I never thought of it that way before. To me, it's soaring."

"You like those hawks, don't you?"

He didn't answer and instead asked, "When you came up to me at the dance that night, did you ever dream that it would go so far?"

"Well honey, I doubt it. But a girl can hope sometimes that things will work out. That she will meet her dreams in some form of reality. That's what's been the best. That it keeps evolving and in the right direction."

He got up and went into the bathroom again and then brought Charlene a glass of water. She said thanks and put the empty glass on the nightstand. He turned out the light. It was after midnight. They snuggled together again under the sheet and he traced figures on her face and neck. He realized after a few minutes that she was asleep.

Scooter woke sometime during the early hours of the morning and found that he was against her hip. He moved slightly against her and she stirred, and then pulled him to her for a kiss.

"Hi lover! Not enough yet, huh?" she softly asked.

"I can't get enough of you!"

They made love again, this time more slowly and less urgently. They changed positions several times, experimenting. At one point Scooter felt Charlene's fingernails in his back as she swore. It drove him to increase the tempo until he could no longer hold back. Afterwards, they again slept.

It was light outside when he again woke, and he looked at his watch. It was eight-thirty and he heard the rain falling outside. He stretched and gazed at Charlene as she slept. He kissed her lightly until she stirred and snuggled against him. They continued to lie together; he was reluctant to get out of bed, but he mightily had to pee.

Finally, he sat up and said, "Hey sweetie, we better rise and shine soon."

"Um, not yet. Come lie with me some more."

"I gotta go, then I will," he said. On his way to the bathroom he looked out the window. "You know it's raining again . . . going to be a mud-fest today."

"Let's just stay in bed . . . can't we?"

"Yeah, that would be nice. I could make love to you again." Scooter came back to the bed and slid in with Charlene. "Guess we got work to do, though . . . on the way to the pro ranks you know."

They snuggled against each other. Scooter smelled the scent of her hair. "Did you get enough sleep?"

"Well, no, thanks to my lover here. I'm okay, though. Did you?"

"I'm good! We better get going though, or I'm going to start thinking about doing it again." He was running a hand lightly up and down her side and then over one of her breasts.

"You keep doing that and you're going to have to make love to me again. I feel like we just started our honeymoon. I'm supposed to feed the horses though, so guess I better get. You want to help me?"

"Yes . . . and I think I like honeymoons."

Charlene laughed and then said, "An actual honeymoon will be special, though. I'm glad I have good intuition and my resolve to see what you were about."

Scooter laughed and then said, "Resolve is right. I thought you were the most forward and interesting girl I'd ever met. Sonny told me after you took us back to the house—after the dance—that you were after my buns!"

Charlene laughed at this and said, "Guess what? He was right! Come on sweetie, let's get a shower."

"Okay. I better shave first. What if it happens when we shower? I remember what you did to me the last time!"

"It was the other way around . . . remember?"

Scooter kissed Charlene and got out of bed, then rustled through his duffle bag to find clean underwear. He had nearly finished shaving when Charlene came into the bathroom and hugged him from behind.

"I should have brought my toothbrush. I should get one and keep it with you for our trysts."

"Here, you can use mine if you want. We've been exchanging every-thing else anyway," Scooter said. He ran hot water over it and gave it to Char-lene. "Here's some mouthwash too." He took a swallow of it from the bottle, swirled it around in his mouth, and then spit it out. Charlene squeezed tooth-paste onto the brush and brushed her teeth while Scooter finished shaving. While she finished with the toothbrush, he hugged her from behind and nuzzled her neck. He then turned the shower on and adjusted the water temperature. He got into the shower first and then Charlene followed. They soaped up and he squeezed shampoo on his hair. They took turns washing each other.

"God damn, Charlene, it's happening again!" Scooter exclaimed.

He lifted her, and they merged as the night before. He felt the water hit his back, but then everything became secondary except his intentions to make love. He then became aware of Charlene pulling his hair and her tongue in his ear.

Scooter, honey, I love what you do to me!"

"Well, daawlin, it's what you do to me too!"

Charlene smiled and said, "It's both of us. It's going to be hard for us not to have a bunch of kids."

Her statement alarmed him slightly. "Judas Priest, kids! . . . I mean, you know, when it's time," he said.

She smiled. "I know. Don't get skittish on me."

Scooter laughed, and they got out and dried each other. "Well, kids . . . having a kid now is scary, I mean with the rodeo circuit on our minds."

Charlene rounded up her clothes and said, "Oh, I know only too well about that. I just meant, all our lovemaking . . . it's . . . well . . . so sweet."

"Okay, like if we were married and down the road some and had already won several world championships and were sort of settled into a second career on a ranch, you'd be way pregnant!"

Charlene laughed. "Yes . . . way pregnant, huh? You'd like me that way too I think. Look, I need to go to the room and change. Then we can get to work." She was trying to re-braid her hair while looking in the mirror.

Scooter pulled on a fresh set of Wranglers and shrugged into a shirt that had been hanging in the closet. He looked back at Charlene and said, "Yeah, I would like you way pregnant. But, let's not jinx ourselves about that! Right now, it makes me nervous!" He smiled at her.

"Look, I know. Don't worry about it. We've been smart about it, haven't we?"

"I reckon and hope so. Okay, sweetie, we better get. Wear your old stuff, 'cause it's going to be a mud-fest. How about I meet you in the lobby. I forgot to make a reservation for the family, so better see if it's possible."

CHAPTER THIRTY-NINE
FAMILY REUNION

Scooter hustled down the stairs to the lobby and walked into the restaurant. He asked the woman at the cash register about a table for seven.

"Just a moment. I need to check with the manager," the woman said. She came back after a few minutes and asked for a name.

She wrote it down. He told her thanks and sorry for the short notice. He walked back into the lobby to wait for Charlene. After several minutes, she came down the stairs and they walked out together to her truck. It was still raining lightly and there were pools in the parking lot.

"Squirrel wasn't looking too good," Charlene said. "She has a hangover and was out most the night, according to Naomi . . . probably with that wild bull rider, Hank, on your team. Of course, they asked where I'd been all night."

"What'd you tell 'em?" he asked.

"Oh, I just told them making love!" She flashed her bright smile at him and he smiled back.

"Makin' love, huh? I reckon so." He smiled at the thought.

They parked by some stables and walked over to one of the stalls. Star stuck her head out of the open top-half of the door and nickered when it saw Charlene.

"Scooter, honey, there's a sack of grain with a can in it in the front of the trailer. Could you get some for her . . . a can full? I'll get some hay out."

Scooter did as she asked and opened the door to the stall and pushed in past Star to pour a measure into a small trough. Star was interested in the grain and pushed her head against his arm. He rubbed the horse's forehead.

"Your horse likes me 'cause I've got the goods," he told Charlene.

"Yes honey, she knows you have the goods alright."

Scooter laughed at her comment. They took care of Squirrel's and Naomi's horses as well. Scooter helped brush them and ran water into large plastic buckets that were secured by wire to the side of the stalls. Charlene shook out hay into the feeders and carefully walked back around the puddles to her pickup.

He asked, as they headed back to the hotel, "Hey, what's Squirrel's real name? I mean if she comes to the brunch thing, does she have another name?'

"That's funny, isn't it? We nearly forget that she has another name, just like you have. It's Bonnie. I'm sure her parents would be thrilled with her nickname. She didn't look too interested in anything approaching breakfast when I went back to the room. We'll see." They walked back across the parking lot. Charlene had her hand in his back pocket. "I wonder what your family's going to think."

"It'll be okay. They gotta know though that we're, you know . . . involved. "

"They'll know, I think, but don't spring too much on them at once, huh?"

"You mean like telling them we been a little intimate?"

"Yes, honey, let them figure it out for themselves. Don't spring too much on them all at once." Charlene had followed Scooter down the hall to his room, and as they reached it, turned to him and said, "Kiss me now before we get our game faces on."

"Sounds like a great plan—the first part, anyway," Scooter said.

Charlene smiled at his comment and then they kissed several times, grasping each other for one that lingered.

"Is it love?" she asked.

"You know it! Think how you feel and multiply it by one hundred . . . no, a thousand and you'll know how it is with me."

"I like the math, and it's a great feeling . . . exciting too!" Her eyes searched his.

"Yeah, very exciting . . . all the lovemaking."

She smiled at him and they broke apart. "I need to go to the room and freshen-up," she said.

"Okay, I'll wait for you . . . and don't worry. It'll be alright. You'll see." Scooter went into his room and washed his face and then ran a wet comb through his hair. He then pulled out his duffle with his tack and sorted through it. He concentrated for a few minutes on what he thought his bareback ride might be like . . . rearing back and spurring up and out with each jump of the horse. When Charlene had said, "Put on our game faces," he already had known what he needed to do. This needed to be a continuation of the ride he had made in Laramie, because he was determined that this was the start of a journey into doing well at the regional competition and into the pro ranks. He placed his rigging and glove back into the bag along with his riding boots and spurs. He carefully smoothed his rolled-up chaps and placed them into the bag as well and set it near the door. He got down onto the floor and did a series of pushups until he could feel the sting in his arms and shoulders.

He sat on the chair by the small desk and again visualized his ride and then got down on the floor and grunted through a second series of pushups. He didn't want to do too many, but enough to warm up again. He hadn't worked out since Thursday, although yesterday's ride had been something of a warm-up too. The phone on the desk interrupted his routine. He picked up the receiver and said hello.

"Hey Scooter, it's Ron. We're down in the lobby."

"Go on into the restaurant, the reservation's in my name. I'll be down in a few minutes," Scooter said.

Scooter phoned Charlene's room. "Hey sweetie, you about ready? I guess the folks are here."

He heard her say, "Well, okay. I'll be out in a few."

Scooter walked out into the hallway near the top of the stairs and waited. Charlene appeared and walked over to him. She had redone her hair and had put on pink lipstick. Scooter held his ground for a few seconds, taking in her tall, lithe build, her face with its lilting mouth and sapphire eyes; her features still stunned him.

"Damn you look good," he said.

She took his hand. "I need you to say that occasionally. By the way, I talked to my mom and she was about to leave the house. I told her she needed to meet you. Of course, she . . . ah, questioned me. I told her it's serious."

Scooter nodded, "Yeah, but we still joke around."

Charlene laughed, but gave him a poke in the ribs with her elbow. They walked down the stairs together and to the restaurant. He told the cashier about the reservation, and she led them to a room off to the side of the main dining area. "We reserved a side-room since there were so many of you," she said.

Scooter and Charlene entered the room and his dad and brother got up to greet them. He shook hands with them and then they hugged.

"I want everyone to meet Charlene O'Brien. Charlene, this is my mom, Connie, my sister, Rachel, and my future sister-in-law, Denise. Then my dad, Evan, and last but not least, Ron, my brother."

Ron had features more like their dad than Rachel and Scooter, with dark hair. He was several inches taller than Scooter and although thicker in the waist, work had honed his physique. Being outside most days had given his face a ruddy tan below a forehead that had been held white by his hat.

Scooter stepped over to his mom and gave her a hug and kissed her cheek and then did the same to Rachel. He gave Denise a hug and said, "Nice to see you."

Everyone started talking at once and Charlene shook hands with Scooter's mother, and then with Denise. Rachel then got out of her chair and hugged Charlene. Rachel was shorter than Charlene by several inches, and had wavy, auburn hair, even lighter than Scooter's and she, like Scooter, had their mother's brown eyes, which, in Rachel, slanted slightly. *Sloe-eyed or cat-like,* Scooter had often thought; *don't know who in the family those came from.* He thought they gave her a sultry quality and figured it likely attracted boys—probably her current boyfriend.

"So, how's your love interest coming along? Ryan . . . isn't that what you said?

Rachel flashed a smile. "Yes, Ryan." She turned the conversation back toward Scooter and Charlene. "We . . . well, I've been wondering who put a rope on ol' Scooter, 'cause he's been wild and free up 'till now."

Charlene's face colored slightly, but she smiled, "He's still a little wild and free." This caused some laughter.

Scooter's mom smiled and said, "We're glad you could join us. He mentioned that you're a good barrel racer."

Scooter broke into the conversation. "Not only good, but yesterday's go-round winner!" He felt Charlene grab his hand, as everyone told her congratulations.

She looked at Scooter and smiled back uncertainly toward his family, saying thanks.

Scooter's dad took control. "Well, come on, let's sit down." They pulled out chairs and pushed them up to the table. To Scooter, he said, "You still have a pretty good mouse around your eye."

"Yeah, you should have seen it early in the week," he said. "Hey Dad, before I forget, one of your old rodeo buddies is here, wants to say hello. He's the chute boss for Flying A . . . Bud Simmons. He knew Uncle Jake, too."

Scooter's dad bobbed his head. "That takes me back. We rodeoed on and off together a couple of years. He was a pretty good bull rider."

Rachel, Denise, and Charlene were already talking about college and courses. Rachel was interested in courses for education. Scooter was relieved that they had made Charlene feel welcome.

He talked to his Dad and brother about the first go-round, telling them about "Little Joe" and scoring in the mid-sixties and then didn't get a re-ride. They talked about "Mucho Blanco," which Ron knew about. Scooter mentioned that he thought it bucked similarly to the "Popcorn" horse of Summit's, the one in Laramie, but with even more power. "It's a big, stout horse!" Their conversation drifted to plans for the summer and the large operations of haying and thrashing the grain.

"If I do well in Central Wyoming at the regionals, I want to go to nationals in Texas," Scooter said.

"I don't get it," Ron countered, "we need you on the ranch. There's a lot to do."

Scooter felt the heat rise in his face and said, "Well, I don't mind working, but I might be scarce on weekends. That's just the way it has to be. Sonny and I need to see if we can stack up against the pros . . . the pro circuit. Dad, what do you think?"

Their meals were starting to be served. Scooter looked over at Charlene, but she was still talking to Rachel and Denise. He noticed his mother studying him from across the table and he smiled at her.

"Well, we should be able to figure this out with a schedule," Evan said. "We need you for sure during haying, as you know. I also know there's a prime time in a person's life to rodeo. We had this same problem with your Uncle Jake. Course, Dad—your grandpa—wanted both of us to be slaving away twenty-four-seven on the ranch."

Scooter looked at Ron to see if there was going to be more discussion, but he was starting to dig into a plate of scrambled eggs. Scooter followed suit. He changed the conversation by asking about Ron's and Denise's upcoming wedding. Denise said they had already reserved the church and talked to the minister but indicated there was a lot to do yet. Her blue eyes sparkled when she talked about the wedding—the plans. She flashed a smile. Scooter thought her smile was used to defuse any hard parts of a conversation or uncomfortable circumstances, flashing occasionally through the introductions and conversations like light glancing off a chrome grill. With her blonde curls and Ron's dark brush-like hair, they seemed to fit together—a natural-enough couple; *like salt and pepper shakers.*

"So, are you guys?" Rachel asked him. Her question jolted him out of his thoughts.

Scooter put a forkful of eggs back on his plate and felt his face flush. "Are us guys what?" he asked. Scooter looked at Charlene, who had a serene smile on her face, as she observed the exchange between him and Rachel.

"Don't get so jumpy. I'm just kidding you," Rachel said, "but you surprised us all." She turned to Charlene and said, "So tell us about how you met . . . we need to know."

Charlene told them about meeting at the rodeo dance in Fort Collins and about looking for Zeke afterwards and one thing led to another. Scooter explained that Zeke had a concussion and had gone missing. Scooter and Charlene linked hands again under the table. Charlene said they had several more weeks of school, but her mom was driving over and was going to take her horse back to Colorado Springs, as there were no more rodeos.

"I told my mom that I was meeting you, and of course she . . . well, she wants to meet Scooter and y'all, as well."

"She wants to make sure Charlene hasn't got hold of some rodeo bum, I guess," Scooter said.

Charlene smiled and said, "That's right. When she sees his black eye, she's going to start wondering."

They all seemed to think this was funny, but Ron said, "Well, she wouldn't be far off."

Scooter took a hard look at Ron, but he was smiling.

"Tell us the story . . . the one about Basin. Word is that some drunk beat you up," Ron said.

Scooter laughed at this. "You know it. The guy was weaving back and forth so much I couldn't get a good lick on 'im."

"I don't like the fighting," Connie said. "You need to be more careful." She changed the subject. "So, you thought you did well on your courses. Have you decided about next year?"

"Well, I don't know . . . probably A&M. It seems like a logical choice." Scooter was thinking that now it was the only choice with Charlene there. He continued, "I already spoke to the head of the rodeo team, and he thought there could be a scholarship available, or at least a partial one to start." He turned slightly to be talking to his dad and brother too, "That's one of the reasons why the regionals are important."

"A scholarship would help," Evan said.

Scooter put a smear of jam on a piece of toast and noticed that his mother and Charlene were talking about teaching school and its challenges.

"Have you thought about diversifying the stock?" Scooter said turning back to his dad and Ron.

Ron replied for their dad, "You mentioned this before. Why do we need to diversify? We have good stock now."

"Well, there are breeds now that have a higher rate of gain—Angus for one, and Charolais. I just think we ought to think about it."

"Well Angus are okay, but they're spookier than Herefords, harder to handle," Evan said.

"Well, we ought to think about it. I bet in five years a lot of the ranches are going to have more than just Herefords," Scooter said, trying to reinforce his point.

"It's just more money, and I don't know if you get it back," Ron replied.

"We could figure that out. Belkys now have some Shorthorn, and

Chuck said they like them . . . are getting more gain and they're leaner meat. When you get home this week we can discuss it some more," Evan said.

"I'd like to get a really good Quarter horse too, maybe a stud with some good papers," Scooter said.

Ron exploded at this and said, "Jeez, where do you think the money's coming from . . . off the trees? You go to college and come back with all these big ideas."

The conversations among the women halted, as they listened to the exchange.

"Hey, don't get your shorts in a knot. It's just ideas," Scooter calmly said. "We haven't spent anything yet. Here's something, do you think a good barrel horse would benefit . . . I mean be faster, if it had a little Thoroughbred in it? I mean, if you didn't lose too much time around the barrels, but faster on the home stretch."

Ron thought about the question, calming down some. "Maybe. If the right combination could be achieved. I'd think one-fourth Thoroughbred might be about right."

"That's what I was thinking. Charlene, you know more about this than we do," Scooter said.

"I think a fast sprinter is still best, 'cause it's a relatively short run," she said. "I don't know anyone that uses a Thoroughbred. Be worth looking into though. How would you do it?"

"You'd have to be sure that it was worth it, because it would take a breeding program and maybe two or three generations to see if it was panning out. Why, are you going into the horse-breeding business?" Evan asked.

"Oh, just thinking about it," Scooter said. "I think a person could develop barrel horses, you know, a defined objective, but it's just an idea."

"One thing a person could do is check with the women in the pro ranks and see what they're running. I think most are using Quarter horses, but some of them seem a little rangy to me," Charlene said.

"Be interesting," Scooter's dad said. "You'd need to use the Thoroughbred as the filly though." He smiled at the others and explained, "Well, the size difference you know."

"I don't know. Seems like a lot of risky investment to me," Ron said, "I still think you're tryin' to convert book learnin' into reality."

Scooter looked at his watch. "Maybe. Look, I gotta get soon. I need to be out at the arena by noon." The waitress served more coffee and filled up the water glasses.

"Scooter mentioned he had invited you to visit, and I want to extend the invitation to you as well. You're welcome to come out any time," Scooter's mom told Charlene.

"Thank you. I can't now because of classes and finals are coming up in two weeks. But I'd like to sometime," Charlene replied. "Scooter's told me some about your place and it sounds nice." She looked at Scooter as she said this, and he smiled back at her.

"Yes, it's been home for this family for a long time now," Connie said.

"How did you two meet?" Charlene asked.

Scooter perked up. He knew the story, but always liked to hear it told.

"Oh, strange, but it was at a dance, too. My father worked for the railroad and we were in Eastgate for the summer. My cousin and I decided to go to a dance—some western days celebration. This strapping cowboy came along and asked me to dance and didn't take me back to my cousin for four or five sets."

"Yes, and I hardly knew how to dance back then . . . tells how desperate a guy can get to meet a good-looking girl before some other yahoo asks her to dance," Scooter's dad said. "Then I had to figure out a way to get the old car and head to Eastgate every chance I got. The old man—I mean your granddad—'bout had a fit with me going off all the time and Jake was off on the rodeo trail."

Those around the table chuckled.

"He told me," he continued, "'Goddammit, can't you marry her and bring her here so's you could do some work?'"

Scooter laughed at this along with the others.

"I thought he was the most dashing boy with his big hat and fancy boots, but he couldn't dance worth a lick, stepping on my feet about ten times it seemed," Connie said. "Then he disappeared after the dance and I didn't hear from him for several weeks. So, he finally phoned and stammered around and then asked if I wanted to go down to Deer Trail for a rodeo. I kept him on the hook for a while, and finally said I would, only to realize after we got there that he was in it—rode a saddle bronc." She smiled at Scooter's dad. "A real cowboy. He was hooked then, but didn't know it!"

Evan beamed at the others as Connie told the story. "We had just gotten a phone out there anyway, so was a big deal to use it . . . took me a week to get up the nerve."

Connie turned to Charlene and said, "I hope Scooter was a better dancer when you guys met."

Charlene looked at Scooter and smiled, "The first dance he was stiff as a board. It was like dancing with a mannequin." The others laughed at her analogy.

"He cuts it up now, though. We have a good time." They were holding hands again under the table.

"Sheesh, stiff as a mannequin. Well, you had me thunderstruck. I have to admit, I had two left feet, but she's a good teacher," Scooter said. He stood up. "Look, I'm getting antsy, so I better start to get ready for this bareback horse."

Charlene stood up as well. "I really liked meeting everyone. I should get ready, too."

Scooter's family scraped chairs and stood up as well. Rachel hugged Charlene and then Denise did as well.

"I think we're sisters," Rachel said.

Charlene took this in stride. "I think we are. You're very perceptive."

Rachel smiled and said, "Well, it's obvious." Charlene looked over at Scooter and smiled.

He winked at her and then said to his family, "I'll see you guys after."

His father and brother stood up and shook his hand, saying. "Good luck!" They told Charlene that it was nice to meet her and hoped she had a good run.

Scooter's mom said to Scooter, "I need to talk to you before you head out."

He paused and then said, "Okay. I'll be back in a few."

He and Charlene walked out of the restaurant and went up the stairs to the hallway.

"Well, it wasn't too bad, was it?" Scooter asked.

"No, I like your family. Rachel is a little barby though. I think she's jealous."

"Maybe. I spoiled her as we grew up, so could be, but she likes you. She always wanted a sister and now she's going to have two."

They stopped near Charlene's room. "I better go back down and see what's on my mom's mind . . . she was studying me."

"Well honey, she's perceptive too, so she's going to ask you how far this has gone—you and me."

"Yeah, I know. Well, I'm going to tell her that we've been fucking our brains out."

Charlene's laughter rang out and she said, "That'd ease her mind for sure. Come here and give me a kiss!"

He did as she asked, and they embraced for several minutes. "I do love you, all of you," he said.

"I love you more, you buckaroo. Wasn't that a nice story of your mom and dad?" she asked.

"Yeah, I think I'm more like him than I thought. But danced like a mannequin?" He pinched her butt and said, "I don't think so."

Charlene laughed and jerked away from him. "Be careful with that. You don't want to damage your woman. I'll see you out there. Good luck honey."

"Okay, yeah, give 'em hell today, sweetie. Remember it's muddy. Although, Star seems to like the mud. In any case, you can win the whole thing."

"Well, honey, I hope so. We'll do our best!" They came together for another kiss.

Scooter walked back down the stairs to the lobby and into the restaurant. His mom was the only one of the family that remained.

"Sit down for a minute. I just want to talk to you for a few minutes. This girl, well, she's a surprise to us . . . to me. One thing that's . . . well, she's very striking, attractive. How long have you guys known each other?" Connie asked.

"Believe me, I know she's attractive . . . Charlene. I realize we only met less than a month ago, but we're serious about each other—in a relationship," Scooter said.

"That isn't very much time to learn about each other. I could tell you're serious about each other, but I just wanted to know since she's come into the picture so suddenly."

"You know mom, it just happened. That we ran into each other and things just fell together. When I say together, I mean everything. So, we've talked about . . . well, plans like we're serious about rodeo and well, eventually . . . what if we get married? That's how fast things have progressed."

"My God, Scooter! That's what I mean! You guys should learn more about each other. You go from one extreme to the other."

"Look, I know it seems that way, but we love each other. How long did you and dad go together before you got married?"

"Well, that was different . . . a different time."

"I don't think it's different. You know that ring you have of Grams? I'd like to give it to Charlene."

"Scooter, that's promised to Rachel." She paused for a few seconds. "Maybe you can have that one of mine . . . the garnet, if you're that determined."

"Yes, I need to give her a ring . . . well, sometime. I told her she needed one . . . a special one, not just a store-bought one."

"Look, I love you and want the best for you. You have so much potential and I don't want you truncating that with an early marriage. I think you need to slow down some. Don't get me wrong, we like her . . . your dad and I."

"Mom, this potential includes Charlene. We're going on a journey together. We help each other realize our potential in rodeo, and we're going in completely the same direction. For one thing, we're going to raise Quarter horses—barrel racing horses. That's my idea, but I wouldn't consider it if she wasn't part of the picture. The thing is, we will not, and I emphasize 'will not' jeopardize what we want to do in rodeo . . . you know, competing at the highest level. If marriage would jeopardize this, we won't do it."

He looked at his mother, trying to see if she understood. He knew his mother was usually understanding, but in being so, also had her hand on the pulse of how they all functioned. His dad took care of the business end and made sure things got done at the ranch. But his mom took charge of the rest of the family functions. Scooter looked at his watch.

"Look, I better get. I have to get my mind set for the competition." They both stood up and Scooter gave his mother a hug. He continued, "I love you too mom. Don't worry, I know she's the one."

"I know you think that, but realize relationships evolve. Well, be careful today. It'll be good having you home for a while. Your dad and I are very proud of you. Your brother needs you too. He has a big responsibility with the work."

"I have a question about that. He thinks it's unfair for me to be going to college and to follow rodeo. Maybe it is. If he'd have wanted to, could he have gone to college?"

His mother looked at him for a few seconds. Scooter thought his mom was still pretty, although there were a few lines at the edges of her mouth and the corners of her eyes. He could see why his dad didn't want to let her go—way back when—at the dance in Eastgate.

"He could have. We were going to hire someone to help, and you were still in high school."

"Well, I don't want him to put it across that I've had an unfair advantage. If things pan out the way I want them to, like if I'm good enough to follow a dream into pro rodeo, maybe we should hire someone to help, at least during the summer. I can put a lot of what I make into the ranch. I mean, if I don't make it, then I'll be there . . . no choice."

"That's something for you to discuss with him and your father," she said.

"You'll see today if I have any ability," he continued.

"Scooter, we never doubted you have ability. You've had it since before you were in high school. We'll need to have a family meeting on this whole thing."

He stood up. "Okay mom. I love you and dad, all you guys." He hugged her, and it seemed as if she had shrunk slightly. *Maybe I've grown a little since Christmas.* "I have to check out yet, too."

CHAPTER FORTY
MUCHO BLANCO AND MUD

Scooter wore his old hat and pulled on a yellow slicker. He stored his duffle bag of equipment under the announcer's stand, trying to keep his gear dry. Several other bareback competitors also placed their gear in the same area as they said hello.

"This is going to suck today with all the mud out there, slippin' and slidin' around," one of the other contestants said.

Scooter agreed. He hadn't seen Johnny or Hank yet but walked through the alleyway to the pen of bareback horses and asked one of the roustabouts if he could point out Mucho Blanco.

"Be that big white in the middle there with a black spot on its head."

Scooter climbed up onto the fence to look over the horses, which had been sorted for the day's competition. Mucho Blanco stood quietly while munching hay that had been thrown into the pen. It was larger than most of the other horses, and well muscled. Several horses snorted at him, not enjoying his presence on the fence. Mucho had angled over and seemed to be gazing at Scooter with an evil eye. Scooter frowned at the horse and said, "So you think you're tough, huh?" Blanco snorted at him and flinched as Scooter jumped down. He headed back to his bag of gear, then changed to his riding boots and began strapping on his spurs. Other bareback riders were gathering as well, and people were starting to file into the grandstand.

Scooter noticed Vince Claypool and said, "Well, here we go again."

"This mud will make it interesting. Could be low scores," Vince said. "By the way, on that Blanco horse . . . it'll take a jump out of the chute on you. I think a guy needs to spur down with it for the mark out. If ya try to hold into it from the start, may blow a foot out. And, I'd say, really stay up on the riggin' 'cause it's stout. That was my main problem!"

Scooter nodded his understanding of what Vince was saying. "Okay, thanks for the tips. Do you know your horse for today?"

"No. Supposedly it goes straight down the arena, so guess I'll see."

Scooter noticed that Johnny was also getting ready and went over to him and they talked for several minutes. Johnny mentioned that Hank hadn't wanted to get out of bed and had been out most of the night with that Squirrel person. "You know, your honey's friend, so he's not going to be much good today fer nothin'."

"Well," Scooter replied, "we can pull for each other. Maybe Zeke will get here soon, too."

He no sooner had said this when he heard his friend say, "Looks like a couple of tender feet here. You guys think ya kin ride sumthin' today?"

Scooter and Johnny shook Zeke's hand and Scooter said, "We think we can. Johnny here garnered a second yesterday, so he at least can ride."

They gave Zeke details of the previous day's rides, Johnny explained about Scooter's ride on a horse that didn't know whether to buck or go blind, and that he should have been given a re-ride, but wasn't.

"The word was that since I wasn't fouled on the way out or anything and had scored, that was it. Look, you might have to help us set the riggings. But before all the excitement starts, I want to introduce you to my family if they're here yet."

"I left Molly over by the stands, so maybe she could sit with 'em."

They walked back through the alleyway to the grandstand. Scooter gave Molly a hug. It took him a few minutes to locate his family and he introduced Zeke and then Molly to them. He introduced her as Zeke's fiancée. Zeke had a strange look on his face but didn't say anything different. Molly shook hands with everyone. He reminded his mom and dad that Zeke was the guy on the rodeo team he and Sonny had traveled with most of the spring; the one that had gotten a concussion in Fort Collins. His mother had a large umbrella out and asked if Molly wanted to share it with her and Rachel.

"The guys are too manly to use an umbrella, but us women-folk have more sense," she said. Molly looked uncertain, but finally said, "Well, I appreciate it," and scooted in with them.

Zeke mentioned that he was glad to have met everyone. Scooter asked his dad and Ron if they wanted to come over. "Bud's over there somewhere." The four of them walked along with Scooter back to the chutes.

Scooter took his dad and brother to the front of the chutes to where Bud was talking to some of the chute crew. They slapped each other on the back and said how long it had been since they had seen each other.

Scooter and Zeke left them and headed across the chutes to the alleyway.

"So, wanting to get me married off already? Where'd that come from?" Zeke asked.

"Well, it's easier to explain it. You might as well be married to her. You need to actually, the way you've been doin'."

"Isn't that like the pot calling the kettle black? You and Charlene been humpin' plenty too," Zeke said.

"You don't know that."

"Don't tell me you're not. She's a happy woman. It's written all over her face," Zeke laughed.

Scooter smiled as he looked at Zeke. "Well, we're going to get hitched someday, I reckon," he said.

"Well, I'm glad for you! Maybe we'll all get hitched someday."

Scooter laughed at Zeke's comment and replied, "Yeah, if we're lucky to find someone wants some rodeo bums."

Zeke smiled, and replied, "Sheeit!"

"You checked out the bull you got today?" asked Scooter

"Yeah, a long brindle, whirly bastard. Been to the National Finals! Y'know, Vacquero Roja."

"Don't know it but sounds like a tough out!"

"Yeah, but most are you know. I'm actually looking forward to it. I think I'm good on a flat-spinning bull, I don't care how fast they go!"

Scooter laughed at Zeke's assessment.

They walked back to the alleyway behind the chutes where Zeke started conversing with Johnny and some of the other contestants. Scooter began to warmup with a series of calisthenics and stretching exercises. He found a brace running across from the top of the chutes to the holding-pen fence above the alleyway and used it to perform a series of chin-ups. He grunted with the effort at the end and did one more. The muscles in his upper arm—his triceps felt hard, which satisfied him. He then buckled on his chaps and began to work rosin into the handhold of his rigging and when satisfied that it was tacky, put an old towel over it to keep it dry. Scooter applied extra rosin to his glove, but then had trouble striking a match to heat-up the material. Instead, he pulled the covering off the rigging and worked the rosin into the handhold with his glove until it seemed tacky. He covered the handhold again and stuck the glove into the belt of his chaps. He continued to loosen the muscles in his arms and then leaned over to touch the ground, stretching his hamstrings.

The first six bareback horses were loaded into the chutes and he checked to see if Mucho Blanco was among them. Scooter noticed Bud Simmons in front of the chute calling out the names of the riders that were up. He noticed Scooter and said, "You should be up in the second group. Good luck on that horse today. This mud's goin' to slow everythin' down."

Scooter continued to keep loose during the grand entry stretching the backs of his legs again and squatting to limber his knees. He stood with his hat off while a recording of the National Anthem played and felt the rain on his face. He felt good and could feel the power in his arms as he pushed and pulled on the top board of the chute. He felt the buzz in his core—the electric current that started in the center of his stomach and radiated out into his extremities. He casually watched the first group of bareback riders. Vince Claypool made a respectable ride, and Scooter thought it put Vince in a good position to win the event average. Scooter had checked the posted list from the first go-round and saw that he was in tenth place. He had smiled at this, as it was way better than he had thought after the ride on Little Joe; there had been a fair share of buck-offs and missed mark-outs.

Johnny came over to Scooter. "I'm the last one out today, so will give you a hand. I don't know much about the horse—Marshmallow Whip—a big gray. Well, it might be white if it wasn't so wet. That Bud said it bucks pretty good . . . straight. We should put some rosin on our butts though. I hate riding in this stuff."

Scooter nodded his head thinking about putting some rosin on his jeans; if it would do any good. "Glue might be better, course I don't know how a guy'd get off. Likely have a bunch of horse hair stuck to your ass!" They and several other nearby contestants laughed at the picture.

"You guys already look funny enough without hair stuck all over yer asses," Zeke said.

"Well anyway, you ride as good as yesterday and you'll be in the money, so let's figure on it," Scooter told Johnny.

Johnny nodded and continued to stretch his arms and legs. The nervous energy among the contestants was evident, as they bounced on their toes or shuffled back and forth while waiting their turn. The second batch of horses was loaded into the chute. Scooter figured he knew which horse was Mucho Blanco. Johnny and Zeke helped bring up the latigo, and then Zeke pulled the cinch tight as Scooter positioned the rigging. He had felt nervous before, as he had waited and watched the other rides, but now felt relatively calm. He was cognizant of the other rides ahead of him. He noticed that one of the contestants, a rider from Baca Junior College, make a good ride, scoring in the mid-seventies. Scooter ran the image of what he wanted to do during the ride, using the "Popcorn" horse as a model, about lying back and spurring with each jump. It was a risk to do what Carl had suggested, but Scooter understood the advantages of going up with the horse with his feet loose and then clamping down as the horse's front feet hit the ground for the mark-out.

The rider in front of Scooter had trouble when the horse lunged in a new direction and he double grabbed before the horn sounded.

"You're next pardner," Bud Simmons said.

Scooter heard the announcer mention his name and college affiliation, and that the horse, Mucho Blanco had been to the National Finals rodeo four times.

"You know what to do. Be tough!" Zeke said.

Scooter meticulously threaded his gloved hand into the handhold and pulled the ends of the fingers around to be under the grip. He was cautious, after having been warned by Carl, but the horse seemed to weather his attention without fighting him. He slid up to be tight with the rigging, tugged his hat down, squashing his ears outward slightly and pulled his chaps back away from his feet. Mucho Blanco's ears flicked as Scooter settled onto its back, but otherwise the horse seemed calm.

"Let's go, boys!" Scooter exclaimed.

The chute gate was flung open and Mucho Blanco arced out with an upwards lunge, as Vince Claypool had said it would. Scooter reared back and followed the horse upwards and then clamped his spurs to its shoulders as its front feet landed for the first jump out of the chute. He was certain that he had successfully marked the horse out. Starting the ride in a positive way gave him confidence as he set his spurs firmly into the horse's shoulders. Mucho Blanco took a second arcing jump, as if headed for outer space, and Scooter felt a surge of force go through his arm and shoulder. He spurred up and out with this jump to begin his spurring action, but realized he better not get behind on a horse like this and hustled his spurs back down to its shoulders as its front feet came back to earth. Mucho Blanco angled out in a different direction, and Scooter quickly followed. This to-and-fro action set him up with the bucking rhythm of the horse.

Mucho Blanco then wheeled hard to the left back toward the chutes. Scooter followed the direction, again spurring up high into the air. He became conscious of the horse emitting low, throaty grunts as it continued to spring upwards. There was no doubt that Mucho Blanco would like nothing better than to plant Scooter into the arena mud. He reared farther back to help propel his legs from the horse into the air each time it left the ground. The strain from holding on was demanding; his hand burned from the friction between the glove and the hard leather of the handhold. The force that occurred each time the horse leaped into the air sent a shock wave into his arm and shoulder. He was determined about using the horse though, to aim for a high score, so reared back even farther until suddenly the horse's rear hit him in the back of the head. This satisfied him though that now he was getting everything he could out of the ride; that each time Mucho Blanco exploded into the air Scooter spurred up and out, throwing himself back. He felt that he was in control; in time with the horse, a complete opposite of the ride on Little Joe the day before. Scooter felt the horse's rear end hit him again as it went high up into the air another time. It again jarred him, and several chunks of mud splattered across his shoulders and neck. His hat had sailed away, but he hadn't been aware of when. Suddenly he felt a stinging swat from Mucho Blanco's tail. It surprised him; *damn . . . like a big fly swatter!* He was aware of being close to the chutes again but kept spurring. Finally, when he thought he could no longer hold on, he heard the horn sound and he double grabbed the hand-hold of the rigging. As had been the case with Popcorn in Laramie, Scooter had not been aware of any noise while the ride was in progress. But now, a swell of cheering from the grandstands on both sides of the arena washed over him as if a wave. He then felt the horse slip out from under him and he tried to push away, but the world seemed to have inverted—Mucho Blanco on top and him on the bottom and against a chute gate. He felt the crushing weight of the horse, having had no success of pushing away from it.

A series of images flickered through Scooter's mind as if part of a slide show; him as a young boy holding the lead rope of Rags, his first pony. They were posed for a photograph, and he gazed toward his mother who was looking down into a box camera she was holding; with Ron and Rachel, it seemed to be at a family picnic. Rachel said, "Either one of you can help me with my project: teaching that stubborn steer how to lead instead of being rooted there in the corral like a block of granite." Ron shook his head that it wasn't going to be him. He was cooling his heels with Sonny as they waited by a burned-out pickup for Zeke to return. He tried to hear Sonny explain something, but the words were elusive, and Scooter responded several times, "You need to use these crutches I made up to remember the scientific names." He took his time looking and absorbing details as a scene with Char-lene came into view. She was at the far end of a hallway; he understood it was in a church. Even from a distance, he could see that she wore a straight, white, silky dress that reached the floor. Scooter had never seen her in any-thing but jeans or western-cut slacks, but she looked beautiful. She turned her head to gaze back, smiling at him. She moved through a door out of the structure, and Scooter followed her, but found her image only partially visi-ble as he exited because of a bright light that reflected from her white gown. More light streamed through tall cottonwoods and washed across a verdant meadow. She moved in that direction; he sensed, rather than saw, that there was a tumbling brook nearby. She held out her hand, and turned looking back at him, waiting. He tried to close the space between them, but it seemed like his feet had been mired in mud. The space between them remained, and a sense of frustration washed over him. He called for her to wait-up.

The noise of the crowd swelled during Scooter's ride on a rank horse. When Mucho Blanco slipped however, the crowd let out a collective "Oh!" as the horse fell heavily against the bottom of a chute gate with the rider underneath it. The horse struggled to its feet and drug Scooter along for several jumps until his hand came out of the rigging. He fell limply to the ground and was still. Several of the men handling the chute gate, and then Zeke, raced over to where Scooter lay. They bent over him and one of them waved to a person on the main gate and hollered, "We need an ambulance!"

One of the emergency crew from the ambulance came into the arena and knelt by Scooter. He laboriously ran back the way he had come and then came back with another EMT and a gurney. They had trouble walking through the mud, carrying the gurney between them. The EMTs worked to put on a neck brace, and one of them then gave Scooter CPR. Bud Simmons and then Scooter's father came over to see if they could help. Scooter's father paled slightly and took Scooter's limp hand.

Charlene had been standing on the lower board of a fence near the edge of the chutes and continued to stand there transfixed. She had linked her hands on top of her head and bit on her lower lip. She had experienced the extreme of emotions in the span of eight seconds. Now she barely breathed as she waited to see if Scooter would spring upright and walk back to climb over the chutes as if nothing had happened.

The announcer said, "Ladies and gentlemen, we have an unheard-of score of eighty-seven points for that young cowboy, but we need your prayers and thoughts now while we try to help him. Injury is part of this sport, but we never like to see it happen."

The stands were silent, as the crowd seemed to hold its breath. The EMTs finally put Scooter onto the gurney and, with help from the chute crew and other contestants awkwardly struggled through the mud of the arena and to the ambulance that had been parked on relatively solid ground.

Ron had come over to meet them, and Scooter's father brusquely told him, "Bring your mother and sister," before climbing into the back of the ambulance.

Zeke came hurrying out from near the ambulance and said to Charlene, "Come on, we better get to the hospital!"

Once there, Charlene, Molly, and Zeke hurried into the Emergency Room and were given directions to a waiting room. They joined Scooter's mother and siblings, all waiting for word on his condition.

"It didn't look good to me. That horse came down right on top of him!" Zeke said.

Charlene looked scared and had tears in her eyes. Rachel came over and they held hands. Rachel said, "My big brother . . . he's always been so strong, but I'm praying for him now. We need him . . . you and me."

Charlene nodded her head but didn't respond. Tears were trickling down her face and Scooter's mother came over and put a hand on her shoulder and then gave her a tissue.

Squirrel came into the room with Charlene's mother, and after they introduced themselves to Scooter's family, Squirrel came over to Charlene and hugged her. Finally, Charlene said softly to no one in particular, "I can't lose him. It took me most of my life to find him!"

CHAPTER FORTY-ONE
A COWBOY'S LAMENT

Evan and Connie

Services for Scooter Henry were scheduled in the Lutheran church in Bunting for the Saturday after his accident. The force of the horse falling on him had wedged his head against the base of a chute gate and the weight of the horse had broken his neck. The emergency physician at the La Junta hospital noted that a shoulder had also been dislocated. Scooter's father, Evan, had been in the emergency room with Scooter, but had told Connie that Scooter had never been conscious from the time they had taken him out of the arena.

"Such a natural . . . guess he had some of his Uncle Jake in him," he said. "I hadn't realized how good the kid had become. That's what I hate so much . . . to have all that potential taken away like that."

Connie had seldom seen her husband cry, but she did during this time. She, on the other hand had wept with him and then in private. Scooter may have had some of his Uncle Jake in him, but he had a lot of her too. He could have been many things. Sometimes he had tried her patience with his hot temper and the penchant to fight at the drop of a hat, especially with Ron, who was larger, but that hadn't deterred Scooter . . . but wasn't that so much like her dad? And he could be impulsive, like with this willowy girl, Charlene. Did he know what he was getting into? A girl with her looks could be trouble. Yet it seems they were in love, or at least thought they were. Conversely, he could be very set in what he wanted to do. Maybe the impulsiveness was determination after he had made up his mind. Ron is going to be lost for a while too. He may not have known it, but he needed Scooter to be a partner with him, to be the innovator of their partnership. It's more than what Evan said. It takes so much away from our family—our future. And Rachel is devastated. *How do we all get over this, or will we? Guess not.*

Evan thought about how they always knew about the risks of rodeo, yet no one ever expects it to take someone's life. They had received a call from the Intercollegiate Rodeo Association with condolences. The man said that there had been no fatalities the last three years, but this year there had been two; Scooter's and a bull rider in south Texas. He had said they had expected Scooter to qualify for the Collegiate National event. Yes, it's all a dream . . . to be chasing the Nationals and then among the pros to qualify for the finals by being one of the top fifteen in winnings. Jake and he had chased that dream.

They had the same problem that Ron and Scooter had talked about that fateful morning . . . the fine line between having a job and going on the circuit full-time. Only a few of those who try have the talent and the fortitude to make it on the circuit . . . rough life. So, now what do we do here? We'll need to hire on someone full-time. He reminded me of Jake some, but different too, not quite so rough around the edges, but had that natural ability to ride the broncs . . .

Zeke and Sonny

Zeke had phoned the reservation and left a message for Sonny at the store; left Molly's phone number for a return call. Sonny had called on Wednesday and had asked for details of what had happened. He had told Zeke, "I doan believe it. Tell me again. How could somthin' like that happen? He was just gettin' started. He was going in the pro ranks fer sure. He was my pardner." He had said something else in Apache that Zeke thought might be swearing.

"I called his folks. The service is in Bunting on Saturday afternoon. Can you come?" Zeke asked.

Sonny said he'd be there. Zeke continued, "A lot of people are in shock about this. I turned out my bull. I wasn't even thinking about it after that . . . Hank and Johnny too just stood around with me after the rodeo. We couldn't even think of anything to say. Johnny rode 'cause he didn't know the full consequences of what the injuries were. He ended up fourth overall. Here's what's so weird, Scooter ended up fifth in the ave and had won the second go-round. If he'd had a horse in the first go, he'd won it all!"

Sonny asked what the scores were again. "I tol' him after Laramie he should go pro and I guess he would have fer sure," he said. "I have to say somethin' at the funeral. I hate to get in front of a bunch a people—white-eyes even worse, but I gotta. We both gotta."

"I was wondering about it. I'll mention it to his folks," Zeke said.

He had called Southwestern State College and had left a message for the Dean of Students, Doctor Walters. Many of the staff had taken some time off, so Zeke didn't know if the Dean had received the message. He couldn't get a grip on the finality. Sometimes he thought it might be a dream. They had been so happy-go-lucky all spring. He had lain for a long time staring at the ceiling with Molly cradled inside an arm and not saying anything, and she seemed to understand. She had said though that she didn't know what she would do if that happened to him and that she felt sorry for Charlene.

Zeke understood that what Molly was saying without saying it, is that she had misgivings about him continuing to compete in rodeos.

After talking to Zeke on the telephone, Sonny told his father and mother what had happened. Then Frank, too, after he had come into the house from outside. "It isn't fair t'have this happen, innit? I mean it wasn't bull riding where bad things happen all the time, uh?" Sonny said. "I need t' go to that thing fer 'im on Saturday." His father said that he would tell some of the others and maybe a few of them from the reservation would go with him.

Charlene

Charlene was in another world, not wanting to come to grips with reality. What she had seen was on the opposite ends of an emotional spectrum of triumph and despair; of her feelings soaring as Scooter had made such a spectacular ride and then her heart shattering into a million pieces in a split second. It was like she had been thrown into outer space. Her footing was gone, there was nothing solid to grasp. At times, she was physically sick when some form of reality penetrated her being. She told herself, "It was meant to be!" and the next second she would say, "It wasn't meant to be!"

Squirrel had driven Charlene's truck and horse back to Colorado Springs after the rodeo. Charlene had ridden with her mother late that evening, but they hadn't said much. Charlene had told her mother, "I loved him so much!"

"I know, honey," her mother said, pulling Charlene to her for a hug.

Now, her mother and father had wanted her to go back to Fort Collins and try to finish her classes, but she could not fathom doing anything. Squirrel was going to talk to Charlene's professors. She didn't know how she would finish the semester and really didn't care about it.

"What did I do to deserve to be broken, to have my world shattered?" she had asked her mother.

"It wasn't anything you did," her mother said. "I think you have to look at it differently somehow. What if you had never met? Would that have been better? Think of the good things that happened while you two knew each other, even if it was brief . . . that he loved you above all others . . . that he wanted to make his life with you, however short it was. Can you do this?"

Charlene put her head onto her mom's shoulder. She tried to dwell on these thoughts; on the times they had been together and how he had enriched her life. She reviewed their telephone conversations and how they had danced around what they really wanted to say about their feelings and how she would let him know a little by calling him "honey." He did get it finally but was he at first just being coy or shy, because he hadn't said anything in response to this endearment. She had torn open the letter she had received after their first weekend, but he had only said that he had enjoyed feeding her horse with her. She had read between the lines and thought she knew what he meant, or had hoped he meant, and figured that they had started to be boyfriend and girl-friend. She again pulled out the note that he had written her in Laramie—his poem to her. No one had ever written her a poem, and she read it over again and tears flowed until she could no longer see his rounded, cursive script.

Squirrel had called several times and asked how she was. Beyond that, they didn't really have very much to say. Scooter's mother had phoned about the service and then Rachel had come on the phone and they had chat-ted and then had cried together. Charlene had decided that she and Rachel had a lot in common and would likely become good friends.

Charlene's sister, Lorraine, came into her bedroom to sit with her to say how sorry she was. They hadn't been especially close the last few years since Charlene had gone to college, but Charlene said that she wished Lor-raine could have known him. She had asked what he was like. Charlene took a deep breath and told her about the light in his eyes, his wide smile and hair that looked like it had been highlighted with gold. "His kisses would light a fire in me," she said. "You should have seen him ride those broncs. He was my buckaroo." This statement caused her tears to start again, as if this image of him opened a tap. They sat hugging each other.

CHAPTER FORTY-TWO
A CELEBRATION OF LIFE

Charlene went with her family to meet Scooter's parents at the funeral home in Bunting for the visitation the morning of the funeral. Charlene's and Scooter's mothers had talked about this. Connie had invited them to attend and to come out to the ranch after the funeral.

Charlene attended the visitation with misgivings. She dreaded it and yet needed to go and see him one last time. His family greeted them as they filed in. Connie and then Rachel had come over and hugged her and then her mother. One of the funeral officials stood by the casket. Finally, Charlene slowly walked over to the area and looked in among the sprays of flowers to see him. He looked peaceful, as if sleeping. He was pale, though. She reached in and laid her hand lightly on his chest. He had on a western-cut suit with a white shirt and string tie.

"I miss you so much," she said. "I'll always love you!" She couldn't continue and had to hurry out of the room and outside to get fresh air. Rachel followed her out to make sure she was alright.

"I'll be okay in a while," Charlene said, as if trying to convince herself.

They left for the church and the service after Scooter's family had left. The church parking lot was filling up. It seemed everyone in town was there.

"They're well known out here, a close community," Charlene's father observed.

After they had taken seats about halfway back, Charlene noticed Squirrel was sitting across the room with Zeke and Sonny. Hank and Johnny were there too. Squirrel got up and walked across the aisle and then leaned over, gave Charlene a hug, and kissed her cheek. "I love you, Char. Be strong," she said. Charlene nodded. There were some relatives near the front, Charlene thought perhaps some cousins.

Rachel looked back toward Charlene from where she sat with the rest of her family. She said something to her mother, then came back and took Charlene's hand. "Come sit with me. I need you."

Charlene was startled by the request but followed Rachel to the front of the church. She sat beside Rachel, and Connie reached over and squeezed Charlene's hand. As she sat there waiting for the service to start, she glanced at the memorial notice that had been handed out at the entry. She put it aside, having no ability in her grief to read it. She looked at Rachel and their glances met. Rachel reached over, hugged Charlene and kissed her cheek. The funeral directors brought in the casket and set it up near the altar. Charlene was conscious of part of the service, the music, and the minister talking about eternal life and that death is but a passing into a new everlasting state. Rachel and Ron went to the podium and she talked haltingly that Scooter had been the best big brother and had been the only way she had gotten through algebra. Ron said that he would miss his little brother, who had suddenly not been so little, and, as he tried to smile, said that now he had no one to spar with.

An older man in a tailored suit then took the podium and introduced himself as Dean Walters, Dean of Students at Southwestern State College. "We don't have to do this very often and this is especially difficult," he said. "Scooter was a good student and we think would have done the college proud. He already had as a part of the rodeo team this year and, as most of you may know, was a terrific athlete. I checked with the Registrar's office before I left the college and Scooter had a three-point-five average this last semester, which qualifies for the Dean's list. He was on this list the fall semester also. It's quite an achievement for a student-athlete to be on this list, especially with the training and traveling that the rodeo team does in the spring. But, I want to tell you a story about him that perhaps illustrates more of what he was like—his grit.

"He and Sonny Valverde ran into trouble on their way back from a rodeo in Laramie where he had won the bareback riding event and had gotten into a scrap with several men in Basin. We wanted to make sure that the boys knew that as ambassadors of the college, they needed to be careful in their travels. Scooter thought about this for a few seconds and then told Dr. Mills and me that they weren't about to slink out of town like 'yellow, egg-sucking dogs with their tails between their legs.' We took this comment in stride during the meeting, but had a good laugh about it after the boys had left about the graphic analogy." There was scattered laughter through the church. He continued, "The college is really like a big family and we become fond of the students, no matter their triumphs and failings. Scooter Henry was one of the special ones. We offer condolences from the college to his family and friends."

After Dean Walters vacated the podium, there was a pause. People started to crane their necks and to look around. Finally, Zeke and then Sonny stood up and walked slowly to the front, stopping briefly by the casket. They then walked up the steps to the podium, as if dragging a weight. Zeke tapped the microphone and bent it upward slightly.

"I'm Zeke Eckhardt, one of Scooter's teammates and a good friend," he said. "We traveled to a lot of rodeos together this spring. He was a great traveling partner, no matter what happened, whether we had car trouble and had to ride a bus all night to get to a rodeo, or got head butted or some other injury, or actually won some money. We'll miss his quick wit and excellent riding style that set the standard for the team."

Zeke stepped aside for Sonny to step up. Zeke then stepped back up and bent the microphone down. Sonny haltingly started to speak. "I'm Sonny Valverde, also of the college rodeo team. Scooter was my travelin' partner all spring. Like Zeke said, he set the standard for the rest of us. Not only that, but he was my friend. What the Dean said was right. He never ran from anything and he stuck up fer me. We had a thing 'bout keepin' a roll of nickels handy." Sonny paused, suddenly realizing he was in front of an audience that had no idea what his reference to a roll of nickels meant. "Well, it's one of those inside story things . . . he'd know what I mean."

Sonny paused again to compose himself and took a deep breath. It looked like he was going to leave it at that, but then stepped back up to the microphone and said, "He and I were going t' travel together t' the regional rodeo up north and then try the pro circuit. I have no doubt that Scooter at some point'd be in the National Finals and would win the whole thing some-day. I just want to say, so long, you bronc rider."

Charlene smiled slightly through her tears. It seemed to her that Sonny was silently crying, but it was hard to tell. He, as did Zeke, had on dark glasses. They descended to the floor of the church and Sonny walked over to the casket and laid something inside it.

At the end of the service, people walked slowly by the casket to show their respect. When everyone had left, Charlene went with Scooter's family and they stood by the casket for several minutes. She noticed a sprig of sage and a length of what looked like braided horsehair. It had a loop on one end. Sonny had laid it near Scooter's crossed hands. Charlene's eyes were drawn to them. His hands still looked strong, as if they could grasp her hands again with his innate, gentle, solid strength. Tears again clouded her vision and she felt her knees become weak, but she walked outside, took a deep breath of fresh air, and met her parents.

They followed the slow procession to the cemetery, and Scooter was interned in a grave beside his Uncle Jake. Charlene read the inscription on the headstone. Jake Henry had passed away five years ago. There was a buck-ing horse and rider inscribed into the marble.

After the internment, Charlene was thinking that perhaps they would not go to the gathering at the Henry ranch; it had been a long day. Yet, Connie and Evan both had asked them if they would, and Charlene was reluctant to let the day pass, to let go of any ties to Scooter and his family.

She had visited with Squirrel and also Sonny and Zeke. They were somber, except when they were telling a story about Scooter; then all of them seemed to brighten for a minute or two.

Finally, Rachel said that she would ride with Charlene to show the way. They followed several other cars that were also traveling the same direction. They increased the distance between them and the car ahead of to stay clear of the dust when the roads changed to a gravel surface. Charlene's parents asked Rachel questions about her grade in school and if she did sports. Charlene was curious about Jake and if he had a family.

"He did, but he and my aunt split up a long time ago . . . maybe fifteen years ago," Rachel said. "She and their kids moved out of state. It's something my mom and dad don't talk about much."

They followed Rachel's directions and pulled into a long lane that went past a large barn and out buildings to a large grove of cottonwood trees and a rambling two-story house. "This is it . . . the old home place," Rachel said.

They parked among several other cars and some pickup trucks. Charlene and her parents followed Rachel into the front door and to the living room. They were introduced to a number of people, both friends and relatives. Scooter's mother introduced Charlene as Scooter's friend. It seemed a little awkward. There was a buffet set up in the kitchen, but Charlene just had coffee.

Rachel came over and asked, "Would you like to see his room? You have to forgive Mom, she hadn't accepted the fact that Scooter and you were talking about marriage already."

Charlene nodded. "Yes, it came together so quickly, as if our relationship had just been waiting to happen. He so attracted me early . . . at the first spring rodeo. We talked about destiny. I'm not so sure I want to see his room, but yet I do."

"Such a strong attraction . . . must be like chemistry!" Charlene studied Rachel, as her comment was so like Scooter. "Come on, it's upstairs," Rachel said.

They climbed a steep staircase and Charlene followed Rachel to a room at the back of a hallway. "He sort of camped out up here sometimes, even in the summer when it gets so hot," she said. "He was always doing things, interesting things. He and I did a 4-H project together. I entered a sheaf of oats in the Lincoln County Fair one year and he helped me prep it. We took razor blades to peel off the outer sheath from the stems. That exposed the gold, shiny part of the stem. We mounted it on plywood, and then he suggested we cover the plywood with purple velvet to offset the gold of the sheaf. Even got Mom involved to help. It looked nice. Well, I won first at the county fair and then first at the State Fair. We were both quite proud; he was proud for me . . . happy.

"But, he could be cantankerous sometimes, not to me so much, but more with Ron. They didn't see things the same way. Ron is more meat and potatoes . . . bullish. Scooter had . . . ah, a good imagination. Goddammit! I'm going to miss him so!"

Rachel's sudden outburst startled Charlene. She looked around the room. There was a large poster of a bareback horse and rider in an action shot from a National Finals Rodeo, and several framed photos of Scooter on bucking horses; one from the National High School Rodeo Finals. A pair of boots sat near the foot of a small bed. An old felt hat and a straw one with dark sweat stain around the band were lazily hanging on pegs set in the wall. Several rodeo trophies and a belt buckle sat on a bureau. Charlene touched the engraving on them.

"Yes, I'm going to miss him something fierce. I think we had found something . . . the destiny. I sort of knew when I saw him at the first rodeo this spring that he was the one. Isn't that strange? I'm not sure I know why I thought that. But, I thought he was really handsome. I wished later that I would have introduced myself to him then. I had plenty of nerve at College Days . . . or was it determination? You should have seen him at the dance when I went over to him. He and Sonny were just spectating. He told me later that he may as well have been struck by lightning."

"I can see it," Rachel said. "He wasn't really comfortable in asking girls out in high school. A lot of them liked him and sometimes asked him out . . . funny. He was interested in schoolwork and was on the high school rodeo team too. As you know, he was determined about that. He was happy when he won a go-round at high school nationals and was accepted at Southwestern for their team." Rachel held Charlene's hand as both had tears in their eyes. "We better go down."

Charlene went over to her mother, who was talking to Connie and several other women. Her mother asked her how she was doing. Charlene put her head on her mother's shoulder and said, "I'm really tired now."

"We're going soon," her mother said. "Your dad and Mr. Henry went out to see a horse. We'll go when they get back."

"Charlene, I need you to come with me a minute. I have something for you, something Scooter wanted you to have," Connie said.

Charlene followed her to a main floor bedroom near the back of the house. Connie turned on a light and dug through a jewelry box. She pulled out a ring that shone dull red. It was etched in gold with a red stone set in the center. "Scooter asked about a ring for you. He said it had to be something special. Here, I think you should have this. I've had this since I was a young girl."

Charlene took it and then started to weep as she viewed it. Connie hugged her. "I know, I know, it's going to be so hard for a while. He thought you were special—'the one,' as he said. As far as we're concerned, you're part of our family. Don't forget that."

Charlene just nodded her understanding, and then said, "I appreciate that. I'm sorry we didn't have a chance to live our dreams. It seems so unfair."

"Yes, very unfair for all of us, and for him too," Connie said.

The road back to Colorado Springs seemed unending. Charlene was tired and drifted off occasionally while her parents talked softly in the front seat. A jolt from the road jarred her awake and from a dream that had recurred several times. She had been having trouble sleeping anyway and when she did sleep, the dream came to her almost immediately, as if someone was turning on a movie projector. It always seemed so real, that upon waking, she thought it was, and then wished it was, yet parts of it were illogical. In the dream, she had been lying with Scooter alongside a mountain creek among conifers, but then the trees had changed to willows and the stream to slow water. She decided that the image was a hybrid between her vision of the pristine area on the reservation he had regaled her about, and what he had told her of the special area on his parent's ranch. She dreamed that they were lying naked together in thick, soft grass and the sunlight had been beautiful, streaming down in golden shafts of light through a forest canopy. He had been so tender with her; so warm with kisses near her hairline and in her ears as he used to do. But the image changed; she was lying inside a white tent, and at first, sensed, rather than saw, that there was a horse outside and had thought it was Arabian. It came near, and its faint shadow played on the tent wall, moving back and forth. She also then sensed that Scooter was outside taking care of the horse, perhaps brushing its mane. She realized then that the horse was not an Arabian, but was her horse, Star. She awoke from the dream hungry for Scooter, but the black vacuum of reality quickly returned.

Charlene had decided that she had to endure somehow the week of finals, or otherwise all the work she had done would be lost. Squirrel had reminded her of this, but she already knew. She just didn't have any incentive to think about classes and the course work. She sleepwalked through her final exams. It had been completely the opposite when all of them had been studying together in Laramie. *Seems so long ago now, another lifetime.* Now her period was late, and she had been nauseous the last two mornings. *It couldn't be. We were so careful. Must be the stress of this whole thing. Is this all a dream and I'll wake up and have him again? How could he just disappear from my life like that? What a painful journey this has been since . . . since it happened. Mom is right. We had everything, but for too short a time. Maybe Scooter was right; it was too good to last . . . like the flaming, brilliant light of a shooting star, or what did he say once? . . . Like a fleeting, soft spring rain.* Charlene pulled Scooter's obituary once again from a book where she had kept it pressed, pristine. Every time she read it, her tears would start. But she again studied it through her watery vision. It read:

Llewellyn "Scooter" Henry, December 10, 1941 – May 21, 1961. A photo of him, possibly from his high school graduation, had been inset above the dates. It was a younger version of the Scooter she knew, but there was that wide grin and the light in his eyes. There was a verse below this, and her eyes were drawn to it.

Farewell! For I have ridden through the canyons in the silvery moonlight, through the thick grass of the prairie, and crossed the river, the wind at my back. I am heading for the great divide, leaving the valleys and my family, friends, and my true love behind. Farewell, but fear not, as I will eventually circle back, bringing in the herd. — Connie and Rachel Henry

EPILOGUE

Jake

Jake O'Brien had a conflict. He had been hard on the rodeo circuit and occasionally winning money in the saddle bronc event. On this particular day however, he and his two traveling partners had gone into an Indian jewelry shop in Cortez because Jake had wanted to buy his mother, Charlene, something for her birthday. They had been kidding around and his buddies, Bobby and Paul, had been giving him a hard time about being a momma's boy. He had retorted though that he knew on which side his bread was buttered, whereas they apparently didn't. They had cruised through part of the store, and Jake stopped at the display cases of turquoise jewelry. Bobby and Paul had quickly tired of looking through the displays and wandered over to a series of Native American weaponry artifacts that were mounted on a wall of the store. Jake had continued to gaze at a series of silver bracelets of different turquoise designs that had caught his eye.

A girl who he hadn't noticed before came over and asked, "May I help you? Those are Navajo. Zuni work is on this side. It's more inlaid."

He looked up and was startled to see an attractive girl with dark eyes framed by long, dark lashes. She was trim and had on a sleeveless white blouse. Her dark hair was gathered by a silver clasp into a kind of up-right ponytail with the ends falling back toward earth in a kind of circular spray. He thought it resembled a fireworks starburst explosion. She looked at him wide-eyed, expectantly. *Perky . . . a perky, cute girl.* He stammered something unintelligible.

He then struggled to recover his normal verve and asked, "What would you recommend? It's for my mother and she's partial to turquoise. Could you try some on?"

She smiled, and he noticed her even teeth and curved, full lips. Her smile seemed to brighten the space between them. She had a narrow, straight nose. *Angular and high cheekbones.* Her cheeks had a skiff of color. He wasn't sure if it was natural or a light application of rouge.

She opened the back of the case and removed several bracelets, then asked, "Are you here for the rodeo?"

"Yeah, does it show?"

"Well, the big hat and . . . yeah, somehow you guys look like rodeo."

He chuckled at her comment. "That's us, alright. Would y'like to go? I can get you tickets to tonight's performance."

She smiled at him. "Are you asking me out? We haven't even met."

He had laughed outright at her comment and offered his hand. "Hello, I'm Jake O'Brien. I'm very glad to meet you."

The girl laughed too and after a few seconds delay, shook his hand. "Hi, my name is Marie . . . Langineau."

"Oh, French. It's a nice name."

She laughed again. He enjoyed making her do it.

"Well, my dad is. My mom's family name is Sandoval. That's Hispanic."

He smiled at that, "Well, I know. I mean, I would know. So, you coming to the rodeo? I'm riding saddle broncs. I'll take you out for a coke or something afterward."

Her bright smile appeared again, as she placed several bracelets on her arm, but she said, "I don't think so."

He tried to use his charm and teased her, "You're not afraid of me, are you? I won't bite. Do you have a boyfriend?"

She paused before answering, "Yes, I do."

Bobby, who had the opposite features of Jake, with dark hair and eyes, sauntered over and asked, "What y'doin', tryin' to get a date?" He said to Marie, "You have to watch him, he ain't had a date since we been travelin' together, which is considerable. He wouldn't know how t' act." To Jake he said, "Well, we're going to that café down the street. If you ever get done, come on."

Jake looked over and saw that his other companion, Paul, was already by the door. Jake grinned at Marie but felt that he was blushing.

"Yeah, yeah . . . you guys go ahead, I'll catch-up," he said to Bobby.

He turned back toward Marie to continue his probe about her status. "You're not married, are you? You're not engaged, are you? That'd be a downer. I'd be sad most the rest of the day, maybe even into tomorrow!"

Bobby said, as he heard this, "See what I mean? He's pathetic. Don't fall for that stuff." To Jake he said, "Okay, lover boy, see you over there."

"Yeah, alright already!" Jake said more stringently.

Bobby's statement made Marie laugh again, but she said to Jake, "No, I'm not engaged, but I do have a boyfriend, at least part of the time."

He continued pressing her and said, "Look, I'm not trying to take his place, you know, displace him. I'm just trying to be friendly. I'll leave a ticket for you at the gate, in an envelope with your name on it. If I spell your last name correctly, we'll get a coke or milkshake somewhere. I don't drink, see, if'n you're wondering." He had smiled at her. "You want me to leave you two tickets, one for you and one for your boyfriend that I'm actually going to displace?" He laughed at his own change in tactics as if it was a joke.

His sudden change of intention about displacing her boyfriend and teasing caused Marie to laugh again too. She said, "You're ornery . . . an ornery boy. Leave one, I'll think about going. Are you going to buy anything?"

The bell on the shop's door rang and another customer entered. An older woman, who Jake thought quite attractive, came out from the back of the store to wait on the new customer.

"Okay, that's a deal," Jake said. He meant about the rodeo ticket. He continued to look over the bracelets that Marie had brought out of the display. He liked one of the Navajo bracelets that she had placed on her arm. The bracelet flared to a large silver base on which silver roses had been set around a large piece of turquoise in the center. He touched the roses and circled the turquoise with an index finger.

"I like this one on you, so I'll take it." He noticed that it had a tag with $50.00 written on it, but he thought it was worth it. His mother would like it, although she might wonder if he'd paid too much.

Marie touched it where he had. "That's very nice and it's on sale. It's probably for your girlfriend. I think you're giving me a line." She smiled when she said it, but Jake decided he better respond.

"Well, you never know about us rodeo guys I guess," he said. "I could have you mail it to my mother though." Marie nodded and smiled as she thought about his statement.

He paid at the cash register and Marie placed the bracelet into a gift box. "To your mother, huh? Well, we mail gifts all over, so could, or to your girlfriend too."

He laughed at her nerve. "Well, if I had one, I would y'know, just to be that kind of a guy—you know, a considerate rodeo guy." Marie laughed at this. "It was my pleasure to meet you!" he said. "Don't forget . . . check the spelling! I'll meet you after near the announcer's booth."

"Thanks! About the rodeo, don't get too confident." she smiled though as she said this.

Jake noticed that the older woman, whom he figured was the manager, was inspecting him with a questioning look. He headed out the door to catch up with his buddies, gift box in-hand.

His conflict though was whether he could get back to Cortez to see this girl. The three were traveling in Bobby's car and had planned to head back to Colorado Springs for a week and then back west for three different rodeos. Maybe he would drive his own car for the next stint and stop back here in Cortez somehow. *Well, I'm getting way ahead of myself.* He couldn't stop thinking about her though. He had to move her image into the background, however, and start thinking about the competition.

Jake had an average horse in the saddle bronc event and scored in the middle of the qualified rides. He thought he might make a little money but began to think of the next go-round on Sunday afternoon and possibly placing in the average. He helped Bobby with his horse and then Paul in the bull riding. Bobby lost a stirrup and didn't score, but Paul made a qualified ride on a spinning bull for fourth place that Jake thought would likely result in a nice check.

After the bull riding was over, Jake slowly cruised the area near the announcer's booth, but didn't see Marie. He began thinking that she had decided not to show up. He hollered at Bobby, who was hauling tack with Paul from the alley behind the chutes, to wait for him before heading back into town. He then saw Marie standing near the grandstand, as if lost.

He sauntered over toward her. She acted nonchalant, as if she was looking for someone else. "Hey, you're not lost, are you?" he asked. "I was sent over to provide a rescue."

She smiled. "No, I was just waiting. It was too busy by the announcer's stand. I see that you can ride bucking horses. Do you do it full-time?"

"Well, nearly," he said, "I'm on a scholarship at Wyoming . . . Laramie. Been there two years in Business Ag. But I help on my grandfather's ranch during the summers . . . out near Bunting, if you know where that is. My Uncle Ron runs it now, mostly. I was practically raised there. My mom lives in Colorado Springs. Come on, let's go get a milkshake or whatever. I mean, a deal's a deal, right?"

She stared intently at him, and then said, "I guess it's a deal. Were you just lucky or are you a good speller?"

He laughed. "A guy shouldn't leave something like that to chance. I checked the phone book."

She laughed, too. "Sneaky. When you say on a scholarship, do you mean to rodeo?"

"Yeah, isn't that a hoot? But a guy has to keep his grades up, so that's somethin'. Do you have a car? 'Cause I'm traveling with Bobby, one of the guys that was with me today in your store."

They headed back to town and Marie angled the car into a parking spot. They went inside to a booth, and Jake bought two milkshakes. He continued to study her. He thought she was very attractive. He was curious about her job in the store and she said it was her mother's, that she usually worked there during the busy summer season, but was going to Southwestern State in the fall, her first year.

"You mentioned your family. You didn't say anything about brothers or sisters."

"Nah, just me," he said, "I have a younger step-brother though, my step-dad's.

"Where's your dad?" she asked.

He paused and took a deep breath, "Well, that's a hole in my life. My dad . . . well, that's interesting you mentioned Southwestern State, 'cause he was on that rodeo team . . . a long time ago. He was killed in a rodeo in La Junta—a freak accident I guess. Apparently, he was hot, y'know . . . riding bareback horses and winning quite a lot. I checked Southwestern out after high school, 'cause they offered me a scholarship too. There's still a picture of him in the Phys Ed building on a bareback horse at a rodeo in Laramie. My grandparents have the same one in their house. I often wonder what he was like. My mom doesn't want to talk about it much." He took a drink and looked at Marie over the rim of the glass. She was studying him in return.

"My Aunt Rachel and Mom are good friends. I asked my Aunt about it. She said that they were a hot couple . . . that he was the love of her life, so guess she never really recovered . . . y'know? My step-dad is okay though . . . good to her."

"I'm very sorry for you." Marie said. He thought there were tears in her eyes and he wanted to reach across the table and take her hand. She looked down and then brushed her eyes. After a pause, she continued, "It's interesting . . . my mother went to Southwestern. Wonder if they knew each other?"

He studied her for a few seconds. "You should ask her. His name was Scooter Henry. I'm named after him, but they always called me Jake . . . a nickname on a nickname." He laughed at his explanation. "What's your major going to be?"

"I think business . . . marketing. My mom needs a buyer and some-one to advertise. Her business is slowly growing, and she thinks it will need both of us. I'm on a scholarship too."

He waited for her to continue, but she seemed hesitant. "Well, okay, I know it's not wrestling or football."

She laughed. "No, it's academic and running . . . cross country. My mom did it, too, and I didn't want to be the same, but it just happened. I mean it just seemed that it was something I could do . . . was on the high school team. Were you as well? I mean on a rodeo team. We have one, but it's only a couple of guys."

He watched her as she spoke, following her expressions. Her dark eyes mesmerized him, as if he could dive into them and find out what she liked, what she thought. He liked her curved lips and how she pursed them when she was thinking. Her smile came easily and gave him incentive to make her laugh. *A runner, no wonder she's so trim, but with those nice buns.* He shook his head to get the thought of her shape out of his mind. She was a little younger than he had thought while she had waited on him in her shop, but her conversation with him added a few years. *She's a quick study is what.*

"Yeah, we had a good team, even a coach," he said, "Two of us guys and one of the girls went to High School Nationals in Oklahoma, so it was okay."

He laughed at his own joke, and then Marie caught on and laughed as well. "You're a funny guy. Did you do well there?"

"Well, that's why I had scholarship offers. I think too that people remember my dad and then his Uncle Jake was in the National Finals for the World Championships—won some of the go-rounds, way back when. So, as you can see, there's a long lineage of bronc riders for me. My mom was a good barrel racer too."

"Talk about something being in your blood, that's what it means," she said.

"But running's apparently in your blood. You have natural ability and then you overlay it with hard work."

She smiled. "You think so, huh? That I work at it?"

"Yes," he said, "I know you work at whatever you need to and want to do." She looked intently at him. He continued, "You haven't mentioned your family."

"I have a younger brother. He's twelve and a pain. My dad's in construction and in Utah right now. He wanted us to move, but Mom is determined to make a go of her business. So, it hasn't been the best of times between them . . . for us."

He nodded his understanding, "Life sucks sometimes at what we have to do. Come on, let's go visit some bucking horses."

"Really?" she asked.

He stood up. She hesitated and studied him for several seconds, but then slid out of her side of the booth. They drove back through town and out to the rodeo grounds, which were dark except for one yard light near the corrals.

He guided her over to a pen of horses and they climbed onto the top rail of the corral. The horses snorted at them.

"They don't like this. It scares them," Marie said uncertainly.

"They'll get used to us," Jake confidently said. The horses sidled over to the far side of the corral. He continued, "I could teach you to ride sometime."

"You don't mean horses like this, 'cause I'm not that . . . crazy!" He laughed at her expression.

"No, just regular horses."

"I used to have a horse for a while until I was in high school and got too busy. My dad decided it was a 'hay burner' so we sold her. I was sad about it for a while."

"Well, in that case, we could just go riding . . . explore some country. But, tell me about this boyfriend, the one I want to displace."

Marie reached over, whipped Jake's hat off and placed it on her head. He looked at her quite amazed but didn't take it back.

"Do I look like a bucking bronco rider?" she asked.

He laughed. "You do, like a regular buckaroo is what. A cute one, too."

He waited to see if she would answer his question, and there was a thick pause. She avoided his question though with one of her own. "Isn't rodeo, I mean riding bucking horses dangerous? A person could get hurt doing it. Don't you think about it, about your dad?"

"Well, yes, I know that after what happened to my dad . . . that it has its dangers. I just started riding the rough string for my grandpa though and he helped me then, my uncle Ron too, when I was just a little shaver."

Marie laughed. "A little shaver, huh?"

He chuckled and said, "Yeah, y'know, eleven or twelve. I've been lucky though, nothing major. I had my nose broken once and a dislocated finger. The way I look at it, it's pretty simple. It's has to do with the Law of Gravity."

"The Law of Gravity? You mean you want to stay up in the air?"

"Well, not entirely," he explained, "the horses are trying to enforce it and I'm trying to defy it."

Marie laughed and said, "You've put some thought into this gravity thing."

"Yes, I saw how it was quite a few times from the ground in an arena somewhere as the horse continued to buck without me on it, the Law of Gravity having prevailed." They both laughed at his explanation. "You never answered my question," he said, "about that boyfriend."

"He's working in Durango this summer," she finally explained. "He was going to go to Southwestern too, but now he doesn't think so. I guess we're not as thick this summer as we thought we were during high school. I don't think he needs replaced though. How's that for honesty?"

"I like honesty," he said. "Well, don't you think I'm a good candidate though?" It seemed his comment made her smile. "We're going to go back to Colorado Springs tomorrow after the performance. There's a little tourist rodeo there on Wednesday nights and we sometimes pick-up pocket money at it. Then I need to do some work at the ranch for my uncle. But then . . . well, there's a rodeo in Farmington and we were going to Spanish Forks in Utah after that and then back to Prescott in Arizona. Late in July I'm going to Cheyenne for the amateur bronc riding. But, what I'm getting to is that I was going to travel with Bobby and Paul, but now what if I came through here some? Would you go out?"

"You mean you want to just go back and forth, traveling through as some kind of candidate?" she asked.

The way she put it made his suggestion seem ridiculous. He laughed loudly though and said, "Well, I mean if I came through here anyway?"

"Maybe. You'd have to spell my name correctly again, though . . . each time."

He laughed hard again at her comment. Finally, when he could talk, he said, "You're a funny girl!" His butt was starting to get a crease in it from sitting on the fence and he climbed down. He caught her by the waist as she began to climb down also, and gently set her onto the ground. They were standing close together and he realized that their fingers had interlocked. "If I came through here and spelled your name correctly and you went out with me, would you let me kiss you?" he asked.

"Even if you did all that, I'd have to think about it," she said.

"But what about now?" he asked. "Do you have to think about it?" She still had his hat on and he tipped it back and kissed her for several seconds. He readjusted and kissed her again. Her lips were moist and opened slightly. He felt her fingers on his upper arm, then on the back of his neck. She leaned into him and he felt her breasts and thighs pressing into him. After they broke apart, he said, "Jeez!"

They started to walk slowly toward her car still holding hands. "Okay, my turn." she said. "So, tell me about your girlfriend, or should I say girlfriends."

"Well, I don't have any right now, but suddenly, I think I want one."

She laughed at this and said, "You sound so lonely."

Yeah, the cowboy trail is a lonely journey and we're poor waifs like children lost in the woods."

"If I had a violin I'd play some dirge for you," she said. "I don't believe you about the girls. Some just hang around rodeo. What do you call them?"

"Buckle chasers, buckle bunnies . . . but I've still got mine as you can see," he said.

He pulled her toward him and tipped her head back for another kiss. The intensity increased, but finally they broke apart for air, and he then kissed her neck and ear. He felt her move against him and heard her say, "Oh!" She felt nice, she smelled nice. He tried to figure out what the scent was, and thoughts of lilac and a fresh spring evening came to mind.

She finally pushed against him with her hand to gain some space. "I need to get in. I have to work, you know. I'm not like some bronco rider who can sleep all morning."

He laughed and said, "I have no idea who you're talking about."

They walked under the starlight toward her car and saw a sheriff's vehicle circling the parking area. A light was shined on them for a split second.

"Oh-oh," Marie murmured.

"Don't worry, just checking the area I guess. Probably saw the car," Jake said.

The car pulled up and a voice from inside it asked what they were doing in the area. "Just out walking, officer." Jake said. The voice mentioned that they shouldn't be out by the rodeo stock. "Yeah, officer, we were just leaving."

Marie drove them back to town and they stopped at his direction in a motel parking lot one block from Main Street. He took his hat from her and kissed her again.

"Come to the rodeo tomorrow and I'll show you something. I have a rank horse, so should be interesting," he said.

"Interesting, huh? Doesn't it scare you to do this, if a horse is rank, as you say?"

"You know how you get that concentrated feeling—butterflies or whatever—before a cross-country race? That's how it is. I'll put a ticket for you again. Name spelled right too! Will you give me your telephone number?"

"I don't know if you should have it yet. I have to think about it."

"But what if I came to town and asked you out and spelled your name correctly and kissed you ever so sweetly, would you give me your phone number?"

Marie laughed at his plea. "Kiss me ever so sweetly . . . what a bull-shitter you are. Like I said, I'll think about it. Ride that horse tomorrow!"

He watched her drive out of the motel parking lot and said to himself, "God damn, that's a girl!"

Marie

Marie had seen the three cowboys come into the shop. She and her mother had been in the back room that serves as an office and had been look-ing through a catalog. The three young men had scouted out the store and stopped by one of the glass cases. Marie's mother started to go out to wait on them, but Marie said, "I'll get it," and hustled out to make sure she did.

Two of the young men drifted over to the historic weapons display on one of the walls of the store. One was slight and had long black hair that he had tied behind his ears. The other was slightly taller and square with a pug nose. Marie thought he looked like a boxer. She walked over to the third, who was gazing intently through the glass of the display. Marie thought he was quite handsome with his large tan-colored hat. It was decorated with a dark, braided leather band. He had a thick mob of golden curls that cascad-ed onto his neck, and was trim, but thick in the shoulders. He wore a dark blue western-cut tapered shirt and a wide belt with a silver buckle with gold engraving. His jeans were creased and long over his boots. Marie thought; *he's lithe*, and that he resembled one of the early wild-west heroes; maybe Kit Carson or Buffalo Bill.

She slid behind the counter and asked if she could assist him but was quite amazed as he looked up with striking, indigo-blue eyes and then flashed a smile. He had stuttered something, but then asked about the brace-lets. He said for his mother and was bold enough to ask her to try some on.

Marie thought: *Yes, handsome with those bright, blue-green eyes, and flash of a smile, but cocky, too.*

Her dilemma though, after he had asked, was whether she should go to the rodeo. He had aroused her interest by teasing her about displacing her boyfriend. She very much wanted to go see more of what he was about, yet she didn't want to. She had heard about the love 'em-leave 'em fast action of rodeo. But he seemed nice. Later, she asked her mother about it.

"I saw him sweet-talking you," her mother said. "You're asking for trouble. What about Martin?"

Marie thought about Martin. It seemed their relationship was stale—in a rut. *But this new boy . . . Jake with sparkling eyes like turquoise and the sunrise, ready smile. He likes to laugh . . . makes me laugh. Talk about fresh air. Wonder if he can spell. He's older . . .*

Marie decided she needed to find out more about this Jake, to see him ride a bucking bronco; *saddle broncs, he called it*. Her mother was con-cerned and asked how old he was. Marie wasn't sure, but said, "Twenty." Her mom thought he was a little old—too experienced.

"Mom! Two years?" Marie exclaimed. She asked for her mom's car and said she wouldn't be too late. Her mom said she should go to the rodeo with one of her friends and to be careful; to be in by midnight. Marie retorted that her mom didn't need to set a curfew anymore, but didn't press the issue.

She checked in at the ticket booth, and there was an envelope with her name on it and a ticket inside. He had written in large letters, *Marie Langineau.* She smiled at the spelling. She took a seat partway up in the grandstand and watched the different competitions but was mostly interested in the saddle bronc event. She watched his ride; he spurred a large roan horse back and forth as it bucked down the arena. His ride thrilled her. The roughness of the event was evident though as the horse and Jake came back along the fence in front of the grandstand after the horn had sounded to end the ride. He had both hands on the thick rein, but the horse still bucked jerkily until another man on a saddle horse caught up to take him off and the bucking horse was controlled. He had made the ride look quite easy, and she realized that he was good at what he did. *He's a real cowboy. Handsome, too.*

She nearly left afterwards, yet hung around to see if he would meet her and if he was really interested in her, or was just dallying, looking for another girl on a string. *What did cowboys call their string of horses in the old days? . . . Remuda, that's it. Well, I'm not going to be one of his horses.* The atmosphere of the rodeo and his ability excited her though, and she thought back over their conversation in her mom's shop. His brashness about replacing her boyfriend and teasing made her smile.

At the drive-in restaurant, she found their conversation interesting and he was attentive to what she said. She thought it was a strange coincidence about his dad and her mom perhaps being in college at the same time. She wanted to reach out to him about his dad being killed, and his mother losing the love of her life. But also, wondered why he would want a career, or whatever he was doing in rodeo, with such a legacy. Maybe that didn't figure into the equation.

She softened toward him when they sat on the corral fence at the rodeo grounds talking. Then when he lifted her down off the fence, and she felt his strength, as he set her down as if she was a feather, she nearly melted into him like a cube of butter. She wondered if he wanted to kiss her. She wanted him to, and when he did, she found her hand in his hair. She felt the firm muscles of his upper arms and shoulders; his leg against her thigh. He did something to her during the kiss; or had she done something to herself with him? She felt warmth start in her center, as if a small fire had been lit, and when he kissed her ear and throat she felt the warmth flair out like a flame fanned by the wind. It thrilled yet scared her. *I'm like those bucking broncos in the corral . . . leery of something new. Yet, I like this new excitement. Strange, because Martin and I made out some, but it wasn't like this. Wonder if this Jake knows what he's doing to me? Then he talks about ever-so-sweet kisses and coming back as he travels to the different rodeos . . .*

Another thing she noticed was that she felt safe with him, sitting on the corral near the herd of wild horses and even when the sheriff had shined the light on them. So safe that she had wanted to stay and hear more about him, to tell him more about herself. She liked it that he had kissed her again, had stirred her as before with kisses to her ear and throat, and that he wanted her phone number.

Marie's mother was still up when she got home and asked how everything went. Marie said fine and, that they had a nice chat. "You know what, Mother? His dad might have been at Southwestern the same time as you. His name was Scooter . . . I think Henry or something. His last name's O'Brien though. I mean Jake's.

Her mother looked startled and paled slightly. "Oh my God! I knew him. He and I were in an English class together." She sat down on a kitchen chair. "We went out some . . . well, more than just going out. He and I . . . that was before your dad . . . he was unique . . . a good student."

Marie glanced at her mother, wondering about her mother having been involved with Jake's father. Her mother had a strange expression on her face, her eyes glistening with tears, and she seemed lost in thought. She finally continued, "I knew that he had been killed in a rodeo, of course, right after finals. I couldn't believe it . . . a real blow to me, to the college, I think. What did you say this boy's name is?"

"Jake O'Brien. He said he was nearly raised on his dad's ranch out east. Well, he said his grandpa's ranch. But he can really ride bucking horses. He's on a rodeo scholarship to Wyoming. He wants to see me again . . . wants my phone number. I think I like him."

"You should be very careful. I know he might be exciting and maybe nice, but rodeo . . . He's just going to be drifting, not settling down if that's even in his blood," Marie's mother said. "If he comes back this way, you better have him over. I need to talk with him."

"Mother, I'm not in high school anymore!" Marie said. She noticed her mother carefully studying her and then staring at nothing, as if lost in time.

Marie thought about Jake off and on while she waited on customers the next day, and as she filled out an order form for one of their artist groups on the Navajo Reservation. She sometimes went with her mother to see the new pieces being marketed and she looked forward to these trips. Today though, she was wondering if maybe Jake was going to appear at the store. She tentatively hoped not, but she looked up in anticipation every time the bell on the door rang as it opened.

Sharon, one of her friends from high school, came into the store and asked if Marie wanted to do something when she got off in the afternoon.

"I've been invited to the rodeo by one of the saddle bronc riders," Marie said.

"You mean a guy from the rodeo?" Sharon's voice went up an octave. She wanted to hear all the details and then asked about Martin. Marie mentioned that she wasn't too concerned right now and that maybe they were breaking up.

"Wow!" Sharon said. "This must be some guy! Maybe I'll go with you and see him for myself."

Marie smiled and suggested, "You should 'cause he has two friends who are kind of cute too in a rough way. One's a bull rider."

"Sounds interesting. I shouldn't let you have all the fun. If there are three though, we need to find a third," Sharon said. "I should ask my cousin. She's been out with rodeo guys before. Actually, one of them brought her home drunk though and left her passed out on the lawn, so she might be leery. It didn't seem to have lasting effects though . . . she's been out with the guy since."

Marie shook her head and said, "My guy isn't like that . . . doesn't drink . . . or at least he said so last night." She didn't want to be saddled with Sharon and her cousin or whomever she brought along and said, "Well, I'll meet you at the ticket booth if you're coming out to it."

There was a similar envelope with her name on it at the ticket booth, but Jake had penciled a line and had written *Phone #* beside it. Marie smiled at his persistence, realizing he could get it from the phone directory, but apparently wanted her to provide it. She waited for Sharon and was about to go in through the entrance gate when Sharon hollered at her to wait up. She introduced a companion, as Rose, who was dressed in tight bell-bottom western-cut slacks and a low-cut western shirt. Marie noticed that Rose was showing some cleavage and had on heavy purple eye shadow. She was holding a long, smoldering cigarette. Marie contemplated that perhaps she should distance herself from Rose and possibly Sharon, too. However, they found seats several rows up in bleachers near the edge of the chutes and Marie mentioned to the other girls that she only knew Jake's friends as Bobby and Paul, but if she saw them, or recognized them in the saddle bronc and bull riding, she would tell them.

They talked during parts of the intervening events and occasionally, Rose would light up another long cigarette. The smoke was giving Marie a headache. Finally, the saddle bronc event started, and they were more attentive. They heard Bobby's name announced with his hometown as Jicarilla, New Mexico. Marie had not known that, having assumed he was also from Colorado Springs and had thought he might be Hispanic, but realized he was likely Jicarilla Apache.

"That's one of the guys," she said.

Bobby made a qualified ride and Sharon said, "He's cute!" as he walked back toward the chutes.

There were several other rides and then Jake's was announced. Marie could see him getting down onto the horse. "That's my guy!" she said, letting the other girls know he was off limits to them. "The one helping is Paul, the bull rider."

The horse came out of the chute bounding in a high arc and continued to leap and kick in a circle. Jake sat upright, spurring with each jump, and there was a swell of cheering from the crowd. However, near the end of the ride it seemed he caught his foot forward and suddenly pitched off over the front of the horse. He skidded into the arena's gravelly surface. Marie found herself standing and she let out a loud, "Oh!" with the rest of the crowd. She was hoping he wasn't hurt.

Jake sprang or jack-knifed up from a squat to regain his feet and gazed at the horse as it was being controlled by one of the pick-up men. He gathered up his hat from the ground and walked back toward the chutes.

"I want that one, he's cute!" Rose exclaimed.

Marie felt a flash of anger go through her. "Keep your hands off him, he's taken!" Her intuition had been right . . . that she should distance herself from these girls, especially Rose, who seemed to be a little on the wild side. Marie took a pen out of her purse and wrote her phone number on the envelope that Jake had left with the ticket.

They watched the rest of the rodeo, including Paul, who made a qualified ride on a bull that started out spinning, but then went straight and by the end of the ride seemed to be looking for the exit gate that led to the holding pens. Paul threw a leg over and bounded away from the bull, leaping onto the side of a chute gate to be away from the bull's horns.

"He's kind of cute too, I think," Rose said. "He can ride bulls!"

Marie observed Rose and thought that she likely had a lot of experience with a whole bunch of men. Another plume of smoke from Rose's cigarette drifted over and Marie held her breath.

The three girls waited as most of the crowd filed out. Marie saw Jake come through the small gate near the chutes with a large kit bag and his saddle that he had somehow wrapped up into a bundle, using the cinch and stirrups.

"I'll go talk to him and see if he can introduce you to the other guys," she told the other girls.

She walked over and realized the two girls were trailing along, but said, "Hey cowboy. You okay?"

Jake looked over and smiled, "Yeah! Like they say, you can't ride 'em all, I guess. I'll get that horse again somewhere down the road, so we'll see then. I spurred over the rein, which weren't too good!"

"Well, you were right, it was interesting. I'll have to say that!"

"Yeah, almost too interesting," he grinned.

"I want you to meet two friends. This is Sharon and Rose. This is Jake. They came to watch you guys . . .y'know, your buddies," she said.

They all said hello and he said, "Come on, I'll introduce you to the other dudes. I think Paul might have won some money in the average. Good someone has. They might be over at the car."

The three girls followed him through the parking area. As they walked, Marie said, "Your persistence paid off." He looked at her, and she handed him the envelope.

He smiled. "Thanks. What changed your mind?"

"You unsuccessfully defying gravity. I felt sorry for you!"

Jake laughed at this. A wave of happiness coursed through Marie. *I like this . . . just being with him. I might be falling for him. This is ridiculous. Two days.*

They stopped by an older Mercury four-door car and Jake opened a front door and popped the trunk. He threw his saddle and duffle bag into it and closed the lid.

"Those other two hombres should be along soon. I don't know, those guys might sign an autograph or two," he said.

"What would they sign? We don't have anything," Rose said.

"Oh, that never stopped them before. They just have you lift up your blouses. Back or front, it's up to you."

Rose's face turned slightly red, but she and the rest of them laughed at his joke. "Anyway, why don't y'all join us for some grub, then we're hitting the road. Paul has to be back in the Springs by morning for some job."

Marie realized that Jake had taken her hand. She looked up at him; he smiled and softly said to her, "I'm coming back through the end of next week. How about we ride some horses?"

She looked into his twinkling blue-green eyes and murmured, "That'd be fine, cowboy." He pulled her closer to him, and she thought he smelled like what she would later define as rodeo: a combination of leather, horse, and sweat. She didn't mind and leaned her head into his shoulder. She felt him kiss her hair. The melting in her continued and she realized he was true to his word; he had become her boyfriend. She laced her fingers through his, thinking that the evening had become especially balmy.

THE END

ABOUT THE AUTHOR

Kale Gray was raised on a farm in eastern Colorado and competed for two years on the college rodeo circuit while pursuing a degree in pre-forestry. Between college terms, he worked for the Forest Service on trail maintenance, fence building, fire suppression, and timber thinning; as a wrangler and rough-string rider on a northern New Mexico ranch; and competed on an amateur rodeo circuit. His background includes a PhD in ecology and a long career as an environmental scientist throughout the western U.S., Alaska, and Canada. Kale has written short stories for Terrain.org, and resides with his wife and family in Colorado. This is his first novel.

www.ingramcontent.com/pod-product-compliance
Lightning Source LLC
Chambersburg PA
CBHW050859250626
47155CB00001B/22